Cur
3332700495 W9-AVN-290
Curran, Thomas Rendell,
Undertow /

undertow

Thomas Rendell Curran

undertow

Thomas Rendell Curran

"Library Discard"
Non-returnable

PALLISER REGIONAL LIBRARY 20234N

BREAKWATER
100 Water Street
P.O. Box 2188
St. John's, NL
A1C 6E6

National Library of Canada Cataloguing in Publication Data

Curran, Thomas Rendell, 1939-
Undertow / Thomas Rendell Curran.

ISBN 1-55081-193-2   I. Title.

PS8555.U68U5 2002   C813'.6   C2002-904937-7
PR9199.4.C87U5 2002

© 2002 Thomas Rendell Curran
Reprinted in 2003

Design & Layout: Rhonda Molloy
Cover photo courtesy of Ray Fennelly
Author photo by Kristina Curren

ALL RIGHTS RESERVED. No part of this work covered by the copyright hereon may
be reproduced or used in any form or by any means—graphic, electronic or
mechanical—without the prior written permission of the publisher. Any request for
photocopying, recording, taping or storing in an information retrieval system of
any part of this book shall be directed in writing to the Canadian Reprography
Collective, 6 Adelaide Street East, Suite 900, Toronto, Ontario, M5C 1H6. This applies
to classroom usage as well.

The Canada Council | Le Conseil des Arts
for the Arts | du Canada

We acknowledge the financial support of The Canada Council for the Arts for our
publishing activities.

 We acknowledge the financial support of the Government of
Canada through the Book Publishing Industry Development
Program (BPIDP) for our publishing
activities.

Printed in Canada.

This is a work of fiction. Any resemblance to actual events or persons, with
the exception of certain historical and public ones, is entirely coincidental.

Curran has evoked the time period beautifully, adding just enough telling detail, and moves the story along at a good pace. And the ending, while violent, is both unexpected and believable. *Undertow* is well-delivered, and sure to garner fans.

Joan Sullivan, *The Telegram*

The time is 1947 and the feeling one gets is of a black and white film...The book starts slowly, giving you a sense of place and time...This is not a light mystery, it has substance and local interest.

Independently Reviewed

Newfoundland continues to export literary stock well worth its salt. A case in point is Thomas Rendell Curran.

Mike Gillespie, *The Ottawa Citizen*

Undertow is a great read and its author is to be congratulated for keeping his readers in suspense throughout this book. Curran has also managed to provide a great sense of place in his descriptions of St. John's of that era... It is to be hoped there will be other Inspector Stride mysteries to come from the pen of Thomas Rendell Curran!

John C. Perlin, *Newfoundland Book Corner*

For Leah Rendell Curren

undertow: a current below the surface of the sea that moves in the opposite direction to the current on the surface

prologue

St. John's, Newfoundland
The Evening Telegram, 22 June 1943

The body of an American soldier has been found on Southside Road, near the Mill Bridge on the Waterford River. The body was discovered by Constable Walter Williams shortly after one o'clock this morning in the course of his duty as patrolman in that area. The deceased has been identified as Marco (Mark) Petrelli, a corporal in the United States Army stationed at Fort Pepperrell.

Dr. Thomas Butcher, coroner for St. John's, said that Corporal Petrelli met his death as the result of an attack on his person. No details on the nature of the injuries have been released. Inspector Eric Stride, speaking for the Criminal Investigation Division of the Newfoundland Constabulary, said that Corporal Petrelli's death was being treated as a homicide and a robbery, and that the investigation was continuing. Inspector Stride said that the United States Military Police would be acting in close co-operation with the constabulary throughout the investigation.

Colonel James Marsden, United States Army, speaking for the Newfoundland Base Command at Fort Pepperrell, said that servicemen from the United States had been warmly welcomed by Newfoundlanders from all walks of life and made to feel that St. John's was their home away from home. Colonel Marsden emphasised, however, that there are dangers for troops in every foreign posting, just as there are in the United States itself. Servicemen are advised to exercise appropriate caution at all times, particularly late at night when in unfamiliar surroundings.

The *Telegram* has learned that Corporal Petrelli spent the evening preceding his death in the company of two other servicemen, one of them a Canadian sailor, and three young women from the city. Two of the young women, Rita Fleming and Jenny Cole, reside on Macklin Place in the city's west end. The two women last saw Corporal Petrelli shortly before midnight when he escorted them to their residence. Miss Fleming told our reporter that Corporal Petrelli had intended to wait on the street corner for his American comrade to return, and drive with him back to Fort Pepperrell. Miss Fleming could not say how or why Corporal Petrelli came to be on the Southside Road. Macklin Place is approximately one mile from the place where the young man's body was found.

Corporal Petrelli arrived in St. John's on January 25, 1941 aboard the United States Army Transport *Edmund B. Alexander*. He was a member of the first contingent of 1,000 American troops to arrive in Newfoundland after the outbreak of war in 1939. He was a native of Brooklyn, New York, and his remains will be returned to his home for interment. He is survived by his parents, Mr. and Mrs. Vincenzo Petrelli, two brothers and three sisters. The deceased was twenty-two years of age.

o n e

St. John's, Newfoundland, May 1947

It was the sound that she was most aware of, a resounding boom that echoed inside her head, blotting out almost every other thing.

She had been immersed in the water up to her chin, absorbed in soft contemplation of the evening ahead, drowsy in the hot fragrance of bath oil, too late aware that someone had come into the room.

She spoke only one word before she was seized by the hair and her head was slammed against the edge of the cast-iron tub.

"You," she said. Almost a question.

She had only a few moments to wonder that she felt no pain, moments when she looked at the person looming over her, at the calm, cold expression on the pale face in the light that was softly misted with steam.

Then another distant tugging at her hair, and again the same heavy sound, though not so loud this time. And again. The light exploded, then dimmed abruptly into final darkness.

Edith Taylor slipped under the water, a stream of bubbles briefly disturbing the surface. A soft red cloud gathered around the web of her dark hair. One last bubble, rainbow-sheened, held for an instant on the surface, then vanished without sound.

Music crept into the warm and scented air from a radio in the bedroom. Frank Sinatra was singing a song about love.

t w o

Eric Stride lay on his bed, one hand under his head, watching the play of lights on the ceiling and walls of the room. The window was open a crack, and he could hear the occasional sound of a car as it hissed by on the rain-slicked street below.

It was Saturday night, and it had been raining all day, starting early in the morning, before dawn, the heavy, determined rain that can signal the change of seasons in the North Atlantic. A week earlier, a storm had blown in from the north-east and dropped more than a foot of snow on the city. Most of the snow had disappeared, though, even before the onset of the rain, only traces lingering in sheltered areas.

The light had faded quickly in the late afternoon and it was almost dark by eight o'clock. An overcast hung above the city like a spell of bad temper. For a change, though, there was little wind to speak of. There was even a hint of spring in the air, a suggestion of the warmth to come. If one enjoyed walking in the rain, this was a good night for it.

Stride picked his watch off the bedside table. It was nine-ten. He put the watch back, studied the random lines in the plaster of the ceiling for a minute, inventing patterns and portraits, then turned his head and looked at the woman lying beside him. Her eyes were closed, her breathing slow and even. He wondered if she was sleeping.

"I can feel you looking at me," Margaret Nichol said then. She was smiling now, but her eyes were still closed. "I think I must have fallen asleep. I thought we were dressed and we were going out for a drive. In the rain. I was wearing white rubber boots and a blue raincoat. And you were wearing a black leather coat."

"You were asleep," Stride said. "I don't own a black leather coat."

"I know," she said. She raised herself on an elbow and looked at him. She touched his chest, tugged at the dark, curly hairs. "You looked very nice, though. I think black becomes you."

"So I've been told," he said. "First thing Monday morning, then, as soon as the stores open." He turned towards her, touched her hand, then kissed her breast.

She pushed him away, laughing.

"Don't get me started again. Food is what I need."

"Food it shall be."

Stride rolled away from her and swung his legs over the side of the bed. He sat still for a moment, the sudden movement making his head spin. Low blood pressure, Thomas Butcher had told him. Nothing to worry about. Just be aware of it.

Margaret placed her hand on the thick muscles of his upper back, frowning now. Stride reached over his shoulder and covered her hand with his, their fingers intertwining. After a few moments, he stood up and stretched to his full height, reaching towards the high ceiling with his fingertips. He was tall, over six feet, heavily built. His hair was dark, almost jet black, thick and curly.

Stride tilted his head slowly back and forth, then from side to side, loosening the muscles in his neck and upper back. He went to the window, pulled the drapes further open and leaned on the sill, looking down at the street. The subdued light from the street lamp three doors away highlighted the curtain of rain.

"Still raining to beat hell," he said. "Well, at least it will take the rest of the snow with it."

"Small mercies," Margaret said. She sat on the side of the bed, flexing her arms and shoulders, the movement causing her breasts to rise and fall. She ran her hands through her long dark hair, lifted the tresses, then let them fall about her shoulders. She saw that Stride had turned away from the window and was watching her. She looked at him and grinned.

"Do you need the bathroom? I know I do."

She stood up and stretched again, preening almost. She was tall for a woman, slender and fit. She was very attractive and she knew it. No false modesty there.

Stride shook his head, smiling, and started to dress as Margaret ran down the hall. He heard the bathroom door close, then the sound of water running into the sink. He finished dressing while he walked to the kitchen, tucking in his shirt and buckling his belt.

He took two halibut steaks from the fridge and dredged them in seasoned flour. He reached into the pantry for the bottle of olive oil, shook it, and uttered a mild curse. It was almost empty. He opened the fridge and took out a block of fatback pork and cut a half-dozen slices, then dropped them into a large cast-iron skillet and placed it on the stove. While the fat was being rendered, Stride pulled the cork from a bottle of white Burgundy, poured a small amount into a glass and drank it, letting the cold wine run slowly down the back of his throat. He closed his eyes for a moment, savouring the full, rich taste. Then he took a bowl of parboiled potatoes from the fridge. He had sliced half of them when the telephone rang.

t h r e e

Detective Sergeant Harry Phelan was waiting on the sidewalk under a black umbrella on the corner of Queen's Road and Victoria Street when Stride's dark blue MG pulled up to the curb. Stride leaned across the passenger seat and pushed the door open. Phelan shook the water from the umbrella, rolled it tightly, and stepped down into the car. He placed the umbrella between his knees and settled himself against the leather seat.

"Sometimes I think it will never stop," Phelan said, brushing the rainwater off his coat. "This is the kind of day that inspires my old man to say that this country's not fit to live in, wishes he had stayed in County Kilkenny."

Stride looked at Phelan and smiled.

If latitude alone could dictate climate, Newfoundland would be a pleasant place to live. Most of the island lies to the south of London, England, and St. John's, the capital, is to the south of Paris. But Newfoundland has a stridently northern climate, decreed in part by the cold Labrador current that sweeps from the north down its coast, the chill sharpened early in the year by Arctic drift ice that often barricades the coastline, producing spring weather that is usually cold and damp. Summer, such as it is, arrives late and is almost always too short. Winter sometimes seems to last forever, and snow in May is not unusual. A day when the wind does not blow is worth talking about.

"The call came in to the station at nine-twenty, sir." Phelan looked at Stride and tried to gauge his mood. He hadn't been happy to hear from his sergeant on a Saturday night. Especially on a rainy Saturday night when he was with Margaret Nichol. Stride's expression was neutral.

"Billy Dickson was the desk officer," Phelan continued. "A man identifying himself as Edward Taylor said he had found his stepmother dead in her bathtub. Drowned, apparently, but Billy said the gentleman wasn't very clear about that, and he did say something about blood. The lady's husband, Jonathan Taylor, wasn't at home at the time. The house is in the west end. Leslie Street."

"She was alone in the house, then?" Stride turned the rear-view mirror towards him and combed his hair with his fingers.

"Apparently. Dickson said the man sounded distraught."

"Distraught." Stride re-adjusted the mirror. He was smiling now. "That's a good word. I expect I might be distraught if I found my stepmother drowned in her bathtub, blood or no blood. Just having a stepmother might be enough by itself to make me distraught." He shook his head then. He was annoyed with himself for making light of a woman's death. Stride glanced at Phelan. "Did you manage to get hold of Noseworthy?" Kevin Noseworthy was the CID's fingerprint and evidence expert.

"Yes, I did. He could be at the house already."

Stride grunted his approval. He checked the rear-view mirror, waited for a taxi to pass, then shifted the MG into gear and pulled out onto Queen's Road, heading west.

"I know a man who lives on Leslie Street," Stride said after a minute. "He's a sort of friend, actually. Tommy Connars."

Phelan looked at him.

"It's a small world, sir. Tommy Connars is a friend of my father. Connars was a blacksmith, like his own father, and so was my old man before he got into boats and marine engines. My dad's blacksmithing was back in the old country, though. When I was a young boy, my old man would sometimes work with Connars in his forge. He liked to say that he and Connars would work together after hours for the pleasure of their craft. That was the phrase my old man used. The pleasure of their craft. It has a nice ring." Phelan was silent for a moment. "But that was ages ago. Connars started out working in his father's forge, had a good business on Holdsworth Street. He gave up blacksmithing in the early thirties and went into merchandising."

"Jack Taylor," Stride said. He had been only halfway listening to Phelan. "He's called Jack, not Jonathan. The name didn't register right away. And I've met him. Small bloody world, indeed." Stride eased the MG towards the centre of the road, skirting around a large puddle. "Connars introduced him to me. I think he's with the Colonial Stores." Stride ran names through his mind. Jack Taylor. Edward Taylor. "Ned Taylor. Shit!" The words leaked out and the MG leapt forward as Stride jammed his foot against the gas pedal, the small car rattling fiercely over the cobblestone surface, the engine keening. Phelan looked at Stride. They were driving west along Water Street now, well above the speed limit. Stride eased back on the accelerator and the car slowed. The black iron fence fronting the sloping lawn of Victoria Park was on their right.

"We're just about there, sir. It's the second turn on the right, maybe a hundred and fifty yards."

Stride nodded and drummed his fingers against the leather-wrapped steering wheel. They drove in silence until they reached the intersection. Stride geared down, turned onto Leslie Street, and accelerated up the hill.

The Taylor home was a modest two-story house on the west side of the street, painted dark green, fronted by a small patch of tired grass that lacked the ambition to be a lawn. A short flight of wooden steps led to the front door. A constable in a dark blue uniform, and wearing a rain cape, stood guard on the veranda. He nodded to Stride and Phelan.

"You're the first to arrive, sir," he said to Stride. "Dr. Butcher is on his way, and I understand Mr. Noseworthy will be coming along with him. Right now, there's just Mr. Edward Taylor inside with another gentleman. His name's Shaw. He's a friend of Mr. Taylor, so he says."

Ned Taylor sat on the chesterfield in the living room of his father's house, looking pale, his hands shaking. He took a package of cigarettes from his jacket, stared at it as if expecting to find a message encrypted in the label, and then put it into his shirt pocket. Taylor was a tall man with fair hair that was beginning to thin and a medium build. He was about thirty years old, Stride judged. And he looked much the worse for wear. Distraught, Billy Dickson had said.

"Just start from the beginning, Mr. Taylor," Stride said. He sat on an armchair facing Taylor. Phelan stood in the entrance to the living room. "Start from when you first got to the house this evening."

Taylor looked at Stride, sat upright and smoothed his hair with his right hand.

"From the beginning," he repeated. "Of course."

The two men looked at each other for a moment. Taylor nodded slowly, then looked over his shoulder at the man standing beside the chesterfield.

"George and I were at our club. For a meeting." He looked over his shoulder again. "George Shaw," he said. "George and I are in business together."

"What time did your meeting start?"

"It started at seven. Seven sharp. And it ended at about eight-thirty. Maybe a little earlier, or a little later. Then we drove here, to the house. This is my father's house." Taylor paused. "But you already know that. I was returning a chest of silverware that we had borrowed. That my wife and I had borrowed. For a dinner party last week." He smiled uncertainly. "Joanne. My wife's name is Joanne."

Stride stared at him for a moment, then wrote the name in his notebook.

"What time did you arrive here at the house?"

"I would guess that it was about eight-forty, or eight-forty-five. Something like that. I didn't pay much attention to the time." He shrugged. "There was no reason to, really. I was only returning some silverware. I rang the doorbell, but there wasn't any answer. I think I rang the bell a couple of times." He looked over at George Shaw who nodded agreement. "When I didn't get an answer, I let myself in. I have a key, of course. Anyway, I let myself in. Edith's raincoat was hanging on the coat rack in the vestibule. And her boots were on the rubber mat. There was water on the mat. I remember that. There were lights on in the house. In the hall. And in the kitchen, and upstairs. I could hear a radio playing upstairs. In Edith's bedroom, I think." He stopped, then looked towards the staircase that led to the second floor. His head drooped, his chin almost resting on his chest. George Shaw placed his hand on Taylor's shoulder.

"Edith is your stepmother's name?"

"Yes." Taylor stared at Stride. "It is. Was." He looked away. "I went upstairs. I could see that there was a light on in the bathroom. The door wasn't closed all the way. I called out, called Edith's name. It felt very strange. Calling her name, I mean, and not getting an answer. I knocked on the door. I assumed that she must have been in there. I could feel the heat from the bathwater, I think. You know, the warmth and the moisture." Taylor leaned forward and put his hand on his forehead. He stared at Stride again. "I started to feel nervous then. That something might be wrong. It was the silence. There wasn't a sound, except for the radio. I know I stood by the door for a while, afraid to open it. I don't know how long."

He paused again.

"Anyway. I pushed the door open. She was in the bathtub. The water was red. Reddish. She was under water." Taylor took a breath. "Her eyes were open."

He slumped back against the chesterfield, chin on chest, staring at the pattern on the carpet.

"What did you do then, Mr. Taylor? Did you touch the body?"

"Touch her?" He looked at Stride for a moment, as though offended by the suggestion. "No. I didn't touch her. God, no." He blinked several times. "I think I knelt by the tub. Yes, I did kneel by the tub. And I think I may have put my hands on the side. Yes, I'm sure I did." He nodded his head, confirming his own statement. "Then I came downstairs and I called the police. I asked the operator to connect me with the police station."

Taylor took out his package of cigarettes and stared at the label again. He put the package back into his shirt pocket.

"My father doesn't really approve of smoking," he said, almost apologetically. His voice had a distant quality now. "Doesn't permit smoking in his house." He ran his hand through his hair. "Actually, Dad didn't really care much one way or the other, until after he married Beryl. He smoked himself when he was young. But Beryl was very strict. No tobacco, no alcohol. Not much of anything, really." Taylor looked around the room. His gaze came to rest on the upright piano in the far corner. "She played the piano every evening after tea. Hymns. Always hymns." He looked at the two policemen and smiled awkwardly. "I don't know why I'm talking about Beryl. Beryl's been in her grave for two years, and it's Edith who's upstairs now, dead in the bathtub."

He fell silent, placed a hand over his eyes.

Stride glanced at Harry Phelan. We have a stepmother named Edith and a second stepmother named Beryl. Three wives. Any more surprises? he wondered. And where was Jack Taylor?

"Can you tell us where your father is, Mr. Taylor?" Stride looked at his watch. It was just past ten.

"My father is at his cabin at Tors Cove. Trouting. He went there yesterday afternoon after work. He has a cabin on the pond." He paused. "I thought I told you that. I guess I must have told the officer who answered the phone. He went with Uncle Tommy." His voice trailed off.

"Uncle Tommy?"

"Tommy Connars. He lives next door. They aren't really related to us, but they've been Uncle Tommy and Aunt Becky for as long as I can remember. They're family, for all intents and purposes. They would look after the house when we were away, and we would return the favour. They have a key, of course." He rubbed the back of his neck. "Much good that it did Edith tonight."

"I take it there's no telephone at the cabin?"

"No, of course not." Taylor smiled. "There isn't even electricity."

"When do you expect your father to return to St. John's, Mr. Taylor?"

"Tomorrow. Tomorrow evening, I think, around suppertime."

Taylor pulled out his cigarettes again. He looked at the package, then shook a cigarette loose and placed it between his lips. Harry Phelan stepped forward with his lighter. Taylor inhaled deeply and held the smoke in his lungs for a long time.

"Thanks. I really needed that." He looked towards the piano and smiled again. "I almost expect to hear a hymn tune start up on that thing. Beryl will be spinning in her grave."

"I gather your father was married three times, Mr. Taylor. And the late Mrs. Taylor," Stride gestured towards the stairs, "is his third wife?"

"His fourth, actually. I'm sorry. I should have explained. It's wallpaper to me, of course, but our family story always comes as a surprise to third parties. Edith is—was—my father's fourth wife. Beryl, who died two years ago, was his third. My mother, Bobby's mother, too, was Jean. Bobby—Robert—is my younger brother. Jean was my father's first wife. Our mother died when we were both very young." Taylor paused and took a deep breath.

"Dad's second wife was Irene," he went on. "He married Irene a year after my mother died, and Irene died of cancer two years after that. And then he married Beryl." Taylor spoke quickly now, mechanically, without emotion. "It's complicated, I know. Did I leave anything out? Oh, yes. About Edith. Edith was our housekeeper. She came to live with us when we were just boys, Bobby and me. She was Edith Wright then. She was Dad's—our—housekeeper for about twenty years, all told. They were married last year."

Taylor made a resigned gesture with his hands, smiled. "The Taylor family tree is complicated."

And had been rigorously pruned, Stride thought. He tried to imagine being married even once. Four marriages in a lifetime took his breath away.

The front door opened and closed, and Dr. Thomas Butcher walked into the living room, Kevin Noseworthy following close behind him. Noseworthy took Butcher's raincoat and hung it on the coat rack in the hall, then took off his own.

"Thomas Butcher," he announced, and extended his hand to Taylor. He nodded at Stride and Phelan. "Please accept my condolences, Mr. Taylor. My information is that you arrived home this evening to find your mother deceased. While bathing, I understand?"

Taylor stood up.

"My stepmother, in fact, Dr. Butcher. This is my father's home, not mine. I had stopped by to return some silverware."

"Well, I had half the information correct. Par for the course."

Thomas Butcher was in his late fifties, a first-generation Newfoundlander who had come to the island after the Great War. He had managed to retain his soft Devonshire accent after almost three decades of immersion in the largely Irish intonations of St. John's. Butcher had been a British Army surgeon attached to the Newfoundland Regiment in France in 1916. He had been in France, at Beaumont Hamel, on the first of July that year, when almost the entire regiment had been wiped out on the first day of the Battle of the Somme.

Butcher was slightly taller than medium height, with a ruddy complexion and dark brown hair, neatly trimmed. He dyed his hair because it pleased him to do so, and he didn't care who knew it. He was slender of build, careful about his weight, and took pleasure in telling people that he could still fit comfortably into the army uniform that he had last worn in public almost thirty years ago.

He paused now to light a cork-tipped cigarette that he had taken from a silver cigarette case. The heavy sweet smell of Turkish tobacco filled the room.

"You have no objection to my smoking, I hope, Mr. Taylor? Something of an occupational hazard, I'm sorry to say. Do find me an ashtray, Sergeant Phelan. Don't want to scatter ashes all over the place. Sorry to be such a nuisance." Butcher smiled and looked towards the staircase. "Shall we have at it, then, gentlemen?"

Edith Taylor's body lay in the bath, in the same position that Ned Taylor said he had found her. Noseworthy took photographs while the others stood in the hall. Harry Phelan lingered behind the group, out of sight of the bath-tub. He had an aversion to blood, at best an inconvenience in his line of work, sometimes an embarrassment.

"I take it that Mr. Taylor did not attempt to lift her out of the bath? I dare say the blood in the water by itself dissuaded him. Just as well, really. She's not a large woman, but it's always a surprise to the uninitiated to discover how very heavy and cumbersome a lifeless body can be."

Butcher took off his jacket and rolled up his sleeves. He knelt by the bathtub and surveyed the scene.

"Can't tell much while she's still under water. Noseworthy, pass me a vial and one of those filter papers." Butcher filled the vial with bathwater and then positioned the filter over the drain and pulled the plug. He sat on the floor and lit another cigarette. The water made its way down the drain, gurgling softly.

"One can never be certain what one might find in bathwater," Butcher said. "I've read of cases in the States where the medical examiner identified semen on a filter in a situation similar to this one. Intriguing what some men will do."

The water gone, Butcher knelt by the tub and made a cursory examination of the dead woman. There was a delicacy, almost a grace, to his attentions.

"I wager she was an attractive woman in life. A little past her prime, I think, if that is not too crude a comment, but an attractive woman indeed. Did Mr. Taylor say how old she was? I would estimate that she was in her late thirties." He glanced at Stride and raised his eyebrows. "Not a great deal older than her stepson."

Butcher turned back to the body and began a careful examination. He hummed softly to himself while he worked.

When he was finished, he stood up and smoothed his vest and trousers. He lit another cigarette, staring at the woman in the bath, silently smoking. After a minute he tapped his cigarette ash into the toilet bowl and rolled his sleeves down.

"I've not seen anything quite like this before. There is an injury on the top of the lady's head. The injury by itself isn't serious, but I would say it's consistent with someone having grasped her violently by the hair. There's also a serious injury on the back of the head, indicating that she was struck a very violent blow. That's where the blood came from. Taking the two together, I will speculate that her assailant grasped her hair and then slammed her head against the tub."

"Did she drown, Thomas, or was she killed by the injury to the head?"

"I won't say for certain until I've done the post-mortem, Eric. There's been considerable bleeding, obviously, which indicates she lived for a time after being struck. Drowning's more than a possibility." He looked at Stride. "She's not been dead for very long. For one thing, the bathwater was still warm. I would guess no more than a half hour. It's possible her stepson arrived here almost at the time her killer was finishing up."

"That's one possibility," Stride said. He glanced at Phelan. "We'll leave you to it, Kevin. Do the whole place, especially the tub. Door, doorjambs, stair banister." Noseworthy smiled patiently. Stride turned to Phelan. "Take a look around downstairs, Harry, and out back. If the front door was locked, as Taylor says it was, our man probably came in through the back. Unless, of course, he had a key."

Ned Taylor and George Shaw were sitting on the couch smoking cigarettes. Shaw had his hand on Taylor's shoulder. The small amount of life that had been in Taylor's face during the initial interview was gone now. He was very pale and he looked tired.

"Our man is dusting for prints upstairs, Mr. Taylor. He'll be a while yet, and he'll also want to do the same down here. When it's convenient, he'll fingerprint you and Mr. Shaw. And the rest of your family." Taylor stared at him. "It's routine. We'll need the fingerprints of everyone who has normal access to this house. It allows us to focus on those that don't belong here."

Taylor looked at him blankly, circles already visible under his eyes. Stride wondered about the extent of the man's reaction. But then, Edith Taylor had been a member of the family, one way and another, for twenty years. It was hard to guess how people might react, or why. Perhaps the Taylor family was especially close-knit. He recalled Butcher's observation about the dead woman's age. Then Thomas Butcher spoke to him from the doorway.

"I'm finished here, Eric, so I'll be off. I have surgery early tomorrow morning at the Grace, Sunday notwithstanding." Butcher gestured to him. Stride walked to the hallway.

"Your Mr. Taylor looks very much the worse for wear. I doubt you'll get a lot more out of him this evening."

"Probably not, but I want him to think about who might have wanted his stepmother dead."

"Yes, of course." Butcher said. "Did you say that his father had four wives? A remarkable man." Butcher shook his head. "The ambulance chaps have just arrived out front, by the way. I'll get to the post-mortem early tomorrow afternoon at the General. Say about two? Join me if you can."

Butcher turned and left. Stride watched as the two ambulance men carried the stretcher up the stairs. He went into the living room and sat on a chair, facing Ned Taylor.

"I have to ask you a few more questions, Mr. Taylor."

"Yes, I suppose so. I'll try to answer them, of course."

"What brought you here, this evening? To your father's house?"

"I was returning some place settings, silverware, that we had borrowed for a dinner party. I thought I mentioned that." He shrugged. "George and I were at our club for a meeting earlier in the evening, then we drove here afterwards."

"Where was Mrs. Taylor this evening? Your wife."

"As far as I know, my wife was at home." Taylor stared at Stride, his look questioning. Then he turned away. "Now that I think of it, though, she told me she would probably go to a movie."

"Was there anything unusual about the house when you arrived here? Anything at all out of the ordinary? Any unfamiliar cars parked nearby, or moving on the street?"

"No, there was nothing at all. I didn't notice anything. Except for the fact that Edith didn't answer the doorbell. I rang a couple of times, then let myself in. There was a radio playing upstairs. Sinatra. I recognised his voice." Taylor shook his head. "I'm sorry. That doesn't mean anything. What does it matter who was singing? It's just that it stuck in my mind."

"That's all right, Mr. Taylor. Every bit of information helps." He paused. "I have to ask you this. Can you think of anyone who would want to kill your stepmother? Anyone who might want to harm her?"

Taylor looked at Stride, trying to find some hidden meaning in the question. Then he blinked rapidly and shook his head.

"No. Of course not." He looked around the room as though the modest furniture and collection of family photographs provided ample confirmation. "I can't think of anyone, or any reason for this."

Stride decided that Butcher was right. He might as well send the man home. Taylor was looking in Stride's direction but his eyes no longer seemed completely focused. There was a fragment of cigarette paper stuck to his lower lip, adding an odd note of sadness to his appearance.

"I have no further questions at this time, Mr. Taylor. If you should think of anything else that might be of help, please call me."

Taylor nodded and then seemed to withdraw further into himself. George Shaw was looking at Stride, his lips moving soundlessly, as though he was preparing to say something, but he remained silent. Taylor stood up suddenly. He smoothed the sleeves of his jacket and straightened his tie.

"Yes," he said, as though answering a silent question. "I have to go home.

None of this makes any sense to me. Thank you, Inspector. I will call you if I remember anything else." He walked to the vestibule and pulled on his coat, then he turned abruptly and came back. "Someone has to tell my father about this."

"We'll look after that, Mr. Taylor. I'll contact the station at Bay Bulls and have them send someone out to the cabin to contact your father first thing tomorrow morning." He didn't add that he preferred having a policeman deliver the news, rather than a family member. Someone who could gauge Taylor's reaction with a degree of professional detachment.

There was a noise from above. The three men looked towards the second floor. The ambulance men stood at the head of the stairs holding the stretcher. Edith Taylor's body was wrapped in a red blanket.

The front door opened and closed quickly. When Stride looked back, Ned Taylor and George Shaw were gone.

Stride and Phelan stood in the front doorway of Jack Taylor's house watching the red taillights of the ambulance move slowly up the hill. The rain had slackened now but it was still an impressive downpour.

"At this rate, half the town will be floating in the harbour by morning," Phelan said.

"Not to worry, Harry. We're a seafaring people."

"Small mercies," Phelan replied. Stride stared at him, remembering the last time he had heard those words, conjuring up an image of Margaret Nichol sitting on the side of his bed. After the phone call, Margaret had started cooking her own dinner. She had told Stride she would probably go home afterwards.

The two detectives walked back to the kitchen.

"It looks as though our man came in through the back door all right," Phelan said. "Wet footprints on the canvas to here, halfway into the kitchen, and then he remembered his manners and went back to the porch to wipe his feet on the mat. The back of this chair is still damp and there's water on the floor. I'd guess he dropped his coat over the chair. Water on the door here, maybe where he took the coat off and brushed up against it."

"That suggests he left not so very long ago." Stride touched a fingertip to the door. "Back door still unlocked?"

"Yes. But properly closed. Our man may have left in a hurry but he was careful to pull it shut all the way, even though the hinges are a bit rusty. But he couldn't have locked it going out. It's a sliding bolt. You can only lock it from the inside."

"Which means the door was left unlocked. Do you leave your doors unlocked, Harry?"

"As often as not. But I'm a big, strong policeman. Who would want to go fifteen rounds with the likes of me?"

"Can't think of anyone off-hand. Does Kitty lock the doors when you're not at home?"

"Always. But to no avail. I have keys for both of them, back and front."

"She could change the locks."

"I'd get in through a window. Just like before we were married."

Stride laughed and took out a cigarette, passed the package to Phelan.

"Nice modern kitchen," Phelan said. He touched a cupboard door with his fingertips. "This is oak, and expensive. Kitty would love a set like this. Maybe when I get promoted to inspector."

"Maybe we'll both get promoted if we solve this in jig time. Did you take a look at the back yard?"

"Yes. There's a low fence that backs on a field."

"Ayre's Field," Stride said. The Ayres were one of Newfoundland's wealthiest families, owners of a department store on Water Street, among other things. "The company pastures its cart horses in the field, spring, summer and fall. I expect they're out there now in the rain. Bloody great beasts with hairy feet."

"Too bad they can't talk. Might have seen our man climbing the fence."

Noseworthy walked into the kitchen and set his equipment on the table. He was tall and thin, with a pale complexion that looked almost unhealthy, and lank, dark hair that fell in a swath across his forehead.

"Any joy, Kevin?" Stride asked. He offered Noseworthy a cigarette.

"Some. But the bathroom is very clean." Noseworthy leaned towards Phelan's proffered lighter. "Someone was careful about wiping surfaces down after he finished his business. Also, the paint looks quite new. No more than a year or two old is my guess. But I have a number of prints, mainly from the cupboards and the drawers and some from the tub. Places a nervous Nelly in a hurry would likely miss in the wiping up. Two full handprints on the side of the tub, just where you would expect them, according to what Mr. Edward Taylor told us in the interview. I do have some interesting latents from a left hand. These came from the left doorjamb, on the outside. Left-hand partial palm print, two full fingers and one partial."

"What do you make of that?"

"Looks to me like someone stood there in the doorway, holding onto the jamb, looking into the bathroom. But there's no way to know how long they've been there. Might have been one of the painters come back to admire his work after the paint dried. But I don't think so."

"Why?"

"I found a clear print of the same index finger on the doorknob."

"The one from the doorjamb."

"Yes. I'm guessing that after our man was done looking at the scene, he closed the door behind him."

"Will the fingerprints you have be good enough to run through our system and make an identification?"

"Not easily, and it'll take a while. I did the bedrooms as well. Quite a collection from the lady's bedroom, and some of them appear to match the prints from the bathroom."

"The lady's bedroom?"

"I'm not an expert on the nuances of domestic arrangements, sir, but it looks to me as though the master and the late mistress sawed wood in separate digs."

"That's interesting," Phelan said. He couldn't imagine himself and Kitty sleeping in separate rooms.

"I'll get started down here now, if that's all right, sir." Noseworthy pinched off the end of his cigarette and shook it into the sink. He put the butt in his jacket pocket.

"We'll leave you to it. Take a walk outside, Harry. See which of the neighbours is paying attention. There's an umbrella in the hall stand. The Taylors won't mind if you borrow it."

Stride went back upstairs. There were four bedrooms; two small ones, one that was considerably larger, and the main bedroom. On a hunch, he went into the largest of the three smaller rooms and switched on the light. There was a double bed, with a dark blue quilted bedspread, a dresser with a mirror and a small chest of drawers. The closet contained a half dozen dark-coloured suits and four pairs of black shoes. The room was comfortable, but Spartan in its appointments.

He went to the master bedroom and stood in the doorway for a few minutes, smoking and looking over the room. A double bed covered with a puffy pink eiderdown filled a third of the room. The furniture, in a rich dark wood, appeared to be new. A dresser with many drawers and a large mirror against the far wall. A vanity in the same wood and design, with a small padded stool, faced the triple window that looked out on the street. So that madam could tend to her appearance and monitor the comings and goings of the neighbourhood. Or enjoy the morning sun whenever it deigned to appear.

Stride walked into the room. Six framed photographs stood on the dresser, three on each side. They appeared to be divided according to families, Edith Taylor's family on the left, Jack Taylor's on the right. A picture of Edith that must have been from almost ten years earlier. She stood with a young man who wore the rough khakis of the British Army. A formal pose, slightly awkward, a platonic closeness between the two. The background scenery suggested an outport community. Stride let his imagination run. A brother or cousin, perhaps. The last visit to the family home before the trip overseas in a crowded troopship, fearful of U-Boats or surface raiders. The photo kept as a tangible memory of someone who was never coming home, perhaps.

A photo of Edith with a second woman, a bit older than she was, dark-haired and attractive. They were wearing party frocks and ridiculous hats. Dressed to the nines, Harry would say, ready to kick their heels in the air. A black sedan was parked to one side, a Buick, 1938 model. The wind must have been blowing when the picture was snapped because their skirts were flared to the right and they were holding on to their hats. Better to have let them be blown away, over the hills and into the sea, Stride thought. He realised then that he was grinning, like a small boy with a stone in each hand.

Edith Wright and her parents in the third photograph. Her mother was a tiny woman, made smaller by her years and by what was almost certainly a hard life in a small outport village, with too many children and too much toil and too little money. Her smile was cautious, half-hearted, her eyes tired. The father was a large square man, a foot taller than his daughter, towering over his wife. He was heavily built, with a thick moustache but with an oddly timid expression, as if he feared having his person captured on film. He held his derby hat in hands that seemed too large to be real, and one foot slightly in back of the other as though ready to run from the scene in an instant.

On the right side of the dresser, a picture of Jack Taylor and his most recent bride, each smiling careful smiles at the lens. Stride judged that Taylor was a good twenty years older than his wife. He tried to capture his memory of the man from the one time he had met him. Taylor had changed, older than should have been dictated by the four years between that meeting and this photograph. And Butcher had been right. Edith Taylor was a very attractive woman, even if slightly past her prime. But that depended on how one defined the term. Stride looked closely at Jack Taylor's image in the photograph. There was something odd about the position of his right hand and the right eye seemed slightly out of focus. One celebratory drink too many? Then Stride recalled Edward Taylor's comments about smoking and drinking.

There was a photograph of a young man with a fair complexion, fine features, and very sharp eyes. Almost handsome, but not exactly that. He wore the cap and uniform of a naval officer but his hands were behind his back, in the at-ease position, and his rank was not apparent. Stride guessed that this was the brother, Robert Taylor. Ned Taylor had called him Bobby. A boy's name carried into adult life.

A photograph of Ned Taylor and his wife. Stride looked back to the photo of Jack and Edith. Same background, same sky, same photo studio. The two pictures had been taken on the same day, the day Jack and Edith were married. A year ago, Taylor had said. Stride reached for the picture, pulled his hand back, then remembered that Noseworthy had already been through the room with his fingerprint powder. Noseworthy had cleaned up, after a fashion, but there was still powder on a number of surfaces. Not on the picture, though. He carried the photograph to the vanity stool and sat down. Two more formal smiles, captured on a day of formality.

Ned Taylor looked a lot like his father, tall, not at all bad looking, but starting to put on weight. Stride tried to remember what Ned Taylor did for a living, but the answer didn't come. Taylor had introduced George Shaw as his partner. Stride should have known what business Ned Taylor was in. He wondered if he had consciously erased the information from memory. Taylor and his wife stood slightly farther apart from each other than the photographer might have liked on an occasion of family togetherness. Stride wondered about that, tried not to read anything into it.

He studied the image of Taylor's wife, a young woman more handsome than pretty, taller than average height, with light brown hair, strong facial features and large dark eyes. She was as lithe and slender in the photograph as Stride remembered her from three years earlier, when she wasn't married to Ned Taylor, when her name was Joanne Bartlett. When they had known each other.

four

It was almost midnight and they had returned to Fort Townshend after leaving the Taylor house, too restless to go home just yet. There really wasn't much more they could do until tomorrow, but they could put their feet up, smoke and drink tea, discuss the case, and bullshit for a while. Phelan stood by the hot plate in the lunch room, waiting for the kettle to come to a boil. It seemed like it had been rumbling forever, teasing him.

Fort Townshend, where the constabulary was headquartered, really had been a fort at one time. In 1762, when France and England were battling for overseas supremacy, a French force of eight hundred men captured St. John's from the British, then settled in to await reinforcements from France. Instead, they were routed by fifteen hundred British troops dispatched post-haste from New York, in what would be the last engagement of the Seven Years War. A year later, in 1763, the conflicts between France and Britain over the New World, including Newfoundland, were finally settled by the Treaty of Paris.

The treaty notwithstanding, the occupation of St. John's by the French in 1762 inspired the British to construct a fortress on high ground overlooking the harbour, a fortress that included a battery of 24-pound artillery pieces. The site was named for the Master General of Ordinance at the time, one Lord Townshend, and upon its completion in 1781, the British governor established his summer residence there. A century of relative peace followed, and the British troops were withdrawn from St. John's in 1881. The ramparts of the fort were levelled, and part of the remaining structure was converted into a barracks for the Newfoundland Constabulary, which had been created that same year.

The history of St. John's went back a lot farther than 1762, of course. It was already a "place very populous and much frequented" when the English mariner Sir Humphrey Gilbert sailed into the harbour in 1583. Even then, St. John's had long been the meeting place each spring for merchant vessels from Europe that came to the island to exploit the fishery. Permanent settlement anywhere on the island was for a long period actively, and sometimes brutally, discouraged by the British government. The island itself was likened by one writer to a "great ship" moored near the Grand Banks during the fishing season.

In spite of everything, a city did gradually arise around the perimeter of the harbour, one of the finest and most secure created by nature. The entrance to the harbour, only five hundred feet wide and appropriately known as the Narrows, is guarded on both sides by rocky cliffs seven hundred feet tall. The city itself was mostly built on the harbour's northern hillside, dauntingly steep in many places. It was, and is, a motley collection of mostly small houses built of wood, often brightly painted, many large churches, and an array of commercial establishments. St. John's was the commercial heart, if not the soul, of Newfoundland. In addition to its bracing climate and rugged countenance, the city claims an enduring attachment to another of nature's brute powers, fire. Three times in the nineteenth century, most recently in 1892, St. John's went up in flames. And three times it was rebuilt.

Phelan shifted the kettle so that it was more squarely on the red-hot element. He stared at it, fists on hips.

"You know what they say about watched pots, Harry."

Phelan shrugged and sat down at the table across from Stride and took out his notebook, turning the pages slowly. He had canvassed the neighbouring houses on Leslie Street while Stride toured the Taylors' bedrooms.

"The house next door, up the hill, was dark," Phelan said, "so I didn't ring the bell."

"That's the Connars' house," Stride said. "Rebecca Connars would have been home alone. Probably in bed asleep by the time you went out calling."

"Across the street, I could see lights at the back of the house and upstairs, and someone at the living room window. The family name is Gatherall. Henry Gatherall said that he and his wife had seen Edith Taylor arrive home around eight, in a black car, a two-door model. He couldn't say what make it was, and of course he didn't have any reason to look at the licence plate."

"You said Gatherall was standing in the living room by himself. Did you speak to Mrs. Gatherall?"

"Not really, no. Gatherall said she had just gotten out of the bath when I came to the house."

"Saturday night tradition," Stride said. "But what do you mean, not really?"

"She made an appearance of sorts, but only came halfway down the stairs in her dressing gown, with a towel wrapped around her head."

"Did she actually say anything?"

"Not very much. She left most of the talking to her husband, but she agreed with everything he said. That Mrs. Taylor had arrived home in a black car, that they might have seen the car before, but couldn't be certain. That Jack Taylor was away at his cabin for the weekend with Tommy Connars."

"Did Gatherall have anything to say about Edith Taylor, or about the family?"

"Nothing much, really. I would guess the Gatheralls are about Edith Taylor's age, late thirties. But Gatherall said they weren't friends with the Taylors, just knew each other well enough to say hello-how-are-you-nice-day-isn't-it."

"Was there any animosity, do you think?"

"Hard to say. People aren't usually at their most open and affable when the police come calling late at night. The Gatheralls are Catholic, the Taylors are Protestants. Different churches, different schools. That doesn't mean they were at drawn daggers, but might mean they didn't socialise. You know the drill as well as I do."

"Yes," Stride said. He knew the drill. The religious divide between Protestant and Catholic, English and Irish, was an enduring characteristic of the city, of the island, founded in history and perpetuated through tradition, with prejudice on both sides.

And Leslie Street was an odd place. The houses ran the gamut from the elaborate to the very simple, rich and poor families living in close proximity. The economic spectrum changed as one moved along the hill, and from one side of the street to the other. The Taylor house was firmly middle-class, but three doors up the hill on the same side, were two small row houses, barely above the poverty line. Two doors down the street was a large house whose owners, Stride knew, were very well off. There might have been more than religion separating the Taylors and the Gatheralls and others on the street.

"There were lights on in two other houses across the street from Taylors'," Phelan said. "I spoke to the people there, the O'Keefes and the Chaytors, but they said they hadn't seen anything apart from the cavalcade of visitors after Ned Taylor called the station. Neither said anything much when

I asked if they knew Edith Taylor."

"Interesting. Purposeful silence, do you think?"

"Hard to say, really. If I let myself, I could probably invent something. But I'd rather not."

Stride looked at Phelan, shook his head, then stared at the kettle which continued to rumble towards the boil. He wanted his mug of tea. He paced back and forth, now and then punching a fist into the palm of his hand.

Phelan shook the kettle and placed it back on the hot plate.

"You talked to O'Brien in Bay Bulls?"

"Yes," Stride said. "He said he would go out at first light to give the news to Taylor."

Phelan looked up from the kettle, which was finally producing a flow of steam. He poured boiling water into a large teapot. "He knows the cabin, then?"

"O'Brien knows every cabin on Tors Cove Pond, and in the district for that matter. Which is what you would expect. Taylor parks his car in a gravel pit just off the side road and takes a twenty-minute hike over the barrens to his cabin. O'Brien says it's good blueberry ground. Also a good area for partridge hunting. No end of information."

Phelan waited another minute, then poured the tea. He added a splash of condensed milk to each mug and brought them to the table.

"Our man could have come through Ayre's Field from a couple of directions," Stride said. He picked up the mug and blew across the surface before taking an exploratory sip. "From Warbury Street on the north side, or from Water Street to the south. Over the fence at the bottom of the yard and into the house through the back door."

"Do you think the lady might have invited someone over for the evening, while the husband was chasing mud trout in Tors Cove Pond?"

"A back-door Johnny who didn't want the neighbours to see him arrive?" Stride shrugged and again blew across the surface of the tea. "That's one possibility."

"There was no indication of robbery, but it could have been a complete stranger just the same. Although that raises possibilities I'd rather not think about."

"Unless we have to," Stride said. He took out a cigarette and slid the package across the table to Phelan. "It's almost certain that robbery wasn't the motive. Nothing obvious was missing, no evidence that anything was disturbed. The house was very tidy. The radio was playing when he got there,

Taylor told us. Thieves don't usually barge in if the folks are at home."

"It was likely a personal thing, then."

"That would be my guess. Murder is usually a very personal thing."

"And usually a family affair," Phelan said. "What do you think about Ned Taylor? Dr. Butcher said he might have got to the house not long after the murderer left. Maybe he was there at the time." Phelan looked at Stride. "So to speak."

Phelan spoke carefully, but his suggestion was valid enough. Stride looked at him, sorting out his feelings about Ned Taylor and his wife. The thought that Taylor could have killed his stepmother had already occurred to him. He acknowledged Harry's comment.

"It bears thinking about," he said.

Phelan nodded and made a note in his book.

"You told me you had met Jack Taylor, sir. Did you know him well?"

"Just met him that one time, and not for very long. It was about four years ago. Connars was part of a group organising sports events to keep the Canadian and American troops occupied when they weren't busy saving the world for democracy. Give them something to do besides drink beer and beat the piss out of each other. Tommy asked me to help out. I spent a couple of evenings with him at his place working on it."

"Taylor helped out, too?"

"No. He was supposed to, but he didn't have the time, he said."

"Taylor and Tommy Connars appear to be close," Phelan said. "Uncle Tommy, Ned Taylor called him."

"The unofficial aunt and uncle. Almost everyone has an Uncle Tommy and an Aunt Becky," Stride said. He took a final drag on his cigarette and crushed it in the ashtray. He was silent for a few moments, staring at a spot on the far wall of the room, thinking. He swung his feet down from the table and stood up. "It's better if we drive down to Bay Bulls tomorrow morning and give the news to Jack Taylor in person."

"You want to see how he reacts?"

"Yes. There may not be anything in it, probably won't be, but it's better that we find out first-hand, instead of asking O'Brien about it afterwards."

"You can tell O'Brien that you decided it would be kinder if we delivered the news ourselves. More appropriate. You having met Taylor and Connars both."

Stride smiled. "You're a born diplomat, Harry."

"'Tis the Irish in me, sir," Phelan said, thickening his accent. "Sure, it's large hearts that we all have, indeed, indeed."

"O'Brien will understand at once, then," Stride said. "Anyway, you're right. I know Connars well enough, and I've at least met Taylor. I won't be a complete stranger to him. I'll phone O'Brien now and tell him that we'll be down early tomorrow."

"Perhaps the rain will have stopped by then, and the sun will shine."

"We live in hope," Stride said.

Stride drove slowly along the wet streets, making extra turns, spinning out the drive. He had dropped Phelan at his home on Victoria Street on the way, and he was enjoying the solitude now, trying to clear his head after too much talk and too many cigarettes. It was past midnight, and he knew that he should go straight home, try and get some sleep. In the morning, he and Phelan would leave early to drive to Bay Bulls and from there make their way to Jack Taylor's cabin on Tors Cove Pond. Stride attempted to construct the upcoming scene in his mind, using the image of Taylor from the wedding picture, augmented by his memory of the man from four years earlier. But he knew it was nonsense, that he couldn't script these things. Taylor's reaction, after all, was the main purpose of the trip.

It was almost one when Stride finally reached his house on Circular Road, in the east end of the city. It was a street of large houses, in a very affluent neighbourhood, populated by families whose fathers were successful in business, or who had a store of old money. The area was known in the city as "Millionaire's Row." Government House, where the British Governor resided, was close by. Not far from that was the Colonial Building, nominally the seat of government.

For the official record, Thomas Butcher was the owner of the three-story house, and Stride rented a flat on the top floor. In fact, Stride owned the house, and had for ten years. Butcher's nominal ownership saved Stride the necessity, and potential embarrassment, of explaining how a policeman, even an inspector, could afford such a home. Stride's car, a 1938 MG TA, which he had purchased before the war, had caused enough of a stir. Stride's district inspector, Jack McCowan, had blanched when he first saw the car, but finally rationalised it through reference to the fact that the constabulary, operating on a modest budget, possessed only a couple of working vehicles. The MG was a wonderfully inappropriate vehicle for Newfoundland, and it was Stride's pride and joy. He'd had the suspension modified to cope with the sometimes vestigial roads in and around St. John's, but if he drove carefully, there usually wasn't a major problem.

Stride leaned against the garage door and lit the final cigarette of the evening, enjoying the feel of the cold, rain-freshened air on his face. There was a light in the kitchen window of his flat on the top floor, but he knew that Margaret had gone back to her own place for the night. They sometimes spent the night together, but not often, an acknowledgement of the traditional and conservative society in which they lived, as well as their individual need for solitude. And perhaps some doubt about the extent to which they wanted to combine their lives. But they had been together for almost a year now, comfortable with what they had. They had not talked much about the future. Not yet.

But now, with the unexpected reappearance of Joanne Bartlett, the past had thrown the future into sharper focus. Stride hadn't seen Joanne, except for occasional random encounters, since they had parted almost three years ago. Their relationship had lasted less than a year, had been intense and passionate, punctuated by frantic hopes and raging disappointments, each of them taking turns retreating into furious solitude. It had ended with each of them angry and feeling betrayed by the other, their expectations finally crumbling under the accumulated burden of exaggerated and undefined longing.

Stride had persuaded himself that it was over with Joanne when they parted, had even felt a degree of relief when he heard that she had married Ned Taylor. He told himself that they were each too emotional and volatile for the other, badly matched. When they argued and fought, Stride would go inside with his turmoil and pain, while Joanne more typically vented her anger towards him. Their reconciliations were prolonged and spectacular, almost as exhausting as the angers that sent them fleeing in opposite directions. For all of that, though, Joanne had inspired levels of feeling and passion in Stride that he had never felt for anyone else. Not even for Margaret. He had struggled against Joanne's memory for a long time after they had parted, sometimes successfully, oftentimes not.

And now Joanne was back again. Sort of. He reminded himself that she was married, that she was unavailable. That he was unavailable. But the memories were coming back, and with them, a degree of sentiment and yearning that both surprised and dismayed him.

He took a final drag and dropped the half-smoked cigarette on the wet gravel of the driveway. He ground the butt under his shoe, shut the double doors of the garage, and secured them with a padlock. He walked to the front of the house, up the four steps onto the veranda. He stood there for a minute, looking up and down the deserted street, then unlocked the front door and went inside.

five

They set out for Bay Bulls shortly after eight. With the heavy rains of the past day, and following a hard winter, there was a good chance that parts of the road, mostly unpaved down the east coast of the Avalon Peninsula, would make for slow going. It might take close to an hour's careful driving to cover the approximately twenty miles. The penalties for driving too fast on rain-scoured gravel roads could include a sojourn in a roadside ditch, even a broken axle. Today Stride drove with great, and atypical care.

By the time the massive headland of Bay Bulls came into view, the sun was shining brightly, and the waters of the bay were sparkling in the morning light. Several small vessels rode at anchor in the harbour or were tied up at the wharf. Two boats could be seen moving on the horizon.

The scene was postcard-peaceful now, but Stride remembered the day two years earlier when the Canadian Navy towed U-190 into this harbour, the first German submarine to surrender at war's end. Stride and Phelan had stood together on Signal Hill in the shadow of Cabot Tower when the U-boat was finally towed from Bay Bulls into St. John's Harbour. Phelan had produced a flask of dark rum from an inside jacket pocket and they drank a succession of toasts to the end of the war in Europe.

Constable Joe O'Brien was attaching feathered flies to a catgut leader when Stride and Phelan arrived at the Constabulary station. Three sections of an expensive fly rod stood in the corner by his desk. Most anglers would get their start on the trouting season on the traditional 24th of May holiday. Enthusiasts like O'Brien would be out much earlier than that on the ponds and rivers. He finished tying the last fly to the leader.

O'Brien was a short, dark-haired, ruddy-faced man of middle age. He had been a policeman since he was twenty years old, almost twenty-five years. He was shorter than the minimum height for the Newfoundland constabulary. Not that anyone really cared, even at headquarters in St. John's. O'Brien was good at his job and, if he had to, and occasionally he did, could easily lay out a man half again as big as he was. Bay Bulls was Joe O'Brien's home. He had been born there, had never lived anywhere else, and had never wanted to.

"I took a run out this morning, Inspector Stride, and Mr. Taylor's car is still there in the gravel pit where it was last night. The day having turned out so nice, I expect himself and Mr. Connars will be there until late afternoon. Yesterday was a terrible day. It rained so hard that there were times I couldn't see the shoreline from here."

O'Brien carefully rolled the leader with the attached flies and placed it in a small tackle box. He was uncomfortable. He didn't often receive visits from detectives from headquarters in St. John's.

"That was an awful bit of news you gave me last night. I hesitate to ask, sir, but is there any chance that the lady might have drowned by accident? Terrible thing enough to have to tell a man that his wife is dead, but to have to tell the man that she was murdered..." O'Brien shook his head. He picked up a pipe and a leather tobacco pouch from his desk, studied them for a moment and put them down.

"The injuries on Mrs. Taylor's head leave no room for doubt," Stride said. "Dr. Butcher is doing the post-mortem this afternoon. It will only confirm what we already know."

"Awful business." O'Brien sighed. "Can I get you gentlemen a mug of tea, then, or will you want to start for the pond straight away?" He gestured towards the wood stove in the corner. A large copper kettle was rumbling on the right-hand side at the back.

"I think we can let Mr. Taylor enjoy a bit of trouting before we give him the bad news from home. A cup of tea and a biscuit will be appreciated." Stride nodded in Phelan's direction. "It will give us a chance to chat a little bit before we set off."

O'Brien made the tea and set three mugs on the table.

"Jack Taylor has been coming down to Tors Cove Pond for going on twenty-five years, Inspector Stride. Maybe a bit longer than twenty-five years. The cabin he owns now is not the same one he owned when he first started coming down, though. He built a new one about, let me see, about eight or ten years back. It was not long before the war, I remember."

O'Brien filled the three mugs with tea and glanced back and forth between the two detectives, somewhat guarded now. He returned the enamel teapot to the back of the stove and picked up his pipe and tobacco pouch again, this time proceeding with the ritual of filling the pipe. The rich tobacco smell drifted across the table.

"What can you tell us about Jack Taylor, Joe?" Stride nodded at the fly rod. "Perhaps you've wetted a line with him once or twice?"

"Well, yes, I have, Inspector. Mr. Taylor has been kind enough to invite me to his cabin on occasion."

"You've gotten to know him fairly well, then?"

O'Brien drew on his pipe. He looked evenly at Stride and nodded his head slowly.

"I know you have to ask me questions about Jack Taylor, Inspector. When someone is murdered, the family's life gets torn open. Twenty-odd year ago, we had a fella murdered down the road a ways. We found out things about him and his family then that would lift the scalp off your head." O'Brien swallowed some tea. He tapped the stem of his pipe against his lower teeth. "Mr. Taylor has always been very decent to me. He enjoys his time on the pond, often by himself now, but there was a time when his two sons would be with him on the weekends in the summer. Sometimes he brings a friend down with him, more often than not Mr. Connars, who is there with him this weekend."

Stride took out a cigarette and rolled it between his fingers. He leaned forward in his chair, his elbows resting on his knees. He didn't think this discussion would move them any farther ahead in the investigation, but it was part of the routine.

"Did the late Mrs. Taylor often join him at the cabin?"

"Mrs. Edith Taylor? No, sir. I met that lady only the one time, and that was years ago when the boys were still quite young. She wasn't much more than a girl herself at the time. They had all come down only for the day. Mrs. Beryl Taylor was with them. But herself didn't come to the cabin very often." O'Brien grinned around his pipe stem. "My missus called her a 'city lady.'"

"And the previous Mrs. Taylors? Jean and Irene?"

"Mrs. Jean Taylor came down on many occasions. That was a long time ago, of course, because she died very young, 1923 or 1924, I believe it was. I was just starting out with the constabulary then, just a lad. But I remember that she was a nice lady, Mrs. Taylor, very pleasant to talk to. As for Mrs. Irene Taylor, I never met her at all."

"Does anything stand out in your memory about Jack Taylor that you think we should know, Joe?"

O'Brien sat back and raked a thumbnail across the stubble on his chin. It was early in the day, but O'Brien looked almost as though he needed another shave. Five o'clock shadow, seven hours early. He was shaking his head.

"I'm sorry, Inspector Stride, but there really isn't very much to tell. Mr. Taylor is respected in the town as a decent sort of man who keeps his own company well." O'Brien's eyes brightened and he laughed. "And there was a time when he travelled in very good company, indeed. Something that impressed the local folk, your obedient servant included."

"How's that, Joe?"

"Oh, that was quite a while ago, sir, some years after Mrs. Jean Taylor died. Mr. Taylor had been spending a lot of weekends by himself, as well as a week or two in the summer. On a couple of Sundays that year, though, there was a very large car, a limousine, that went through the town. Later that day, one of the local boys saw the limousine parked near Mr. Taylor's car on the road by Tors Cove Pond."

"A limousine?" Stride was interested now.

"Yes, sir. And with a driver wearing a sort of chauffeur's uniform. Very formal it was. And a very distinguished-looking gentleman sitting in the back seat. I thought the car was a Rolls Royce, but Joseph Hickman, who owns the local garage, he said it was a Bentley. They are similar cars, of course."

"A Bentley? I am impressed. Who was it?"

"Well, I didn't know at the time, but I saw the gentleman's picture in the city paper a few weeks later. His name was Hudson. The paper said he was a lawyer in the city, and that he had his own firm."

"Ralph Waldo Hudson?" Phelan raised his eyebrows in response to Stride's glance.

"Yes, that's the name, Sergeant Phelan. It caused no little interest in the town at the time. Some people even wondered if the governor might have stopped by for a bit of trouting on the pond."

"Hudson is one of the most prominent lawyers in the city," Stride said. "He counts some of the highest and mightiest among his clientele, and he's very wealthy in his own right."

Stride flicked open his lighter and lit the cigarette he had been rolling around in his fingers. He remembered the last occasion Ralph Waldo Hudson had cross-examined him in court, an experience he likened to having a vital organ removed under a local anaesthetic. Jack Taylor had suddenly become more interesting.

"I suppose we should be getting along, then," O'Brien said. "It will be a wet walk to the cabin, gentlemen. If you didn't bring rubber boots of your own, I have a few pairs here you can choose from."

O'Brien opened the door and stepped outside. He looked at Stride's MG for a moment and shook his head. He walked to a small black Austin sedan and opened the door on the driver's side.

"I'll lead the way, Inspector. Mind you keep well back. The road's still very rough this time of year. A lot of mud and loose gravel, and all the worse after yesterday's rain."

He stepped into the car and slammed the door twice before the latch caught. He started the motor and moved slowly to the main road, then turned south towards Tors Cove.

O'Brien led the way across the barrens towards the Taylor cabin. As he had said, the ground was wet from the rain. The pond came into view after a few minutes walking, but the cabin was well inland from the road, more than a mile, O'Brien said. O'Brien set a fast pace although he did not seem to be hurrying. Stride and Phelan found after a few minutes that they had to concentrate their efforts to match the smaller man's pace. Stride put it down to a lifetime spent walking over hills and rough country. He watched as Phelan carefully planted his feet on the narrow path between clumps of low-growing bushes, taking care not to catch a foot on the small ropy roots of stunted trees that crossed the trail at irregular intervals.

Harry Phelan had been a sprinter in his schooldays and, in spite of an additional twenty-five pounds, he still won the 100 and 220 at the annual police games, leaving younger, apparently fitter constables gasping in his wake. But Phelan was struggling now. He looked back over his shoulder at Stride, his face red and shiny with sweat. The toe of his rubber wellington caught on a root and he pitched forward, arms flailing like an ungainly bird straining for flight.

Stride was having an easier time, his height advantage over O'Brien just about making up the difference in lifestyles. Stride had been born on the rugged south coast of the island and he had hunted and trapped with his father when he was a boy, but that was a long time ago, and scarcely counted now. His adventures as a young man, off the island, had also been demanding, dangerous sometimes, but had not done a lot for his physical stamina. For a policeman in the city, Stride was in very good shape, well above average, but this was a different world. O'Brien was in his element here; Stride wasn't.

He looked towards the bright sun that was climbing higher in the cloudless eastern sky. He could feel sweat trickling down his spine, start to puddle at the waistband of his trousers. He tipped his hat back on his head, loosened his tie and undid the top button of his shirt. He looked around him at the woods and water, happy now that the city was a long way off, recapturing, however briefly, a sense of where he once had been.

O'Brien had paused at the top of a small rise and waited until Phelan and Stride caught up to him. Phelan took off his hat, wiped a sheen of sweat from his head and dried his hand against the leg of his trousers. He looked at Stride and shook his head, grinning.

Ahead of them were three small cabins, each set back from the pond by twenty or thirty yards. The cabin farthest away was the smallest of the three. Its door hung awkwardly from one hinge and the glass in the one window that could be seen was shattered. Stride wondered if that was Jack Taylor's original cabin.

"That's the Taylor cabin, there," O'Brien said, pointing to the largest of the three, the one closest to the pond. "He has a boat, Mr. Taylor has, with a Johnson five, and it's maybe that himself and Mr. Connars are up at the head of the pond since first light. I know that's where I'd be. But we'll know something about that before we get to the cabin. You can see the mooring from just down there."

They walked towards the spot that O'Brien had indicated, slowly now, no longer in a hurry, the information they carried weighing them down, slowing their pace. O'Brien stopped again. There was no boat at the mooring, a thick stake driven into the bank, with a rusted iron ring for securing the painter.

"Like I said, sir, they're off in the boat." He gestured towards a spit of land that thrust out into the pond to their left. "They'll come back around that point, and like as not we'll hear them before we catch sight. The wind's in the right direction." He looked at Stride and Phelan in turn, his expression clouded, and set off towards the cabin alone, walking very slowly now.

"This won't go down as O'Brien's best day, sir."

"Likely not," Stride said. He buttoned his shirt and snugged his tie back in place. The sun had a promise of warmth but the air was cool and now that they weren't walking briskly, he was feeling slightly chilled.

Just as O'Brien had said, they heard the motor before the boat came into view, a small persistent buzzing noise puncturing the quiet of the wilderness.

O'Brien was sitting on the step in front of the cabin, smoking his pipe. He looked at Stride and tapped the dottle from the bowl against the concrete. Phelan had wandered off to look at the derelict cabin but now came walking quickly back, pointing in the direction of the sound.

Stride drew on his cigarette, flicked the ash from the end, and rubbed the back of his neck. He had slid easily, even happily, into the role of sleuth, a murder to occupy him, the search for the killer. He had begun to enjoy himself, excited at the break from routine. Now he recalled the image of Jack Taylor in the photograph on the dresser in the bedroom, older man, younger wife. Taylor had counted on this relationship lasting him to the end of it all. Stride was here to tell him that it wouldn't, that he was a widower for a fourth time, alone again.

"About five minutes, now," O'Brien said, thrusting his hands into his pockets, shoulders hunched. A small wooden boat, clinker-built, white with red trim, rounded the point. The two men in the craft looked towards the visitors on the shore, pointed and waved. The boat slowed as it neared the land. Then Taylor cut the motor and suddenly it was very quiet, with only the gentle sounds of the water caressing the shore.

Jack Taylor sat in a wicker chair in a corner of the main room of the cabin. He had kicked off his long-rubbers by the concrete step, keeping his balance by leaning heavily against the door frame. Even at that he had difficulty. O'Brien had helped steady him, a hand on Taylor's upper arm, support and comfort both. Taylor wore heavy grey woollen socks, calf-length, hand-knit, one red and one white stripe near the top. The right-hand sock was worn at the toe, Stride noticed, and would soon be in need of darning. He found himself wondering if Taylor would know how to do that.

O'Brien, as much friend as policeman, busied himself in the kitchen, heating tinned soup for a lunch that Taylor probably wouldn't feel like eating. He had already tended to the two dozen trout that the men had caught that morning. Phelan stood near the open door, smoking, occasionally looking out at the pond. A solitary crow pitched awkwardly on a tree near the water, rasping a salutation to anyone who cared to listen.

"There's no doubt that Edith was murdered?" Tommy Connars looked anxiously at Stride. Absently, with his right hand, he patted Taylor on the shoulder. Probably anyone would ask the same question. Stride fought back a sense of impatience.

"No doubt at all, Tommy. Sadly."

He wondered then why he had added that. It didn't seem the appropriate word. Outside, the crow bleated once more, almost like a rebuke. Stride watched Taylor closely. The man's first reaction had been a stunned silence, a sense of terrible shock. He had started to speak, to ask a question perhaps, Connars' question possibly, but in the end had said nothing. Then he had begun the struggle to remove the thigh-length rubber waders. His silence continued now in the cabin. From time to time, Taylor's lips moved slightly. He sighed and rested his chin on his hand, then looked up at Stride. He seemed tired. And very old.

"I met you once before, Mr. Stride. I just remembered. Tommy," he turned to look at his neighbour, "introduced us one evening. It was during the war."

"That's right, Mr. Taylor. We did meet then."

"I remember because I had just learned that Bobby had been wounded, and was in hospital in Liverpool." A smile appeared, then vanished. "Bobby is my son. My younger son. He was in the navy. It was Ned, of course, that you met last night. Ned is married. Joanne. She's a fine girl. A fine girl." Silent again, although his lips formed half-words. "I suppose Joanne wasn't at the house, though, or you would have mentioned her. Just Ned," he said finally, and looked off into the distance.

"How did it happen, Eric? Was it a robbery?" Connars had trouble getting the words out. There was fear in his expression. Stride remembered then that Connars' wife was home alone in the house next door.

"We don't think so, Tommy. We don't think robbery had anything to do with it." That was clumsy. Trying to comfort Connars, an old man worried about an ageing wife alone in their home, Stride had thunked the nub of the matter straight down on the table. Phelan shifted his position in the doorway and lit a cigarette. He snapped his lighter shut, a sharp sound of metal on metal. A cloud of smoke drifted on the soft breeze outside.

Connars spoke again. He was very agitated, alternating between offering comfort to his friend, and trying to hold his personal anxiety in check.

"I'm worried about Rebecca, you see, Eric. You can understand that? Can I ask you one more question?" He placed his hand on Taylor's shoulder once more. "Was Francis Morgan at my house last night? With Rebecca, I mean. Francis is her cousin and I asked him to look in while I was away."

"I don't believe so, Tommy. By the time we got there, all the lights in your house were out. Rebecca must have gone to bed early."

"I see," he said. The old man nodded his head and walked towards the small kitchen at the rear of the cabin.

Taylor looked up, his eyes now focused and clear. Stride sensed a nervousness, and a hint of caution, in his expression.

"You're saying that someone went into my house to kill my wife? That someone wanted her dead?" It was half statement, half question. Taylor turned his head sharply away.

"We can't be certain, Mr. Taylor, but that is the way it appears at the moment." He paused. "I have to ask this, sir. Can you think of anyone who would want to kill your wife?" The standard crude question. Routine.

"Kill Edith," Taylor said. He looked at Stride for a moment, then at his hands that now rested in his lap. Stride noticed the brown age marks on their backs. He glanced at his own hands, trying to imagine what they might look like in twenty years. "Kill Edith," Taylor said again. He seemed to be testing the phrase, trying it on. "I wouldn't have thought so," he said. And then he seemed to drift away once more.

six

Stride and Phelan drove to the Grace Hospital on LeMarchant Road when they returned from Bay Bulls. They had spent more than an hour at Taylor's cabin, letting him set the pace and direction. Taylor had not added much to the first utterances he made after Stride had told him about his wife's death. He had talked randomly about his family, about Ned and about his younger son, Bobby. He talked a little about his third wife, Beryl, and how Edith Wright had stayed with him after Beryl died.

Taylor had remained detached, though, and Stride couldn't guess if he was simply dropping words and phrases into an emotional void that he was otherwise unable to deal with. Taylor was just shy of sixty years old and had outlived four wives, Stride was thirty-eight and had never been married. More than years between them.

They found Butcher in his office in the basement of the hospital. He was sitting in his desk chair, feet on the desktop, reading and smoking a cigarette. Typically, his ashtray was about to overflow and the air in the room was heavy with old smoke. He swung his feet down from the desk and stood up to greet the two detectives. He cleared papers and journals off two straight-backed wooden chairs.

"My day moved faster than I expected, and I went ahead and did the post at the General without you. I didn't think you would mind too much." Butcher smiled at Phelan. "My surgery this morning, which I thought would take at least two hours, ended very abruptly when the gentleman expired on the table. I therefore had time on my hands. A luxury I am loathe to squander." He shrugged and lit a fresh cigarette from the stub of the first. Stride knew that Butcher's apparently casual attitude to death was a front, born in the trenches of France and Belgium.

"Did you find anything to contradict your first impressions about Mrs. Taylor's death, Thomas?"

"More the contrary, Eric. The wound on the back of her head was more severe than I initially thought. In fact, there were at least three blows to the head, two of which were much more serious than the third. I couldn't tell which came first, not that it matters a lot in the final analysis. I would hazard a guess, though, that the first and least serious injury might have stunned her. That injury, I believe, came from her assailant thrusting Mrs. Taylor's head against the back of the tub. I'm speculating that her attacker then actually lifted her by the hair part way out of the bath and slammed her head at least twice more against the rim of the tub. A smaller surface, so a greatly more focused impact. Those blows literally crushed the base of the skull and caused a massive trauma." Butcher shook his head slowly. "There was a tremendous violence in that assault. Frightening."

"Did she drown, then, or did she die from the blow to the head?"

"Death was the result of drowning, although she would have succumbed eventually, probably soon, to the head injuries. The person who killed Edith Taylor is a very strong individual, and someone with a lot of rage."

"Rage?" Stride's eyebrows lifted.

"Yes. It suggests some kind of personal involvement, certainly. It could be an actual involvement, or simply an imagined one. We won't know which until you find the laddie who did this."

Stride paused and tried to process the new information. He looked at Phelan. Harry was frowning. He shrugged his shoulders in response to Stride's look.

"And the bathwater?"

"The paper filter? Nothing unusual there."

Stride nodded. He turned back to Butcher.

"We're just back from Tors Cove and Bay Bulls. We spent some time with Jack Taylor." Stride summarised the encounter, Taylor's detachment.

"That doesn't surprise me," Butcher said. "People react in all manner of different ways to a sudden death in the family. Some burst into fits of hysterical weeping, others try to make jokes, some just sit in silence. And an infinity of variations in between. In any event, Jack Taylor is no longer on your list of suspects, if he ever was. Which doesn't mean of course that he wasn't involved in some way."

"Yes," Stride said.

"I have some additional information for you about Jack Taylor. It's probably not important, but you might as well have it. Taylor was a patient in this hospital fourteen months ago. Technically, this information is confidential, and I know you'll respect that. He was here for only a short time, four days. He had suffered a stroke, the result of a small hemorrhage, left side of the brain. It was his right side that was affected. He recovered quickly, although I expect he still has some debility. Perhaps you noticed something?"

Stride nodded slowly. He thought of the marriage photograph, and the difficulty Taylor had at the cabin shedding his waders. It all made sense.

"Even if Taylor wanted to kill his wife, and had the opportunity, Eric, I doubt he would have had the physical wherewithal to do it." Butcher evaluated the expression on Stride's face. "There's something that bothers you about this?"

"Not directly, no. I wondered about Taylor's physical state, in fact. What I'm still wondering is why a relatively young woman marries a man twenty years her senior, one who's also incapacitated? We also noticed they slept in separate bedrooms."

"An act of kindness, for kindnesses received? A mutually advantageous domestic arrangement? Edith Taylor—did you tell me her name was Wright before she was married?—lived in that household for twenty years. After all those years, it must have seemed like home to her. People will do remarkable things to hold on to their homes."

"It didn't work very well, or for very long."

"No, it didn't."

"Thanks, Thomas. I'll be in touch."

Stride stood up and moved towards the door, Phelan following behind him.

"I hate the smell of hospitals," Phelan said. "One small step from there to the undertaker and his vats of preservative, cosmetics, and hair goo. Christ." He lit another cigarette and sucked the smoke deep into his lungs. He laughed then, exhaling a cloud of smoke. "And this," he held up the cigarette, "makes all kinds of bloody sense, doesn't it?"

"Contradictions and the human condition," Stride said, staring through the windshield and fiddling with the handle on the side window. "Do you want to rescue what's left of your Sunday, Harry? You have a marriage to look after."

"You're asking me to choose between Taylor's dead wife and my live one?"

"You've nicely captured the essence of the matter."

"In my lilting Irish way, you mean? As a matter of fact, Kitty and I are having Sunday dinner with her brother's family. And that includes Kitty's mother, God bless the old dear. A monthly ritual."

Stride continued to stare through the windshield. Three young nurses in crisp white uniforms and winged hats exited the hospital and trotted along the sidewalk. Two of them wore the dark blue woollen capes that were a part of their uniform. The third hugged a brown cardigan sweater close to her body. Stride drifted off for a moment, all but one of the Taylor clan forgotten for the nonce. He sighed and pushed the memory of Joanne Bartlett away.

"I'll drop you off at your place, Harry. I'm going to nose around the Taylor neighbourhood for a bit."

"Soak up the local atmosphere."

"Something like that."

Stride drove down Leslie Street and halted at the intersection with Warbury to permit a car to pass. He glanced to his left towards Macklin Place, then turned west onto Warbury. He drove a short distance and parked the MG. A double garage backed on Ayre's Field near the corner of Leslie Street. A low wire fence ran from the garage along the width of the field, perhaps a hundred and twenty yards, and terminated at the laneway of a small grocery store that was also a family home. Stride could just read the name Parkins on the banner above the display window. A wooden fence enclosed the long backyard behind the store. The backyard had two small sheds, low piles of stacked firewood and lumber, and an antiquated car body.

Beyond the Parkins yard a wire fence again took over from the wooden one, enclosing a second field. Tall trees and another wooden fence marked the far end of the field. A half-dozen large cart horses stood in the field, nuzzling grass left over from the previous year. Stride remembered that there was a feeding station and a water trough near the gated entrance to the field on Leslie Street. A group of five small children, all of them rubber-booted, were playing in the field near the double garage. A small brown and white dog, a Jack Russell terrier, yapped noisily around them.

He got out of the car, looked at the sky and decided to put the top up. Dark clouds were rolling across the South Side Hills from the west. He walked over to the fence, stopped for a moment and then walked as far as the Parkins store. The wire was unbroken along its length but bowed at various spots where people had climbed over to enter and leave the field. A man emerged from a side door of the Parkins house and stood on the landing, hands on hips, staring at him. Stride tapped his index finger on the brim of his cap in salutation. The man made no response, stood for a moment longer, then tossed the fag end of his cigarette onto the ground and went back inside.

Stride walked the length of the street back to the double garage, running his hand along the wire from time to time, looking for nothing in particular, but looking carefully just the same. He went back to the middle of the fence, near where he had parked the MG. A couple, late middle-age, dressed in dark blue uniforms of the Salvation Army were walking towards him, the woman with her hand on her husband's arm. The man carried a small black book that was probably a bible. The woman smiled shyly from under her large formal bonnet. Her husband touched the peak of his uniform cap, a gesture halfway to a military salute. Stride nodded, and when they had passed he stepped over the fence into the field.

If the killer did come through the field from Warbury Street he would most likely have hopped over the fence about here, away from the houses, where he was less likely to be observed. Stride thought this was probably a waste of time, but he walked into the field anyway. He looked down at his shoes and saw that they were already covered with water. He wore heavy leather oxfords with extra-thick soles but he expected that the water would soon seep through and he would drive home with wet socks. He bent down and rolled up the cuffs of his trousers. The neighbourhood children had the right idea, or their mothers did, decked out in rubber wellingtons.

How did the man feel, Stride wondered, walking through the field in the dark and the rain, past the sleeping cart-horses, their coats slick and shiny with water. Did the animals pay attention to him, able in some instinctual way to discern that the human who walked past them in the night had death on his mind? Well, it would make a good scene in a movie, he thought. He pulled out his package of cigarettes.

"Give us a fag, Mister?"

A small boy, maybe ten years old, dark-haired, with pale skin and a face like a clenched fist, had detached himself from the group and come up unnoticed to Stride. The designated moocher. The others stood back and watched. The dog sat beside the group, eyes bright, mouth open, pink tongue on display.

"You're a bit young for smoking, aren't you?" Stride said.

"Nah. I bin smokin' fer years, boy. Old stuff."

"Old stuff, is it? Do you know that it's against the law to give cigarettes to young lads like you?" Stride wondered if that was actually true.

"I don't care. I smokes anyway. It's good."

"Smoking will stunt your growth. How would you feel about that?"

"Don't care. Me father's not very big and he can beat up fellas twice his size. And he smokes like a tilt."

"You live around here?" Stride asked, changing the subject.

"Yah. Over on Leslie Street. You gonna give me a cigarette?"

"No, I'm not. Your father might hear about it and beat me up. I wouldn't like that."

The boy grinned at him.

"Your feet is all wet, Mister."

"Yes, they are, aren't they? I should have a nice pair of rubber boots like yours."

Stride set off towards the Taylor property, the boy trailing behind. He came to a stop near the green picket fence. A wooden pole was bolted to the upright at the corner and a double clothes-line on a metal wheel ran to the corner of the back porch. A ladder with four narrow steps was nailed to the fence by the pole. Its twin was attached to the fence inside the Taylor's garden, the wood on both ladders weathered and old. Jack Taylor had probably put the ladders there years earlier to allow his sons easy access to the field. Stride ran his hand over the wooden steps. The steps would have been washed clean by Saturday's downpour, assuming that there had been anything there in the first place.

The small band of children had followed Stride and the boy to the fence, the little dog trailing behind. A young girl, perhaps a year or two older than the boy, had moved to the head of the pack. She looked at him with interest, and a certain amount of defiance. She was a sturdy child, solid as a brick. The neighbourhood tomboy, Stride decided. He imagined that she could match any of the boys in any game they might play. He made a quick comparison between the girl and the boy who had asked for a cigarette. There was sufficient resemblance to suggest that they were brother and sister, cousins at least. But where the boy had dark hair, the girl's was reddish brown with a deep lustre that caught the light. She wore blue dungarees and a red wool sweater that had seen better days, probably on other children of another generation.

"What are you looking at, Mister? That's not your house." Her tone was firm, but carried as much curiosity as aggression. And it was a fair question. A tall stranger in a dark suit on a Sunday afternoon, walking through a field that they probably considered their private territory, looking into someone else's garden.

"You're right, young lady. This isn't my house." Stride tried a smile. Her face softened slightly, but a smile did not quite form. "Do you know who lives there?"

"Yah. I know who lives there."

"Would you tell me who lives there, then? I'd like to know."

"That's Mr. Taylor's house. Mr. Taylor lives there. Mr. and Mrs. Taylor. But she's dead now, Mrs. Taylor is."

That surprised him. Perhaps she meant Beryl Taylor.

"Is she? When did Mrs. Taylor die?"

"Last night."

"Last night?" He paused. "Are you sure about that?"

"Yah." The girl had drawn herself up to full height, now, puffed with a sense of importance, the holder of secrets, the dispenser of information. "My Dad saw the ambulance last night, he said, and he saw them take Mrs. Taylor out of the house on a stretcher, wrapped up in a red blanket, and put her into it. And the police was there too. My Dad saw them. They stayed for a long time and one of them walked up and down the street looking at all the houses. And he came to our house and talked to my Dad and my Mam." She stopped to catch her breath. Her eyes were shining now.

"What else did your Dad tell you?"

The girl looked at Stride, closed her eyes for a moment, thinking, uncertain now that she should be talking so freely to a stranger.

"I don't know." She looked at the children grouped behind her. Her confidence came back a little. "I heard my Dad and my Mam and Grampy talking about it this morning at breakfast. My Grampy said that if Mrs. Taylor was dead, then it was the Lord's willing, and the Lord knew what he was about."

"Your grandfather said that?"

"Yes. That's what he said." The little girl drew herself up as tall as she could. "My Grampy knows lots of things."

"Did your grandfather say anything else?"

"He said the police would probably come back and ask people questions about Mrs. Taylor." She paused again and looked at Stride, shyly now. "Are you a policeman, Mister?"

"Yes," Stride said. "I'm a policeman."

"Are you the policeman that talked to my Dad, last night?"

Stride shook his head. "No, that was another policeman, a man who works with me."

The girl nodded her head, and appeared to think about that. Her uncertainty had returned, and she took a step backward.

"I think I have to go home, now," she said.

"I've enjoyed talking to you," Stride said, trying out his best paternal smile. "Would you tell me what your name is?"

She looked at him doubtfully for a few moments, then smiled tentatively, politeness winning out over reticence.

"Gatherall," she said, finally. "My name is Anna Mary Gatherall. And I live on Leslie Street, right across from the Taylors' house. Over there." She pointed towards the driveway that separated the Taylor and Connars houses. The front steps of the Gatherall house were visible in the gap.

Stride nodded and looked at the other children. They had all stepped back while Anna Mary Gatherall was speaking, concerned perhaps that Stride might ask them questions also. And her initial boldness had made them uncomfortable, perhaps afraid of what his reaction might be.

"Is that your brother, there?" Stride pointed to the boy who had asked him for a cigarette.

The girl looked at the boy, then back at Stride, and nodded. "His name is Michael," she said. "Michael John."

"Do you have other brothers and sisters?"

The girl shook her head. Stride patted her on the shoulder and started to turn away from the fence. Just then, the back door of the Connars house opened and Rebecca Connars stepped out. She walked down three wooden steps to the concrete landing and stood there looking into the field, her heavy arms folded across her chest.

Anna Mary Gatherall looked at the old woman, then at Stride, and backed away from the fence. She stood still for a moment, then pulled a length of heavy twine from her pocket, bent down, and slipped it through the metal ring on the dog's collar. She wrapped the ends around her right hand. The terrier stood on his hind legs and rested his front paws against her thighs, his stump of a tail wagging in anticipation. The girl jerked the string and walked the dog down the field towards the garage on Warbury Street. Her pace accelerated from a walk to a skip, and then she broke into a full run. The rest of the children followed after her, all of them running hard now, and in a pack they turned the corner onto Leslie Street, out of sight. The yapping of the terrier could be heard for a short while after they had disappeared, and then faded.

Stride turned back towards the Connars house, but the yard was empty now. As he watched, Rebecca Connars appeared in the kitchen window, looking in Stride's direction. Then she turned and disappeared into the interior of the house.

He walked back up the field to Warbury Street and leaned on the wire fence, smoked his last cigarette while he looked back at the Taylor's yard. The horses had gathered in a group at the bottom of the field, standing very still. Stride tossed his cigarette into the field and walked towards Leslie Street. He paused at the intersection with Macklin Place, reached into his pocket and took out the empty cigarette package.

He crossed Leslie Street onto Macklin Place and stopped at a small store on the south side of the street. He wasn't sure it would be open on a Sunday, but a single bulb was burning inside and he could see a man behind the counter. A bell tinkled as he went through the door.

He walked up to the counter and pointed to a carton of Royal Blends on a shelf, held up two fingers and placed a dollar bill on the counter. There was an open package of cigarettes by the carton. Small shops like this one usually sold single smokes at two cents apiece. The shopkeeper handed two packages of cigarettes to Stride, pulled open the cash drawer under the counter and made change.

"Your name be Stride, I believe." The shopkeeper pulled at his pipe and exhaled a stream of smoke. He was a tall, thin man in his sixties, Stride guessed, with a large nose, a prominent Adam's apple, and a cadaverous appearance. He wore a cardigan sweater, worn at the elbows, a soft brown cap, and a white half-apron secured around his waist with a length of stout twine. "I'm not supposed to be open on a Sunday, but I 'llows you won't arrest me for selling you some fags." The shopkeeper smiled.

"I won't. It's supposed to be my day off, too," Stride said. The man's face was somehow familiar. Stride opened the package and took out a cigarette. The shopkeeper struck a wooden match on the edge of the counter and held it out for him.

"You was in here four years ago, Mr. Stride, when that Yank got himself killed on the South Side."

"Yes, I was," Stride said. He remembered the man now, but he had greatly changed in appearance. Four years ago, he had been robust, even overweight. Stride searched his memory for a name. It was just beyond reach. He started to work through the alphabet and got as far as "f". "It's Mr. Foley, I believe."

"Not too much wrong with your memory. Foley it is." The shopkeeper looked pleased. "You never cotched the fellow did the Yank in, did you?"

"No," Stride said. "That case is still open."

"And now you has Mrs. Jack Taylor to look after. So they say." The man shook his head. A half-smile played at the corners of his mouth. "Us will have a reputation now. Dangerous folk to be around, bodies to right and left."

"Unhappy coincidence," Stride said. He wondered how fast the news had spread through the neighbourhood, what version Foley might have heard.

"I 'llows," Foley replied. He puffed at his pipe and continued to look at Stride, unblinking.

"Do you know the Taylors, Mr. Foley?"

"Some," he said. "Neighbours. My son did a job of work once for Mr. Jack Taylor. Painted his house and garage for him, back before the war." He paused, his eyes bright, tapping the stem of his pipe against his chin. "Generous farmer, is Jack Taylor."

"A farmer?" Stride looked at Foley, smiling, but confused. The man's small blue eyes contrasted with the unhealthy pallor of his face.

"Some would say so," Foley said. "Ploughed many a furrow, so I've heard, not always inside his own fence. Might have slowed down a bit over the years, though." Another cumulous of pipe smoke. "So I hear," he said again. He lowered his eyes, seemed suddenly embarrassed.

"And Mrs. Taylor?"

Foley shook his head and did not reply. He walked to the black iron stove near the back of the store and tapped his pipe into it. He took a small knife from his trouser pocket and scraped the residue of ash from the inside of the bowl, then blew through the stem until it was clear.

"Sad business about Edith Taylor," Foley said at last, shaking his head. "Sad business. She were just a young woman." Foley dropped the pipe into his cardigan pocket and walked back behind the counter and began to wipe the surface with a cloth, rearranging various small items as he did so.

"Yes," Stride said. He waited to see if Foley would say something more, but now the man was busily rearranging boxes and cans on the shelf behind the counter, his back turned to Stride. It was obvious that he wouldn't say anything else. Stride walked to the door, took a last look back at the shopkeeper, then opened the door and left, the bell tinkling in his wake.

seven

Stride saw the black Citroën sedan parked on the street across from his house as soon as he rounded the corner onto Circular Road. The sun was lowering in the western sky, and the shadows were lengthening now. He pulled up alongside the black car, stopped for a moment to look inside, then turned into his driveway. He left the MG outside, close to the garage door, and went into the house.

A male voice greeted him when he came through the door into his flat. "It's about time."

Jean-Louis Marchand stood in the middle of Stride's living room. He held up a glass half-filled with red wine. "It's a good thing you have arrived now. I am almost starving, and I've already had at least one glass of wine too many."

"It's difficult to change a lifetime's habit, Jean-Louis."

"Impossible, *mon vieux*. It is for me and wine, as it is for the nun and her attire."

They shook hands. Stride took the glass from Jean-Louis and swallowed half the remaining wine. He raised his eyebrows in pleasure.

"This is very good," he said.

"It is pre-war," Marchand said. "To be precise, 1935. A very fine lot that *les sales boches* did not get their hands or their primitive palates on."

"But you did."

"Of course." Marchand smiled. "I have my sources. As always."

Jean-Louis Marchand was short, stocky, with a dark complexion. His hair was thinning, but what was left was black and curly. His facial features were oversized, the nose especially prominent, suggesting a Semitic heritage that he would neither confirm nor deny. He radiated a restless energy even while standing still. Marchand claimed to be forty-five but Stride believed he was at least fifty, maybe older than that.

Marchand had been born in Marseille, lived there, he said, until he was in his teens, when he joined the French Foreign Legion and spent an unspecified number of years in North Africa. After that he wandered about the world, touching down in any number of places that flew the French Tricolour, sometimes working on the fringes of the law, sometimes not, always accumulating money. He lived in Indochina for several years, then moved on to French Polynesia. Jean-Louis Marchand was never very precise about the amount of time he lived in any one place, or about the dates of his various moves.

The one thing that Stride was fairly certain of was that Marchand had arrived in North America in the mid-1920s. More precisely, he had, by choice, come to the small archipelago of St. Pierre and Miquelon, a short distance off the south coast of Newfoundland, a territory ceded to France in 1763 under the Treaty of Paris. Marchand settled in the town of Saint Pierre, and he lived there still. When asked how he could have managed all that he had done, all of his world travels, and still be only forty-five, Marchand merely offered a grin and a Gallic shrug. But there was no sense of calculated deceit or malice in Marchand's vagueness, and Stride accepted his stories with a knowing smile.

St. Pierre was a good place to be in the 1920s, if a man had a taste for adventure and risk, and a certain mindset. Jean-Louis Marchand possessed both qualities in abundance. On January 16, 1920, the Volstead Act had become law in the United States, outlawing the manufacture and sale of alcoholic beverages in that country. Prohibition, America's great experiment, created almost unlimited opportunities for huge profits through smuggling. It was not exactly what Volstead and his supporters in and out of the Congress had hoped for, although there were rumours that some who had voted for the legislation had precisely that end in mind. The period became known on the French islands as the "Golden Years."

Marchand quickly established himself in the smuggling trade, the owner of two fast vessels that carried contraband from the islands to destinations on the east coast of the United States. It was a bonanza time for many people, from adventurous entrepreneurs to established criminals. Jean-Louis told Stride that he had once met Al Capone on St. Pierre, at Capone's preferred residence in the town, the Hôtel Robert. Marchand said he hadn't liked Capone because the man was not a gentleman, a thug in fact, and that they had never done business together. Stride took him at his word, whatever doubts he might have had about the veracity of it all.

Eric Stride had met Marchand in 1928, some years after the supposed meeting with the Chicago gangster. Full of youthful exuberance and an equal measure of indiscretion, and ready to do almost anything that promised excitement and financial gain, Stride looked on the smuggling of wine and liquor as a crime without victims. He worked on one of Jean-Louis's vessels for a year, then accepted a partnership with him, shipping alcohol to destinations on the eastern seaboard of the United States.

It was a grand time, and Stride enjoyed almost every moment of it. His companions were as adventurous as himself, but older, and different from him in their backgrounds and ambitions. Jean-Pierre Fréchette, like Marchand, was a French national. He had been living on St. Pierre for ten years when he met Marchand, and, like many of the islanders, had happily traded his fisherman's toil for the relatively light work of smuggling booze to thirsty Americans. Nico Zafiriou was a Greek from the island of Samos near the coast of Turkey. He was a wizard with engines, a fanatic reader of eighteenth-century English poets, and once a champion wrestler in his homeland.

But everything changed for Stride one night in 1932, the year before the Volstead Act was repealed. Stride's vessel was overtaken by a rival rum-runner who made an attempt to board her. A gun battle broke out, two men were killed, one of them a member of Stride's crew. Stride himself took a bullet in the shoulder. The attack was beaten off and Stride delivered his cargo on schedule, but the adventure was over. He ended his partnership with Marchand and went back home to Newfoundland to recover from his wounds, and to think about his future. He was able to take his time about that. His years in the smuggling trade had made him a lot of money, and he had saved most of it.

The close friendship with Marchand had continued, though, and they met from time to time, usually when Marchand was in St. John's on business.

"You're almost a week early," Stride said. "I didn't expect you until Friday."

"Circumstances," Marchand said with a shrug. "They are as unpredictable as women, and often as bothersome. But what can one do? With neither, life would be unremittingly grey, without interest. I am here, believe it or not, because I am thinking of investing in a vineyard in Portugal, of all places, in the Douro region." Another dramatic shrug. "Port is hardly my favourite wine, but there is a good market for it, and I think it will only get larger. A countryman of yours, one Bertram Cartwell to give him a name, has recently expressed an interest in the port wine trade. You know of course that the association between port and St. John's goes back more than two centuries. The climate here, I am reliably told, is perfect for ageing the wine."

"Bertram Cartwell?" Stride was intrigued. He knew the name, of course, although he had never met the man.

"Yes, Cartwell. He is a crude man, much unrefined, but—how may I put it?—not without a certain quality. He knows his enterprise well and, unlike me, he has a fondness for port. For him, a happy union of business and pleasure. For me, it is just business. We will have conversations about it tomorrow, and perhaps the day after that. So, here I am."

Marchand made a dramatic gesture.

"But, no more talk of business, Eric. We shall eat well, drink well, and—how do you say it?—catch up on things." Marchand poured two glasses of red wine, then held up the bottle. "When we are finished this, there are two bottles of *Bordeaux blanc* chilling in your refrigerator. I have also brought with me oysters and lobster and calamari. And olive oil for your pantry. I will be the chef, you will be the loyal helper. We shall feast."

Almost two hours later, heavy with food and wine, they talked comfortably over cigars and cognac, Marchand's restless energy banked for the moment.

"I see some of the old gang from time to time," Marchand said. "They are scattered now, with different irons in different fires. Nico Zafiriou is back in Greece, fighting against the Communists. I ran into him in Marseille six months ago. He was there to purchase weapons for the cause. There is much available now, you understand. Parts of Europe are sagging under the weight of contraband weapons, left over from the war. But it is not something I am interested in, although once upon a time," he grinned and shrugged, "I might have been. Wisdom and discretion come with advancing age, I suppose. But I wished Nico well, of course."

"One war ends, and another starts," Stride said. The civil war in Greece had continued since the Allied victory in 1945, but its origins went back much farther than that. He poured more cognac into their glasses.

"It is too true." Marchand was silent for a moment, staring into his glass of cognac. He looked at Stride.

"Jean-Pierre is dead."

Jean-Pierre Fréchette had retired in comfort to St. Pierre in 1932 after the liquor trade dried up. Like Stride, he had saved most of his earnings, had invested carefully and well. Then, in 1940, when the Germans marched into Paris, and the island government sided with Vichy, Fréchette made his way back to France to fight with the Résistance.

"I hadn't heard," Stride said. He closed his eyes for a moment. He hadn't known Fréchette as well as he wanted to, wasn't drawn to him in the same way he was to Marchand. But he had liked Fréchette, considered him a friend. "I saw Jean-Pierre two or three times after I came back to Newfoundland. He was greatly amused, but also pleased he said, that I had become a policeman. And then the war started. Not so long ago, I was thinking about him. I wondered if he was still in France."

"He is there forever," Marchand said, shaking his head. "It was a tragedy. I myself heard about it only a short time ago. Jean-Pierre survived the Nazis in France for four years, fighting with the Résistance, and then he was killed in a stupid auto accident a month after Paris was liberated. Justice is a capricious bitch. That is not a blindfold that she wears, I often think. It is really the mask of a brigand."

"Sometimes," Stride said. "Sometimes, it does seem that way."

"Yes," Marchand said.

They were silent for a minute, attending to their cigars, their cognac, their memories. Marchand spoke first.

"This case you have, Eric. A murder. Tragic, of course, but interesting for you, *n'est-ce pas?*"

"Yes. Murder can sometimes be interesting."

"More often it is only banal and ugly," Marchand said. He smiled at Stride, then, his dark eyes twinkling. "But you tell me that your lady, your *grande passion*, has made another appearance in your life? Mademoiselle Bartlett?"

"Yes," Stride said. "She's Joanne Taylor now, though. Her husband is the victim's stepson, Edward Taylor."

"How will you deal with that? And the lovely Margaret, what about her? It has been my experience, sometimes a very bothersome experience, that the feelings from a great passion lost do not all go away. And when the person makes a reappearance, it is like a stone in the shoe. One starts to walk strangely, sometimes loses his balance."

"I don't know, Jean-Louis." Stride picked up his glass and swirled the golden liquid around, then swallowed a large portion of it. Marchand, in his typically blunt way, had gone straight to the heart of it. "I will have to wait and see. I haven't actually met with Joanne yet."

"But you will. It is an inevitability. And then you will have to see. You will have no choice." He reached across the table and gripped Stride's wrist, squeezing it. "Be true to yourself, *mon vieux*, whatever happens, whatever you feel. Be yourself. Don't make faces."

He raised his glass and smiled again.

eight

District Inspector Jack McCowan sat behind his desk and stroked his mutton chops. He was looking over the report on the Taylor murder that Stride had put together late Sunday night after Marchand had gone back to his hotel. McCowan grunted benignly several times and then went back to the beginning and ran his finger quickly down the two pages.

"Succinct and to the point." He looked up and smiled at Stride and Phelan.

McCowan had been with the constabulary for more than twenty-five years. He was from an established and well-to-do St. John's family. His father and two brothers were lawyers. McCowan's first choice had been for a military career, and he had served with distinction as a junior officer with the Newfoundland Regiment in the Great War. The incompetence and butchery on the Western Front had soured him on a military future, but some of the trappings of the military carried forward into McCowan's police career. The men in the Criminal Investigation Division typically referred to his military bearing and approach to command, and for as long as anyone could remember he had been known within the constabulary as the "Field Marshal." Although not to his face. He continued to affect a handlebar moustache and large mutton chops, decades after they had gone out of fashion. They suited him.

"This Foley chap, Eric. Do you suppose his comments about Taylor are valid? Might be just malicious gossip, some old grudge brought forward for the occasion."

"That's a possibility, sir," Stride said, "although he appeared sincere enough. We'll keep his story in mind, but we won't give it much weight at this point."

"Best not to, but don't discard it entirely. It might be relevant. Keep it strictly to yourselves, though, no beer-glass chatter after hours. I don't want to think about the yellow jays flocking over to Macklin Place to interview Foley, or anyone else for that matter." McCowan typically thought of the press, local and otherwise, in the context of yellow journalism.

McCowan tapped his fingers on his desktop and stared through the window for a few moments, savouring his distaste for newspapermen. His office location afforded him a good view of Signal Hill and Cabot Tower, the stubby granite memorial to Newfoundland's fifteenth-century discoverer, John Cabot, that looked over the harbour entrance. He turned back to Stride and Phelan.

"Still, the press is not your responsibility, Eric." He frowned. "But I trust we will do better with this case than we did with that Macaroni affair during the war."

"Petrelli, sir," Stride said, softly.

"Eh?" McCowan looked at Stride and grunted, half-smiling. "Of course. Petrelli. Eye-tie names all sound the same to me." He picked up Stride's report, then put it down again. "Wasn't that fellow's body found somewhere around the Taylors' neighbourhood? Petrelli?"

"Not exactly, sir. Petrelli was found on the South Side, near the Mill Bridge. But he had been in that neighbourhood that evening, escorting two young women home."

"Ah, yes, the two tarts. I remember now." McCowan pulled at his facial hair and went back to the report. "You say here this Taylor fellow was married four times? Remarkable. And all four wives are dead. I suppose one could say that Mr. Jack Taylor is simply not very lucky in marriage."

"Nowhere near as unlucky as his four wives, sir," Phelan said.

"Well put, Harry," McCowan snorted. "Enlighten me, Eric. What is the story on the four marriages?"

"The first wife, Jean Taylor, was the mother of his two sons. After she died, Taylor married again." Stride consulted his notes. "Ned Taylor said that the second wife, Irene, died of cancer two years later. His third wife, Beryl, died from a heart attack, about two years ago."

"And the first wife died how?" McCowan sat back and frowned again. "Interesting that young Taylor was specific about how two of his stepmothers died, but didn't mention how his own mother met her maker. Find out. There's not likely anything in it, it was a long time ago, but it's worth looking at. And Taylor has two sons, you say? The older son, Edward, seems like a sound chap. Married, has a good business, lives in a decent neighbourhood. And belongs to a service club, you say.'

Stride nodded and looked away, towards the window with its view of the harbour.

"Something you wanted to add, Eric?"

"No, sir."

"What about the second son, then? Robert is his name?" He looked up. "They call him Bobby?"

"Yes, sir. He's quite different from his brother," Stride replied. "He lives on the South Side in a boarding house, his father told us. He was in the Royal Navy during the war. He was commissioned as a sub-lieutenant in 1941, promoted to lieutenant in 1942. His ship was torpedoed on convoy duty and he was wounded, quite seriously. He works as a merchant seaman, now, although not steadily. There appear to have been problems since the war. He's been arrested twice for brawling in taverns."

"A hot-tempered fellow, eh? That might prove to be of some interest to us. And his father may have a reputation as a skirt-chaser, if we can credit Foley's statement. Interesting family." McCowan stood up and walked to the window. He leaned on the sill and looked towards Signal Hill for a few moments.

"That bit about Jack Taylor is a dicey matter, of course, and I'll be interested to see if the yellow jays pick up on that eventually, and just what they might do with it, if anything. If they dance too close to the line with the neighbourhood gossip, Taylor will have grounds to sue their collective balls off. And the best of luck to him say I." He smiled at the happy prospect, then seemed to reconsider. "Not that I have a high opinion of adulterers, you understand."

McCowan turned away from the window, consulted the mirror on the wall beside his desk and carefully arranged the facial foliage. He stood back and straightened his tie, pleased with what he observed.

"Time to give a statement to the gentlemen of the press. I shall make it very short." McCowan put a hand on Stride's shoulder as the three men walked towards the door. "A word, Eric."

Phelan paused, saw that it was a private word with Stride that McCowan wanted, and carried on down the corridor.

"Something about the case, sir?"

"No." McCowan was wearing his warmest smile. "Not the case. Your friend Marchand called yesterday morning, at my place, while you and Phelan were around the bay. I was eating breakfast when he called. Took me quite by surprise."

"I had dinner with him last night, sir. He had a change in plans, arrived here a week earlier than he'd anticipated."

"Yes, so he said. He delivered my two cases of claret, though, as promised." McCowan was beaming now. The district inspector liked his wine, and the supply available locally through the government-controlled outlet fell far short of his wants. "I just wanted to say thanks, once again, for putting us in contact. The man's a treasure. Can't imagine what I would do without him now."

Someone had once told Stride that the South Side was as much a state of mind as a community, separated from St. John's by the harbour and the eastern extremity of the Waterford River. There was a strong sense of "them" and "us" on both sides of the divide.

Bobby Taylor's room at the boarding house surprised them. Given the location and Taylor's reputation, Stride and Phelan had expected to find at best a modest accommodation with only the bare essentials for sleeping and daily survival. Instead, they found themselves in a large room, comfortably appointed with an expansive four-poster bed, an antique wooden rocking chair, two matching leather armchairs, and an ornate sideboard in what looked to be walnut. Above the sideboard, a mace with an iron head and a wooden handle hung on the wall, crossed over the blade of a small sword. There was a large bookcase in heavy dark wood near the window. Stride thought at first it was an antique like the rocking chair and the sideboard. A second look revealed that it was quite new, and patterned after a type popular in the Victorian era. The room was decorated with photographs and memorabilia, most of them from Taylor's career in the navy.

If one looked closely at Bobby Taylor, the family resemblance slowly revealed itself. But where Ned was drifting towards comfortable and fleshy middle age, Bobby was thin almost to the point of gaunt, even leaner than in the photograph on Edith's dresser. A long white scar ran across his left cheek. Phelan fixed his gaze on the scar. Taylor touched it with his fingers as though checking to see that it was still there. He smiled briefly and turned away from the door, beckoning the two detectives into the room. He settled himself in one of the leather chairs and crossed his legs. His right hand tapped a slow beat on the arm of the chair. He waited for one of the policemen to speak.

"It was rude of me to stare the way I did," Phelan said. "I apologise."

"No offence taken, Detective. It's a normal reaction. Even flattering in an odd way."

"War injury?" Phelan asked.

"Nothing that honourable, I'm afraid. Although I do have some picturesque souvenirs from my happy days in the Royal Navy. This one," he touched the scar again, "was awarded for a heated debate in a local watering-hole. A personal weakness of mine, heated debates. Perhaps my brother or father have mentioned something along those lines?"

"We need to ask you some questions about your late stepmother," Stride said, pulling them into the subject at hand.

"I'm not surprised. Ned told me you were treating this as a homicide, although at first he said only that Edith had drowned in her bath. I found that possibility surprising." Bobby Taylor grinned at the detectives. "I knew Edith was no Florence Chadwick, but I didn't think an accidental drowning was likely in the confines of my father's antique bathtub. I was almost relieved when I heard she had been murdered."

Stride and Phelan exchanged surprised glances.

"Your stepmother was some twenty years younger than your father," Stride went on. "What was their marriage like?"

"I assume it was adequate for the time, the place, and the circumstance."

"Meaning?"

"Meaning what I said. If you want to know about their marriage, I suggest you ask my father. I didn't take all that much interest in it."

"I take it you were not close to your stepmother, Mr. Taylor?"

"Not as close as some," Taylor replied, and looked away from the detectives towards the window. He was silent for a moment. "I'm not all that close to anyone in my family. The ones I share blood with, anyway."

"Is that a recent development?" Stride asked. He wondered about the reference to blood, assumed he was referring to Joanne.

Taylor looked at Stride, and then at Phelan, and didn't answer at once. He shifted uncomfortably in his chair.

"I don't know if I want to say anything about that. But this being a murder investigation, I suppose I have no choice." He looked at the two detectives. "So, in response to your question, it's not a recent development. I've had little to do with my family since some time before the war."

Taylor stood up and walked to the window. He took a cigarette from a silver box on the bookcase and lit a wooden match with his thumbnail. Blowing a cloud of smoke towards the ceiling, he pulled the window open a few inches and tossed the match outside. He turned and faced the two detectives, then walked back to his chair. He gestured to the second armchair and the wooden rocker.

"We don't have that many murders in St. John's," Taylor said. "The local scribes should be happy. Things have been dull for them since the war. Even then, of course, there were strict limits on what they could write or photograph. But perhaps that comment is unkind, crude perhaps?" He fixed Stride with an even look, but he seemed to be grinning behind his eyes. "Am I a suspect, then? The wastrel son who lives on the wrong side of the bridge?"

"All I can tell you, Mr. Taylor, is that we're gathering information from family members, as well as from people who knew your late stepmother."

"Carefully said, Mr. Stride." Taylor tapped his cigarette against an ashtray and gestured with his right hand. "Ask your questions."

"Can you tell us your whereabouts on Saturday night?"

"You want to know where I was Saturday night? Certainly sounds like you suspect me of something. Ah, well. I had my tea at about six. Right here, as a matter of fact. Mrs. Casey, my gentle hostess, will be able to confirm that. We had rabbit pie. Mrs. Casey is famous in these parts for her rabbit pie. Her pastry shell is quite wonderful. As light as dreams should be."

"And after you had your tea?"

"Well, after that, I adjourned to Mr. Harvey Button's establishment down the road, for refreshments and possible heated debates with selected members of the clientele on matters of current interest."

Taylor smiled at the detectives. He's enjoying himself, Stride thought. Either he's innocent and feels free to indulge in wordplay with us, or he's guilty as hell and doesn't give a damn. He also was thinking that Taylor's flippant speech pattern was starting to grate on his nerves. He fought back an urge to pick the man up and smack him. Or throw him through his partly-opened window.

"Dear old Harvey was not there at his usual spot Saturday night. I was given to understand that he had recently become a recipient of your institutional hospitality. Yet again. The man truly is a caution."

"How late did you stay at Button's tavern?" Phelan took over the questioning, sensing that Stride was nearing the point where his temper might be wearing thin. He ignored Taylor's comment on Harvey Button.

"Well, that is a little problematic. I believe I was there until sometime around eight. Perhaps a little after that. I had a second drink, possibly a third, perhaps even a fourth, but my debating skills were not at their peak on Saturday evening, so to speak. So I left."

"You're not certain of the exact time you left? Perhaps one of the other patrons could assist you?"

"I doubt that. They're not a punctual lot, Harvey's regulars. Getting the day right is a challenge for some of them. And they really are not at their dubious best on a Saturday."

"Assuming that you left Button's tavern around eight, where did you go next?"

"I went for a long walk. I was restless and didn't feel like going home just then."

"It was raining very heavily Saturday night. But you went for a walk anyway?"

"I like walking in the rain. The streets are usually deserted when it rains. I like that."

"You said it was a long walk. Where did you go?"

"Here and there. I crossed over the Mill Bridge onto Water Street, up Topsail Road, up Craigmillar to Cornwall, to Hamilton Avenue. Then back down Patrick Street to Water, and back to the Mill Bridge and the South Side. I could draw the route on a city map for you, if you like."

"You didn't happen to walk down Leslie Street, then?"

"No. I was in the area, of course, but I prefer to avoid my father's neighbourhood."

"What time did you get home?"

"Around nine o'clock, give or take twenty minutes. I'm not certain of the exact time. I didn't make notes, had no reason to."

"Can Mrs. Casey confirm that you came home then?"

"Unhappily, no. She went out that evening after we had our tea. She has a friend that she visits several nights each week for a sleep over, the lusty wench, and Saturday was one of those nights. I am afraid there is no one else I can turn to for corroboration on my whereabouts. All I can offer is my word. And I have a feeling that will not quite do the trick." Taylor stood up and walked to the bookcase again and lit another cigarette. He picked up the box and offered it to the detectives. "No? Filthy habit, anyway."

"We'd like to ask some questions about your family," Stride said.

Taylor nodded.

"Your father was married four times."

Bobby Taylor nodded again but said nothing.

"Your mother, Jean, was his first wife, I understand?"

"A matter of historical and civic record. Yes, Jack's first wife was my mother. Ned's also. And her name was indeed Jean."

"How did your mother die, Mr. Taylor?" Stride surprised himself by asking the question. There was no particular reason to have raised the matter just now. Perhaps he asked because Bobby Taylor had annoyed him with his attitude towards his stepmother's death. Stride couldn't imagine what Taylor might be thinking now. He didn't react in any overt way, only stood there staring back at him. The silence in the room was suddenly oppressive. Taylor turned towards the window.

"I suppose you have some good reason for asking me that, Mr. Stride." He took a final long drag on his cigarette and tossed the butt through the open window. Then his posture visibly changed as he appeared to make a decision. "As a matter of fact, my mother's death also is on the civic record. You can look it up, if you want to. As I am sure you will, now."

Taylor was silent again for a few moments.

"My mother drowned in Conception Bay, near Bell Island, in 1924. She'd been on an excursion on a schooner with my father, and a group of people from the store where he worked. I was very young when it happened, just a small boy. There was an inquest. I expect the constabulary has a copy on file."

The room was silent again, but the tension had dissipated now. Taylor's expression had softened while he was speaking, the arrogance and sarcasm gone, and for just a moment he looked something like a small, lost child.

"I really don't have anything else to say about that, Inspector. But perhaps you have more questions?" Stride shook his head and stood up.

"We'll be in touch, Mr. Taylor. We understand you work with the merchant navy. Are you planning any trips in the near future?"

"None at all, Mr. Stride. I shall be here for the duration, as they say."

"What do you make of him, sir? He was walking around in the rain just about the time his stepmother was gasping her last. And with no witnesses to say where he was."

"Yes. But he doesn't know what time she was killed, does he? Unless, of course, he's the one who killed her."

"He seems an odd sort, sir. I wonder if he isn't a cod or two short of a quintal. Do you think it's possible he's just playing games with us?"

"I have no idea, Harry. But I agree that he's cut from a different bolt of cloth."

"The bit about his mother was a surprise," Phelan said.

"I wonder if he would have told us about her, even if I hadn't asked the question directly. It all seemed a bit calculated somehow."

"He did seem to take a certain satisfaction from it," Phelan said.

"It has to be just coincidence, of course. Jack Taylor's first wife drowns in Conception Bay, and his fourth wife drowns in a bathtub. It's almost like some awful comedy."

"I thought you didn't believe in coincidence, sir." Phelan was grinning. "And can you deny there's a certain symmetry there?"

"Symmetry? Bloody symmetry?" Stride laughed out loud. "Jesus, Harry, you truly are a romantic."

"I keep telling you I am, sir," Phelan said. "Can't help it. It's the Irish blood, you see."

nine

Bernard Crotty had been in charge of the constabulary's records office since 1944, when he was released from hospital in London and, soon after, discharged from the British army. Crotty was with an artillery regiment in Tunisia when they had come under attack by German fighter bombers. A shell fragment tore through his left leg below the calf muscle. Four operations later, the leg had been amputated below the knee when an adequate blood supply failed to re-establish and gangrene had set in.

Invalided back to St. John's, Crotty had faced an uncertain future. He could no longer expect to discharge the normal duties of a police officer. But it was decided after surprisingly little discussion that Crotty would be in charge of the constabulary's records.

Crotty not only kept the records in an accessible state, he spent a lot of time familiarising himself with the information in the files. He had developed an impressive memory for names, places and events. When Harry Phelan asked for the file on the death of Jean Taylor, Crotty was able to supply pertinent information while he located the dossier.

"I went through that file about two years ago, Sergeant, when I was still in the process of organising and indexing things to my satisfaction."

The two men walked down a narrow aisle between rows of filing cabinets. Phelan was intrigued that Crotty showed little sign of his infirmity.

"The accident with Mrs. Taylor occurred more than twenty years ago. Going on twenty-five, actually. It happened during a day-long outing from Portugal Cove. A group from the Colonial Stores had chartered a schooner for a Sunday sail to Bell Island and back, with a boil-up and a picnic on the island in the middle of the day. They had decent weather for it, according to the constable's report. Sometime after they left Bell Island on their way back to Portugal Cove, Jean Taylor apparently fell off the boat into the sea and drowned."

"Who was the investigating constable?"

"That would have been George Fox. He retired in 1944. His full name is George Arthur Fox, but everyone calls him Gaffer. Did you ever meet him, I wonder?"

"I remember him. He was a nice man."

"Still is a nice man, Sergeant. I had a glass of beer with him last month at his house. He's living in a place called Caitlin's Cove, which is not far from Portugal Cove, in fact. Gaffer and I have something in common. I'm the keeper of the official records and Gaffer is putting together a history of the constabulary. He might write a book about it some day, he says. We stay in touch."

Crotty opened a file drawer and pulled out a manila folder.

"Here we are. Taylor, Jean Elisabeth Snow. Date of death, August 1, 1924." Crotty handed the file to Phelan. "Snow was her maiden name."

"I'll keep this for a few days, Bern. The Taylor family is in the news again, as you probably know."

"The lady who was killed on Leslie Street? I read about that in the paper this morning. When I saw the name Jonathan Taylor, it rang a bell. I wondered if he was the same Jack Taylor. I was going to pull the file today, just to check, when you called me. The paper said that the lady was Taylor's fourth wife." Crotty shook his head. "I can't imagine there'll be a lineup to become his fifth."

"I'll take good care of this, Bern," Phelan said. "Many thanks."

"You're entirely welcome, Sergeant." Crotty put his hand on Phelan's arm as he was about to turn away. "You might want to speak to Gaffer himself after you've read through the file. Just a suggestion." He smiled. "And when you do, give him my regards."

Stride poured tea into two enamel mugs. He added a dollop of condensed milk to each and pushed a crock of sugar across the table to Phelan. Stride sipped his tea while Phelan stirred sugar into his.

"Jean Taylor went missing from that schooner in the middle of the afternoon, sir. No one actually saw her fall into the water."

"Which raises a question. Why did no one see her go in, I wonder? We're talking about a small fishing schooner, not the Queen Mary."

"The report says there were whales in the bay that day, and they were spouting on the port side of the boat. That was part of the reason for the outing. It seems everyone on board was distracted by the whales."

Stride nodded. "It makes sense, I suppose. I would have been hanging over the port side with the rest of them. But why wasn't Jean Taylor also on the port side looking at whales, I wonder?"

"That's a good question." Phelan looked at the report. "It says here that her disappearance might not have been noticed until long after the fact but for the fortunate happenstance—that will be my new word for the week—that a crew member caught sight of a bright yellow oilskin in the wake behind the boat. The fellow suspected right away that someone might have gone overboard."

"And when that happened, people started looking for their nearest and dearest?"

"Right. Jack Taylor had been whale-watching with the rest. Any number of people testified to that fact. When he couldn't locate his wife, the cry of alarm went up for real."

"So, however Jean Taylor came to fall into the bay, it had nothing to do with her husband?"

"Apparently not. The odd part of the story is that when the skipper brought the boat about, they found only the jacket in the water. Jean Taylor was nowhere to be seen. Her body was found three days later. By then, of course, the word had gone out and the fishermen and boaters in the area had been alerted to keep an eye open."

"The inquest returned a verdict of accidental death by drowning. It sounds straightforward enough to me. What do you suppose Crotty was on about, saying that we should talk to Gaffer Fox?"

"This is where it gets interesting. I read through the inquest report twice, sir. The first time, I didn't see anything unusual, so I read it a second time."

"And?"

"In the transcript of the actual testimony, one of the witnesses stated that Jean Taylor had said she was feeling quite chilled on the return trip. That's not necessarily surprising. We both know it can get perishing cold out on the water, even on a sunny day." Phelan swallowed the last of his tea and pushed the mug to the centre of the table. "But the thing is, it was a warm afternoon, and most of the people on board were in their shirtsleeves. And the witness testified that Jean Taylor was wearing the oilskin jacket over her sweater, and the jacket was buttoned all the way up to the neck."

Stride had taken out a cigarette and held it, unlit, between thumb and forefinger. With his other hand, he tapped his silver lighter against the table-top. Stride and Phelan looked at each other.

"So how does a person fall out of a jacket that is buttoned tight around her?" Stride asked.

"That's a question that no one asked at the inquest."

Stride stood up and lit the cigarette, snapping the lighter shut. He stood by the window looking out towards the South Side Hills. There was only a partial overcast, soft white clouds playing tag with the sun.

"It's not a bad day for a drive around the bay. We'll take Crotty's suggestion, Harry, and have a talk with Gaffer Fox."

Caitlin's Cove was a short drive from Portugal Cove over a narrow gravel road that diminished to a cart path at the edge of the small village. The place was a collection of frame houses, brightly painted, perched on small lots carved out of the rugged hillside that circled the shore. Most of the houses were enclosed by whitewashed picket fences.

"We could almost have left the car in Portugal Cove and walked here." Stride said. "This road does not qualify as the King's highway."

"Might have been faster, at that," Phelan replied. He looked up at the sky. The cloud cover had increased. "There might be some rain later, though, and at least we'll stay dry in the car."

"Ever been here before, Harry?" Stride surveyed the village and the surrounding area.

"As a matter of fact, yes. Once, when I was a boy. My old man came down to work on one of the boats. Most of the time, the fishermen can manage their own repairs, but this was a major job and required a shipwright. I spent the day playing on the shore and walking around the community. Everyone knew that I was Mr. Phelan's boy, the man who had come to work on Felix White's boat. I was stuffed to the eyelids with cups of sweet tea and slices of lassy bread—bread and molasses to the uninformed."

Phelan was smiling now.

"It took almost an hour before the local kids decided that I wasn't from Mars and that it might actually be safe to play with me. But, you know, we never did quite get past the fact that I was from the city."

"A townie. You can take the boy out of the town, but..."

"...you can't take the town out of the boy."

"The general store is just over there," Stride said. "The source of all local knowledge. They'll tell us the way to Gaffer's place."

The storekeeper smiled at them from behind the counter. He was a short stout man in his late sixties, with a deeply lined face. The smile seemed to be a permanent feature. He wore a black derby hat, a white collarless shirt and a black vest. A gold watch chain ran across the vest, linking the small pockets on either side.

"Now, if you two boys aren't policemen, I'll eat this hat. And without salt or vinegar." He smiled and extended his right hand. "Isaac Squires at your service, gentlemen. And was I right about your status in life?"

"Quite right, Mr. Squires," Stride said. "Guilty as charged."

"Then," Squires said, "as I've heard nothing of major criminal activity in the area, I'll assume you've come to visit Gaffer Fox. In fact, you have missed bumping into the bold Gaffer by no more than ten minutes. But you'll find him at his house, most likely digging in his garden in the back. The snow's not quite all gone, but Gaffer likes to get an early start on things. He's a man of the soil, Gaffer is, not that there's much of that around here."

Squires gave them detailed directions to Fox's house. As they were about to leave the store, Squires looked closely at Harry Phelan.

"Might you be Walter Phelan's boy, then?"

"I would be," Harry replied. The question didn't really surprise him.

"I knew there was something familiar about you when you walked in. 'I knows he,' I said to myself, 'sure enough I do.' Then your friend said your name, and I knew who you were. It was a long time ago, young Phelan, and you've grown a bit, upwards and outwards, but the boy is still there in the man. Your father is well, I hope?"

"Very well, Mr. Squires, and still working with boats and engines. I'll tell him you asked after him." Phelan paused before heading for the door. "My old man came down that day to work on Felix White's boat. I remember that Mr. White had one of the largest boats in the cove. How is he these days? Well, I hope?"

Squires looked down at the counter and shook his head.

"I'm sorry to say not, Mr. Phelan. Felix White drowned at sea, a few years after you and your dad were here. It was a bad storm that night and Felix probably lost his bearings. Ran his craft onto the rocks near Cape St. Francis. They all went down with her, Felix and three others." Squires shook his head. "It was a tragedy. The world can be a hard place, sometimes."

Gaffer Fox looked very much the country squire in a navy blue wool sweater, corduroy pants and rubber wellingtons. As Squires had predicted, Gaffer was digging in the garden behind his small frame house. Stride hadn't seen Fox in more than a year and he was surprised to see how much he had changed. The seaside climate must agree with him, Stride thought. Gaffer was leaner now, and he looked younger than he had in St. John's. His face was tanned even this early in the year, tribute to time spent outdoors during the unfriendly months. One thing had not changed, though. A hand-rolled cigarette was clenched firmly in his lips.

"Eric. Harry." Gaffer was beaming a welcome at them. "Grand to see you both. Couldn't have been happier when Bernard called to say you were on your way."

"You're looking well, Gaffer. You seem to have found your element."

"Damn true, Eric. A very nice place to live, as long as you don't have to pull a livelihood out of the sea. I am quite the retired gentleman now." Gaffer leaned his prong against the back fence, pushing the tines into the ground with his foot. "Come inside and take a seat, lads. I'll put the kettle on."

Fox poured tea into three mugs and placed the teapot on the back of the stove.

"There's an interesting little history to this place," Gaffer said, blowing across the top of his mug of tea, "and it goes back a century and a half. There was a well-to-do fisherman in Portugal Cove, Raymond Kelly by name. Raymond took up with a young woman named Caitlin Jones. Now, he was Catholic, and the lady was Protestant, but they were in love and determined to marry, in spite of the religious divide. And remember, the religious wars were even fiercer in those days than they are at the present time."

Gaffer snorted and lit a fresh cigarette.

"So the bold Kelly, fed up with the eternal arsing around between the minister and the priest, gives the finger to them both, hires a crew to put floats under his house, waits for a favourable wind, and has the place hauled down the shore to this spot. Must have cost him a bloody fortune, but he did it, and he called the place Caitlin's Cove, after his true love.

"And as far as I can determine, they lived happily ever after and raised a flock of children. The graveyard, back of the hill behind my place, is full of Kellys, and there are three Kelly families living here today. The village even has its own church, built by Mr. Raymond Kelly himself. It's a Free Church, in case you were wondering. The villagers refer to it as St. Raymond's."

Gaffer Fox poured more tea, sat back and crossed his legs. He looked at Stride and smiled indulgently.

"But you lads didn't journey down here to listen to the history of Caitlin's Cove, charming though it may be. Bernard's message said that you want to talk about the drowning death of one Jean Taylor back in 1924."

"Crotty told Harry we should talk to you about that," Stride said. "Harry's read the file twice, and one thing that stands out is the matter of the oilskin jacket that Jean Taylor was wearing the last time anyone saw her on the boat, but which she wasn't wearing when her body was found three days later."

Gaffer Fox rubbed the side of his nose with a tobacco-stained finger, nodding his head slowly.

"That affair is not one of my cherished memories. I was a young man, and still learning the ropes, so to speak. There was no constable stationed in Portugal Cove, where the schooner sailed from. The nearest station was in Torbay. Still is. And yours truly was stationed at Torbay in 1924. I made it to the wharf in Portugal Cove not long after the schooner tied up." Fox closed his eyes for a moment.

"The husband, Jack Taylor, was carrying on like a man gone mad. He was actually howling, tears running down his face, and he had to be held back by friends to keep him from throwing himself into the harbour. I never saw such a sight. It chilled me. There was no talking to Taylor, of course, so I found the skipper, and when I was finished taking his statement, I started on the passengers. Then one of the women grabbed me by the arm and started to have at me, mad as hell. She was looking back and forth between Taylor and me, and her language was ripe enough. She said Jack Taylor was a "goddamned son of a bitch." Her exact words. I can still hear them."

Fox tilted his head, as if he really could hear the voice echoing down through the years.

"Try and picture that scene, lads. We've got a young woman missing and presumed drowned in the bay, the husband is howling like a wounded dog, his friends are crowding around to give him comfort, and a nice lady is telling me the man is a son of a bitch."

"What was she on about, Gaffer? The inquest put no blame on Taylor for his wife's death."

"No, it didn't, and I didn't know what to make of it at the time. Later on, the lady came to see me, after the inquest was over and done with. The long

79

and the short of it is that she told me Jack Taylor was a regular ladies' man. She said he had been keeping company with a young woman at the store, had even set her up in a flat in town for a time."

"Do you suppose Taylor's wife knew this?"

"I wouldn't know about that. Some kind soul might have told her, of course. People will do the goddamnedest things sometimes, with the best of intentions." Fox shook his head and picked up the box of matches and tapped it against the table top. "Family situations were probably the worst things I had to deal with, Eric. I hated it. A domestic disturbance because a husband was cheating on his wife. Men who beat their wives. Sometimes a wife beating up on her husband." Fox took a deep breath, seemed almost in pain. "Even fathers who raped their daughters." He sighed and placed the box of matches on the table and sat with his head bowed.

"There's still the question of the yellow oilskin," Stride said, bringing Gaffer Fox back to the matter at hand. "Jean Taylor was wearing the oilskin just before she disappeared, and a crew member spotted it floating in the water. It's unlikely she just fell out of the thing when she went over the side."

"I know where you're going with this, Eric." Gaffer swallowed some tea. He looked at Stride and Phelan. "I don't think it was an accidental drowning. It's more than likely that Jean Taylor committed suicide. I've thought about it, and I've thought about it. And I believe that's what really happened that day on Conception Bay."

They drove back towards St. John's in silence for a time. The day had remained pleasant and sunny and Stride had the top down, the cool fresh air blowing through the small car. Phelan sat in the passenger seat, looking out at the passing countryside. His right hand, folded into a fist, rose and fell against his knee in an even, slow rhythm.

"Well," he said at last, "I have a problem believing that Jack Taylor was genuinely eaten up with grief about his wife's death when in fact he was having it on with another woman. What was it Gaffer said? Howling like a wounded dog? I think the lady had it closer to the truth."

"That Jack Taylor was a son of a bitch?" Stride laughed, then, matching the two descriptives. "Maybe. There's a phrase to cover that, Harry. You have to suspend your disbelief."

Phelan grunted. "And maintain an open mind? You're right, sir. I shall suspend my disbelief, just as you say." But he didn't look any happier.

"Although you would feel better if you could hang Jack Taylor up by the balls."

Phelan looked at Stride, smiling this time.

"Twenty years ago, yes. Probably. But now he's almost sixty years old, he's had a stroke, and someone has murdered his latest wife. I don't know if he's the same man any longer."

"He's the same man, Harry. Just older and frailer. Unlike some of the reptiles, humans don't have the luxury of shedding our skins and moving on. I wouldn't be surprised if Jack Taylor has had occasion over the last couple of days to think about that outing on Conception Bay."

"Perhaps one or two others have had occasion to think about it too. Do you suppose?"

"That wouldn't surprise me, either," Stride said.

t e n

Tommy Connars had managed to squeeze a decent selection of plants into his small backyard. A patch of thin grass covered most of the yard between the porch and the fence that separated his property from Ayre's Field. A large dogberry tree grew near the fence, its branches reaching into the field. The leaf buds had not yet opened, testimony to a long winter that was reluctant to depart. To the right of the tree was a dense stand of lilacs that covered the rest of the fence line and crowded against the side of the garage. A flower bed had been dug in front of the lilacs, and another bed ran the length of the Taylor garage on the opposite side of the garden. Connars was busy raking up the winter's debris when Stride arrived.

"I had a fine rosebush there by the garage for years, Eric," Connars said, "but the fungus got into it over the summer and killed it off. I think I might try again this year, though." He leaned on his rake and rearranged his thinning white hair with his right hand. "Do you garden at all, Eric?"

"I'm afraid not, Tommy," Stride said. "I think I lack the temperament. Not enough patience to wait for things to grow."

"I believe it may be an acquired taste. There was a time, when I was younger, that I probably felt the same as you. But as I've slowed over the years, I've found a certain pleasure in planting things and waiting for them to grow." He laughed. "Mind you, at my age, I tend to go in mostly for the annuals."

Stride smiled and walked to the fence and looked out into the field. A solitary horse was standing there, eating hay from a small pile that had been carried into the field.

"That fellow," Connars said, pointing to the horse, "has been lame for three days now. He's on holiday, you might say. I went out and had a look at him yesterday. Not a serious injury, just a bruised sole from having a stone lodged between shoe and frog. He'll be back pulling carts in a few days, though, earning his keep."

"You like to keep your hand in, Tommy?"

"Not in any real way, no, but I will always like horses. It's a pleasure for me to have them pastured out there. I often go out of an evening in the decent weather, just to stand near them and feel their presence. It's a nice feeling and it keeps the memories strong."

Stride turned his back to the field.

"What can you tell me about Jean Taylor, Tommy?"

Connars looked at Stride for a moment, then nodded.

"Poor Jean. I knew her as a neighbour, and as the mother of two young boys who would sometimes talk to me, the way young boys will talk to an older man who is not their father. Jean was a quiet girl, pretty, and very much involved with being a wife and mother. She was Jean Snow before she was married. The Snows lived up the hill, on McKay Street. They weren't well off, but through no fault of the father. Albert Snow was crippled in a railway accident when Jean was a young girl, and he was unable to work afterwards. It left a mark on Jean, seeing her father like that. He died just two years after the accident, and the family was almost destitute. Poverty had a terrible effect on Jean, accepting charity, wearing clothes that other families had discarded. When she married Jack Taylor, Jean made a total commitment. Her family, Jack and the two boys, they were her universe."

"Did Jack Taylor make the same commitment?"

Connars looked away, less startled than sad. He turned his attention to the grass again, but gave it up after a few half-hearted pulls with the rake.

"I see you've heard some things about Jack. He has a reputation, yes. I'm fifteen years older than Jack Taylor. I've known him all his life, and we've been friends, off and on, for almost all of that time. I suppose he felt that he had made a commitment to Jean, after his own lights. But it wasn't according to any generally accepted rule, no."

"I've been told that Jack's reaction to Jean's death was unusual. For want of a better word. Was it the reaction of a man who was involved with other women?"

"I will tell you a little story about that. I went to Jean's funeral, of course. When they lowered the box into the ground, it took three men to keep Jack from jumping into the grave after her. It was a disturbing thing. I didn't know what to make of it, then, and I still don't. I knew Jack had been involved with other women. Quite a few people knew it. Jack Taylor was a prick where women were concerned, no doubt about it. But he was a complicated prick."

"And a year later he married again."

"Yes. Irene was very much like Jean. She even looked like her. I felt at the time that Jack was trying to bring Jean back by marrying Irene."

"I suppose that's not unusual."

"I've seen it happen more than once. One of the dubious advantages of being old, Eric, if your brain hasn't turned into hardtack. If you've kept your eyes open at all, you've seen most of the peculiarities of human nature, and you spend a few minutes now and again reflecting on it all." Connars bent over and picked up a short piece of wood, a twig from the lilac. He tossed it over the fence into the field. "We almost adopted Jack's two boys for a time, Rebecca and me. That's when we became Uncle Tommy and Aunt Becky."

"That must have been about the time Edith Wright came to live with the Taylors," Stride said.

"Yes," Connars replied. "Edith came on when Irene was ill. Irene had cancer, you see, although she didn't linger for very long. A blessing of sorts."

"It must have been difficult for Edith, moving into a house with two young boys and a seriously ill woman?"

"I imagine it was. But she managed well enough. She was young enough that the boys could almost see her as a sister, I think, but old enough that she could have some authority."

"Where did she come from? Not from the city, I take it?"

"Oh, no," Connars said. "Not from here. She came from a little place up the coast called Harrows Bay. Edith's father was a fisherman. The family wasn't at all well off." Connars rubbed a hand over his head as though arranging memories. "Her parents passed on a number of years ago. I believe her mother went first, and a year after that the father died. That was before she married Jack, of course."

"I know where Harrows Bay is," Stride said. He drew into focus the picture of Edith and her parents. "As you said, it's a small place. I'm curious, though. How do young women from the outports come to find jobs as housekeepers in the city?"

"There are different ways, I suppose. We've never had a maid so I've no first-hand knowledge. Word of mouth has a lot to do with it, I think. I believe it was Irene who told me that Edith had an aunt who was a housekeeper or a maid in the city."

"When Jack Taylor married Edith, was that a surprise?"

"It was and it wasn't. I'd expected Edith to take her leave for good when the boys were older, when Jack was settled with Beryl. But I think she had become almost a part of the family. It's not unusual. Anyway, she was there when Beryl died quite suddenly. It was a heart attack that took her, one morning after she had driven Jack to work."

"Edith was an attractive woman," Stride said. "Were you surprised that she didn't marry and start her own family?"

"Well, it wasn't for lack of company, certainly. She often went out with young men, but nothing ever seemed to come of any of it. I suppose it's difficult when a young woman is in service. The job takes up most of her life, and she doesn't have the freedom that she would have in a home that is her own. Although Edith had quite a lot of freedom, especially during the war years."

Connars looked towards the kitchen window.

"Rebecca baked a cherry cake last night, Eric. I expect she'll have the kettle on for tea now." He leaned the rake against the side of the garage and motioned towards the back steps.

A large copper kettle was rumbling on the stove, a faint cloud of steam coming from its spout. Rebecca Connars looked at Stride from across the kitchen. She cradled a large brown teapot in her hands. Stride nodded a greeting.

"Make yourself at home, Eric," Connars said. "Take a seat at the table there. I just have to make one quick phone call and I'll be back."

It was the custom. If you were welcome in the home, you were invited to take tea in the kitchen. Strangers and the less well-favoured were treated more formally.

"How do you take your tea, Mr. Stride? Milk and sugar?" Rebecca Connars spooned loose tea into the pot from a green canister and poured in the boiling water. She placed the pot on the back of the stove and covered it with a tea-cosy decorated with the Union Jack. Stride wondered about that in the context of Connars' Irish heritage. Then he remembered that Connars, Irish surname notwithstanding, was a Presbyterian and a member of the congregation of the Kirk on Long's Hill.

"With milk, please."

"Milk in first, or after? Some people are very particular."

"Milk in first, thanks."

"That's the proper way," Rebecca Connars said, smiling. "The way my mother taught me. You've been brought up well, Mr. Stride."

"Well, that's done," Tommy Connars said, coming back into the kitchen. "Have you tried the cake, yet, Eric? Rebecca makes a grand cherry cake. It's my favourite."

Connars touched his wife's shoulder and then seated himself at the table. Stride was surprised to note that Rebecca Connars was almost a head taller than her husband, and was more robust in appearance. He conjured up an image of Rebecca Connars assisting in Tommy's forge, then turned the image on its head, making Rebecca Connars the blacksmith and her husband the assistant. It almost seemed to fit.

"I make one every week, Mr. Stride, and the cherries fall to the bottom every time. I can't seem to get them to stay up. My mother could, but I just don't seem to have the knack."

"It's a grand cake, anyway, my dear. I wouldn't have you change a thing. I will even say that I like the cherries on the bottom."

"Get away with you, Tommy. You're a terrible liar." She passed a plate of cake slices to Stride.

"I was telling Eric about my friend out there." Connars gestured towards Ayre's Field.

"The horse that went lame? But he's all right now, isn't he?"

"Almost perfect, my dear. Another few days and he'll be back in harness."

"I have to ask a few questions about the night Edith Taylor was killed," Stride said, reaching for a second piece of cake. Submarine cherries or no, Rebecca Connars made a damn fine cake. "Did you see Edith Taylor that night, Mrs. Connars?"

There was a brief silence before Rebecca Connars replied.

"Yes, I did. I saw her arrive home. I happened to be standing in the window. It was around eight o'clock. I was just cooking my supper then. I had fallen asleep in the late afternoon—it was dark, and the sound of the rain against the roof often makes me sleepy. I woke up about seven. I remember that because Tommy and I always have our tea at six and I remarked it was an hour past that and I hadn't even started to cook. While my supper was cooking I walked into the living room and saw Edith Taylor get out of a car and run into the house."

"Can you describe the car?"

"It was a small black car. It was a man who was driving. And the car only had two doors. I remember that."

"Had you seen that car before?"

"Not that I can remember, no."

She drank some tea and placed the cup on the table. Stride could sense her discomfort.

"Her companion didn't go into the house with her?"

"No. They sat in the car and talked for a few minutes. Edith stood on the sidewalk in the rain and watched him drive away down the hill. Then she ran up the steps and into the house."

"Do you think her companion was a friend of Mr. Taylor's also?" Stride anticipated the answer but he was interested in how Rebecca Connars might respond to the question.

"I wouldn't think so." Her phrasing was curt and she sharply turned her head away. Then she picked up her cup and quickly drank some tea.

"Jack and Edith had separate friends, Eric." Connars smiled uncertainly at Stride. "It was the difference in their ages, you see. You would expect that, of course."

"Did you know Edith Taylor well?" Stride dropped the question between them.

"Well enough," Rebecca said. "I know the type, certainly."

"We were friends with Beryl," Connars said, anxiety in his voice. "And with Jean, too. We never had much chance to know poor Irene, of course."

"I can still remember the day Edith Wright first arrived at the house," Rebecca Connars said suddenly. "She and her father drove up in an old truck, that looked like it would fall to bits if someone slammed the door on it. I was standing at the front window and there they were, that little man and his daughter standing on the sidewalk in front of the house, himself carrying her old cardboard suitcase for her. I told Tommy that I was afraid the thing would fall apart and her clothes would be all over the street."

She wiped her mouth with purpose, her eyes bright and hard with the memory. Stride's mind pulled forward the photograph of Edith Wright and her parents, on the dresser in her bedroom. Rebecca Connars had called him a "little man". Her description had nothing to do with his physical appearance. He saw that Rebecca Connars' hand was shaking slightly. He had seen this kind of enmity before. As often as not, it was the Protestant-Catholic rift, at other times, the entrenched antagonism between city and outport, typically caused by the inherent snobbishness of the townie.

"I'll have another piece of your cake, my dear," Connars said quickly, holding out his plate. He broke the slice of cake into three pieces and selected first the part with the cluster of red cherries.

Stride was sorry for Connars' obvious discomfort, but he wasn't ready to leave yet. If Rebecca Connars was in the mood to declaim, something useful might come forward.

"It must have been a surprise when Jack Taylor married Edith," Stride said. He drank some tea and carefully selected another piece of cake, breaking it into pieces the way Connars had done.

"Edith Wright made a catch, and no mistake," Rebecca Connars said. She seemed about to say more, but then turned and stared through the window that looked out on the backyard.

"It was a surprise," Connars said. "I won't deny that. But it seemed to work well enough for them both."

For the little time that it lasted, Stride thought.

The atmosphere in the kitchen was heavy with tension. Rebecca Connars continued to look through the window. Stride wondered if some of her closely controlled anger might now be directed towards him. Further questions would get him nowhere. Connars looked weary and his face was slightly flushed. Stride swallowed the last of his tea and stood up.

"I thank you for your time, Mrs. Connars. And the cherry cake was a treat." Rebecca Connars' smile was small and fleeting. She clutched the crumpled table napkin in her right hand and dabbed at the corners of her mouth. She went back to looking through the window.

There was a knocking then at the back door. Connars jumped to his feet and walked quickly through the porch. Stride heard a murmured exchange of greetings and Connars returned to the kitchen with a thin man of moderate height who appeared to be in his middle seventies. On a second glance, Stride thought that the man might be younger, but he had a pale, fragile look that aged him.

"Eric, this is Rebecca's cousin, Francis Morgan. Frank often drops by this time of day for a cup of tea with Rebecca and me."

Stride glanced at Rebecca Connars. She seemed more relaxed now that her cousin was standing in the kitchen. He wondered about the phone call Connars had made before. Had it been to Francis Morgan, asking him to come to the house, perhaps anticipating the scene that had developed with his wife and her antagonism towards Edith Taylor? Connars had also mentioned Francis Morgan on Sunday, in Jack Taylor's cabin.

"My pleasure, Mr. Morgan," Stride said, extending his hand. Morgan's hand was cold and limp. Morgan nodded to Stride and smiled, but did not speak. "You'll have to excuse me," Stride said, "I was just about to leave. I'll find my way out, Tommy." He picked up his hat, nodded to Rebecca Connars and her cousin, and went out through the porch.

He stood on the concrete landing at the bottom of the wooden steps and took a deep breath. He patted his pockets, looking for a cigarette. The solitary horse was still on the spot in the field where it had been earlier. The animal looked at Stride for a few moments, vigorously shook his mane, then lowered his head to grasp another mouthful of hay.

e l e v e n

Stride poured a second glass of rum and settled back into his chair. The last movement of Beethoven's Sixth Symphony was on the phonograph. He picked up his book, opened it at the marker, stared at the page, then closed it again. Margaret had phoned earlier, suggesting that they get together for the evening. Stride had declined, and now he regretted it. He was in one of those moods when being alone was a curse, but the thought of company was also unwelcome. He picked up his drink, swallowed a little, and balanced the glass on the arm of the chair.

There was a knock at the door of the flat. Stride looked at his watch. It was just past eight and he wasn't expecting anyone. He sat still for a moment longer. The knock was repeated. He couldn't pretend that he was not at home. He didn't play his music at a low volume, and whoever was there could certainly hear it. He wondered if Margaret had seen through his remoteness, as she sometimes did, and had decided to come over anyway. He smiled at the thought, and opened the door.

Joanne Taylor stood in the doorway looking at him with her large dark eyes. Her hands were buried in the pockets of her navy-blue raincoat. She smiled tentatively. Stride stepped back a half pace and opened the door wider.

"I've been driving around your neighbourhood for the last forty minutes, Eric. And sitting in my car for another fifteen."

"Some decisions take longer than others," Stride said. It was an inane comment, but he couldn't think clearly.

He took a wooden hanger from the closet. Joanne turned away from him and unbuttoned her coat.

"I've taken you by surprise, haven't I? I hope I haven't interrupted something?"

"No. I was just reading and having a drink."

"A drink," she said. "I think I could use a drink, too."

"I'm having a rum and water. Is that still your drink?"

"Yes. Some things don't change."

He brought her a glass. Then he turned down the volume on the phonograph. She had seated herself in the chair next to his. The record was almost at an end. Joanne ran her fingers over the pattern on the heavy crystal.

"These are new."

"Yes."

"A gift?"

"Yes."

"Perhaps I shouldn't ask from whom."

Stride smiled. He knew she could sense his unease.

"Thomas Butcher gave them to me two Christmases ago. A set of eight."

Mention of Butcher's name brought their focus back to Edith Taylor's murder, and the scene in the house on Leslie Street. They fell into an awkward silence.

"How is Thomas?" she said, finally. "I haven't seen him since—well, since before I last saw you. Really saw you, that is. Passing each other on the street doesn't count. I guess it's been almost three years."

"Yes." He resisted the impulse to say something clever about time flying. "Thomas is fine. He works too hard, smokes too much, but it suits him. He'd be unable to live any other way."

"I suppose so." They were silent again. Joanne held up her glass. "This is very good. And I need it just now."

"I expect so. Things must be very disorganised." It wasn't the right word, but it would do.

"Yes." She sighed and sat back against the chair, closed her eyes. Stride watched her. She had changed only a little in three years, less than he might have expected. Less like a girl now, more like a woman. He wondered if she would approve of his thinking that way. The record came to an end and the needle grated on the surface. He walked across the room and turned off the phonograph.

"That was Beethoven, wasn't it?"

"Yes. Some things don't change. Just as you said."

"And some things do." She looked at him for a moment. "I wanted to see you, Eric. Is it all right that I came?"

"Yes. It's all right with me. Is it all right with you? That's more to the point."

"You were always good at getting to the point."

"No, Jo. Getting to the point was more your forte than mine," he said, his tone sharper than he intended.

She turned away from him. Her face was slightly flushed.

Stride sipped his drink. There was a humming in his ears.

"You're right." She sat forward in the chair, poised. "And I really don't know if it is all right with me. I will probably change my mind about that twelve times over the next two days. But I wanted to see you, and here I am."

"It's all right." Too many 'all rights,' he thought. "Did you want to talk about Edith? Or about Jack and Edith?"

"Yes," she said. "Yes and no."

She wants me to add something to that, he thought, but I'm not going to. It's her agenda, not mine.

There was a long silence. Stride ran a scenario through his mind that had Margaret Nichol in his flat when Joanne arrived. He started a second one with him and Margaret in bed together, but cut that one short. The third possibility was that Margaret still might arrive unannounced. She did that sometimes. He didn't want to think about that one.

"How much do you know about the Taylor family?" she asked.

"Some. And I'll learn a lot more."

"Of course. Have you talked to Bobby?"

"Yes."

"What did you think of him?"

"Various things," Stride said after a short pause.

"That was coy."

"Not coy. Evasive. I'd rather not say what I thought of Bobby Taylor. But I would like to know what you think of him."

She smiled, more comfortable now that they were talking about someone else. "I like Bobby. He's difficult, and short-tempered and unpredictable. He drinks too much and eats too little, but I like him anyway. And I know what you're probably thinking. That I like him because he is all of that. And perhaps that's true."

"He's different from Ned, certainly."

"Oh, yes." She paused for a moment and stared at the rug. Stride's mentioning her husband's name had restored the uneasiness. "He's very different from Ned. And he has a lot more character than you might think. He enlisted in the Royal Navy almost as soon as the war started. He had a good record. Better than good. He was wounded. And he was decorated."

"I knew that. His father told us. The day after Edith was killed, on Sunday, when we drove out to the cabin at Tors Cove. He talked a bit about his family then, in a random sort of way." He paused. "Tell me more about your brother-in-law. He doesn't have a regular job, yet he appears to be comfortable financially. I assume he has a pension of some sort, but he must have another source of income."

"You really have to ask Bobby about that, Eric." She looked away and frowned, then smiled. "Bobby spent some time in England and the continent right after the war. There was a lot of activity then, and a lot of it wasn't exactly legal."

"Smuggling?"

"He didn't tell me much, just hints, really. All he said was that there were opportunities for a man with a naval background, someone who knew ships and boats."

"It sounds like smuggling," Stride said. He was silent for a moment, thinking of the days before he came back to Newfoundland from St. Pierre. He and Bobby Taylor might have things to talk about, should the opportunity arise. "I take it he made some money out of it?"

"Oh, yes. I think he made quite a lot of money. Enough to live comfortably now. He rationalised it as an opportunity to be exploited, a bonus for services rendered in defence of king and country."

"Interesting. Very different from his father, then." Stride looked at Joanne Taylor over the top of his glass.

"Yes," she said. "Did you know that Jack Taylor had a stroke just over a year ago?"

Stride almost said yes, but caught himself.

"I wondered about that. He seemed to have some difficulty at the cabin. Nothing major, but he needed help taking off his boots."

"Strokes run in his family, apparently. His father died of a stroke, and so did his grandfather, and an uncle. Jack was terrified when he had his stroke. I'm sure he thought he was going to die. It turned out that it was only a very small stroke. But it changed him."

"How?"

"Jack has—how shall I put this?—a reputation."

"Yes?" Theme and variations.

"Yes. Perhaps it won't seem like such a big thing to you. Men look at these things differently than women."

"And some men look at things differently than other men."

"I'm sorry," she said after a moment. "That was unfair." Joanne traced the pattern on the crystal with her finger. "Jack was an unfaithful husband. Someone told me once that Jack Taylor has had more women than the average man has had hot meals."

"And his stroke changed all that?"

"Yes, I think so. That's the popular view, anyway. The stroke reminded him that the men in his family die fairly young, and it brought home the fact that he was no longer young. The change in him seemed quite dramatic."

"Is that why he married Edith?"

"I'm sure it had a lot to do with it."

"Which begs a question. Why did Edith marry Jack?"

"A number of reasons, I suppose. Security would be close to the top of the list, I think. But I'm guessing. I really wasn't privy to the whys and wherefores. Edith lived with Jack Taylor and his family, in their various incarnations, for almost twenty years. I think they agreed on an arrangement, an understanding of some sort."

"To their mutual advantage? He would arrange for her over the long term, and Edith would look after him in the short term. For as long as it took?"

"That sounds very cold-blooded, but it might have been like that, I suppose."

"How was your relationship with Edith?"

"Not close."

She placed her glass on the small table between the two chairs, stood up, and walked to the window. She pulled the drapes apart and looked out at the street.

"It's started to rain again." She drew a line on the condensation on the glass, then turned to face him, hands behind her back. "I wish we had talked more about things, Eric. Back when it might have made a difference."

"We'll never know, will we?" His voice had a harder tone than he wanted. He wished he hadn't said anything.

He wasn't surprised that she was trying to bring the past forward. She had started seeing Ned Taylor almost as soon as they separated, which made Stride wonder if Taylor was part of the reason for their arguments. Not long afterward, Joanne and Ned were engaged, and they were married soon after that. "Unseemly haste" was the phrase Thomas Butcher had used to describe the engagement and marriage. Stride had pretended to be amused.

"I don't know." She started to say something else, but offered a brief smile instead. She seemed agitated now. "I probably should go. I probably shouldn't have come in the first place."

But when she moved, it was only to turn back towards the window. Stride walked across the room and stood behind her. He wanted to touch her, remembering what that felt like. He didn't, but stood close enough for her to know that he was there.

"I was pregnant," she said. She continued to look through the window. "I had a miscarriage two weeks after Ned and I were married. I spent a week in the hospital." She shook her head and made a sound that might have been a try at laughter. "It wasn't much of a honeymoon, anyway. The stay in the hospital seemed almost appropriate somehow."

She had taken him by surprise. He hadn't known about the pregnancy. But, then, they hadn't had mutual friends. And though St. John's wasn't a large city, neither was it a hamlet where everyone knew everything about everyone else. It was large enough for family secrets. He went to the table and picked up his glass.

"And the marriage?" The question sounded cold, and Stride winced at his clumsiness. Still, it was a fair question under the circumstances. Joanne was setting the directions for their conversation, for the evening.

"It's not perfect," she said, "but we get by." She turned and looked at him.

"Have you gone back to work? I hadn't heard that you had." When they had met, Joanne worked for a solicitor, Brendan Madigan, who had originally trained for the priesthood but, after two years, had fled the seminary in Ireland. Madigan had lived in New York City for a time before returning to St. John's to article as a lawyer.

"No. I probably will, though. I don't think Ned and I will have a family, and I don't much enjoy idleness."

"The time hangs heavy?"

"Yes. Sometimes."

"Do you still have the property at the pond?" Her family's home, east of St. John's. She had lived there with her mother, had cared for her through her final illness. But that had been a long time ago, before she and Stride had met. She had moved into the city when her mother died.

"Yes." She seemed surprised that he mentioned it. "I still have it, but I never go there now." She picked up her drink. "Memories," she said.

He nodded, although he wasn't certain which memories she referred to. Memories of her family? Their one visit to the place? He wondered if perhaps she and Ned had gone to the house sometimes, but he didn't want to ask her about that.

"Our lives weren't complicated enough," she said. She wasn't smiling exactly. "My coming here tonight, I hope it was all right. You were going to have to see me eventually, Eric, and I'd rather it was like this than in some horribly formal interview."

"The horribly formal interview will have to take place anyway, Jo." The sensitive policeman speaks.

"I know. But I'm still glad that I came to see you this evening. I hope you're not too unhappy about it." She walked to the closet by the door. Stride took the coat from the wooden hanger. The metal hook clanked against the coat rail.

"I'm not unhappy," he said, but no convenient adjective presented itself to him. "Can I ask you a question about the Taylors? Don't answer if you don't want to."

"I'll answer if I can."

"Have Ned or Bobby ever suggested to you that their mother might have committed suicide?" Spoken out loud, the question sounded unexpectedly cold and harsh. Joanne's expression didn't change much, but he knew he had surprised her.

"Yes," she said after a moment. "Bobby told me once that he thought Jean had killed herself."

"And Ned?"

"He's never said it in so many words. He's almost never talked about it. But I believe he thinks she committed suicide."

"Do they blame their father for that?"

"Oh yes, I think they do."

"Does Jack know that?"

"I think so, yes. In the way that people know such things, without ever talking about them. It shows up in other ways."

For an instant she looked sad, thoughtful. She started to open the door, then turned back to him.

"I'd like to see you again, Eric." The words tumbled out, taking them both by surprise.

"Well," he said, then paused. He didn't know what to say, wasn't able to think clearly. "There's the interview, of course."

"I know," Joanne said, thoughtful again. "The interview. But I wasn't thinking about that. It's probably a bad idea, though. All things considered." She looked away from him. Her face was flushed, an unfamiliar trace of uncertainty in her eyes.

"There's a lot going on, now, Jo." He looked for the right words, wondered why he didn't simply decline. And knew why.

Joanne reached out and touched his face. She looked into his eyes.

"I'm sorry, Eric. I see that I've made you uncomfortable." She smiled. "Made us both uncomfortable, I guess." Then she turned and left, the door closing softly behind her.

Stride went back into the room and picked up his drink, rolled the crystal glass between his fingers. He walked to the window, looked down at the street. He watched as Joanne got into a small English car, a Hillman it looked like, and started the engine. She turned on the headlights and pulled away from the curb. Stride dropped the curtain back into place and sat down in his chair. He held the glass up to the light, looked through the amber liquid for a moment, then drank about half of it. He laid his head back against the chair and closed his eyes. The images of Margaret and Joanne competed for his attention.

"Christ." He spoke the word softly, but it seemed loud in the still and silent room.

twelve

Kevin Noseworthy knocked at the door of Stride's office in the middle of the afternoon.

"I have some results on the fingerprint analysis, sir. As I suspected, most of the prints in the bathroom are Mr. and Mrs. Taylor's. The two sets of prints on the tub are Mr. Edward Taylor's, just as we thought."

"And the others?"

"No identification, yet, I'm afraid. I'm still working on the set I took from the doorjamb. And the one from the doorknob. That's the most useful lot. But, it's a difficult process when you don't have all ten fingers together."

"Was there anything useful from downstairs?"

"Excluding those of us who were officially on the scene, including Dr. Butcher, and Mr. Taylor's friend George Shaw, they're mostly prints from the family members."

"Mrs. Edward Taylor?"

"Yes, sir. Quite a few of those, all over the house, actually, including the bathroom. Not many from Mr. Robert Taylor, though, as you suggested. I guess he didn't visit very often."

"Did you find any of his prints in or around the bathroom?"

"No, sir. None at all."

"Interesting. If he visited, presumably he never had to take a leak."

"Superior holding tank, maybe. Mark of the seasoned drinker." Noseworthy grinned. "Or he cleaned up after himself the night of the murder. But some of the prints I found match those from the bathroom, including the set on the doorjamb and the knob."

"Where did you find them? The ones that match the prints from the bathroom door?"

"All over the place, including in the lady's bedroom. I get the impression that he might have been a regular visitor. With privileges."

Stride thought about that.

"Anything else?"

"A random collection of prints that don't match any of the family members, or our mysterious visitor. They could belong to anyone, sir. Neighbours, visitors, plumber, electrician. Rich man, poor man, beggarman, thief." Adding the last four in a sing-song. "As usual, sir, our best hope is that you arrest a suspect so that we can do a comparison. But if the killer is someone in the family, the fingerprint evidence won't be worth much."

As Noseworthy was leaving, Harry Phelan walked into Stride's office.

"We have a witness of sorts," Phelan said. He was smiling. "She just walked in off the street and said she had something to tell us about last Saturday night."

"Are you kidding me, Harry? What do you mean "of sorts" and what's that grin all about?"

"Come see for yourself. Her name is Ida Furlong. She's a very feisty lady, our Mrs. Furlong is. And she'll only speak to the officer in charge. She doesn't intend to waste her time and energy on the likes of detective sergeants. She was quite definite about that."

Ida Furlong looked to be at least seventy-five years old, a tiny bird-like woman with sharp features, bright blue eyes, and blue-rinsed hair. She sat stiffly on a wooden chair in the interview room, knees and feet close together, a black leather handbag resting on her knees and clutched tightly in both hands. She wore a grey woollen overcoat, a black hat, and rubber overshoes. Her thin legs were encased in heavy brown stockings.

"This is Inspector Stride, Mrs. Furlong. He's the officer in charge of this case."

Ida Furlong looked at Stride, running her eyes up and down his frame.

"Well, you're big enough. My Percy always said they chose policemen for the height and the weight."

"Percy?" Stride said.

"My late husband, God rest his soul."

"Would you like a cup of tea, Mrs. Furlong?" Stride tried not to sigh openly. "Sergeant Phelan will be happy to get one for you."

"Yes I would. And thank you. It's Phelan, is it?" She had raised her voice a notch. "That's an Irish name, Phelan. And what kind of a name is Stride, if I may ask? I don't know of any Strides that I can think of."

"I'll just go and get that tea, sir. Can I bring you anything while I'm at it?"

Harry was still smiling.

Stride shook his head and turned back to Ida Furlong.

"It's an English name, Mrs. Furlong. One of my ancestors came from Hampshire, I believe."

"English," Ida Furlong said. Her features hardened a bit. "And you're a Protestant, I suppose."

"Yes, ma'am. Guilty as charged." Stride doubted that he would score many points if he said he wasn't a regular churchgoer. He took a seat and rested his forearms on the table. He wondered if this might be a long interview. "Sergeant Phelan said you had some information for us about Mrs. Taylor's death?"

"I have."

Stride placed his notebook on the table and screwed the cap off his pen.

"What's that for?" Ida Furlong shifted in her chair.

"I always make notes when I interview a witness, Mrs. Furlong. To make sure that I don't forget anything important. It's a standard procedure."

"Is it, now? Well you just be careful what you write down."

"I will, Mrs. Furlong. You can trust me." He gave her what he hoped was his warmest smile. "Can you tell me what you saw on Saturday night?"

"I'll have my tea first. Is that boy going to be long?"

"I'm sure he'll be back very soon, Mrs. Furlong." And if he isn't I'll wring his fucking neck, Stride thought. "Where do you live, Mrs. Furlong?"

"I live on Warbury Street, almost to Shaw's Lane. I lived there with my Percy and now that he's gone ahead, God rest his soul, I live there by myself. Almost fifty years I've lived there." She looked towards the door. Phelan came into the room and set a tray down in front of her. It contained a small pot of tea, a cup and saucer, spoon, milk and sugar. Ida Furlong lifted the lid of the pot and stirred the tea. She poured milk into the cup first, then the tea. Finally she measured out a spoonful of sugar and stirred it in.

Stride smiled again while Phelan seated himself at the table.

"Can you tell us what you saw on Saturday night?"

"I was at Mass on Saturday night. As I am every night and every morning of the week." She set her cup carefully on the saucer. "You make a nice cup of tea, Sergeant Phelan."

"Thank you, ma'am. I am happy that you think so."

"Twice a day, every day." She turned towards Phelan, her expression serious. "Do you attend Mass, Sergeant Phelan?"

"Yes, ma'am. Every Sunday."

"Every Sunday? The Lord does not relax on the other six days, Sergeant Phelan."

"Yes, ma'am. Can you tell us about last Saturday night?"

"I was at Mass, as usual, and I stayed on at the cathedral for a while afterwards. That's St. Patrick's Cathedral on Patrick Street. I stayed longer than usual. It was that quiet and peaceful, I lost track of the time, like. Father Reagan it was that put his hand on my shoulder and told me that it was going on for eight and asked if I shouldn't be thinking about getting along home."

"You're sure of the time, Mrs. Furlong?"

"Yes, I am. I had my watch on, and I set it every day by the radio, and anyway, Father Reagan said what time it was when he spoke to me."

"And you left the church then?"

"Yes, I did. Father Reagan asked me if I wanted a drive home as it was raining outside. He's a sweet man, Father Reagan, good as gold to his mother, and she was a widow all these years after old Mr. Reagan died of the cancer. But I said no, that it was the Lord that sent the rain, and that I had walked through the rain to get to the cathedral, and I would walk through the rain to take myself back home. A drop of rain never hurt anyone, I told him. And anyway I had my rubber boots and my umbrella."

"What did you see that you think would interest us?"

"I saw a man is what I saw. On Warbury Street."

She gave her head a little toss and her eyes flashed.

"Tell us about that, please." Stride felt his right leg start to twitch. "Where did you see this man?"

"On Warbury Street. I just told you where I saw him."

Stride put a hand on his leg to hold it steady. "Yes, of course. What was it about the man that caught your attention?"

"He was the only other person on the street that I saw. And he didn't have an umbrella, and I thought that was some foolish of him. But he was wearing a hat. A big hat it was, with a wide brim."

"Was there anything else that caught your attention? Did he do anything or say anything unusual?"

"Of course he didn't say anything. He was on the other side of the street and passed me by. But he looked right at me, very bold. He didn't smile or speak, he just looked at me and then he looked ahead, and then he was gone."

Stride glanced at Phelan and made a note about the hat. It was the only remarkable item that she had mentioned.

"Well," he said, clearing his throat. "Thank you Mrs. Furlong. That was very interesting."

"I'm not finished yet, Mr. Stride. I wouldn't have walked all the way down here from Warbury Street if all I saw was a man walking, now would I?"

She walked? Christ, it was more than a mile to Fort Townshend from Warbury Street. And there were steep hills along the way.

"I'm sorry, Mrs. Furlong. Please continue."

"I saw him in Ayre's Field. The man. He was in the field after he passed me by. I saw him there. And I thought that was a very strange thing."

"You saw this man go over the fence into the field?"

"No, I never did. I didn't see him go into the field. You're not listening to what I'm telling you. I saw him in the field. After he passed by me, I turned to take a look at him and he wasn't anywhere on the street, and I thought that was odd, so I stopped and had a look around. And there he was walking across the field, very fast, and I believe he was heading in the direction of the Taylors' backyard."

Phelan spoke. "Are you certain it was the man you saw in the field, Mrs. Furlong? It was dark and it was raining. Is it possible that it was one of the horses you saw?"

Ida Furlong sat up very straight in her chair.

"My eyes aren't what they used to be, Sergeant Phelan. But I can still tell a man from a horse." She fixed Phelan with a cold stare. "Although when the horse is turned back on, it's easy enough sometimes to confuse the two."

Harry Phelan cleared his throat. Stride's right leg had stopped twitching. Stride stared at a picture of the King and Queen on the wall to the right of Ida Furlong. He hoped he wasn't smiling.

"What time would that have been, Mrs. Furlong?" Phelan was carefully polite. "When you saw the man in the field, I mean?"

"I would say it was about twenty of nine. I say that because I got in the house when it was almost a quarter of nine. I always look at the clock in the hall when I get home. It's a fine old clock that my Percy gave me for a present on our thirtieth wedding anniversary, and it keeps wonderful time."

"Can you describe the man you saw on the street, Mrs. Furlong?"

"He was taller than I was. But almost everyone is." She smiled for the first time, her old blue eyes twinkling. She had one-upped the two detectives and she knew it. Stride wondered if old ladies with time on their hands sat down and plotted this kind of ambush, rehearsed it over and over so they would get it exactly right when the moment arrived. "But he wasn't as tall as my Percy. He was a fine, big man, my Percy. I would say the man was just about Sergeant

Phelan's height, perhaps a little shorter."

"About five-eight. Anything else?"

"He could do with a few good meals. He was very thin, to my way of thinking. Not like my Percy at all. And he wasn't a dark-complexioned man. Fair of skin I would have said, although it was dark and he was wearing his big hat and he had his coat collar turned up."

"Do you think you would recognise the man if you saw him again?"

"I think I might, Mr. Stride, but I'm not completely sure and certain. I don't have a really clear picture of his face in my mind's eye. Just a picture of himself in the rain, with a big hat and a coat with the collar turned up." She paused for a moment and seemed to reflect.

"Was there something else?"

"His eyes," she said, a little uncertainly. "He had very keen eyes, I thought. I think I would recognise his eyes if I saw them again."

"What do you think, sir? Do you suppose she really saw our man? It almost seems too good to be true."

"I think that's one blue-haired old dear who misses very little that goes on around her, and doesn't forget a thing. The time is about right. Remember, she had no way of knowing what time frame we're looking at. I think it's very likely that she did see our man."

"Might very well be the case," Phelan said. "It occurs to me, though, that it's a tight little neighbourhood out there, sir. Like most neighbourhoods in the city."

"And she didn't recognise him, did she? A stranger who wears a hat with a wide brim and who stares boldly at devout old ladies on their way home from Mass. It's not much, but it's something."

"Maybe he lives in a different part of town, then."

"Like the South Side, maybe?"

"That would be too good to be true, sir."

"It's easy enough to check out, Harry. Go see Jack Taylor and ask him for a photograph of Bobby Taylor. Then drop in on Mrs. Furlong. If she gives us a positive ID, I'll buy you a beer."

"And if she doesn't?"

"I'll buy you a beer, anyway."

"That's the best offer I've had today," Phelan said. "In fact, it's the only one. I'm on my way."

He picked up his hat and mackintosh and headed for the door.

thirteen

Margaret Nichol phoned a few minutes after Phelan had left for Jack Taylor's house.

"I missed you last night, Eric. I almost came over to your place, anyway." Stride leaned back in his chair and stared at the ceiling, a dismal scenario taking form in his imagination. He thought about Margaret, and all the things he liked about her, and wondered why in God's name he had given a second thought to the overture from Joanne Taylor. Her being married to Ned Taylor was the least part of his consternation.

"I really was preoccupied, Margaret." Some of her friends called her Madge, but it was a name Stride disliked. For him, it conjured up the image of a matronly woman with greying hair and heavy arms.

"The Taylor murder?"

"Yes. I really can't talk about it, but the thing is starting to look complicated."

"It won't be a one-day wonder, then?"

"No, it won't." The rule of thumb on murders was that if they weren't solved in the first twenty-four hours, the trail quickly went cold. But maybe that only applied to big cities where murders seemed to be a dime a dozen. A murder in St. John's was something of an event. Stride thought of Harry Phelan walking up to Ida Furlong's door with a photograph of Bobby Taylor, and being told that the stranger with the large hat and bold stare was someone other than Jack Taylor's younger son. That didn't rule out Bobby Taylor entirely, but it put him beyond their grasp. For the moment.

"Come over to my place for supper tonight, Eric. I'd like to see you. And I might even be able to take your mind off your job for a few hours."

Suddenly, he wanted to see Margaret, have a drink, eat a relaxed dinner, spend the evening. Maybe spend the night. He ran the day's program through his mind. He and Harry were going to interview Ned and Joanne at their home at six. After that, they had arranged to meet Jimmy Peach at a tavern. Peach was their principal source of street information, and an old friend. Peach had phoned Stride that morning.

"Eric?" Margaret's voice brought him back to the here and now. "Are you still there?"

"Yes. Of course. I was getting my ducks in a row." He could arrange to meet Joanne and her husband an hour early. As for Jimmy Peach, he was usually in the Squared Circle tavern on Gower Street anytime after five o'clock. It wouldn't bother him if Stride and Phelan arrived earlier than expected.

"And what do your ducks tell you?" Stride could hear the smile in Margaret's voice, feel her warmth.

"That I'll be there, but it probably won't be until after seven. Maybe well after seven, depending on how things go. Is that still all right?" He fished a cigarette from his package and lit it. Suddenly his day looked brighter.

"That will be fine, Eric. We'll have a late supper. And your coming late, it will give me a chance for a long, soothing bath." She made it sound like the prelude to something very nice. Stride sat up straighter, a warm feeling running through him.

"I'll call you later, then. When I have a better idea of what's what."

He hung up the phone and smoked his cigarette, images of Margaret Nichol and Joanne Taylor competing for space in his mind. He rubbed the back of his neck and made himself think about Edith Taylor, about his job. He picked up the phone and gave the operator the number for Ned Taylor's office. There was no chance that he was going to speak to Joanne just now.

Ned Taylor looked better than he had when Stride had last seen him at his father's house on Saturday night. But there were dark smudges under his eyes and he had an air of weary anxiety. He wore dark grey suit pants, a white shirt that had probably been fresh for work that morning, the top button undone, and a dark-patterned tie pulled down about four inches. Taylor buttoned the shirt and snugged the tie into the vee of his collar as he ushered the detectives into the living room. Joanne was standing by the fireplace, one hand on the mantelpiece, in what she probably hoped was a casual pose. She glanced at Stride, then quickly looked away.

"I've tried to recall as much as I could from Saturday evening, Mr. Stride,

but I'm afraid that I can't add anything much to what I've told you already."
He gestured towards the couch and chairs and took the lead by sitting in
a severely straight-backed arm chair. "I was in the Militia during the war, and
I injured my back lifting ammunition boxes onto a truck. This is the only
comfortable chair in the house."

"Was there anything at all you wanted to add to your earlier statement?"
Stride asked. He was uneasy in this house. He concentrated on not looking at
Joanne and hoped that Phelan would take good notes.

"I think the only thing I might have left out was the fact that the bathroom
door was closed when I came upstairs. I suppose the killer must have closed
it after himself. I wonder why?" He looked at Phelan, then at Stride. "In
retrospect, it just seems odd. That's the only reason I mention it."

"Have you thought of anyone who would want to harm"—silly word, but
it sounded better than kill—"your stepmother, Mr. Taylor?" Taylor had
already told them that the bathroom door had been closed when he arrived at
the house. Stride chanced a quick look at Joanne. "Mrs. Taylor?"

"I can't think of anyone who would," Taylor replied. "Edith worked for
my father for almost twenty years, all told. She was a housekeeper. How many
enemies can a housekeeper make?"

Joanne Taylor stood up.

"I was about to make tea. I'll just go and tend to that." She walked quickly to the kitchen. They heard the sound of the kettle being filled.

"It's not all that difficult to make enemies," Stride said. He wondered how
much, if anything, Taylor knew about him and Joanne. "What can you tell us
about Edith Taylor's life outside your father's house?"

"Not very much. Edith had her own life, apart from us. When Bobby
and I were grown and out on our own, Edith's duties weren't all that onerous.
I know she had friends that she did things with. I didn't know any of them,
really. Just at the moment I can't think of any of their names."

"Why did your father keep Edith on as housekeeper after you and your
brother were grown? He had married again. A housekeeper seems a bit
extravagant."

"He could afford it. And I think Beryl liked the idea at least as much as
Dad did. Beryl wasn't much for cooking and housework. She liked having
someone to do all the things she didn't want to do."

"Beryl wasn't from here, you know." Joanne had quietly returned to the
living room. She was sitting on a small chair near the entrance to the dining
room. Stride had not seen her come back.

"She wasn't a Newfoundlander. She was an American from Boston. Jack met her when he was on holiday there, visiting with relatives, cousins, after Irene died. Her family was well-connected there, although most of the real money had disappeared through bad investments, even before the Depression. But Beryl wasn't poor. By our standards, she was well off. Having a house-keeper suited her. And she was something of a snob."

"In what way?" Stride could see the familiar shine in Joanne's eyes. She had never held soft opinions. Ned was not looking at her. He seemed to focus his attention on a spot behind her left shoulder.

"Not in any awful way. But she believed in the class system. Many Americans do, you know, for all their chatter about equality and democracy. Especially when they come to places they see as being backward by their standards. Beryl was in one class. Edith, coming from a small outport, was in a different, lower class. It was very straightforward. For Beryl, it was no more complicated than shoe sizes."

"And for Edith?"

"It was much the same, actually. Edith believed in the class system as much as Beryl did. They were natural antagonists, Edith and Beryl, almost different species. But they learned to live with each other, according to rules set down generations before they were born. In an odd way, they actually liked each other, in the way that natural antagonists sometimes do."

"It sounds very contentious," Stride said. Joanne's spirited intervention resonated inside him, a familiar feeling.

"It wasn't, really. But it was interesting." She stood up. "I'll get the tea."

Ned Taylor got up suddenly and walked through the dining room to the kitchen. Presently, Stride and Phelan could hear the murmur of voices in earnest discussion, punctuated by the sharp clatter of cups and saucers being arranged on a tray.

"A moment of family intimacy." Phelan winked at Stride.

Joanne returned with the tea on a large tray of dark wood. She glanced at Stride, her eyes still bright, and set the tray on a low Queen Anne table. Ned Taylor came back to the living room and resumed his seat. He was smoking a cigarette. Stride decided it was up to him to break the cool silence.

"What can you tell me about Edith's boyfriends?" He directed his question to both of them. Ned stared back at him. Joanne poured tea into four china cups. "I'm assuming she had boyfriends."

"Of course," Taylor said. "But I don't know anything about that. None of Edith's male friends came to the house. Into the house, I mean. Sometimes they would pick her up at the house, but she was always waiting for them, anticipating when they would arrive. She would meet them on the street, or get in their car. A few had cars. Most didn't."

"Was she seeing anyone in particular around the time she married your father?"

"A rejected suitor, you mean?"

"Something like that."

"I don't know of anyone." Taylor looked at his wife. Joanne didn't speak.

"Did you see your father and Edith often?" Stride asked.

"Not very often," Taylor said. "Only on the odd occasion."

There was no life in the room now. Joanne's candid declaration had drained the energy from herself and her husband. They were now just going through the motions, sipping tea, being polite. Whatever had been said in the kitchen had brought about a sort of truce. They were acting like a husband and wife practised in entertaining guests and defusing personal conflicts. Stride wanted to get out of there. He gulped his tea. It was hot and it burned his throat. He looked at Phelan. Harry would ask the rest of the questions.

"I have to ask this, Mrs. Taylor." Joanne looked at Phelan with some interest, half-smiling. "Where were you Saturday night?"

"I was here until about six-forty-five. Ned and I had dinner. We were finished around six-thirty. Then Ned went to his meeting with George Shaw." The smile grew. "I went out to see a movie at the Paramount. *The Big Sleep*. Humphrey Bogart and Lauren Bacall. Raymond Chandler's book, a murder mystery. It was very good."

"Do you often go to movies by yourself, Mrs. Taylor?"

"Yes, I do, Sergeant." She glanced quickly at Stride, then picked up her cup. "I've done that for years."

"Perhaps you saw someone there you knew?"

"No. I didn't see anyone I knew, at the theatre or on the way. It was pouring rain Saturday night. There weren't many people there at all. A few young couples sitting in the back rows, and the balcony, waiting for the lights to go out." She paused and sipped her tea. "I remember there were two Americans there, in uniform. One of them was a Negro. I suppose that's why I remember them." She smiled again, briefly, a little forlorn. "That doesn't help much, does it?"

Phelan glanced at Stride, who was focused on his cup of tea. He put his notebook away.

fourteen

Jimmy Peach was sitting in his familiar spot in a far corner of the tavern when Stride and Phelan walked in. It was just past six o'clock. The place was about half-filled. Later in the evening it would be standing room only, but already the atmosphere was thick with tobacco smoke and animated conversation. There was an occasional snatch of song. Peach waved to Stride and Phelan as they threaded their way between the tables. Several customers took close notice of the two detectives as they walked past their tables. One of the men hurriedly swallowed his drink and left the tavern.

Phelan nudged Stride and grinned.

Stride had known Jimmy Peach for years, an acquaintanceship he had made even before he became a policeman. Peach took his living where he found it, usually on the right side of the law, but sometimes not quite. His principal currency was information, but if a dollar could be made trading in goods that a certain segment of the public wanted at a bargain price, he would sometimes do that also. But he was circumspect and discreet.

Jimmy Peach was a small man, thin and wiry, with sharp features and one restless brown eye. The other was clouded and sightless. Jimmy never said what happened to it but once, laughing, he had told Stride that looking through keyholes was a risky business. When he was in the mood for it he wore a black eye-patch and claimed to be a descendant of Peter Easton, a pirate who had roamed Newfoundland's waters in the early sixteen hundreds. Stride believed that all of this was nonsense but he didn't care. He liked Jimmy Peach. And Peach was useful to the policing trade.

"Eric, Harry. Grand to see you both. I was wondering if you had got my message." He signalled to the waiter. "I've just come back from two days in Clarenville, doing a little bookkeeping, you might say, taking a walk on the shore." He sipped some beer. "Did you know that Clarenville was originally named Clarenceville, I wonder?"

"I didn't know that, Jimmy." Stride took a bottle of beer from the waiter and poured half of it into a small glass.

"Well, I can't vouch personally for the accuracy of the tale, of course, but the story is that it was named for the Duke of Clarence, a grandson of Queen Victoria. The Duke was the oldest son of the Prince of Wales, who became Edward VII when his mother passed on. Of course, the old Queen had herds of children and grandchildren. And it so happened that when the Duke died in 1891, just about the time Clarenville was being established, someone thought it would be a nice gesture to name the place after him."

"You sure you haven't got the sequence mixed up, Jimmy?" Phelan drank some beer and wiped the foam from his upper lip. "Isn't it more likely that they called the town Clarenceville first, and when the Duke heard about it the shock did him in."

"Oh, you are a bugger, Harry, and no mistake. You suffer from a serious lack of national pride."

"How have you been keeping, Jimmy? It's been a while."

"I've been keeping out of trouble, Eric, or you would have heard about it, I'm sure." Jimmy Peach patted his jacket pockets and looked hopefully at each of the detectives in turn. Stride passed his cigarettes across the table and then produced his lighter.

"Ta, Eric. I neglected to pick up some fags before I came in here this evening, and you know that they charge double the store rate in this place."

"You have something for us, Jimmy?"

"Well, perhaps I do have something that might be of interest. I was reading the *Evening T* on the train coming back from Clarenville. The paper was a day old, but it was the one with the story about that lady getting herself killed on Leslie Street. Very sad case. Died in her bath, the paper said. And meself, sure I've always enjoyed the occasional long, hot bath. Made me shiver when I read about it. Did she drown, then?"

"Whatever the *Evening T* said, Jimmy."

"I get your drift. They print what they're told. It's a sound practice to hold back on some of the specifics."

"Lay on, MacDuff," Stride said. "What do you have for us?"

"*And damned be he that first cries, 'Hold! Enough!'*" Peach delivered the line with a practised flourish and winked at Phelan. "That's Shakespeare,

Sergeant Phelan. The tragedy of *Macbeth*." Phelan shook his head and smiled. Peach drank from his beer. "Well, now, I happen to know a little bit about Mr. Jack Taylor, you see. I get around in my line of work, as you know, tending to the books of the not-so-rich-and-famous, and a few others besides. People are in the habit of telling me things. Tit for tat, so to speak." Jimmy Peach scratched his head. "I'm trying to think of the appropriate Latin phrase, Eric. Perhaps you can help me?"

"*Quid pro quo.* I think that's the phrase you're looking for."

"Exactly. *Quid pro quo.*" Peach beamed across the table at them.

"We just might have something to trade at the moment, Jimmy. You may have heard that our mutual friend, Harvey Button, is currently a guest of the state?"

"I had heard that. The story told to me was that he was apprehended on the road from Argentia with a rather large consignment of American cigarettes, and a quantity of gin and other medicinals. It's wonderful how these stories get around."

"Did you also hear that some of both might have fallen off the back of Harvey's truck while we were driving it up to St. John's?" Phelan refilled his glass.

"No. Is it a fact? I had not heard that, although it doesn't surprise me one little bit. That road is very rough in places, of course." He took another cigarette from Stride's package. "Well, that's grand, then, isn't it?" Peach tilted his cap back on his head and leaned forward, serious now.

"You are both familiar with the name John Henry Harriston, I expect?"

"The Harriston family founded the Colonial Stores," Stride said. "John Henry was the eldest son of the founder, Josiah Harriston. I understand he died some years ago."

"That is the rumour," Peach said. "But in fact he's alive, if not very well, and living in faded splendour in a large house on Waterford Bridge Road. It's his wife's house, in case you were wondering, more precisely his wife's family's estate. She was an Archibald, and her family made a fortune in munitions in England in the last century, which was as grand a time as ever there was to be in the mass murder business. Her father, as much a ne'er-do-well in his youth as her husband eventually turned out to be, left England as a young man and came out to Newfoundland to escape a variety of scandals. After he arrived here, strangely enough, he straightened himself up and did very well. Perhaps it was our bracing climate did the trick. Daisy

Archibald, Daisy Harriston now, was his only child.

"At the time, the union was seen as a coup for both families, but John Henry badly let the side down. Poor fella inherited the job of running the family enterprise when his father passed on, with the Colonial Stores the jewel in the crown so to speak. But he simply wasn't up to it and none of his siblings was any better. You almost had to wonder if the dustman hadn't slipped in between old Josiah and his missus on those nights when the Harriston sprigs were created." Peach threw his head back and laughed. "But, to cut a long and interesting story short, John Henry took to the bottle in the face of adversity, which lifted his spirits for a time, but didn't similarly enhance his management of the company. It's not a widely known fact, but the Colonial Stores was in a very bad way for a time. In fact it was right on the edge. By 1932, a very bad year even for a well-run business, Harriston was the width of a nose hair from plummeting into bankruptcy and losing the entire enterprise, the Stores included."

Stride smoked, sipped his beer, and listened to Peach's dissertation. It had always been a mystery to him how Jimmy Peach managed to know all the things he did and yet appeared to live on the edge of financial ruin, trading information for small change and dubious favours.

"And by now you're wondering what this has to do with the late Mrs. Taylor and her husband. Well, it's just about here that Jack Taylor gets involved. With the firm in danger of going under, a group of businessmen formed a consortium to take over the store and a couple of the related companies that were worth the effort. John Henry was left in place for a time as the titular head of the outfit, strictly as window dressing you understand. A new management group took over."

"And Jack Taylor was one of the group?"

"He was a junior member of the group, yes. Taylor was offered a block of shares in the new company in return for a modest financial investment and an agreement to continue to function as personnel manager at the Stores. In today's terms, Taylor's input might not seem all that great, but remember that this was 1932 when some once-thriving businesses could be bought for a puncheon of cod livers. It was a bit of a gamble for Taylor at the time, but he was very lucky to have been given the chance. There were others who wanted in but found the door closed and bolted."

"If Harriston's wife was well off, why didn't she rescue the company herself?"

"For one very good reason. Her money and property both were tied up in a complicated trust. Harriston couldn't touch it and she couldn't either, even if she'd wanted to. Which she didn't, and a damn good thing, too. Poor John Henry was the problem after all, and it would have been a case of good money going after bad."

"Who headed up the group that took over Harriston's company?"

"That would be Bertram Cartwell," Peach said. He butted his cigarette in the ashtray and reclined against the back of his chair. "Bert to his friends."

"Cartwell?" Stride knew he shouldn't have been surprised. Bert Cartwell was one of the wealthiest men on the island, arising from obscurity early in the century to achieve fortune, along with a kind of fame. He recalled his conversation with Jean-Louis Marchand.

"And Jack Taylor has done well out of his investment?" Phelan leaned forward.

"Very well, indeed. We should all be so wise and fortunate in the disbursement of our limited funds. After the war started, with all the buildings that were put up and all the roads that were built and paved, and all the goods that moved through this island, the Colonial Stores and its associated companies progressed to a state of health that would have brought a tear to Josiah Harriston's eye. And they have moved from strength to strength as the saying goes, playing their full part in the post-war boom, here and elsewhere."

"Are you telling us that Jack Taylor is a rich man, then?" Phelan's eyes were bright with interest.

"Depends on your definition of rich, Harry. He would be rich compared to yours truly, certainly, but let's just say that he is very well off. Well-away, is how my old Dad would have described him. And blessed with a new young wife who would under normal circumstances have outlived him by at least a couple of decades. And be set to inherit when he went to his reward. But I don't need to go telling you lads about your trade."

Peach leaned forward.

"That stuff that fell off the bold Harvey's truck on the road back from Argentia. It's in the usual place, I suppose?"

"The usual place, Jimmy."

"Well, that's grand, then, isn't it?" he said, smiling broadly. He helped himself to another of Stride's cigarettes and raised his glass.

"Do you suppose we can believe all that, sir?" Phelan leaned against the passenger side of the MG and lit a cigarette.

"Jimmy hasn't let us down yet, Harry."

"Assuming it's true that Jack Taylor is a lot better off than his modest house on Leslie Street would suggest, it adds a whole new dimension to the case. I know that I'd feel a little compromised if my rich old Dad took on a young wife. If I had a rich old Dad, that is."

"Well, we know that Ned Taylor didn't kill his stepmother. He has a crew of witnesses who put him at a service-club meeting. As for Bobby Taylor, we have Ida Furlong's statement that he wasn't the man she saw walking in Ayre's Field that night. But I'm not quite prepared to exclude him just yet."

"And we don't really know for sure where the other Mrs. Taylor was at the time of the murder. Ned Taylor's wife. She says she was at a movie, alone, but can't bring anyone forward to vouch for that. Her fingerprints were all over the house, including the bathroom." Phelan's eyes were bright with the possibilities. "Who was it said that the female of the species is more deadly than the male?"

Stride didn't reply. He walked around the front of the MG and opened the door. He didn't get in right away, just stood by the car looking up and down the street, hands in his trouser pockets.

"What?" Phelan asked, perplexed. "Did I miss something?"

"No, Harry, you didn't miss a thing. Jimmy has given us something to think about."

Phelan was cautious now, his enthusiasm curbed, aware that something was going on with Stride. He had picked up on Stride's discomfort while they were questioning Ned and Joanne Taylor, and now this. It didn't take an Einstein to make the connections. But he also knew that confronting Stride with his thoughts, however brilliantly insightful they might seem to be, was not the way to go. He would have to bide his time until Stride was ready to talk about it. It was also getting late, well past supper time, and Phelan was hungry. He made a small ceremony of looking at his watch.

"It's past seven, sir. It's girls' night out tonight, so to speak, although I should say girls' night in. Kitty has her weekly bridge and natter party, and this week it's at our place. Do you want to get a meal at the Chinaman's on Water Street? We could walk there from here."

Stride felt suddenly weary. Harry was just doing his job, adding up the numbers, rounding off the fractions. Stride wanted to believe that Joanne had been at a movie by herself the night of the murder. It was possible that she had been; it was something she did when they were together. He didn't want to think about the possibility that she might have killed Edith Taylor. But he knew that not wanting to think about it was a tacit admission that it was possible. He believed that almost anyone was capable of murder, given the right—or the wrong—set of circumstances. History was on his side in this one, but the insight brought him no joy.

"Sir?" Phelan was starting to feel annoyed. The case was difficult enough without having to deal with a complication that somehow linked the senior investigating officer with a prime suspect.

"It's nothing, Harry. I haven't been sleeping well for a couple of nights." He knew it was lame, and guessed that Phelan wasn't buying it. But it didn't matter. "The fact is, I have a date. Margaret is making dinner for me, even as we speak. I can drop you off at home, or anywhere you like, if you'd prefer to avoid the bridge party."

"Avoiding the bridge party is a priority, sir. You go ahead and enjoy your evening. I'll have my supper at Hong's."

"I can drive you, Harry. Jump in."

Phelan nodded and opened the passenger door. Whatever was going on, it wouldn't help matters if Phelan added his irritation to the mix.

Stride finished wiping the serving platter and placed it carefully on the top shelf of the china cabinet, inserting the rim in the plate rail and leaning the platter against the back. Margaret had served them roast chicken with savoury dressing, roast potatoes, carrots and peas. Stride had brought a bottle of wine, a white Bordeaux. He had confronted the meal without much real enthusiasm, but after a glass of wine, he started to relax and attacked the food with gusto.

Margaret dropped the last pieces of cutlery in the dish rack and pulled the plug from the sink. She dried her hands on a dish towel and took off her apron, hanging it on a hook near the ice box. While Stride finished the drying-up, she put the leftovers away.

Stride was closing the cutlery drawer when she came up behind him and put her arms around his waist, pulling him close. He placed his hands on hers and they stood that way for a minute, not moving. He turned and drew her close. She tilted her face up, smiled, and their lips touched briefly. Then she pulled away a little.

"I wasn't sure that you were really here, Eric. At first. Is it anything you can talk about?"

Talk about. Stride suppressed a sigh and looked away, his mind edging towards the tangle of feelings that the wine and Margaret's presence had pushed to the side. He turned back to her, touched her face with his fingertips.

"Not really. Like I said, the case is becoming complicated."

A half-truth. He closed his eyes, hating that he wasn't being open with her. But he didn't know how, not without putting their relationship at risk, and he couldn't deal with that. She was watching him, her eyes sharp, the appraisal process under way. He knew she sensed his evasiveness. And he also knew that she wouldn't grill him. She seemed able to accept the part of him that was available, and to let the rest go. He worried sometimes about how long she would continue to do that.

Stride picked up their glasses and the bottle of wine and carried them to the living room. He sat on the couch and topped up the glasses while Margaret pulled the drapes. She stepped out of her shoes and sat beside him, tucking her legs under her, and picked up her glass.

"We started with the assumption, Harry and I, that Edith Taylor was meeting someone the night she was killed."

"At her home, while her husband was away?" Margaret made a face, somewhere between amusement and mild disapproval. She sipped her wine.

"Yes. The back door had been left unlocked and there was evidence that someone came in that way. It might have been the killer. It probably was the killer, in fact. We have no evidence that anyone other than Ned Taylor entered the house by the front door after Edith came home."

"But you don't know if the killer was someone Edith Taylor had arranged to meet, do you?"

Stride looked at her and smiled briefly, nodding.

"No, we don't."

"Then, it's possible that there were two people in her house that night. The killer, who must have arrived first, and then the person, the man, she had arranged to meet. Her assignation." She gave the word a dramatic touch. "And a third visitor. Her stepson, Ned. A busy night at the Taylor house. It's a wonder they didn't all trip over each other."

"Yes." Stride leaned over and untied his shoes, arranged them carefully under the coffee table, heels in line. Margaret watched, smiling. "All that's complicated enough," he said, "but now we've discovered that Jack Taylor's first wife may have committed suicide. Although that was a long time ago, more than twenty years. And we've found out that Taylor is really quite well off."

"It all distorts the focus, doesn't it?" She was about to add to that, but caught Stride's small reaction and sensed that he was uncomfortable again.

"Yes," he said. He sat back and lifted his feet onto the coffee table, crossing one ankle over the other. He closed his eyes and willed the discomfort to go away. He held out his hand, palm upwards, and was pleased when he felt her fingers interlock with his. He didn't want to discuss the case any more. He turned his head and looked at her, grateful for the smile that she gave him, the warmth of her touch.

She looked at him steadily, smiling still, her eyes holding questions that he knew she wouldn't ask. She placed her glass on the table and set his alongside it. She would take her time, now, set the pace that pleased her, knowing that it would please him also. The room was very quiet. He could hear the ticking of the clock on the mantel. She loosened his tie, slowly pulled it from under the collar, the fabric whispering softly. She draped the tie over the back of the couch and worked on the top button of his shirt, tilting his chin back with a fingertip.

Her lips followed the progress of her fingers, soft against his chest, pausing frequently, teasing with her tongue, then moving on. Stride closed his eyes again, slid along the back of the couch until his head rested against the arm. A soft light danced behind his eyes, a humming sound in his ears, as Margaret explored and caressed his body with her fingers and her lips. The only sound was the ticking of the clock.

Kitty Phelan was clearing away the last of the glasses and dishes from the bridge party when Harry arrived home. She had opened windows at the front and back of the house to clear the smoke, but the odour of too many cigarettes still lingered. Kitty and some of her friends smoked as much as Harry did. Someone said it was a legacy of the war years, women smoking, and maybe that was generally true, but Kitty had always smoked a lot.

"I was beginning to wonder if something happened to you, Harry. It's been hours since you phoned me from the station."

"It just seems like hours, Kit. It was barely an hour ago."

"Then, it must be because I miss you so when you're not here, my darling man." She put her arms around him and pulled him close, resting her head on his chest. Harry put his hand on the back of her neck, stroking the short soft hairs at the nape. She pushed him away.

"Stop that now, or I won't get this place cleared up tonight." Then she caught the expression on his face. "Something's up. What is it, Harry?"

"I'm not positive, but I think there's something going on between Stride and the wife of one of Jack Taylor's sons. And I went back to the station to think about it all."

"There's only the one of them that's married, you said. The older one, Edward?"

"They call him Ned. Joanne is his wife's name. We interviewed them earlier this evening. Then we met with Jimmy Peach—I think you met Jimmy, once?"

"Little fella with the eye-patch?"

"That's Jimmy. Anyway, we were talking after that, going over what we knew and what we didn't know, and I said that Joanne Taylor had to be a principal suspect because she didn't really have an alibi for that Saturday night."

"What motive would she have had for killing the woman?"

"It turns out that Jack Taylor is a lot more well off than anyone might have thought. He bought into the Colonial Stores back in the thirties when shares were going cheap. Jimmy says he's done very well out of it."

"Are you sure Jimmy Peach knows what he's talking about?"

"Pretty sure. Jimmy has his sources, and I can't remember that he's ever given us a wrong steer."

"That does make it interesting, doesn't it? If Jack Taylor is well off, and has a young wife to outlive him, his sons would stand to lose a lot on the inheritance when the old man goes to his reward."

"That's about the size of it. Money is one of the great motivators." Phelan wondered what Jack Taylor's reward might be when he got to wherever he was going.

"You said Joanne Taylor doesn't have an alibi. Where does she say she was at the time?"

"She said she was at a movie, but that she went alone, and didn't see anyone she knew there, or on the way."

"What movie was it?" Kitty Phelan didn't miss many films that came to town.

"*The Big Sleep*, at the Paramount."

"Bogart and Bacall." Kitty smiled in anticipation. "I want to see that, Harry. Even if you do supply the expert running commentary all the way through." Then she was serious again. "There's nothing to say she didn't go, is there?"

"No. But it would help if she could bring someone forward to say she was there." Phelan poured a large portion of rum into a glass.

"Why do you think there's something going on between Joanne Taylor and Eric? Did they know each other before?"

"Stride's very close about his personal life, Kit. But I remember that he was seeing someone a few years ago, and I think her name was Joanne. He didn't talk about it, and I never met her, but it could be the same woman."

"You still haven't told me why you think he might be involved with her." She took his glass from him and drank some rum. "And, anyway, he has a girlfriend. Margaret Nichol?"

"Yes. In fact, he went to her place for supper after he dropped me at Hong's."

"Are you telling me that Eric Stride has two women on the go, one of them married?"

"I don't know. He could have a half dozen for all I know."

"Well, I don't believe it, Harry. He's not the type. And I think I'm a pretty good judge of character. My taste in husbands notwithstanding."

Phelan laughed and touched his wife's cheek.

"I think you're right about Stride's character, but I also think something's going on. He was uncomfortable when we interviewed the Taylors tonight, and I think she was, too. I learned a long time ago not to ask Stride about his personal life. If he wants to tell me something, he'll tell me, but in his own time." Phelan retrieved his glass. "And I remembered something else. The night we drove to Taylor's house, the night of the murder, Stride had a funny reaction when I told him whose house it was. He said a couple of the Taylor names. I remember he said 'Ned Taylor.' Then he swore. It seemed peculiar at the time, but now it makes sense. At least, I think it does."

"Is that why you went back to the station tonight? To worry about Eric Stride, and try and figure out some way to make everything all right?"

"Yes, I suppose so. But I'm no further ahead than I was."

"Harry, you are a sweetheart. And you know what?"

"What?"

"I think it's really interesting."

"Interesting?" Kitty could still surprise him sometimes. "Why?"

"Because it is." She wrapped her arms around him again and began moving her hips against him. "And it's romantic. The inspector could be in love with a married woman who's related to the murder victim and he's all upset at the thought she might have done it. And just to complicate matters, there's a second woman in the picture. And his trusty sidekick, Sergeant Plod, is going to come to the rescue and provide the lady with an alibi, sort everything out. Bogart and Bacall would be great in the movie."

"With Ronald Reagan as Sergeant Plod."

"You got it, Sherlock. You've caught the spirit of the thing." She held him tighter. Her hip movement became more insistent.

"What about the dishes?" Phelan had begun nibbling at the soft part of her neck, just under her chin.

"Screw the dishes."

"First things first," he said.

She giggled into his ear.

Stride awoke with a jolt, falling into consciousness from a dream-tossed sleep, his heart racing. They were lying spoon fashion, Margaret's back close against his chest, her legs drawn up, her breathing slow and even. She lay on his right arm and his hand still touched her breast. He moved the arm a little, slowly flexing the fingers, coaxing a flow of blood into the numbed extremity. Deep in sleep, Margaret was unaware of his movement. Carefully, slowly, Stride pulled his arm from under her, and rolled over onto his back, lying still until his breathing slowed.

When he first awoke, he didn't know where he was. He had dreamed he was walking on the shore hand-in-hand with Margaret, slowly making their way between the sea-smoothed rocks that littered the shore. Then Margaret became Joanne. She was laughing, challenging him to a race along the water's edge, reckless, finding footfalls in the small spaces between the rocks, winning the race as she always did, because she didn't care about risk, looking back over her shoulder at him, waving, mocking.

He slid from the bed, tucked the covers around Margaret's back, reached down to touch her shoulder, but stopped, his hand hovering inches away. He pulled the covers a little higher, then turned and walked into the living room. Their clothes lay where they had fallen, and seeing them he revisited their love-making, remembering the closeness, the barely controlled urgency, the climb and the descent into mutual release.

Their glasses, half-filled with wine, still stood on the table. He decanted one into the other, lifted the glass in a mock toast and drank. The wine had warmed, but it still tasted good. He found his cigarettes under a pile of clothing. The air in the flat was cool. He went quietly back into the bedroom and took his bathrobe from the closet. It was just past two, and he doubted that he would sleep very much more tonight. He lit his cigarette, drank some wine, and looked down at the street. He stood there for a long time, smoking, sipping warm Bordeaux, and thinking.

Around two-thirty, a black sedan, one of the large, cumbersome pre-war models, rolled to a stop in front of a house two doors away. A couple emerged from the front seat, passenger side. The woman searched for keys in her handbag walking towards the house, while her companion leaned against the car, talking with the driver. He closed the door, stood in the street while the sedan moved on, then walked towards the woman on the sidewalk, stumbling when his foot caught the edge of the curb. The woman laughed and slapped him on the shoulder, then ran across the sidewalk and up the front steps of the house. The man paused briefly to dance a few steps on the sidewalk with an imaginary partner, then climbed the steps after her. They disappeared into the shadows of the veranda.

Stride pulled the drapes closed and walked over to the couch. There was a small amount of wine left in the bottle, so he poured it into his glass and sat back, his feet on the table. He took out another cigarette and picked up his lighter. The ticking of the clock was loud in the stillness of the room.

fifteen

Phelan sat with his feet up on the desk. He was eating a thick roast beef sandwich that Kitty had packed for him. Usually they ate their midday meal at home. Today was an exception. Stride was drinking a mug of Bovril and trying not to think about another cigarette. They were talking again about Stride's visit to the Connars house. Rebecca Connars' hostility towards Edith Taylor had bothered him then, and still did.

"It's hardly unusual, sir. The hostility between Mrs. Connars and Edith Taylor, I mean." Phelan washed down a mouthful of sandwich with hot tea. "And it's a tide that flows in two directions. I told you about the time I was in Caitlin's Cove with my old man, when he worked on that boat? I was pretty worried at the time that the local lads might decide to take me around in the back of a shed and rearrange my features. And there were a couple of them who might have if their mothers hadn't been watching."

"It's not quite the same thing, Harry. A lot of boys naturally grow up thinking they have to jowl the kids on the next street over."

"Granted. But I wouldn't put too much store in Rebecca Connars' dim view of Edith Taylor. It might not have been personal, might have had as much to do with a young housekeeper marrying her older employer as anything else."

"Crossing the class lines?"

"Something like that. We haven't quite reached the democratic ideal."

"Here or anywhere."

"Maybe in Mr. Stalin's workers' paradise."

"Maybe in your dreams." Stride gave up the struggle and took out a cigarette. "Odd that they never had children, though."

"Who? Tommy Connars and his missus?"

"Yes. Uncle Tommy and Aunt Becky."

"They have a daughter, actually."

"Do they?" Stride was surprised. Tommy Connars had never mentioned children and Stride couldn't recall seeing pictures of a daughter in the Connars house on the several occasions he had visited.

"Yes. I remember her from visits to their house with my old man when I was a boy. She was a plain girl, nice, very quiet. Always seemed to tip-toe around the house. Her name was Patricia. I believe she's married and living in the States somewhere."

"She must have married before the war, then," Stride said.

"Oh, yes," Phelan said. "She left home a long time before the war, but I think her husband was an American sailor, in fact. I remember my folks talking about it. And if I remember correctly, she ran away from home with her sailor boy. I'm pretty certain there was a story there, but my old man never told me what it was. I remember him talking about it to my mother, though. I think maybe Patricia and her mother didn't get along very well."

Kevin Noseworthy had been standing unnoticed in the doorway for a few minutes, listening to them talking. Now he cleared his throat noisily. Phelan turned towards the door, brushing crumbs of bread from the corner of his mouth. Stride looked hopefully at Noseworthy.

"One of the people you would like to talk to, sir, is named Ambrose White."

"The prints from the bathroom door?" Stride set his mug on the desk very carefully. He stared at Noseworthy. "Who is he?"

Noseworthy held out a file folder.

"Everything we have is in here, sir. Arrested September 3rd, 1936, for assault. Date of birth, August 2nd, 1918. Both parents dead. The constable's notes say that White was drinking in a tavern—underage, at that—and got into an argument with a group of longshoremen and then started a free-for-all. Pretty ferocious little fellow according to the constable's notes. He bloodied some noses and split a couple of lips before they managed to get him under control. He spent the night in jail and was arraigned and tried before a magistrate the next day. Since it was a first offence, and none of the men he attacked wanted to press charges, the judge let him off with a two-dollar fine and a lecture about the evils of drink."

Stride looked through the file.

"It says here he was living on Kelsey Row, off New Gower Street."

"That whole block burned down years ago," Phelan said. "Before the war."

"The first year of the war, actually," Noseworthy said. "I remember that fire. My uncle was living there and he moved in with us for a while. I had to bunk with my brother for a week until he found another place."

"It was a bit of toil to suss out the match?" Stride asked.

"When you don't have the full set of prints, sir, it's a lot harder. But I eventually managed to create a set, using prints from the door and the collection from the bedroom. It was a bit of a long shot, but it worked. And I did put in a few extra hours. All in the name of justice and the greater good."

"You'll find your reward in that special place in heaven reserved for dedicated public servants," Phelan said.

"I'm looking forward to that, Harry. I'm told that not a single Irishman has ever made it there."

"Up yours, Noseworthy," Phelan said, gesturing with his middle finger. "Or you can crawl up my arse, if that suits you better."

Noseworthy laughed and pulled up a chair, turned it around and sat down, propping his elbows on its back. Phelan lit a cigarette and tossed his package to Noseworthy. He took the file from Stride.

"There isn't much here to go on, sir. Home address no longer exists. No parents. No information on place of birth. How did he support himself, I wonder? The court record says he paid the fine himself."

"Who was the arresting constable?"

"Duffett."

"Which one? Charlie or Walter?"

"Charlie Duffett. Why?"

"You didn't know Charlie Duffett, did you Harry? Poor Charlie died in November of '36. Basically, he drank himself to death. The number of days that Charlie was sober that year, or the year before, could be counted on your fingers and toes. I'm surprised he managed to make an arrest at all. The third of September must have been one of his last good nights."

"So, we may have to do it the hard way. City directory for 1936 and see who was living on Kelsey Row, then cross-index it to the most recent listings, and hope that someone remembers an Ambrose White." Phelan turned to Noseworthy. "Where's your uncle now, Kevin?"

"General Protestant Cemetery between Waterford Bridge and Topsail Road. Look for a large lilac bush near the east fence, about one-third of the way up from the lower road. But Uncle Carl was never very talkative and the passing years haven't brought much improvement."

"That helps a lot."

"I suppose now you'll want your cigarette back. Well, you can have it. I don't want it any more." Noseworthy held up the inch-long butt and grinned. He stood up and pushed the chair back against the wall. "Now I see that my popularity has waned. *Sic transit gloria.* So be it. I have to get back to work anyway."

Reginald Kelsey had come to Newfoundland in 1853 from Devon in the south of England as a boy of fifteen, apprenticed to a cooper who had established a successful business on Water Street. The cooper, Wilfred Bastow, was a widower and, as a consequence of a diphtheria epidemic, childless. Young Kelsey proved to be more than Bastow could have dreamed of. He was a hard worker and unusually bright. Not only did Kelsey learn all there was to know about the cooperage trade, but when the opportunity arose he urged his employer to expand the firm into fish exporting which was the principal user of Bastow's barrels in the first place. When Bastow died in 1880, Kelsey inherited the much enlarged business. He continued to expand and diversify while maintaining the cooperage as the core of the enterprise.

In 1889, Kelsey decided he wanted to further expand the cooperage, but was frustrated by the lack of space in his established location on Water Street, and the land that was available was too expensive. He made a decision that was considered at the time to be risky, even foolhardy. He sold the property on Water Street and moved his enterprise to the city's perimeter on the north. Three years later, in 1892, on an unusually hot and dry July afternoon, a drayman named Tommy Fitzpatrick accidentally dropped his pipe onto a pile of hay in Timothy O'Brien's stable and started a small fire that quickly roared out of control, fanned by high winds. A large part of St. John's went up in flames, including the former Bastow property and all its neighbours.

When the fire was finally put out, most of the city was in ruins, charred to ground-level, and eleven thousand people were homeless. But Reginald Kelsey was still in business, and mostly unscathed by the holocaust. Moreover, there was now land available for much new building and Kelsey purchased some of it at a good price. One of his projects was the construction of a long row of houses off New Gower Street near the centre of the city. Although the houses weren't formally given a name, they were popularly known as Kelsey Row.

Originally owned and inhabited by upper-middle-class families, the property went into decline in the 1920s, a decline enhanced by the Depression, and subsequent owners continued to subdivide the structure into a warren of small flats and rooms whose single attractive feature was the low price of rental. In 1939, another fire completed the historical circle: Kelsey Row burned to the ground when a kerosene heater exploded in one of the centre units. Eight people died in the blaze.

"There's no Ambrose White listed on Kelsey Row for 1936," Phelan said. "I suppose that's not a great surprise."

"He was probably bunking with another family for the time he was there. The place was a catch-all for transients. There are two ways we can do this, Harry. We can painstakingly work our way through all the names in this directory and then start phoning and calling on people of the same name in the current directory. Or we can take a short cut and ask someone who might have known some of the people who lived on Kelsey Row in 1936."

"I lived on Kelsey Row myself once," Jimmy Peach said. "A long time ago. It was a very fine place to live at one time, you know. I couldn't have afforded to live there at the beginning, and wouldn't have been comfortable there in any case. But then the general tenor of the area began to migrate south while my own fortunes were moving modestly northward, and one day I found that I could afford one of the smaller flats. So I packed a cigar box full of my worldly goods and made the move. It was a grand place for a while, with a rare assortment of characters. Hilda Penny had a place there at one time, one of the end-houses. You remember Hilda, don't you Eric?"

"Only by reputation, Jimmy. She was a little before my time."

"Of course, she would be, wouldn't she? Ah, but Hilda was a grand girl, a heart as big as all outdoors, you might say, and appetites to match. At the peak of her career Hilda had as many as ten young women working for her. And they were fine girls too. One of them, it was said, was the niece of a prime minister. But perhaps that was just a story. I can tell you that some very outstanding people came to Kelsey Row in that period. My son, there were some Saturday nights at Hilda's establishment, and I am a witness so help me God, when the Prime Minister could have convened a cabinet meeting on the very spot without having to raise his voice unduly." Jimmy smiled happily. "Grand memories, Eric. But I digress."

Jimmy Peach went through the ritual of patting his pockets and Stride produced his package of cigarettes.

"Now, who is this laddie you're trying to find?"

"His name is Ambrose White," Stride said. "We have a record of him from 1936 and that's the address he gave."

"I take it this Ambrose White has something to do with the Taylor killing?"

"He may have had. We won't know until we ask him some questions."

"Then it's important that you find him, isn't it? I can't help you myself, but I'll give you a name. Agnes Duder. She was a schoolteacher at the Methodist College on Long's Hill and she's quite old now. Lives in a home on Torbay Road. St. Jude's. Agnes will tell you that she lived on Kelsey Row most of her life, even after it went into decline. Provided the place with a centre of gravity, you might say. Anyway, the long and the short of it is that Agnes knew most of the people who lived there for the almost fifty years that the place existed, and, well along in years though she may be, I doubt she's forgotten many of the names."

"I usually have a cigarette at this time in the afternoon," Agnes Duder said. "I wonder if you can oblige me, young man? I seem to have mislaid my package."

Stride produced his cigarettes and his lighter. He considered asking Agnes Duder if she was related to Jimmy Peach, but thought better of it.

"You smoke Royal Blends? I would have thought an inspector would manage something better than a local brand. Myself, now, I like Luckys. The war spoiled me, of course. All those nice American boys, and some of them so very generous. But never mind. Beggars can't be choosers."

Agnes Duder was a tall, raw-boned woman with heavy features whose age, Stride reckoned, was somewhere between seventy and the century mark. Her appearance probably hadn't changed much in two decades and he thought it wouldn't change appreciably in another two or three. Her hair, coiled into an improbable bun on the top of her head, was dyed an intriguing shade of orange. Two evil-looking steel pins with large round knobs skewered the coil of hair. Stride wondered whether the pins were there for decoration or close-order combat.

"Jimmy Peach gave us your name, Mrs. Duder," Stride said and saw her eyes flash and her features stiffen.

"It's Miss Duder, thank you, Mr. Stride. I never married, nor ever saw a need to." She gave Stride a stern look. "The title notwithstanding, I have missed nothing of significance in my years on this earth, and that's a fact."

Stride thought he detected a hint of a smile.

"My apologies, Miss Duder. Jimmy said you would have known most of the residents on Kelsey Row over the years. We're trying to find some information on a young man named Ambrose White in connection with an investigation. He may have lived there in 1936, and he was about eighteen years old."

"Nineteen thirty-six, you say? That was the year that Edna Cowan had triplets. April the fourth. Two of them died the night they were born but the third thrived and was a pleasant little girl the last time I saw her. Edna comes to visit me from time to time, and she's a good woman. She has her own millinery shop on Duckworth Street, not too far from the Newfoundland Hotel, and she does very well for herself. Her husband, now, is another story. A lazy oaf who drinks too much, works hardly at all, and would do the world a favour, and Edna especially, if he drowned himself in the harbour. If I were twenty years younger I might take on the task myself."

She crushed her cigarette in an ashtray. Stride was about to ask a second time about Ambrose White when Agnes Duder crossed her arms over her ample bosom and spoke again.

"Yes, I remember Ambrose White. And if he could be called a young man, he was just barely that, Mr. Stride. You say he was eighteen in 1936? I wouldn't have given him eighteen years. I would have said younger."

Stride leaned forward in his chair. "How much do you know about him?"

"Why do you want to know?" A demand politely phrased as a question.

"His fingerprints were found at the scene of a serious crime," Stride said.

"That doesn't mean he did the crime, only that he was there at one time. I have read that fingerprints can be years old. Decades, even."

Stride sat back and suppressed a sigh. It was the second time in a week that he felt he had been trampled to the ground under an elderly lady's sensible shoes.

"Yes, ma'am, that's true. We want to find Ambrose White and ask him some questions. If he was present at or near the scene when the crime was committed, he may be able to assist us in finding the perpetrator."

Agnes Duder stared at Stride with unblinking eyes behind large horn-rimmed glasses. He imagined she wasn't buying much of this. She probably had a mental picture of a windowless room with insulated walls, a naked light bulb dangling from the ceiling, and two large men wielding lengths of rubber hose. One named Phelan and one named Stride.

"My father was a policeman," she said finally, her features softening slightly. "He was with the constabulary for thirty years."

Stride blinked. He raced through his memory for a name.

"Your father was Albert Duder?" Phelan got there first.

"He was." Agnes Duder smiled broadly for the first time. "He sometimes told me he wished I had been born a boy so that I could have joined the constabulary when I came of age. And there were times when I wished that myself. It's not a sin for a man to want a son, and he was a good man, and a good enough father, for all of that."

She sat silently with the memory for a moment and then she was serious again. "I won't ask you what the crime is. I know that you aren't permitted to say. Do you think that Ambrose committed this crime, Mr. Stride?"

"We have to consider the possibility. So it's important that we find him as soon as we can."

"Yes. I can understand that." She closed her eyes for a moment. "Ambrose White said very little to anyone about himself, or about anything at all for that matter. At first I wondered if he was mute. To the extent that he talked to anybody, I think it was me that he spoke to most. He shared a room with the two Murphy boys on Kelsey Row. They were hard boys, both of them, and I expect they gave Ambrose a heavy time of it, but he never said a word against them. I didn't know if that was because of his natural reticence or because he was afraid to. He was only half their size and he had learned to tread carefully."

"Would he have told the Murphys anything about himself?"

"I doubt it. They only wanted him there for the bit of rent money he could pay. But it doesn't matter, anyway. The parents are dead. And the two boys enlisted in the navy in 1939. Billy was killed at sea in 1941 and Harold came back in 1943 with a dreadful head wound. He's lived in a home since then, and he doesn't know January from July. I visited him only the one time."

"Can you tell us anything about White? All we know at the present time is his birth date, in August 1918, and you say you doubt the accuracy of that."

"I do, and I'll tell you why. One of the few things that Ambrose told me about himself was that he was born on Regatta Day, and that his father liked to tell people that he'd missed the boat races at Quidi Vidi that year because he had to be with his wife during the birth."

"There wasn't a Regatta in 1918," Stride said, "or any time during the First World War. The period 1915 to 1918 was the only time the boat races were cancelled since the event started back in the early 1800s."

"Well done, Mr. Stride. I'll give you an 'A' in local history." And she did look pleased. "That means that Ambrose White must have been born in 1919 or later. He certainly wasn't around in 1914."

"Did he tell you anything else about himself?"

"Almost nothing. He did say that his parents were dead. And one day when he came home from work, his sweater was covered with sawdust. He looked especially tired. I asked him where he was working but he wouldn't tell me. I had made blueberry pies that day, and he could smell them from the kitchen where they were cooling. I asked him if he'd like a piece with a glass of milk. He didn't say yes, but he didn't say no, either, so I marched him into my flat and sat him down at the table. He ate two large pieces of pie and drank almost a quart of milk. The poor little fellow was half-starved, I believe. He loosened up a little bit then, and although he still said very little, he did mention the name Thompson in connection with the place he worked."

Agnes Duder sat back and was silent. The retrieval of memories seemed to have tired her. Or perhaps it was the circumstances.

"And now I've told you all that I know about Ambrose White," she said. "Not long after that evening he disappeared and that was the last I saw of him."

sixteen

"Ambrose White." Henry Thompson tapped a small chisel on the desk top and pondered Stride's question. "Did you say 1936? Well, I've had a goodly number of men work for me over the past eleven years, sir." Henry Thompson was in his late sixties, a short heavyset man with a grey beard and moustache, and soft brown eyes.

The woodworking and carpentry firm Henry Thompson & Sons had been operating in St. John's for more than fifty years, founded by Thompson's father and namesake.

"He was a young fellow, Mr. Thompson. No more than eighteen years old when he was arrested. Possibly a year or two younger than that."

Thompson nodded his head slowly and stroked his beard.

"My memory is not what it used to be, sir. Show me a picture of the fellow and I could tell you yea or nay in a second. But names are quite another thing. Oh, yes. In one ear and out the same in the blinking of an eye. The ravages of my accumulated years."

Thompson took a ledger from a shelf and blew dust from its top. "Yes," he said, after a careful scrutiny of many pages. "Here we are. Just so. Ambrose White. It starts to come back to me now. I've recorded here that he worked on a dining room table for the Ollerhead family. That is the key that unlocks memory's storeroom. You see, I have to take hold of the face of the man in my mind so that the rest of the information will follow along. I remember that table, and I can see the faces of the men who built it."

Thompson sat down in his desk chair.

"Do take a seat, gentlemen." Thompson propped his head on one hand and gazed thoughtfully at the ceiling beams, pulling thoughts into focus. "Young White came to my place of business on the recommendation of one

Benjamin Downe in Portugal Cove. Yes. Mr. Downe had a carpentry and woodworking business there. Sadly, he passed on some years ago. But he was a good man, very skilled. Ambrose, himself, I remember, had a talent in the working of wood, and he might have been successful in the trade, I believe. But talent by itself is a delicate flower. It has to be nurtured."

Thompson paused and shook his head again.

"There were problems?"

"Problems, yes. The lad had an unfortunate history. He was an orphan, you see, and all on his own when he came to my establishment. His father died when Ambrose was quite small. It all had an effect on young White, of that I'm certain. And most understandable, I'm sure you will agree. He had difficulties in focusing his mind and his energy on the main task. And I was told that he had a fierce temper, and was unable to control it at times."

"Did White tell you anything about himself, or his family?"

"Beyond the fact that his parents were dead, and that he was alone in the world, he told me nothing."

"You say he was alone in the world. Did you take that to mean he had no brothers or sisters? No family at all?"

"If he had family, he made no mention of them."

"So all you know, really, is that he was from Portugal Cove."

Thompson shook his head and smiled ruefully.

"I do not know that he was from Portugal Cove. I do know that he was living in Portugal Cove and working there for Mr. Downe before he came to my establishment. He might have come originally from any one of a number of communities in the area. Or even from the city for that matter."

"How long did White work for you, Mr. Thompson?"

"Not long. In fact, he departed soon after the altercation that you referred to when you arrived here."

"Did you fire him?"

"I believe I suggested that he should find work elsewhere. I do not hold with drinking and brawling, sir. A hot-tempered man who works with tools such as these," Thompson held up a large chisel, "can be a danger to those around him. It was a risk that I felt I could not take. There were many unemployed at the time, and I could replace young White with a steadier sort of man."

"Do you know where he went after he left your shop?"

"I have no idea. I didn't see him after that." Thompson paused then, his expression set. "Can I ask what has brought you here now asking me about Ambrose White? Is he again in trouble with the law?"

"He may be, but we won't know for sure until we find him and ask the appropriate questions, Mr. Thompson. I can only tell you that his fingerprints were found at the scene of a crime."

"You believe he did this crime, then? Was it a serious crime, can I ask? A crime of violence?" The soft brown eyes had narrowed, and Thompson now seemed uneasy.

"It was a serious crime, sir, but the presence of his fingerprints only indicates that he was at the scene at some point. He may have had nothing to do with it. But it's important that we find him."

"I see. Your qualification of the circumstances brings me a small degree of relief. But I confess to being unhappy about this. I wish I could give you more help, but I have had no knowledge of his whereabouts since he left my employ eleven years ago. And so much has happened in our world since that time. It has occurred to you, of course, that he might have enlisted in the forces and been in the war?"

"We're looking into that. Did White have any friends at work? Perhaps someone who knew him a little better, on a personal level?"

"I don't know of anyone. White was the youngest of my employees during the time he was here. I'm not aware that he made any friendships. My impression was that he was a very solitary kind of person. I wish I could be of greater help. But the little I have told you is all that I know." Thompson chuckled, but his eyes held no joy. "All that this grey head can reclaim at the moment, at any rate. If I think of anything else I will call you, of course."

"I'll give you an opinion about all of that if you like, sir."

"You'll give it to me whether I like it or not, Harry."

"That nice old man with the soulful brown eyes is not above cutting corners and dabbling in a bit of bullshit. He knew who Ambrose White was the moment you mentioned his name. That was written all over his face. The rest of it, the dusty ledger and the Ollerhead table, was a performance, albeit a pretty damn good one. Thompson has a boy working for him who isn't quite eighteen years of age. He doesn't ask for a home address, he doesn't ask for any identification? Just that his good friend Mr. Downe in Portugal Cove recommended him for employment. Would I be wildly out of line if I suggested that something is just a little off here?"

"Not wildly out of line, Harry, but where do you want to go with this?"

"I'd like to go back in there and take that old bugger by the lapels and bounce him up and down until the truth about Ambrose White shakes out of him."

"And by tomorrow you might be walking a beat on the Great Northern Peninsula, muttering at seabirds. Or worse. Thompson is a respected businessman, like it or not. No, that won't do, Harry. And, anyway, it isn't likely to get us any closer to Ambrose White."

"You don't believe all that codswallop about nurturing White's talent like a fragile flower, and his concern that White might have been involved in a serious crime?"

"Not all of it, but I believe some of it. I think he is worried that Ambrose White might be arrested and interrogated. He knows that White might say unpleasant things about some of his past employers. And I think he's worried that an older, larger Ambrose White may be back in town. The reference to the war gave that away. An Ambrose White recently experienced in combat would scare the hell out of me if I thought he was carrying a grudge."

"Point taken."

"But for all we know, Harry, the worst that Thompson might have done was exploit the boy by paying him sub-standard wages. If that's all it was, it wouldn't be seen by many people as a great sin. Remember the times. If Thompson paid White any wage at all, most people would probably say that it was a damn sight better than the dole, which you will recall was the princely sum of six cents per person per day."

"Right." Phelan kicked at a small piece of wood that lay on the ground near the MG. "But you don't believe that's all there was to it? Just a matter of slavey wages."

"No, I don't. But I want more information before I send you back in there to bounce Henry Thompson up and down. And I believe that White did leave Thompson's establishment about the time he says he did. And I don't think Thompson knows where he is."

"The Bureau of Vital Statistics is our next stop, then. White's a very common name. But maybe Ambrose isn't. And we can't even trust the birth date he gave the constable."

"Let's just hope he was using his real name," Stride said.

"The thing is, gentlemen, that although we strive for completeness in our records, there are gaps still. The system has been made much better over the last decade. For one thing, government revenue during the war years was boosted tremendously, thanks to our American and Canadian cousins— sunshine in the overcast you could say—and systems such as this require infusions of cash to make them work."

Rodney Staples gestured with his left hand towards the banks of filing cabinets in his office. He was a tall, thin man of indeterminable age with a bald pate that glowed under the harsh overhead lighting. The little cranial hair that he retained was grey and formed a sad little hedge around the perimeter of his skull. His facial features were small and blunt, as though his Maker had become bored with the project halfway through. In compensation, perhaps, Staples had a startling set of eyebrows, dark and thick, that seemed to leap from the region above his small blue eyes.

"Someday, the Bureau of Vital Statistics will have a system that will approach perfection. We will know everything we need to know about almost everyone. And when that happens, I wager, there will be complaints that we know far too much."

Staples smiled, his massive eyebrows quivering.

"How good are the records for 1918 and thereabouts?" Stride already had a sinking feeling about this.

"Well, they're generally not too bad, Inspector Stride, but there are the inevitable gaps. And the farther you get from St. John's, the more likely it is that we will have missed some of the births and deaths. That's particularly the case for small isolated communities along our coastlines. Which, of course, is where most of our citizens outside the city and the larger towns reside." Staples dug at the right side of his grey hedge with the blunt end of a pencil. "And there are some communities that take the attitude that what the government doesn't know about them is like money in the bank, if you get my meaning."

"Explain it to me, Mr. Staples." Stride's spirits sank a little lower.

"Well, sir, in the Great War, there was scarcely a family on this island that didn't lose a loved one, or didn't have a friend or neighbour who did. That was especially the case after the first day of July in 1916 when Haig and his lot made their famous miscalculation and all but gave the war to the Hun. And lost most of the Newfoundland Regiment in the process. Some families were reluctant to register births, particularly of male children. You can see that it does have a kind of logic. If the government doesn't know that young Johnny or Billy exists, he can't be rounded up eighteen years down the road, dressed in khaki, and pushed over the top into the machine-gun fire."

"Are you making this up?" Stride asked. But he wondered if it was possible.

"Let's say that I've perhaps embellished the facts a little." Staples was smiling again. "But, you know, I did hear such sentiments expressed, and more than once, in the years after 1916. The long and the short of it is, though, that not all births and deaths were registered back then. There were many reasons why this was the case. But I'll see what I can find, Inspector, and I'll get back to you as soon as I can. Tomorrow, perhaps, or the day after at the latest."

s e v e n t e e n

Bernice Follett was standing on the sidewalk smoking a cigarette when Stride and Phelan arrived at the beauty parlour where she worked. It was a pleasant day, the temperature above normal for the time of year, but there was a cool east wind off the Atlantic. She wore a red wool sweater over the white frock that was her working uniform. Bernice Follett was slender and fair, with a complicated hair style that probably functioned as a kind of walking advert. They had gotten her name from Edith Taylor's address book. Stride judged that she was about thirty-five, but she wore a lot of makeup and it was hard to say if it made her look younger or older than her age.

"Madge says we can go to her place to talk. She lives upstairs. There really isn't a place to talk in the shop, anyway." She didn't add that Madge also said that having two large cops in her place of business would upset the customers.

"Whatever is comfortable for you," Stride said.

The young woman dropped her half-smoked cigarette on the sidewalk and unlocked the door to the flat. Stride and Phelan followed her up the stairs, past the living room and into the kitchen at the back of the house. They sat at the kitchen table.

"Madge lives here alone. She started the shop after her husband, Mr. Roberts, died. Before that she worked at one of the other places in town. She's doing real well. She took a lot of customers with her when she opened this place."

She lit another cigarette and dropped the match into a glass ashtray.

"You were a close friend of Edith Taylor?"

"We used to be pretty close friends, but that was a couple of years ago. Well, more than a couple, really. When she was Edith Wright. I still did her hair, and sometimes she'd phone me, you know, but I wouldn't say we were really close friends any more."

"Tell us when you met Edith Wright."

"I guess that would have been five, maybe six, years ago. I forget exactly when, but I know it was the year after the Yanks arrived on that troopship. That was in 1941, right? So it was the summer of 1942, probably. She came into the shop where I was working, to get her hair permed. We kinda hit it off, you know? Some people you find it easy to talk to right away. Others you don't. Edie was easy to talk to."

"You spent a lot of time together during the war?"

"Some. I don't know if it was a lot. We both liked to dance, and, you know, guys. We had a lot of fun. For a while, anyway."

"Something changed that? What happened?"

"It wasn't any big deal. What happened, I mean. After a year or two, we started hanging around with different people. Well, actually, I guess it was kind of a big deal. Edie came into the shop one afternoon and told me she was going to a big party that night and she wanted to look especially nice because there was going to be some important people there."

"Did she say who these people were?" Stride's interest began to pick up now.

"No. I thought it was all bullshit, anyway, pardon my French. Her meeting important people. Edie was a housekeeper, for Pete's sake. But two days later there was a picture in the paper, and there she was, standing with a bunch of people in uniforms, formal suits, some of the women in big hats, and all that jazz. Jesus, I almost fell over when I saw it. It was some do at Government House. They didn't print Edie's name under the picture, but I recognised her right away. And her hair looked real nice."

Stride remembered the photograph in Edith Taylor's bedroom, the two young women in large hats, the wind blowing their skirts to one side. The other woman in the photograph wasn't Bernice Follett.

"And it was after that that you and Edith didn't see so much of each other."

Bernice nodded.

"Was there anyone in particular that Edith was friends with? After the party at Government House?"

"Yeah. She got really close to someone named Emma. I don't know her last name, though."

"Emma?"

"Yeah. Like I said, I only knew her first name."

Emma was another of the names in Edith Taylor's address book. But no surname was attached. Stride wondered if the address was still valid. He turned away from Bernice Follett and looked through Madge Roberts' kitchen window. There was a telephone pole near the back fence. Three sparrows sat on the wire, swaying in the brisk wind blowing in from the ocean. He looked back at the young woman.

"Do you know anything about her, this Emma?"

"No, I don't, really. I never even met her."

"OK. Let's move to the present, Bernice. Do you know if Edith Taylor was involved with anyone? After she was married. We're particularly interested in someone who drives a coupe, late model, dark colour."

Her reaction told him that she knew who owned the car. She looked down at her hands, reached for another cigarette.

"Jesus. A week ago everything was normal. Now, Edie's dead." She looked up at Stride almost as if surprised to see him there, as though she had just heard the news. Or just accepted that it was true. Tears filled her eyes, overflowed down one cheek. She brushed a hand across her face. "I still can't really believe it. We didn't really see each other any more, socially, you know, but I still did her hair. I keep expecting her to walk into the shop."

She dug into her handbag and pulled out a handkerchief.

"You recognised the description of the car, Bernice. Tell us who you think owns it."

She looked away from Stride, dabbed at her eyes with the handkerchief. She took a breath.

"It was probably Jake Peters. I know he has a car like that, and he told me he'd seen Edie that Saturday afternoon. The day Edie was killed."

"Jake Peters?"

"Yes. Jacob Peters. He works at Martin Motors. He's a car salesman. He dated Edie for a while, although that was a long time ago. But Jake couldn't have had anything to do with Edie's death. He picked me up at my place around eight that night, and a group of us went to the Old Colony Club. Dancing." She stopped then, and her face paled as her mind registered the intersecting chronologies of the evening. "Oh, God." Then the tears started in earnest.

Stride sat back in his chair and took out two cigarettes and tossed one to Phelan. Harry leaned across the table with his lighter.

"Are we finished?" She snuffled into her handkerchief. "I don't feel very well."

Jake Peters was wiping the mudguard of a new Ford sedan with a chamois when Stride and Phelan walked into the showroom of Martin Motors. Peters probably thought he had two new customers.

"I wondered if my name would come up at some point," Peters said. He looked unhappy, but resigned.

Jake Peters was medium height, pushing forty, and was trying to hide a soft belly under the end of a wide necktie. His greying hair had been creatively arranged to cover an expanding forehead. He probably had a special hatred for windy days. In St. John's that was about ninety percent of the time.

"Yes," he said when Stride asked his first question, "I saw Edie that afternoon. I bumped into her on Water Street. We went for something to eat and then I took her home. Just before eight, I think, but the clock in my car is usually fast or slow."

"The two of you were an item at one time?"

"We used to date. And, yes, we were an item for a while, but that was a long time ago. Five or six years, anyway. I hadn't seen her for quite some time before that Saturday."

"Tell us about that Saturday."

"There isn't much to tell." Peters turned away and looked through the large showroom window at the traffic moving along Water Street. "Which is another way of saying that all we did was have supper together and then I took her home."

"What did you talk about at supper?"

"Mostly about old times, and where people are now and what they're doing with their lives. Chitchat, mostly."

"When it wasn't chitchat mostly, what did you talk about?" The question came out even harder than Stride intended and Peters was jolted. Stride disliked car salesmen, any kind of salesman, just on principle.

"Well, she talked some about her marriage. She told me her husband had a stroke last year, but that he seemed to have recovered all right. Then she said that the men in his family often had strokes and died pretty young. She made a joke about being a rich widow, but I don't think she really meant anything by it."

"You talked for a long time, then." Stride stared at Peters, his face set, with just a hint of a knowing smile. Peters looked away.

"Well, we hadn't seen each other for a while."

"Lots of things to catch up on?"

"Yes." Peters glanced back at Stride, who was staring at him with the same expression. Peters looked away again.

"You bumped into Edith Taylor in the afternoon, you said, and managed to get her home just around eight."

"Yes."

"Is it just remotely possible, Mr. Peters, that you and Edith Taylor went back to your place? Just for old times' sake, of course."

"What if we did?" Peters' face was flushed now and he stood a little straighter than before. Somewhere between angry and embarrassed.

"Reliving old, happy times?" Stride made an effort not to smile. Peters was showing a bit of spirit. He had edged up slightly in Stride's estimation.

"Sure. Just like you said. For old times' sake." Peters took a package of cigarettes from his shirt pocket. Stride produced his lighter.

"That part isn't really any of our concern, Mr. Peters. But it helps to fill out the picture. Your secret is safe with us." He ran his hand along the side of the car. "Did you tell Edith Taylor that you were going to the Old Colony Club that night?"

"Yes," Peters said. He drew on his cigarette and blew a cloud of smoke towards the ceiling. "In fact, I invited her to come along with us. She said that her husband was at his cabin and I suggested that it would be a good chance to see some of her old friends."

"But she turned you down."

"Yes."

"Did she say why? Do you think she was planning to meet someone else, later?"

"She didn't actually say that. But, yes, she gave me the impression she was expecting to see someone that night."

"A man?"

"That was the impression I got, yes."

"Do you have any idea who that might have been?"

"I haven't thought about much of anything else since it happened. The murder. It's impossible to describe how it feels to have been the one to drive her home that evening. But I have no idea who she might have been expecting. We hadn't really had anything to do with each other for years." Peters flopped the chamois against the mudguard, over and over. "Maybe I should have called you people after I heard about the murder, but I was really only guessing that she might have been meeting someone."

"Edith Wright had a friend during the war," Stride said. "Bernice Follett said her name was Emma. Do you know who she was?"

The change of subject took Peters by surprise. He thought about the question for a minute.

"Yes, I remember her. Her name, I mean. I think it was Emma Jeans. I never met her, but I'm pretty sure that's her name."

"You never met her?"

"No. She— Emma—wasn't part of our group. And when Edie started spending time with her, we didn't see her as much."

"Do you know anything about her? Where she worked? What she did?"

"Not really. I think they partied a lot. Emma Jeans knew people. That's what Edie told me, anyway."

"People? What kind of people?"

Peters shrugged. "People who had more money than we did, who moved in a different circle than we did."

"Really. And you don't know who these people were? Edith didn't mention any of their names?"

"No. Which I guess is kind of odd. Although she did mention one name that I remember. He wasn't a part of her new group, though. I think he was a friend of Emma's."

"I'm interested," Stride said. "Who was that?"

"I believe his last name was Button. Yes, it was Button. I remember, because Edie made a joke about life being a lot of fun if you knew which buttons to push."

"Was his name Harvey Button?"

"Yes, I think so." Peters looked from Stride to Phelan and back. "You know him?"

"We've met him once or twice." Stride and Phelan exchanged glances, both of them intrigued at the mention of a very familiar name. "Did Edith Wright tell you anything about Harvey Button? What he did for a living, perhaps?"

"Not that I remember. I think she just mentioned his name that one time. I'm not sure she actually knew him, though. But she did know he was someone that Emma knew."

"This might be of some help," Stride said. He made an extra effort to put some warmth into his smile. "You have a good memory for names, Mr. Peters."

"I'm a salesman. It's part of my business to remember faces and names." He smiled back at Stride. "I hope it helps."

"That part about Harvey Button was interesting," Stride said when they were back in the MG. "It's convenient that Harvey's still a houseguest."

"True enough," Phelan said. "You know, Peters didn't seem like such a bad sort. For a car salesman, I mean. I think I'll come back when this is all over and take a test drive in one of his shiny new cars."

"Do that, Harry. At least you can count on him remembering your name."

e i g h t e e n

Ned Taylor looked blankly at them when Stride asked if he knew the name Ambrose White. They met in Taylor's office in a downtown office building. A bank of long shelves lined one wall of his office, filled with a large selection of canned and boxed food products.

"Food import and wholesale," Taylor said by way of explanation.

"The name Ambrose White doesn't mean anything to you, then?"

"No, Mr. Stride, it doesn't. White is a very common name, of course, but I'm coming up empty-handed here. Who is Ambrose White, and what does he have to do with Edith's murder?"

"We don't know at this point. All we can tell you is that his fingerprints were found in your father's house, and we were able to identify him from records that we have on file."

"You mean Ambrose White's a known criminal?"

"That would be an exaggeration. White was arrested more than ten years ago after starting a brawl in a tavern. We don't have much more information about him than that, and nothing at all to connect him with your stepmother's murder."

"Have you asked my father about this?"

"Not yet. We didn't want to bother your father any more than we had to."

"Thank you. I appreciate that."

"We noticed that the bathroom in your father's home had been painted fairly recently. When was that?"

"It was after Beryl died, before Dad married Edith. I think it was about two years ago. He also had new cupboards installed in the kitchen, and in the bathroom too, now that I think of it." Taylor's brow wrinkled as he tried to remember the details. "It was after Beryl died, but after Dad and Edith decided to marry. Edith made most of the decisions, I remember."

"Who did the work on the bathroom and kitchen?"

"It was the firm of Thomas McKinley and Sons. I remember because Dad asked me if I could recommend them. I did, because my partner—George Shaw, you met him that Saturday night—had some work done by them and he was very pleased with it."

"They did the painting also?"

"Yes." Taylor sat straighter in his chair. "Does this Ambrose White have something to do with Thomas McKinley?"

"It's possible," Stride said. "We'll be asking McKinley about that."

Phelan made a gesture to catch Stride's attention.

"I think we're a bit too late for that, sir. McKinley died last year. I remember Kit reading his obit to me one morning."

"That's right," Taylor said. "The firm's name goes back to Tom McKinley's grandfather, the original Thomas McKinley. Tom took over the business. He didn't have any sons of his own, so the business was closed out and the building was sold. I don't know who owns it now."

"Do you think your father would remember the names of any of the men who worked on that job?"

"I doubt it," Taylor said. "Dad's a bit of a snob, too. Not unlike Beryl, really. He wouldn't have known the names of any of the men who did the painting and the carpentry, or cared who they were. They were just workmen, faceless as far as he was concerned." He frowned, made a resigned gesture with his hands. "I guess this isn't helping very much."

Phelan hung up the phone and made a face at Stride who had just come into the office.

"I got hold of McKinley's daughter. She knew some of the men who worked for her father, but she never heard of anyone named Ambrose White. That's not necessarily a surprise. He could be using another name. She said that her father didn't have much of a regular staff, hired men when he needed them."

"Business records?" Stride already figured this was moving towards a dead end.

"She kept them for a year, until all of the bills and taxes were paid, then chucked them out. She told me she didn't believe in keeping a lot of useless clutter about the house."

"Grand." Stride sat down and put his feet up on the desk. "I just had a few carefully chosen words with the Field Marshal," Stride said.

"Oops."

"Oops is the operative word. McCowan is not quite dancing jigs over the progress we've made. I attempted to place the Ambrose White identification in the best light, but somehow it lost persuasion and charm in the retelling. As the Field Marshal summarised it, we have fingerprints that give us the name of a possible suspect, but we have a trail that turned cold in 1936 and that's where we're stuck."

"Put that way, it does look a bit fragile."

"Thin as gossamer is the way McCowan put it."

"One admires his command of the language."

"One does."

"But he was understanding and supportive?"

"Yes," Stride said, "Absolutely."

"Which, translated, means?"

"Find Mr. Ambrose White, and find him soon."

"Straight and to the point."

"Very. Let's go and share our frustration with Mr. Jack Taylor at his place of residence."

Stride's initial thought on seeing Jack Taylor was that the man must have been spending a lot of time looking back over his life and pondering his sins. Taylor seemed to have aged at the rate of at least one year for each day that had passed since his wife's murder. For all of that, his house was neat and clean. He even invited them to sit in the kitchen, a positive gesture. Everything seemed to be in its place, even to the two cup-towels carefully folded and draped over the handle of the oven.

"Ambrose White." Taylor pronounced the name slowly and with care. He rubbed his chin with his right hand. He looked at Stride, but his eyes didn't seem quite focused. "I have known a number of people named White, of course. It's a common name. But I can't say that I have ever met an Ambrose White. You say the man's fingerprints were found in this house?"

"Yes."

"That is a considerable mystery to me. And I suppose to you also."

"Yes, it is," Stride said. "We're following up on this lead, of course, and looking for other possible suspects." He didn't mention that the possibles included the members of his own family. "Ned told us that you had work done on your house about two years ago by Thomas McKinley's firm."

"Yes, I did." He looked pained suddenly. "We did, Edith and I. There was quite a lot of work done, in fact. You think it's possible that someone in his firm might be responsible for Edith's death? That seems very unlikely to me. As I said, the work was done more than two years ago." He rubbed his chin, thinking. "Tom McKinley died last year."

"Yes," Stride said. "We knew that. We have to consider all the possibilities, Mr. Taylor. One of the things we have to do is eliminate possible suspects. Whoever Ambrose White is, he may have had nothing to do with your wife's murder, but we have to establish that as a fact." Taylor nodded slowly. "Who else, to your knowledge, might have access to your house, Mr. Taylor?"

"Access to my house?" Taylor seemed to stiffen, then shifted his position in his chair and crossed his legs. He clasped his hands and rested them on the table in front of him. "I assume you mean by someone such as an electrician or plumber? That sort of person?"

"Yes," Phelan. "And anyone else you can think of."

"I'm not sure what you mean, Sergeant."

Stride weighed in now.

"Mr. Taylor, from what you and others have told us, you and Mrs. Taylor led quite separate lives. One person used the word 'arrangement' to describe your marriage. Why would someone say that?"

"Perhaps you should ask them." Taylor's colour had risen slightly.

"We did. But we'd like to hear what you have to say about it."

"I don't have anything to say about it. My marriage to Edith is my business. Whether we had an arrangement, as you put it, is none of your concern. Some things are private."

"Unfortunately, that's not the case now. Your wife has been murdered, Mr. Taylor." He thought of saying that when murder walks in the door, privacy flies out the window, and cringed at the homily. "Do you travel very much as part of your job?"

"Are you suggesting that Edith entertained people in my house, when I wasn't at home?" Interesting choice of pronoun, Stride thought. Taylor's outrage was redolent of sadness.

"Yes," Stride said, a little too loudly. He paused for a moment to let Taylor think about that. "That is what I'm suggesting. Mrs. Taylor was the victim of a brutal assault before she drowned. Whoever killed your wife was almost certainly someone who knew her and who had, or imagined he had, reason to be angry. That is the premise of our investigation at the present time."

Taylor stared at Stride for what seemed a long time. He stood up then, walked to the sink and looked through the window into the backyard.

"Edith lived in this house for almost twenty years. She wasn't much more than a girl when she first came to us. Her family wasn't well off, of course. An aunt and a cousin of hers both worked for families in the city. Edith always thought she was fortunate to find work here. Her sister, her older sister, still lives in the village where she was born. She has five children now. Edith told me, not so long ago, that her sister looks almost as old as her mother did just before she died. And her sister is barely forty."

"I am sorry to have to ask again, Mr. Taylor, but did your wife see other men?"

Taylor did not reply at once. He sat down again and crossed his legs slowly. He looked across the room at nothing in particular.

"Yes," he said at last. He turned and faced them. "Your information is correct. Edith and I had an arrangement. You will have noticed that we slept in separate bedrooms. But I had no complaints, really. Edith lived up to her part. She was attentive to me." He sat quietly for a minute or two. "I haven't been well over the past year. I had a stroke. I was told it was minor, although I have to wonder if there really is such a thing as a minor stroke. It's possible you already know about that. I don't seem to have very much privacy left."

"Was there anyone in particular that she was seeing, that you know of?"

"Not that I know of. But neither did I ask." Taylor studied his hands, turned them over, and rubbed at the age spots as if trying to make them go away. "My only concern was that Edith should be discreet. And as far as I know she was." Taylor frowned and considered his words. "I know this may sound bizarre to you, but there was no antagonism between Edith and me. In strict terms, I suppose, she was an unfaithful wife, but marital fidelity had nothing to do with our arrangement. She lived her life and I lived mine. It was what we had agreed on."

Taylor looked tired then, but oddly content. Perhaps, Stride thought, he was relieved that he didn't have to play the prescribed husband role any longer. Stride almost felt sorry that he had to ask him more questions.

"Your wife had a friend during the war. Her name was Emma Jeans. Did you know her?"

"No."

"Is her name familiar to you?"

"Edith may have spoken of her sometimes. There was an Emma in Edith's address book. But you know that already. I suppose that's the person you're referring to."

"What do you know about Emma Jeans?"

"Apart from the fact that Edith knew her, that they may have been friends, not very much. They were about the same age, they presumably had similar interests. I know they spent time together during the war."

"A friend of Edith's told us she had seen a picture of Edith at a party at Government House," Stride said, and Taylor smiled. "I take it you're familiar with that picture?"

"Of course," Taylor replied. "Edith was very proud of it. She cut it out of the paper and pinned it to her bedroom wall. It hung there for years. It's probably still among her things somewhere."

"What can you tell us about that?"

"Not very much. I imagine you already know more about it than I do. Until you mentioned the picture just now, I'd forgotten about it. All Beryl and I knew was that Edith had been invited to attend a party at Government House."

"Did that surprise you?"

"Well, yes and no. It was a large affair and there were a lot of servicemen there, officers and enlisted men both. Naturally, there would have been young women in attendance. It was wartime, after all. Morale was important."

Even if morals weren't, necessarily, Stride thought.

"Was Emma Jeans at the same party?"

"I suppose she was. I really don't know."

"You can't tell us anything more about Emma Jeans, then."

"I'm afraid not. But Edith's friendship with Miss—or Mrs.—Jeans ended years ago. At least, as far as I know it did. Edith hadn't mentioned her name in a long time."

Taylor sat back in his chair. He had begun to swing his foot back and forth in a slow rhythm, as though accompanying a silent melody in his head. Stride wondered if it was one of Beryl's hymn-tunes.

"Does the name Harvey Button mean anything to you, Mr. Taylor?"

"No, I don't think so." Taylor shook his head, and Stride was inclined to believe him. Stride nodded his head slowly and looked at Jack Taylor. A week ago the man was the picture of respectability and middle-class values. Since his wife's murder a different picture had emerged. It was like overturning flat stones in a pasture, and watching what ran out into the light. But that was just part of the process.

Taylor returned Stride's look and smiled. But he didn't say anything more.

"I had a friend," Phelan said, "who held to the principle that you should believe nothing that you hear, very little of what you read, and only half of what you see."

Stride and Phelan had walked down to the waterfront to a place where they knew they could get fresh, hot potato chips that they would drench in vinegar and laden with salt. Now they sat on the running board of a delivery van, enjoying the golden brown chunks of potato and watching the activity on the harbour.

"Meaning?" Stride nibbled on a chip, and licked salt and vinegar off the side of his hand.

"Meaning that I had the impression that Taylor knew more than he told us, but I'm not sure. At first I thought I could read him, but then he kind of got away from me."

"That's about the way I feel, Harry." Stride pulled another chip from the cone of brown wrapping paper. "I don't know how much more he might know about her activities during the war. And I think it's possible that he didn't really want to know what she was up to, not that it made a lot of difference to him at the time. She was a housekeeper with modest duties to perform, and if she did her job satisfactorily, Taylor and his wife were probably happy enough with the situation. What she might have been doing on her nights out wouldn't matter much if she stayed out of trouble."

"Where ignorance is bliss," Phelan said. "And a soiree at Government House wouldn't have had them pulling out the shackles and the lash. Christ, these are good. Kit would hang me up by my heels if she knew I was pushing this stuff into my face."

"Your life would be in jeopardy," Stride said.

"Bloody true." Phelan stuffed another chip into his mouth, sucking and blowing to dissipate the heat. "Edith Wright might have been a naughty girl during the war. The association with Harvey Button, however distant, suggests that she might have been just that."

"I wonder," Stride said. "We don't actually know that she was associated with Button. Or what her relationship with Emma Jeans might have involved." Stride watched as a single-sailed catboat with a man and a woman in it moved slowly past. The woman was at the tiller and kept close watch on the sail, making small adjustments to keep the canvas filled with wind. The man relaxed against the gunwale, smoked a pipe, and drank occasionally from a brown bottle.

Stride and Phelan ate in silence until the chips were gone and then they deposited the papers in a wooden barrel near the edge of the wharf.

"Of course, sir, Emma Jeans might have nothing at all to do with this."

"It's possible, even probable. But we will have to find her and ask."

"She isn't in the phone book, she doesn't own any property in the city. I asked about her around the Fort, and a few of the lads knew her name, knew that she had worked for Harvey Button. Walter Williams said she was a classy lady. He said she had style."

"Williams? His beat was on the South Side, wasn't it?"

"Yes. For a couple of years during the war. He was the one who found Petrelli's body, you remember? He asked for the same beat again, last year. I guess he must like the neighbourhood," Phelan said, smiling. Then serious again. "Emma Jeans doesn't have a record, though. I had Bern run a check on her. Not even an arrest."

"Which means that she was either very careful or very lucky."

"Or chose her friends wisely and well."

"Yes," Stride said. "That, too." He lit a cigarette. It tasted very good after the chips.

"Can I ask you a question, sir?"

"Of course," Stride said. Harry was wearing his reflective look.

"I knew a fella, once, who was having it on with his housekeeper on a regular basis. He told me it was the best arrangement he could imagine, and she enjoyed it, too. I asked him why he didn't marry her and he said that it would have mucked things up, and neither of them wanted that."

"That's not a question."

"The question is about to happen."

"Go."

"You're not married, sir, and you live in your own house, and suppose you hire a housekeeper to do all the things that, as a man, you don't much feel like doing. Unless you've fallen madly in love with the lady, or madly in lust at least, why get married? Marriage is a complicated proposition, even at the best of times."

Stride looked at Phelan. He had been asking himself the same thing.

"What I'm wondering is, what advantage was there for Taylor to marry Edith Wright? They weren't sleeping together, they had separate lives. I can't see the advantage for him. He's well off and he could afford a housekeeper, whether Edith Wright or someone else. I have looked and looked for a reason for his marriage, but the cupboard is bare."

"Maybe Jack Taylor is just one of those people who needs to be married." Stride decided to let Harry run free with this.

"In name only, sir? I have trouble buying that. Taylor may have had a small stroke, and he's pushing sixty, but it looks to me as though he's fit enough, all told. I had an uncle who came back from France in 1917 with only one arm, and a leg shot all to hell. He had trouble walking and dressing himself, but when the knickers hit the floorboards, he needed no help from anyone. Not only did he father four children with his missus, but I know for a fact that he had at least one other lady in the wings for recreational purposes."

"It's shocking what you Irish get up to, Harry."

"It's the magic of the confessional, sir. Liberates the human spirit."

Stride walked to the edge of the wharf and looked down at the water. A dead fish was floating belly-up near one of the pilings, a pale white form just under the surface. After a minute, he walked back. Phelan was leaning against the front of the van smoking a cigarette.

"I agree with you, Harry," Stride said. "I don't see any real advantage for Taylor in his marriage to Edith Wright. There was an advantage for her, of course. Nice home, financial security, the freedom to do whatever she want-ed."

"With whoever she wanted."

"Whomever," Stride said, and Phelan grinned. Stride thought about Jake Peters and his artfully combed hair and expanding tummy. It really wasn't an exciting scenario. Then he thought about Ambrose White. But that only suggested to him that Edith Taylor might have had a keen interest in men and also lacked discrimination. He looked at Phelan and shrugged.

"There was an advantage for her," Phelan said, "but none for him, and certainly none for the Taylor family. Not that we know of, anyway." He paused for a moment. "Do you think blackmail might be a possibility?"

"Edith Wright knew things about Jack Taylor's naughty habits, and traded her silence for a marriage arrangement?"

"It's not unheard of, sir. She wouldn't have been breaking new ground in the field of criminal behaviour."

"Blackmail," Stride said. Jack Taylor's peccadilloes weren't really a closely guarded secret, though. He looked back at the harbour. The catboat was approaching the Narrows, heeling to port as it caught a gust of wind from the west, down the Waterford Valley. A tingle of remembered fear ran up his spine as he thought of the dangers facing a small boat beyond the harbour's embrace. He looked at Phelan, and shook his head. "We can't rule blackmail out completely, I suppose, but I don't think it's a serious possibility, Harry."

"Another dart misses the board." Phelan shrugged and smiled.

"But the question still hangs on the wall," Stride said. "Plethora of metaphors, dearth of ideas."

nineteen

Rodney Staples was waiting for Stride when he arrived at the station. He sat primly on a chair, knees together, with his briefcase in his lap, gripping the top with both hands. He looked happy, his small blue eyes dancing under the canopy of his eyebrows.

"I have something for you, Inspector Stride. Wonder of wonders, the system has come through for us. After a fashion, at least. It will not perhaps be exactly what you expected, but facts is facts, and that's what I have come to deliver."

Stride wondered if members of the public reacted to policemen the way he reacted to some civil servants. He fought back an urge to take hold of Rodney Staples, braid his eyebrows together and hang him on the coat rack.

"Let me have it, then, Mr. Staples." He managed a smile. "Whatever it is."

Staples made a small production of opening his briefcase. He took out a single sheet of paper. Then he settled back in his chair and crossed his legs.

"I went through all of the relevant birth records looking for your man White. You might be surprised, or perhaps not, at the number of Whites there are on this island. You gave me the year as 1918—and I believe you added the qualifier 'thereabouts.' So I covered the period 1917 to 1920."

He paused for dramatic effect. Stride glared at him.

"Well, there was no record of an Ambrose White having been born in that period. But as I cautioned you, there was always the possibility that the birth might not have been registered."

"What do you have for me, Mr. Staples?" Stride sat down and clasped his large hands in front of him. "If not a birth record, what?"

"I didn't have any luck with the birth records, Inspector, so I broadened my search, you might say."

Staples placed his sheet of paper on Stride's desk. Stride read it over. Then he read it a second time. Staples was still smiling when he looked up.

"This is a death record," he said finally. "It says that an Ambrose White died in April of 1939. This can't be the same person. We have a set of finger-prints for White that are less than two years old."

"I can't guarantee you that this is the Ambrose White you're looking for, Inspector. But check the birth date. August 2, 1919. You said that you thought 1919 was more likely to be his birth year than 1918. And the birth date is right on the mark. If it's not the same man, it certainly is an interesting coincidence, isn't it?"

"The cause of death was accidental, and the place of death is given as Friendship Cove. That's on Conception Bay, isn't it?"

"Yes, it is. I consulted a map before I came over here. Friendship Cove is near Spaniard's Bay."

"That's a long hike from St. John's."

"It is, but 1939 was a rough year, Inspector Stride. Like the ten years before it. Jobs were few and far between. Men were in the habit of going wherever there might be some work."

"What's up?" Phelan walked into the office. He smiled a greeting at Staples. "Some news on our man?"

"We found an Ambrose White, Harry. But he's been dead eight years according to our friend, Mr. Staples."

Phelan looked at the death certificate.

"Same name, right birth date, but how can this be our man? Dead men don't leave fingerprints. I read that somewhere."

"Two possibilities, then," Stride said. "The obvious one being that this is not the same Ambrose White who was arrested in 1936. Which puts us no farther ahead."

Phelan shrugged and hung his coat on the rack.

"But no farther behind, either."

"Point taken. Second possibility. And this one has more appeal. Ambrose White liked the idea of being dead, so he nominated someone for the position. He may even have helped him along. And White himself is alive and well, and probably living under an assumed name. Just as you suggested, Harry."

"In or near St. John's. And bashing ladies in their baths."

"One lady only, Harry. So far, anyway. And assuming this wasn't a random killing, there must have been a connection between Ambrose White and Edith Taylor."

"Peters said he thought she was meeting someone Saturday night, after he dropped her off."

"Ambrose White using a pseudonym, perhaps."

"It would explain why no one we've spoken to knows him. The Taylors say they don't know the name."

Stride thought about that.

"I'll leave you to it, gentlemen." Rodney Staples had listened to their discussion and now he clicked his briefcase shut and stood up. "I am pleased to have been of assistance, if assistance it proves to be." He paused in the doorway and smiled one last time, the massive eyebrows fluttering. Stride waved a hand at him. Then he was gone.

"I wonder. Why do people commit murder, Harry?"

"A variety of reasons. Money is close to the top of the hit parade."

"Love and hate. Crimes of passion."

"Jealousy, a part of the love-hate equation."

"Revenge. Another part of the love-hate equation."

"How much passion did Edith Taylor inspire, I wonder?"

"None at all in her husband of record, sir. As far as we know, anyway. And as far as we know for certain, only intermittent passion in Mr. Jake Peters, the automobile magnate."

"Well, she inspired someone enough to beat her to death in her bath." Stride looked closely at Phelan and chose his words. "I'm still not discounting three members of the Taylor family. Ned Taylor isn't completely off the hook, neither is his brother. And then there's Joanne Taylor. She doesn't have an alibi, and we know that she had a motive."

Phelan wondered if he should pick up on that. He decided he should.

"Can I ask you a question, sir?"

"I'll save you the trouble, Harry. I knew Joanne Taylor before she married Ned. Her name was Joanne Bartlett then and she worked in Brendan Madigan's office. We met one day when I was in court to testify for the Crown. We were together for not quite a year."

"I was wondering about that," Phelan said, "but I didn't like to ask."

"I suspected as much." Stride lit a cigarette and leaned back in his chair. Phelan thought he looked weary. He wondered how much effect the reappearance of Joanne Taylor was having on Stride's relationship with Margaret Nichol. "I never really expected to see her again after she married Ned Taylor. But here we all are. Joanne's a prime suspect in a murder case and I'm the investigating officer."

"You don't think she might have done it, do you? Not really?"

"No," Stride said. But he had paused just long enough to make them both think about the possibility. "Not really, Harry. But if we ever find Ambrose White and have enough evidence to bring him to trial, a good defence lawyer will bring forward other possible suspects to muddy the case. My relationship with Joanne wasn't a total secret in the legal community, although we were very discreet. Secretive even." Stride shook his head and laughed. "Which is my way."

"I see your point, sir. A good lawyer will make the argument that the inspector has conveniently overlooked a prime suspect in a murder case because he was once involved with the lady. Front-page stuff, even if it is a crock. The Field Marshal would shit very large bricks."

"The thing is, Harry, it doesn't matter what I think about Joanne. She's a suspect, and we have to treat her that way." He mashed his cigarette in an ashtray. "You know, I used to think that Joanne's habit of going off by herself was a good thing on the whole. People needing their independence, their solitude, and all that. But she picked a bad night for it that Saturday."

"Maybe not, sir. If she'd stayed at home by herself that night, there would have been no one at all to vouch for her."

Stride looked at Phelan, his expression a little brighter.

"But if she did go to a movie, someone might remember having seen her. Even if it was a really bad night, pouring rain."

"Especially if it was a really bad night. There's a chance that she wasn't lost in the crowd, because there was no crowd that night. I have a suggestion, sir. While you're looking into this dead Ambrose White thing, I'll take a walk down to the Paramount and ask some questions." Phelan looked at his watch. "The matinee has just started. Maybe the ticket girl from Saturday night is on again this afternoon."

The ticket girl at the Paramount did not quite live up to her designation. Sylvia Rose was the wrong side of thirty, with bleached blonde hair, too much makeup, and a distracted manner. She could also stand to lose at least twenty pounds, Harry decided. She looked at Phelan's shield with some interest, most of which faded when she noticed his wedding ring. The usher, a tall, thin boy in his late teens wearing thick horn-rimmed glasses and an ill-fitting blue uniform, leaned on a broom and stared at Phelan, mouth open, breathing noisily. Adenoids, Harry thought.

"Last Saturday night?" the woman nodded her head. "Yeah, I was on that night. It was raining buckets, I remember that. There was hardly anyone here for the second show. Not many for the first, either, for that matter. Probably lost money. Good movie, though. I just love Bogart."

Phelan looked towards the usher, who nodded in agreement.

"Did either of you happen to notice a woman who came to the first show by herself? She's in her mid- to late-twenties, fairly tall, brown hair, good looking. She would have been wearing a navy blue raincoat." Phelan wished he had a photograph.

"She in some kinda trouble?" Sylvia Rose drew back a bit, cautious.

"Not if you saw her here last Saturday night."

"I might of seen her. I don't know for certain. I don't look at women much. Unless they're wearing a really nice dress, or jewellery, or have a real interesting hair-do, or something. But everyone was all bundled up Saturday night. I wasn't paying much attention. Phil here would be more likely to notice. Right, Phil?" Sylvia Rose grinned and Phil the usher blushed and looked at his shoes.

"I think maybe I saw her," he said, "but I can't say for sure." His voice was thick and seemed filtered through a bowl of oatmeal. Adenoids, definitely, Phelan decided. "You see," he pulled off his glasses and held them out for Phelan, "I didn't have my glasses on. My grandmother sat on them Saturday morning and I didn't get them back from the eye doctor's until Monday. I can see well enough without them to work and walk around, but everything's pretty blurry. I think I remember the blue raincoat, though."

Phelan stifled an obscenity. Maybe they had seen the two Yanks that Joanne Taylor had mentioned.

"You mean the white guy and the nigger?" Sylvia Rose looked triumphant. "Yeah, they came in together. The white guy was really cute. Blond guy, tall. You remember them, Phil?" The usher nodded. "You don't see white guys and niggers together very much. A friend of mine works at the base and she says they can't stand each other, says that most of the Yanks, the white guys, they treat the niggers real bad. I think that's terrible. Niggers are people, too."

Phelan shook his head, smiled, and left the theatre. He walked across Harvey Road and leaned on the black wrought-iron fence that kept pedestrians from tumbling down a steep hill into the parking lot of Holloway School. The vertical rods in the fence were topped with sharp points that resembled spear-heads. Anyway, that's what Harry had always thought they looked like.

You had a pretty good view of the harbour and Cabot Tower and the flanking hills from this point on Harvey Road. If you felt like it, you could spend a pleasant few minutes on a nice day standing there watching the activity on the water, the ships and boats moving in and out through the Narrows. Phelan lit a cigarette and rested one foot on the concrete foundation of the iron fence. It looked like Joanne Taylor had been at the movies when Edith Taylor was being killed, just as she had said she was. Harry would try to follow that up with their contact at Fort Pepperrell, but it was really just a formality. He knew that Stride would be pleased.

Jack Corrigan was a large man with large features, the crowning glory a red bulbous nose with a patchwork of scars and veins. A pair of small dark eyes critically surveyed the world at large. When Stride located him, Corrigan was about to strike a match on the top of his desk. A hand-rolled cigarette was clasped between two thick fingers. Stride smiled at Corrigan, who stared back at him.

The word on Corrigan was that he was resigned to being a uniform for the rest of his tenure with the constabulary. He had once expressed an interest in joining the CID, but didn't get the appointment. No one thought that Corrigan lacked the intelligence to be a detective, but that he seemed to lack the personality. He was typically crude and frank, sometimes remote and at other times belligerent. Corrigan appeared to have few friends on the constabulary, although it was said that he occasionally spent time with Bernard Crotty.

Stride sat on a wooden chair next to Corrigan's desk. He took out a cigarette and rolled it around between thumb and index finger. He and Corrigan looked steadily at each other. Then Corrigan struck the match on the desk-top and held out the flame for Stride to light his cigarette. After which he lit his own.

"How goes it, Jack?"

"It goes, sir." A bit too much emphasis on the "sir", but Stride had expected that.

"You were stationed at Spaniard's Bay on Conception Bay until a few years ago, Jack."

"Matter of record, sir." Corrigan drew on his cigarette. "I was there, all told, for twelve years, five months and eighty-seven days. Not that I was counting the time, you understand. It's just that I have a good memory for obscure fuckin' statistics."

Corrigan flicked ash onto the floor, ignoring the ashtray on the corner of his desk. Stride carefully tapped the end of his cigarette against the same ashtray.

"I need some information, Jack, and I hope you can help me with that famous memory of yours." Corrigan continued to stare at him. "In April 1939, the 22nd to be precise, a man named Ambrose White was killed in or near Friendship Cove." Stride handed Corrigan the death certificate. "You were the investigating officer and you must have written a report. Do you remember it?"

Corrigan took his time reading the certificate, turned it over and observed that the back of the sheet was blank, then read the certificate again. He passed the sheet back to Stride.

"I remember it. And you can get a copy of my report from Bern Crotty."

"I will. But first I want you to tell me about it. Everything you can recall."

"This is important?"

"Yes."

Corrigan leaned back in his chair and stared at the ceiling. He scratched his chin with a thumbnail that had been gnawed very short, almost down to the quick.

"It was a very bright, sunny day. I remember that because I always remember bright sunny days. Living on this fog-bound rock, a bright sunny day is worth remembering. Anyway, I got the word early in the morning from Mose Robbins who saw a car piled into a rock about two miles from Friendship Cove. He was on his regular morning run when he saw the wreck. Mose drove an outport taxi, big fuckin' DeSoto, owned his own business. Hell of a way to make a living, you ask me, belting along those narrow dirt roads going full-forty, but Mose seemed to like it. I think he must of drove a tank in the First War and never got over it."

"Ambrose White was alone in the car?"

"All by his lonesome and dead as mutton. His neck was broke and the steering column was rammed half-way through his fuckin' chest. Must have died instantly. Leastwise, I hope so for his sake. I had Doc Miller along with me when I went to the wreck. Miller said the man had been dead since sometime the night before. Around midnight was his best guess. Probably ran off the road in the dark and hit those rocks going full tilt. Maybe the brakes give out coming down the hill. Anyway, the poor fucker never had a chance. The car he was driving was a shit-box, a real Tin Lizzie, older than Christ."

"What identification was he carrying?"

"Not much. A black leather wallet with one a them little name cards filled out in pencil. Had his name and birth date on it, and that's all. There was also three one-dollar bills in the wallet. I thought about pocketing them, but my good and honest nature wouldn't let me."

"No home address or next of kin mentioned on the card?"

"Like I said. Name and birth date. The wallet is filed with my report unless they threw it out already. Usually they do that after five years, if no one makes a claim." Corrigan closed his eyes and made a face. "Oh, yeah. I remember now. He was also carrying a letter from someone named Downe in Portugal Cove. Tucked in the wallet with the three one-dollar bills. Benjamin Downe, I think the name was. It was a letter of recommendation; said that the bearer had worked in his shop. Woodworking it was. The letter was pretty faded and dog-eared, hard to read. I followed that up, actually got a hold of Benjamin Downe. He said that he had written a dozen letters like that over the years but that he never heard of any Ambrose White."

"Never heard of him?"

"That's what he said."

"And you told him that White was dead?"

"I did."

"How did he explain the letter?"

"Said that White, whoever he was, musta got it from someone else."

Stride looked at Corrigan and thought about that for a few moments.

"And White is buried in Friendship Cove?"

"He is, sir. All done right and proper, too. We didn't know what church he belonged to, not that it matters much you want my fuckin' opinion, so I had the local Catholic priest and the Church of England minister both do the honours. Bit of a lark, sir. Some of the time you can't get a priest and a minister to even talk to each other in this country. But I happened to know them two been bum-fuckin' each other for years. Unholy communion, you might say." Corrigan shook his large head and chuckled. "And if I could of found a fuckin' rabbi, I would have had him there too. Christ knows there was enough of him to go around."

"How's that, Jack? I don't follow you."

"The dead man, sir. Your Ambrose White. He was a big fucker. Must have gone six-three in his stocking feet, and two hundred pounds if he was an ounce. I don't know how he managed to wedge himself into that little coupe in the first place. We had a hell of a time getting him out, I can tell you. Thought for a while there we might have to bury him, car and all."

twenty

Stride and Phelan left Fort Townshend mid-afternoon and headed for Portugal Cove. Stride was just as pleased as Phelan thought he would be with the news about the two American servicemen that Sylvia Rose and Phil, the usher, had remembered seeing in the Paramount on Saturday night.

"We'll follow that up, Harry, just to be sure. If she saw them at the theatre, they might remember having seen her."

"A Yank in uniform who remembers seeing a single woman at a movie on a Saturday night? Hard to imagine, sir."

"What was it the Brits said about Yanks in England during the war? 'Overpaid, over-sexed, and over here?'"

"Some things don't change. I'll call Muff Conway and ask him if he can locate the two airmen." Master Sergeant Melville "Muff" Conway, United States Army Air Force, was their principal contact at Fort Pepperrell. They had first met him in 1943 during the investigation of the Petrelli murder.

"Do that. Finding them might be a long-shot. On the other hand, a white man and a Negro from Pepperrell hanging around together? Not your standard fare."

Stride's relief was almost tangible. And sufficient to indicate that he had believed that Joanne's guilt was a possibility. He chewed that over while he drove. The afternoon had turned out fine, and he had taken the top down on the MG. There was little traffic and he accelerated to a speed well beyond the legal limit, and just a little faster than was probably safe. He glanced at Phelan as the little car zipped along the road. Harry had that slightly pinched look again. He was never all that convinced that Stride's driving abilities matched the MG's performance, especially on rough roads where he had to manoeuvre around potholes and large stones.

"There's nothing in Corrigan's report to suggest that White might have had anything to do with this fellow's death in Friendship Cove?" Phelan was shouting to make himself heard over the rush of air.

"Nothing at all, Harry. I'm willing to accept the verdict that the poor bastard, whoever he was, lost control of his car and ran off the road. The doctor said he probably died before midnight. He might just have fallen asleep at the wheel."

"He sure as hell doesn't match the description of the Ambrose White that Agnes Duder told us about. What did she call him? 'Poor little fellow?' I wonder who he was and how Ambrose White happened to be on the scene when he died."

"Serendipity," Stride said.

"Serendipity," Phelan repeated. "Another good word." He took out his notebook, chuckling as he wrote.

"Yes, serendipity. Although it wasn't a happy accident for the fellow behind the wheel. We can be pretty certain that Ambrose White, at least the version that Agnes Duder and Henry Thompson knew, is probably alive and well, and living somewhere in or near St. John's."

"Maybe we'll get lucky in Portugal Cove and someone will remember him from his days with Benjamin Downe. If we get really lucky, they may be able to tell us where he came from."

The woodworking shop that had once belonged to Benjamin Downe had been newly painted, and it looked as though the original building had been expanded. The shingles about two-thirds of the way along were clearly of a more recent vintage than the rest of the roof. The sign by the door told them that the business was now owned by a Herbert Rodgers. A workman in the shop told them that Rodgers was in the yard behind the building taking inventory on a shipment of wood. Stride looked around him at the rocky terrain. It was obvious that the wood for Rodgers' shop wasn't cut locally.

Herbert Rodgers was a thickset man of medium height with greying hair and steel-rimmed glasses. He wore heavy khaki pants held up by both a wide leather belt and suspenders. The green elastic of the suspenders didn't go well with the blue of his flannel shirt, but Rodgers didn't look like a man who would care much about the trivia of men's fashions. He was making notes on a clipboard. He put his pencil behind his ear and rubbed the end of a large log and then sniffed his fingers. He made another notation on his pad of paper.

He turned then and saw the two policemen watching him. There was a moment when all three were motionless, Rodgers assessing his visitors and trying to guess who they were, Stride and Phelan taking a measure of the man. There was something in Rodgers' expression that brought a tension to Stride's shoulders. That something increased in volume when Stride and Phelan introduced themselves.

"Yes," Rodgers said, "this used to be Benjamin Downe's establishment. I bought it from his family after he died."

"Did you know Mr. Downe, personally?" Stride asked. "Perhaps you worked for him at one time?"

Rodgers did not reply at once. He stared at Stride, looking for something behind the simple words.

"Yes. I worked for Benjamin Downe." Rodgers tapped the toe of his leather boot against the stack of wood. "I worked for Benjamin Downe for more than ten years. I learned much of what I know about my trade from him."

"You had a close relationship with Mr. Downe, then?" Stride looked at Rodgers, allowed a small grin to play across his face. He didn't know what was eating at Rodgers, but he would try and tease it out of him, one way or another.

Rodgers looked back at Stride, his eyes narrowed. He walked a few paces away and placed the clipboard on a low pile of wood.

"I worked for Benjamin Downe, like I said, and he taught me quite a lot. I don't know if that's what you mean by relationship, Mr. Stride." Rodgers hitched up his belt. His hands were large and the skin was rough and calloused. There was a long cut across the back of his right hand, partly healed, a dark red scab running the length of it. "You come down from the city to ask me questions about Benjamin Downe, maybe about me too, but you haven't told me why. Maybe now you better do just that, sir."

Rodgers stood with his hands on his hips now, feet spread, the right foot just behind the left for balance. It was halfway to a fighting posture. Phelan glanced at Stride, surprised, and stepped two paces to the side.

"We do have some questions, Mr. Rodgers." Stride was surprised, as well, and intrigued.

"Then start asking your goddamned questions, sir, or get off my property. I don't spend my days walking around in a suit with a quiff hat on my head, poking my nose into people's business. I work hard for my living, always have. If you have questions, ask them and be off. I got work to do, a family to support."

Rodgers was sweating now, skin shining in the sunlight, his face red. His eyes danced back and forth between Stride and Phelan. Stride glanced over his shoulder. Two workmen had quietly come out of the shop. They looked towards Rodgers, ready to act on his bidding. One of them carried what looked like an axe-handle. Both were lean and fit.

Jesus Christ, Stride thought. The Little-Big-Horn comes to Portugal Cove, with Stride and Phelan playing the part of the cavalry, and not a saddle-horse in sight. He caught Phelan's eye and flicked his glance in the direction of the man with the axe-handle. They would take him first, together, if it came to that. Then Stride would dance with Rodgers, while Phelan looked after the third man. And they would hope that the entire crew wouldn't come running out of the shop in the meantime, armed with all the sharp and fierce tools of the woodworking trade. With any luck at all, they might both be out of the hospital by Christmas. Better to avoid it though, if they could. Stride held up his hand.

"It's just questions, Mr. Rodgers." He waited a few moments. Rodgers continued to stare at him. The two men behind them moved a bit farther apart from each other, a little closer to Stride and Phelan. This was carrying the townie-bayman rift just a bit too far. Stride tried again.

"It's your call, Mr. Rodgers. We can ask our questions, take note of your answers, and then be on our way. And that will likely be the end of it. But if Paul Bunyan there starts swinging that cudgel, it will all end sooner or later in a Black Maria and a one-way trip to the city." Stride caught Rodgers' eye. "Who'll support your family then?"

It was the mention of "family" that made the difference. Rodgers looked away, then down at the ground. He nodded towards the two men who had come out of the shop, and they walked to the far end of the property and leaned on a fence and lit cigarettes. The axe-handle was propped against the fence between them.

"They're good men, both of them," Rodgers said. "The younger fellow, the one with the stick, he spent most of the war in North Africa. Good men, both," he said again. "They didn't know who you were."

"Do you inspire that kind of loyalty in all your employees?" Stride asked. He wondered if it would have made much difference if the two men had known that Stride and Phelan were with the constabulary.

"I treat my men fair. They respect that."

"You've recently expanded, Mr. Rodgers," Stride said, indicating the new roof shingles. "Business must be good?"

Rodgers looked at him. He took a deep breath and grabbed at the diversion.

"Yes. The war brought a lot of work and prosperity, and things have continued to go well. In my little corner, at least, there's almost as much money around now as there was during the war. We're doing quite well."

"You said you bought the business from Benjamin Downe's family. When was that?"

"That was back in 1943. Mr. Downe died that year, early part of the summer. "

"So, you worked for him from early in the 30's."

"Yes. Starting in 1931. June, 1931."

"You were working for him in 1936, then?"

"Yes." Stride saw that Rodgers was casting about to find some significance for the date. He did not obviously find anything. "Why 1936? Did something happen that year? Nothing comes to mind, but I'll help you if I can." Rodgers pointed to a wooden bench near an old and twisted crab-apple tree. "We can sit over there if you like."

Stride sat next to Rodgers. Phelan stood nearby, one foot propped on the bench, leaning on his knee. From time to time he glanced at the two men leaning on the fence by the road, and at the entrance to the shop.

Stride took out the letter of reference that had been included with Corrigan's report on Ambrose White. Rodgers looked at the letter for a few moments, his lips moving soundlessly. He looked back at Stride.

"Can you confirm for us that Mr. Downe wrote that letter?"

Rodgers didn't reply. He looked away and then took his time reading the letter through.

"Yes, that is Mr. Downe's handwriting. And his signature."

"You're certain of that?"

"Yes. I could show you many examples of his handwriting. Mr. Downe was old-fashioned, very set in his ways. He did all his invoicing and correspondence personally, and all of it hand-written in duplicate. He was proud of his penmanship. He told me once that he had won prizes in school." Downe paused and looked at Stride. "This letter is dated 1936. Is this why you drove all the way out here?"

"That's part of it," Stride said. "Did Mr. Downe write many letters like this? In your experience?"

"I know that he sometimes wrote letters for men who were moving on to other locations and might need the reference. I don't know how many he might have written."

"This letter was in the possession of a young man named Ambrose White. Do you remember anyone of that name working for Mr. Downe?"

Rodgers looked away. He took off his glasses and rubbed his eyes. Then put the glasses on again. He was silent for a moment, breathing slowly.

He remembers Ambrose White, Stride thought, but he's trying to decide if he can deny knowing him and get away with it. He watched Rodgers closely. Phelan was doing the same from his end of the bench, still glancing also at the men by the fence. Stride gave Rodgers a nudge.

"We have testimony to the effect that Ambrose White worked for Benjamin Downe in the 1930s. Can you confirm that?"

Rodgers sighed.

"Yes. I remember Ambrose White. He wasn't much more than a boy when he came to work here."

"When was that?"

"I don't remember the exact date, but I believe it was sometime in 1935. Probably in the spring."

"When a constable contacted Mr. Downe a number of years ago and asked him about White, Mr. Downe denied having given him a letter of reference. Why do you think he did that?"

Rodgers was silent again for a moment.

"I don't know. I wasn't privy to Mr. Downe's private thoughts. He must have had his reasons, I suppose."

Stride sensed the tension rising in Rodgers again. He glanced at Phelan, who nodded agreement. That whole scene with the stand-off and incipient brawl was tied in to this.

"The thirties were hard times, Mr. Rodgers. Business must have been very slow. Was Ambrose White an apprentice? Did he work for a salary, or just for his keep?"

"He worked for his keep. But Mr. Downe also paid him an allowance."

"An allowance?"

"Pocket money. It wasn't much, but it allowed him to rattle some change in his pocket."

"Where did White live? At his home?"

"No. He didn't have a home. His parents were dead. Before he came to work for Benjamin Downe he lived with an aunt in St. Phillips, not far from here. I don't know that she was a relative, actually. I believe she might have been a family friend."

"He lived with this aunt while he worked here?"

Another pause.

"No. He lived with Mr. Downe."

"With Mr. and Mrs. Downe?"

"There was no Mrs. Downe." Rodgers sat back and stretched his legs out in front of him. The cuffs of his trousers rode up over the tops of his leather boots. He wore grey wool socks and the boots were laced halfway, the laces wound several times around the middle of the boot, tied with double bows.

"Tell us about that. Was it usual for Mr. Downe to have his employees living with him?"

"He did sometimes."

"Boys? Young men?" It was making sense. The hostility. The fear that lay under it. He remembered Rodgers' comments about his family.

"Yes." Rodgers paused again. When he spoke his voice had dropped low. "Benjamin Downe was a good man in some ways. He was always decent with me."

"And with Ambrose White?"

There was another long pause. Rodgers took a large handkerchief from his hip pocket and wiped his brow. He stared intently at the piece of cloth. He sighed again.

"Mr. Downe was partial to young men."

"I see," Stride said.

"You might think you do," Rodgers said. He stood up and faced Stride and Phelan, angry again. The two men by the fence also stood up. Watching. But Rodgers had a tired, worn look now. "I didn't have anything to do with that. I just worked here. I had children, a wife. I needed that job. And I had hopes for the future."

He walked a short distance away, stood with his hands on his hips. He came back to the bench and sat down again.

"And Ambrose White's future?" Stride said. "Tell us what you think about that. You knew what was going on?"

"Yes. I didn't like it. But I didn't ask about it. I just did my work, collected my pay and went home at the end of the day." Rodgers leaned forward, elbows on knees. He stared at his building, focusing on the addition he had made, the part with the new roof. His lips were moving slightly, as though he was reading a message on the shingles, something that Stride and Phelan couldn't see.

"I'm not very proud of myself, sir," he said at last. "I knew it was wrong. All of it. I looked the other way. I didn't know what else to do."

Stride took a breath and looked at Phelan. Phelan shook his head.

"How long did White work here?"

"About a year. I believe he left in the spring of 1936."

"Where did he go?"

Rodgers paused again. He studied the tops of his boots for a moment.

"He went to the firm of Mr. Henry Thompson, in St. John's."

"On Downe's reference?"

"I think so. I noticed that the date on the letter you showed me was April 1936. That was about the time Ambrose left."

"What do you know about Henry Thompson? Was he a fellow traveller with Downe?"

"I don't know. I only know that he and Mr. Downe were acquainted, did business together sometimes. Mr. Thompson had a good business in St. John's. That much I can say for sure. I met him only once, one day when he came down from the city."

"Was White here then?"

"Yes. It wasn't long after White started here."

"So Henry Thompson would have met White at that time?"

"I dare say."

Stride took another breath. Damn it all. He silently repeated the phrase. It was like peeling an onion. Sometimes it was like that. But the sins of Benjamin Downe and Henry Thompson would have to wait for another time. Stride needed to focus on the main event, finding Ambrose White. Finding Edith Taylor's killer. One job or two? He didn't know yet.

"How much did you know about White? Who was he, and where did he come from?"

"He never said much to me or to anyone else while he was here. The circumstances being what they were, I had as little to do with him as I could. The whole business was very uncomfortable for me, Inspector Stride."

Rodgers was pleading for some kind of absolution. Stride threw him a bone.

"I can see where it would have been, Mr. Rodgers. I might have felt the same way. But tell us what you can. It's important that we find him."

"White wasn't from Portugal Cove proper. But he was from a place near here. Just a couple of miles from where we sit, actually. A place called Caitlin's Cove. If you don't know it, I can give you directions."

"Ambrose White. Now, that's a name I have not heard spoken in quite a few years, sir. Indeed, I have not." Isaac Squires sat on a tall stool behind the counter of his store in Caitlin's Cove, his hands on his knees. He wore the same derby hat he had worn the day Stride and Phelan had driven down from the city to see Gaffer Fox. "It must be all of fifteen years since I last laid eyes on that boy. Of course, he wouldn't be a boy now, would he?"

"No," Stride said. And what boyhood Ambrose White had, had been cut very short. "You knew the family, sir?"

"Knew the family? Oh, yes. His father was a friend of mine. Felix White."

Phelan started.

"The same Felix White whose boat my father came down from St. John's to repair, years ago?"

"Yes, Sergeant Phelan, the very same. Now, I thought to myself when you asked about Ambrose, that I was telling someone not so long ago about Felix White. I had quite forgotten that it was yourself I was talking to. That was the day you came down to see Gaffer Fox. Ah, this head of mine." He smiled shyly. "Ask me about something that happened ten, twenty or more years ago, and I will straightaway give you chapter and verse. But yesterday has already almost gone."

That will work for us, Stride thought. It's Ambrose White's past that we want to hear about. We'll start there and work our way up to the here and now.

"Tell us about him, Mr. Squires. When we were here before, you told us that his father died a long time ago. We understand his mother died sometime after that."

"I did tell you about Felix. Yes." Squires was staring at a spot on the floor behind the counter. He scratched at a loose thread on his pants leg with a calloused forefinger. "It's been a hard road for the White family. Where should I start, I wonder? I suppose I could say that it all started a long time ago, before Felix was married. Poor Felix was as unlucky in life as he was unlucky in love. Is there not a saying about that?" Squires shook his head.

"Felix fell in love with a girl, Effie Morgan was her name. She wasn't from here, from down the shore a ways. I knew Effie, and she was a fine maid. Not pretty in the way that pretty is, but handsome, and she loved Felix too. They were to be married. Then, two weeks before the wedding she caught the influenza and she died. One day she was herself, strong and happy, and then she was sick, and then she was gone. It was so quick. Felix was almost destroyed. Soon after that—too soon—he married the sister, Martha. It should have made a happy ending for them both, but it was only the start of more bad.

"Martha was never a well person, you see. Perhaps it was the flu she had, same time as her sister, the awful fever, but she was never a well person after she married Felix." Squires made a gesture with his right hand towards his head. "But just as likely it was what she was born with. Where Effie was sunshine, Martha was cloud. That's the best way I can say it."

"Was Ambrose the only child?"

"No. There were two children. Ambrose had a sister, some years older than himself. Perhaps there was four, five years between them. Her name was Jennifer."

"Was? Is she dead?" Stride offered his cigarettes to Squires, who shook his head. Stride took one for himself and passed the package to Phelan.

"Not as such, no." Squires looked up, smiled. "I see I'm confusing you. I'm not aware that Jennifer White is dead, sir. But I haven't seen her for a very long time. Longer even than since I last saw Ambrose. You see, it was very hard for Martha after Felix died. There was some insurance money, but Martha had to find work to support the family. In fact, she worked for me for a time. When Jennifer was just eighteen, she left here and went to the city to take a job."

"To St. John's?"

"Yes. There were no paying jobs here, or close by, and not many in St. John's, neither, for that matter. Jennifer found work, though, with a family, as a housemaid. She had limited education, you see, but she was willing to work and she was a bright girl."

"And you haven't seen her since. That was more than fifteen years ago. What happened to her? Who did she work for?"

"It was the Harriston family. They were very well off and had a large house in the city. A palace by our standards, sir."

"John Henry Harriston? That's who she went to work for?"

"I see you are familiar with the name, sir."

"I know who they are, Mr. Squires. A young woman could do worse than work for the Harristons."

"Yes. She didn't stay there long, though. After a few months she found a job at Mr. Harriston's store." Squires shook his head and smiled again. "I should not call it a store, though. It wasn't a store like this little place, of course."

"The Colonial Stores?"

"Yes. That's the one. Martha was quite excited when she heard the news. It was a big step up from being a housemaid."

"Give us the rest of it, Mr. Squires. What went wrong?"

"At first, there seemed to be only good news following good news. Her first job at the department store was in the stockroom, but she was soon promoted to a sales position. We were all surprised, I must say, but very happy for her."

"How long did the good news last?"

"Not very long. Perhaps four or five months. The day came when Martha stopped talking about Jennifer. The change in her mood was very noticeable. I'd ask her sometimes how things were going in the city, but Martha would only reply that she hadn't heard from Jennifer for some time."

"The girl didn't just disappear, surely?"

"No. I knew that Martha had gone up to St. John's one time but she never spoke to me about it. Nor to anyone. But you can't hide much in a small place like this, Inspector Stride. And if you do try and hide something it makes a lump in the fabric of the community. Bad tidings will come out, the more so for not talking about them. When people have no facts, they make up stories. I think the truth of it was that Jennifer had gotten herself in the family way, and the fellow responsible was either married or unwilling to do the right thing by her. It was very hard for Martha. Worse for Jennifer, of course, but Martha was in a very bad way."

Stride's head was starting to buzz. He looked at Phelan and wondered if he was having the same thoughts. Harry's expression told him that he was.

"And the baby?"

"There was no baby that I ever heard of. I don't know how the story ended, Inspector. I think something bad happened that last night when Jennifer came down here to visit her mother. She had come in a car with someone, and she must have left later that same evening. One of the neighbours said that there was a lot of shouting. She said it was a terrible row. Then there was the slamming of doors, the car started up and Jennifer and her companion were gone."

"And she never came back?"

"Not to the best of my knowledge. And that wasn't the end of it. Martha went very strange after that, drew away from everyone, and was hardly seen at all in the place. Not long after that, she was found one morning in the harbour, under the wharf. Drowned."

"A suicide?"

"There was no note to say so, but there's not many in this place that believes otherwise. Although, to give it a better shine, the doctor who signed the death certificate said it was an accident. And who can say for sure that it wasn't? But there was a lot of bad feeling around here."

"Because of the boy, Ambrose?"

"That was the greater part of it, yes. Poor little beggar. Ambrose was a lot like his mother, you see, where his sister was more like Felix. Chalk and cheese. The lad was quiet enough before all that happened, but he went even more quiet after his mother died. He lived here in this house with us for a short time and then moved along to St. Phillips to live with Mrs. Vera Courtney, a cousin of his mother's. I lost sight of him after he moved there."

"Who was the man, the one that Jennifer was involved with?"

"I don't know his name, sir. And I don't know anyone who does. And just as well, too. A man like that is not well thought of in a place like this. Jennifer White, for all her mistakes, deserved better than she got. She was hardly more than a girl at the time, sir, and far from home. What that man did was a cruelty. There were some here who would like to have evened the score for that, if they knew who the man was. But I don't personally hold with vengeance. It only piles wrong atop wrong. But I know that not everyone feels the way that I do about such things."

t w e n t y
o n e

It was almost seven when Stride pulled into his driveway after dropping Phelan off. Joanne Taylor's Hillman was parked across the street from Stride's house. After he locked the MG in the garage, Stride walked across the street to her car.

"I had almost given up on you," Joanne said through the open window. "I've been here since before six-thirty."

"We're just back from Portugal Cove," Stride said. "More correctly, Caitlin's Cove. It's close to Portugal Cove."

"I know where Caitlin's Cove is, Eric. It's partly why I'm here."

"I don't follow you, Jo. You'll have to explain that to me."

"Offer me a drink and I will," she said.

He opened her door and she stepped out of the car.

Joanne settled in a corner of Stride's couch and sipped her drink. Stride sat on the floor with his drink and an ashtray.

"I should have come to you before this, Eric, but I really didn't know what to do. What I should do. After you and Sergeant Phelan interviewed Ned and me at the house, I could sense I'd been placed on the list of suspects. And why not? My story of being at the movies was pretty thin."

"It's gained weight over the past few days, Jo."

She arched her eyebrows in surprise.

"It wasn't all that difficult to check out. Harry went to the Paramount and talked to the ticket girl and the usher. They remember the same two Americans that you do. You weren't quite so memorable, though. The girl wasn't interested, and the usher's grandmother, if you can believe it, had sat on his glasses that morning."

"But you weren't really sure, were you, Eric? That I might not have been the one?"

"Ask me an easy question. That one's too difficult."

"It's all right," she said. "It wasn't a fair question."

"Tell me about Caitlin's Cove, Jo. How do you know about that? What do you know?"

"More than I should, probably. Ned told me that you had asked him about Ambrose White."

"He said he didn't know anything about White."

"He didn't. And he still doesn't. But I know."

Stride stared at her. His mind was running about, looking for the linkages. He knew it must all come back to Jack Taylor, somehow.

"This will take a few minutes to explain. When I worked for Brendan Madigan, one of my jobs was to look after his filing. Brendan's had a very extensive practice since he qualified as a lawyer. He works longer hours than anyone I know. One of his files was on Jack Taylor." She paused and stared into her glass. "I found it just about the time that I started seeing Ned. So of course I was interested, who wouldn't be? And I looked through it. It wasn't ethical perhaps, but as one of Brendan's staff I did have privilege. Telling you about this probably is unethical, maybe even illegal, but I'm going to do it anyway. There were several items in the file. One had to do with Jack's shares in the Harriston company. I wonder if you know about that."

"I've heard about it."

"That must have compounded your suspicions about me, then. Jack is very well off, well beyond what one would expect for a personnel manager in a department store."

"Yes, I know that."

"So it isn't such a great secret, after all. The file also contained an agreement that Jack had Brendan draft between him and a young woman named Jennifer White, who came from Caitlin's Cove. She worked at the store, and in his typical fashion Jack must have pursued her and started an affair. Except this time it went badly wrong."

"She became pregnant. We found out about that this afternoon. When exactly did all this happen, Jo? Sometime in 1932 or 1933?"

"In 1932. To his credit, Jack wanted to make it easier for the girl. An abortion wasn't a consideration, of course, and Jack didn't want the child. He was married to Beryl then, and I'm sure she would have raised all manner of hell. I don't suppose she ever knew about it. I do know that Ned knows nothing about it."

"You're sure about that?"

"Almost sure. Anyway, it was agreed between them that Miss White would have the baby and put it up for adoption. Jack would pay all the attendant expenses, and Jennifer White would still have a job with the company after it was all over. If she wanted it."

"But it didn't work out that way?"

"No. Jennifer miscarried. She almost died, in fact. I don't know exactly what happened, but I do know that she was in hospital for a time, and that Jack paid the bills."

"Did she go back to the Harriston company afterwards?"

"I don't know. The file didn't say."

"And you don't know where she is now?"

"No."

Stride stood up. His legs were stiff from sitting cross-legged on the floor and his left foot was tingling. He limped to the liquor table, shaking his foot, and picked up the bottle of rum. This time he sat on the couch. He leaned towards Joanne and topped up her glass, then his own.

"The agreement must have mentioned something about Ambrose White."

"Yes. There was a paragraph in it that said something to the effect that if Jennifer died as a consequence of the pregnancy, her surviving relatives—the mother and brother—would receive money from an insurance policy that Jack took out in Jennifer's name."

Joanne suddenly slammed her glass down on an end-table.

"Jesus Christ, I really hate this. I know that Jack has his good qualities, but this business of his screwing young women, it makes me really angry." She looked at the table and picked up the glass. "Damn it! Now I've spilled my drink. It will mark the wood."

Stride went to the kitchen and came back with a damp dishcloth. He wiped up the spill and the sides and bottom of her glass. He handed the glass back to her.

"At least you didn't throw it. You've improved."

"I'm a star." She held the crystal glass in both hands and stared into it. "If I sit very still, I can just see my reflection in there."

"Eighty-proof, Joanne."

"What do you think about all that, Eric?"

"All, meaning Jack Taylor and his winsome ways?"

"Yes."

"I try to stay away from that, try not to be judgmental, and just do my job. It's possible that Jack Taylor's sins have brought about his wife's death. Jennifer and Ambrose White each have reasons to hate him, and as far as we know, they're both alive, and out there somewhere. My job is to find them and see what, if anything, they had to do with it."

"You have to, don't you? Avoid judging people, I mean?"

"Yes."

A murmur of voices drifted into the flat from outside, people talking, a woman laughing. Car doors slammed shut, a motor grated into life and moved down the street, leaving silence behind it.

"It was very hard for me to come and see you last time," Joanne said. "It was easier tonight. Still not easy, really, but easier. It helped that I had something to tell you about the case. Anyway, that was my rationalisation. But I would have come again, sooner or later."

"Sooner or later, this will all be over," Stride said, and immediately wondered if that was a bright remark.

"I think I know what you're saying. When it's all over, I won't be able to rationalise any longer."

He didn't reply, felt he'd already said too much, little though it was. Joanne looked at him and shook her head.

"I've gotten very good at rationalisations. Marriage can do that to you."

"I think I read that somewhere." He shook his head. "I'm sorry. I was trying to be funny. It came out all wrong."

"It's all right. This is very awkward for both of us, isn't it? I could never have imagined we would find ourselves in a situation like this. Well, who could imagine it? Here we are, having a drink, talking about Jack and Edith, and all the time the present is tripping over our past." She paused, reflecting. "Who was it said you can't go home again?"

"I think it was Thomas Wolfe. One of his novels."

"You're right, it was Thomas Wolfe."

Stride was grateful for the diversion. He was weary now, his discomfort growing, and he wished he was alone. Which was not quite the same thing as wanting Joanne to leave. Conundrum. He thought about Margaret, and silently asked himself just what the hell he was doing, anyway. He felt a stab of anxiety and reached for his cigarettes.

Joanne seemed to read the tenor of his thoughts because she stood up suddenly and placed her glass on the table. She hadn't finished her drink.

"I really should go," she said. But then she picked up her glass again, and swallowed a large portion of her drink. She looked at Stride, her eyes suddenly bright, her features animated. "What a pair we are, Eric. We get tossed back together again because my stepmother-in-law—God, what a term!—is murdered, and until very recently, today even, I was one of your prime suspects. And for all I know, you still have some doubts about me. You know all about my temper, after all. I'm married, you're involved with someone, but we find now that we didn't cut all the strings three years ago, after all. Most, but not all. And the bit that's left has us dangling."

Joanne stopped talking then, and they stared at each other. Then she laughed.

"Well, you have to admit it wasn't a bad speech."

Stride shook his head and smiled.

"It was pretty good. You've more or less covered all the bases."

"Well, that's something. Now I really should go." She looked into her drink, took a final sip, placed the glass on the coffee table. "At least you know who you're looking for."

"Ambrose and his sister? We know that we want to question them both, yes. But that's a long way from pointing the judicial finger."

He held her coat and she pulled it on. She took her time with the buttons and the belt. Then she turned around and moved close to him, rested her head against his chest. He touched her hair, cupped his hand around the nape of her neck. They stood like that for a moment, then she pulled away from him and left.

t w e n t y
t w o

Muff Conway was a large man with a fierce appearance, a will of steel, and a hidden soft centre. Well over six feet tall, he struggled every year to meet the military's weight requirements, always dieting strenuously and languishing in a steam bath for days before the annual weigh in. His next physical exam was six months away and his weight was near its apogee for the year, somewhere north of 260 pounds. Conway was drinking a bottle of Coke when Stride and Phelan arrived in his office. A collection of candy bar wrappers spilled out of his wastebasket.

Muff Conway might have looked like a freight engine ten minutes after a derailment, but he was a friendly man. And he was very good at his job, which mostly involved keeping the soldiers and airmen at Fort Pepperrell in line and out of trouble, both on the base and in the city. Conway's appearance at any trouble site was usually enough by itself to restore peace and quiet. He didn't like violence, but if he had to he could pick up the average GI and throw him across a room. Sometimes he did that, but it usually wasn't necessary.

Conway was from Hub Purvis, a town in Mississippi south and west of Hattiesburg. His great-grandfather, together with a slew of male ancestors, close and distant, had fought for the Confederacy in the Civil War. There were slave traders and slave owners in Conway's family tree, and two of his brothers were active in the Klan. Conway had an accent as thick as treacle and all of the folksy trappings of the mythical southerner. Except one. Muff Conway really did believe that all men were created equal, just as his Constitution said they were. And he had the scars and the x-ray records to prove it.

"Eric, Harry!" Conway bellowed when Stride and Phelan walked in. He shook hands with each of them. "Great to see ya both. Kitty keepin' well, Harry?"

"Just fine, Muff. Yourself?"

"Just as you see me, gentlemen." He slammed hands the size of fielders' gloves against his mid-section. "Let me get you boys a coffee."

Conway picked up a metal coffee pot and poured steaming dark liquid into two mugs.

"So you boys got yourselves a little murder to work on. Shit, you guys get what, one, two murders a century? Back home they serve us up murders most every day with the coffee and the mornin' paper."

"It's the climate," Stride said, sipping his coffee. "It keeps us honest." You could float a brick on Conway's coffee. But it was very good and he brewed it with chicory, after the southern fashion.

"So, this lady you were telling me about, Eric. She a real suspect, or you boys just trollin'?"

"The lady has motive, Muff, but we don't really think she had anything to do with it. She says she was at the Paramount the night Mrs. Taylor was murdered, and we think that's probably true."

"I think I detect something, here." Conway's eyes were bright. "This lady a special interest of yours, Eric?"

"Used to be."

"But not now?" Conway cocked his head at an angle and grinned.

"No." Stride drank some coffee. Conway was looking at him closely, his eyes bright, but he let the subject drop.

"Right. Come on in and take the weight off, gentlemen." Conway closed the office door behind them.

"Did you have any luck finding the two airmen we told you about?"

"Luck don't have much to do with it. You know what things are like in these here benighted States. Hell, salt and pepper brings tears to the eyes of most of the fine, upstandin' folks on this outpost of democracy." He grunted and took a swallow of Coke. "Course I know who they are. So happens these two boys are on my boxing team, and that's one reason why they aren't in the base hospital half the time. Or dead." He grinned again. "And I'm the other."

There was a knock at the door.

Conway heaved his bulk out of his chair and across the office. He moved very quickly for such a large man.

"The timing's right on. Here they are. Corporal Tom Addams and Private Jacob Washington."

Stride and Phelan shook hands with them. The two young airmen were about the same size, both about six feet tall, both very fit. Stride wondered if they boxed in the same weight division and if they did, how that worked in their complicated friendship.

Addams was blond, handsome, and had the kind of skin that would tan easily and well. He would be hell on wheels on any beach in the world, Stride figured. Jacob Washington was also handsome, and very dark, but it was obvious there was at least one white in his family tree. Muff Conway called it selective segregation. He said mixing the races wasn't an issue for most Americans as long as it was white men screwing black women. Stride tried to remember if the first president of the Union had kept slaves, and thought that he probably had.

The two airmen looked uneasy. Stride imagined that their lives were punctuated by frequent anxiety, bucking convention the way they did. A local policeman coming onto the scene was just another source of discomfort. Stride nodded at Phelan, let him do the questioning.

"We need some information," Phelan said. "Last Saturday you were at a movie in town—the Paramount—and you may have seen a young woman at the theatre. She claims she saw both of you there." Phelan paused and looked at the two men. Now they were really agitated, exchanging nervous glances. He had phrased it badly. They probably thought that something had happened to the woman and they were about to be blamed. Washington seemed especially ill-at-ease. Phelan looked at Stride, who just smiled back at him and shook his head. Silver-tongued Irishman, my ass, Phelan thought. He took a breath.

"Let me try this again and see if I can get it right. The woman we're interested in is a possible suspect in a case we are working on downtown. If she was at the Paramount when she says she was, the night you were there, she couldn't have been at the crime scene. That's where you come in, why we're here."

The drop in tension in the office was almost palpable, as though a window had been opened and fresh air had blown through.

"We have some photos we want you to look at," Phelan said. "If you recognise one of these women, either of you, make a mental note. We want independent identifications."

Phelan placed four photographs on Conway's desk. Three were stock photos from the constabulary's collection. One was a photograph of Joanne Taylor.

The two airmen looked at the photographs. Phelan watched them closely. There was no communication between the two men. After a minute both stepped back. Phelan nodded at Private Washington. He placed a brown index finger on the photograph of Joanne Taylor. Phelan looked at Addams.

"Yes, sir. That's the lady I saw at the movie. I remember she was wearing a dark blue raincoat. It was raining puppies and kittens that night."

Phelan looked at the airmen, from one to the other.

"Did you want to add something, Corporal?"

Addams grinned, and shuffled his feet.

"Well, sir, the reason I remembered her," he glanced at Stride, "is because she was there alone and, well, she was a nice looking lady."

"Yes?" Phelan smiled. "And you thought maybe she was in need of some company."

"Yes, sir. That's pretty much the way it was, all right. She was standing there under the marquee after the movie, watching the rain pouring down, and I guess my natural chivalry just came right on up to the surface."

"Like it would," Conway said. "Sir Walter Fuckin' Raleigh hisownself. Y'all throw your coat over a puddle for the lady, Addams?"

"I might have, Sergeant, but Jake, here, he gave me the elbow and I saw then she was wearing a wedding ring. That cooled my jets."

"Did either of you speak to her?" Phelan had already mentally closed the file on this one, but he asked the question anyway.

"Well, I said hello, but that was when Jake gave me the nudge, so I didn't really say much else. She kinda smiled at us both, and then she walked down the street and got into a little English car and drove off."

"So now you two can go catch whoever it was did the stepmother in," Conway said when the two airmen had left the office. "You got any good leads?"

"Some," Stride said. He drank the last of his coffee. "We have finger-prints, and we have a witness who might have seen a possible suspect on the night of the murder. And we're chasing down a lead connected to the prints. But nobody is jumping out of the alder bushes waving a signed confession."

"Sometimes they do, though, and maybe you'll get lucky. But it's been a while, so my guess is you're gonna have to do it the hard way, gentlemen. Nose to the grindstone, feet to the pavement, balls to the wall."

"I expect you're right," Stride said. The two detectives stood up. Phelan paused by the door and half-turned to Conway.

"Somethin' else, Harry?"

"I'm just curious, Muff. How tough is it here for a guy like Washington?"

"Bein' a coloured man on a near-lily-white military base in a near-lily-white town, you mean? And hangin' around with a white boy, who, rumour has it, gets more pussy than most of the rest of the population put together?"

"Something like that." Phelan looked at Stride. Stride was shaking his head, but he was interested too.

"Well, from what I hear, Washington does OK. He's more than able to take care of any fool tries to hassle him. Two or three had a go at him when he first got here, and he cleaned their clocks right quick. Now the word's gotten around and they pretty much leave him alone. He is, in his own terms, one very uppity nigger, and I told him he should stay that way, but that he should also watch his back. All the time. The biggest worry is him gettin' cornered by a bunch of redneck assholes and having his head kicked in, or his nuts cut off. Or both. That sort of shit's come down some places, although it gets hushed up real quick. Ain't happened here, though. Not yet."

Phelan shook his head, and the three men walked together to the door that led outside.

"Son of a bitch," Conway said, "you still drivin' that kiddie car, Stride?" He walked over to the MG and ran his hand along the top of the door on the driver's side. He laughed and slapped Stride on the arm. "Maybe you'll take me for a drive, someday, I lose a couple hundred pounds? Better you should get a big old Cadillac first, though. Wouldn't be too shabby." Conway placed a hand on Stride's shoulder, and walked him away from the car.

"I was gonna call you sometime soon, anyway, Eric. I had a message from a Lieutenant Commander Vincent Petrelli a while back. That name ring a bell?"

"Marco Petrelli's brother?"

"Cousin," Conway said. "First cousin. He's career Navy and he's been stationed in the Azores the past eleven months. He expressed what I might call a continuing interest in the case, it bein' still open and all. We can't rule out the possibility that he might catch a military flight to the base at Argentia sometime, drive up to St. John's to have a chat with the officers who investigated his cousin's murder."

"Did he actually say that?" Stride glanced towards Phelan who had been listening to the conversation.

"No, he didn't. Just to be safe, though, you should keep it in mind that he might make the trip someday. Wouldn't cost him nothin' but time. Might cost you and Harry a tad more."

"A man on a mission, maybe?"

"Possible," Conway said. "And we both know they're the worst kind."

twenty
three

"Harvey Button is still a houseguest, I understand?" Stride addressed his question to Constable Dexter Whiteway. He was at the Court House on Duckworth Street, where prisoners were held pending trial and sentencing. Stride knew that Abraham Peddle, Button's lawyer, was working to get his client released on personal recognisance, but he doubted that Peddle had been able to persuade a magistrate that releasing Harvey Button was an acceptable risk. Not with a sheet the size of a bedspread. Whiteway looked up from the paperback novel he was reading.

"He's still here, sir. I take it you want to see him?"

"Yes. Who has duty in the wine cellar this evening?"

"Bavidge," Whiteway said, picking up the phone.

Stride flipped the pages of Whiteway's novel, a western, and looked at the cover, a picture of granite-jawed cowboys and blazing six-guns. He dropped the book back on the desk when Whiteway hung up the phone.

"Bavidge will bring Harvey up directly, sir."

Stride walked down the corridor to the interview room. A few minutes later Harvey Button appeared. Chesley Bavidge stood in the doorway behind him. Button was not a small man, but Bavidge dwarfed him. He was by far the largest man on the constabulary, taller and heavier even than Stride. His presence had a useful calming effect on prisoners. Button looked at Stride, his pale blue eyes intent under a high forehead, and glanced over his shoulder at the immense Bavidge. He shrugged and sat down heavily on the wooden chair. Stride nodded and the constable stepped back into the corridor and closed the door.

The two men looked at each other in silence for a few moments. Button looked away first, crossed his legs and picked at a thread on his jacket sleeve.

"Are they treating you well, Harvey?" Stride and Button had known each other for many years, their first encounter taking place when Stride was still a uniformed constable. They had developed a comfortable informality.

"First class, Eric. As always. Governor's suite, breakfast in bed, a pretty little maid to deliver it. With the morning paper, of course."

"That's grand, Harvey. You've become a valued client. You deserve the best."

Stride took out a cigarette and tossed the open package on the table. Button glanced at it, then at Stride. He took a cigarette.

"A mug of tea would be nice, Eric." Button blew a cloud of smoke towards the single bulb that dangled from the ceiling and began to excavate for something in his right ear canal.

Stride opened the door and spoke to Bavidge. The two men smoked in silence until the constable reappeared with two large enamel mugs.

"My mother drank hot tea from the saucer," Button said, blowing across the surface of the mug. "And she always said that tea brewed on a wood stove was hotter than tea made over a coal fire. Do you think there's any truth to that? I could never tell the difference myself."

"It's a nice story, Harvey, but there's no truth to it." Stride said. "The temperature of boiling water varies with the atmospheric pressure. Doesn't matter what the fuel is."

"I always thought that was the case, but I never liked to contradict my mother. The odd time I did, I got a clout across the ear for my troubles. She was a hard woman, my mother. Hard, but usually fair. A good woman." He sipped his tea. "Makes you wonder how I turned out so badly, I suppose." Button grinned. "But you didn't bring me up here to talk about hot tea and lukewarm parenting, Eric."

"No, I didn't."

"Thought not. But you must know I have nothing to say about our most recent disagreement without I have Abe Peddle sitting alongside me." Button sat back, pretending to be relaxed. "But you already know that, so there must be something else on your mind."

"Yes. I want to ask you about someone you might have known during the war, Harvey. It may be that you can give me some help with a case we're working on." Button's eyebrows moved ever so slightly. It was a few moments before he spoke.

"Ancient history, the war, Eric. Busy time in the old town, of course. Newfyjohn, the Canadians used to call it. A very busy time, and in many ways, a grand time. But ancient history all the same." Button looked contemplatively at his cigarette. He was sitting a little straighter now.

"You were as busy as anyone during the war, Harvey. Busier than most."

"There were certain opportunities at the time, yes. I was too old for the services, but I contributed to the struggle for freedom and democracy in other ways." Button smiled and continued to study his cigarette.

"Your record speaks for itself." Stride leaned forward. "Does the name Emma Jeans ring any bells for you?"

"I would have to think about that."

"Yes or no, Harvey. I don't want to play silly games."

"There are some who say that life's a silly game, Eric. Maybe it was Shakespeare. You have the advantage of me there, being a great reader so I hear."

"At the moment, Harvey, I have the advantage of you in most things." Stride looked towards the door. "Constable Bavidge and I, that is."

Button shifted uncomfortably.

"I hope that's not a threat, Eric."

"Not one that Abe Peddle will be able to hang a brief on. Think of it as a simple statement of fact. Time to stop playing games. I've suggested that you might have some useful information for me. We're both free enterprisers."

"Well, now, you should have made that clear right out straight, Eric. I'm a simple fellow at heart."

"Cards on the table, then. I can make things a bit more comfortable for you. A soft word in the right ear and you could be a free man. Until your trial at least." McCowan had agreed that Button could be released on his own recognisance if he had something to offer to the Edith Taylor investigation.

"And after that?"

"Another kind word in another receptive ear. Possibly no more than a fine and a suspended sentence instead of jail time. I will do what I can."

"Gentlemen's agreement?"

"You know that I can't give you a signed declaration. I will do what I can. Tell me about Emma Jeans."

"Emma was an associate of mine during the war," Button said. "She worked for me, in a manner of speaking."

"She ran your house on the South Side."

"That's a crude way to put it, Eric. I like to think that she was the accomplished and gentle hostess at my establishment of adult pleasures. It sounds so much better that way."

"Any way you want it, Harvey. Mutton or lamb, it all starts with a pair of horny beasts."

"Can I ask why this interest in Emma? My association with her ended quite a while ago."

"Her name came up recently in connection with another matter."

"The other case you mentioned." Button nodded and looked thoughtful. "That surprises me. Business has somewhat declined in Emma's main area of expertise, if I can put it that way. The city still has its cat houses, and the usual clutch of freelancers, but the grand old enterprise is significantly down from its wartime peak. Mind you, there are all those fine American boys at Pepperell, so far away from home." Button snubbed his cigarette and put the butt in his shirt pocket. "But I have distanced myself from the world's oldest. I expect you know that."

Stride nodded.

"Do you know where is she now, Harvey?"

"I'm a bit reluctant to say, Eric, although I imagine that you have the resources to find her."

"Yes. And now you have a personal interest in our success."

"Nicely put." Button studied his fingernails for a minute. "I have recently seen her, as a matter of fact. Emma has made a great change in her way of living. I had a cup of tea with her one afternoon, not long before Christmas. We talked a little about old times, she told me that she had forsaken the old ways, and I wished her well. And that's the last time I saw her."

Button's attitude had become less casual and now he leaned towards Stride.

"Unlike some of us, Emma has made the hard old journey back to the straight and narrow. She's even taken a new name, now. Calls herself Emma Janeway. I don't want to muck things up for her. Call it a sort of honour among thieves." Button sat back in his chair.

Christ, Stride thought, a Harvey Button with a sense of honour. That would take some getting used to.

"Do you know where we can find her?"

"Yes. She makes dresses and hats for a living now."

"Dresses and hats?"

"That's what she told me. Her shop is on New Gower Street. Not in the best section of town, so she said, but she has hopes."

"We're looking for information on an Edith Wright," Stride said. "I was told she knew Emma Jeans during the war."

"Who?"

"Edith Wright. She would have been about thirty years old at the start of the war, but she probably looked younger than that."

"Doesn't ring a bell, Eric. Emma knew a lot of girls during the war. That was her trade, after all."

Stride was looking closely at him. Button seemed genuinely unfamiliar with the name.

"I didn't get to know all of the girls who worked for Emma. Some worked part-time, some full-time. But the name Edith Wright just does not ring a bell with me."

"All right, then. Tell me some more about Emma Jeans. What else did she do for fun and profit?"

"Emma kept her eyes open. She had a knack for meeting people."

"I would have thought that meeting people was essential to the trade, Harvey. Girls like Miss Jeans don't prosper by being blushing wallflowers."

"No need to be unkind, Eric. No supply without the demand, after all."

"Thank you for the instruction, Lord Keynes."

"Eh?" Button looked puzzled for a moment, then shrugged and went on. "Well, I can tell you that Emma was a, what do you say, opportunist? Yes. An opportunist. She kept her eyes open."

"And what did she see that might be of interest to me?"

"Well, I know that after a time she started moving with a better class of people than usually turned up at the house. Perhaps that's where she met your Edith Wright."

"How did she manage that? The better class of people, I mean."

"What Emma told me was that, one night, a taxi pulled up to the house and three American army officers got out. And there was a local feller with them. The Yanks were as drunk as lords, and of course they were looking for a bit of the old in-and-out."

"Not unusual."

"No. The unusual part was that they were officers. Our usual clients were enlisted men, you see. Other ranks. Officers were a rarity at the house."

"And the local fellow. Who was he?"

"Emma didn't say. But he was well connected, apparently." Button leaned forward and helped himself to another cigarette. "That was the how of it. A situation of mutual advantage is the way she put it."

"What are we talking about here? Whoring among the upper classes?"

"Crude, Eric. Very crude." Button laughed. "But I imagine that's what it was, all right. We all look much the same with the trousers hanging from the bedpost. Emma still worked at the house part of the time, but I had to get someone else to manage the place. And I know that some of the younger girls sometimes went out with her. I didn't ask too many questions. As long as business prospered, and it did, I didn't mind what else she was up to. I'm an easy fellow to get along with, Eric. Easy come, easy go. You know that, of course."

"Right." Stride and Button sat silent for a moment. Stride opened his notebook, uncapped his pen, and pushed them across the table. "Write down the address of the shop on New Gower Street."

Stride sat back and tried to imagine what kind of a person Emma Jeans might be, apart from the obvious, and what kind of relationship she might have had with Edith Wright. And if that relationship had continued with Edith Taylor. Button noisily cleared his throat.

"You drifted off there for a moment, Eric." He pushed the notebook and pen back across the table. "I hope you aren't going to forget your good friend Harvey after you leave here?"

"I won't forget you, Harvey. I'm grateful for your help."

Button sat back, comfortable with himself, a man who had done an easy job of work and would have something to show for it.

"I'm pleased to hear it." Then he leaned forward, winked at Stride. "Do you suppose you could spare a few more cigarettes for your new partner in crime, then, Eric? Just to tide me over until I get out of here?"

t w e n t y
f o u r

Four strips of calf's liver lay on the cutting board leaking reddish fluid onto the pale wood. Stride measured a quantity of flour into a brown paper bag, then added salt, pepper and a large pinch of summer savoury. He vigorously shook the bag to mix the ingredients. Then he dropped the strips of liver into the bag to dredge them. He removed the liver to a dry plate.

Stride sliced carrots and potato and turnip very thin, glancing occasionally at the frying pan on the stove. The large square of butter he had placed in the centre of the pan was almost completely melted and small bubbles were appearing as the circle of yellow spread outward. He picked up the pan and turned it back and forth until the melted butter covered the entire surface. He replaced the pan on the stove and sprinkled summer savoury onto the glistening surface, then added fresh ground pepper and a small quantity of sea salt. He put the four strips of liver in the pan, added more savoury and pepper, and turned them until they were nicely browned. Then he removed the strips from the pan and placed them on a warm plate on the top of the stove.

He poured a fifty-fifty mixture of hot water and red wine into the pan, brought the liquid to a boil and then dropped the vegetables in, separating the pieces with a wooden spoon. He covered the pan and timed four minutes. Then he returned the strips of liver to the pan and with the cover off, cooked the lot for three minutes longer, stirring the ingredients occasionally with the spoon. He half-filled a large wine goblet with red Bordeaux, and arranged the food on a warm plate. He sipped the wine and closed his eyes, savouring the aromatic mixture of tannins and acids.

The telephone rang.

'Shit!' was the first word that came into his mind. He glared at the phone for a few seconds and considered not answering. Then he picked up. It was

Harry Phelan. Stride listened intently to what Harry had to say.

"Give me ten minutes, Harry. I was just about to eat. I'll pick you up." Stride placed the receiver back on its hook. He entertained unkind thoughts about Mr. Bell and his intrusive invention. He looked at the plate of food and the glass of Bordeaux. He swallowed another mouthful of wine and then began to eat quickly, standing in the kitchen.

"How badly is Taylor hurt?" Stride asked.

"Not badly at all, really. More frightened than anything, I was told," Harry said. "The shot tore out his kitchen window and sprayed glass all over the place. It was just good luck that Taylor chose that moment to open the door of the refrigerator. The door got between him and almost all of the shit that was flying around the room. If he hadn't, Thomas Butcher might be spending the rest of his evening at the Taylor residence with a mop and a pail. As it is, his presence won't even be needed."

Kevin Noseworthy was standing in the doorway of the kitchen when Stride and Phelan entered the Taylor house. Jack Taylor was sitting in the living room. He was very pale. He had a white bandage on his left hand. He raised that hand in a half-hearted greeting when he caught sight of the two detectives. A short, thin man with thick grey hair and wire-framed glasses walked up to Stride. He parked his serious expression and smiled briefly.

"My name is Kavanagh," he said. "I'm Mr. Taylor's physician. I met you once at the College, about a year ago, Inspector Stride. You gave a talk on the uses of forensic science in police work."

"How is Mr. Taylor?" Stride asked. He wasn't in the mood to discuss his qualities as a lecturer.

Kavanagh placed his hand on Stride's arm and walked him to the hallway.

"I think Mr. Taylor is all right, no real physical injury apart from the cut on his hand, but he's had a major shock. I'm quite concerned about that. I will tell you this in confidence, Inspector. Mr. Taylor had a stroke just over a year ago. His blood pressure is at a higher level than I am comfortable with right now, but there seems nothing else untoward."

"Will it be all right to ask him some questions?"

"I think so. But he won't be able to tell you very much. He told me what happened. He went into the kitchen and opened the refrigerator, leaned forward to take out an apple and then there was an explosion."

"An explosion?"

"That's how he described it. An explosion, and at the same time glass flying all over the place. He realised it was actually a shot, probably from a shotgun. His hand was cut by the flying glass. He said he ran out of the kitchen into the hallway and phoned the police. Then he called me. The telephone is on the wall just here by the living room door. He also told me there was a second shot just after the first. I'm not sure he has anything else to say, but you can ask him. I'll stay and observe if that's all right."

"Yes," Stride said. "That's fine. You tend to Mr. Taylor, Dr. Kavanagh. I want to speak with Constable Noseworthy." He walked to the kitchen. Noseworthy and Phelan were standing in the doorway talking. Noseworthy was pointing at the shattered window.

"Shotgun?"

"Yes." Noseworthy held a number of pellets in his hand. "Twelve-gauge. Two shots as far as I can judge, from just outside the window. It was probably a double-barrelled piece rather than a pump-action." Noseworthy walked them to the window. "One blast came through here, right side, and you can see where the casing is partly torn away. That more or less coincides with Davy Crockett aiming in the direction of the fridge, which is where Taylor says he was standing when he heard the shot. The second salvo came through the lower part of the window, here, where the sill is all chewed up. I'm guessing that our man had a second go at Taylor when he was running out of the kitchen, down the hallway, but his aim was way off and mostly he hit wood."

"So Taylor was lucky both times."

"If he was a horse, I would put money on him in any race that he ran. But whoever did this wasn't one of your top-rank assassins. A shotgun is great for up-close and dirty kind of work, but if you're going to stand outside and fire through a window, my choice would be a good rifle. A Lee-Enfield .303, for example. Lots of those around since the war."

"The doctor said that Taylor heard an explosion."

"It might have sounded like that, if the gun was fired so close to the window that the shot and the glass breaking were almost simultaneous."

"Did Taylor say who might have been shooting at him?"

"He didn't say much to me at all. His doctor kept getting between us. Can't say that I blame him. Someone empties a shotgun at your patient, you want to limit the additional excitement."

"Makes sense to me," Stride said. "But we'll have to shoulder the good doctor aside for a few minutes." He nodded to Phelan and they left the kitchen.

Jack Taylor did not reply at once when Stride asked him who he thought might have tried to kill him. Even if he had suspicions, Taylor might be reluctant to voice them. If he thought that Ambrose White or his sister were responsible, mentioning their names would entail a lengthy dissertation. If he thought someone else cared enough to fire both barrels of a twelve-gauge through his kitchen window, the explanation might not be all that much shorter.

"I don't know what to say in reply, Mr. Stride," Taylor said at last. "The past week, including this awful night, have left me almost speechless. My world is in fragments. Like my kitchen." Taylor looked towards his doctor, then lapsed back into silence. His head slumped forward, chin on chest.

The sentiment was too neatly packaged, Stride thought, as though Taylor had practised the speech while Stride and Phelan were in the kitchen with Noseworthy. Stride walked Harry into the hallway.

"If he won't talk, we have nothing to listen to," Stride said. "I vote that we call it a night. If we force the issue and upset him, and he has another stroke, the boffins at the sharp end, McCowan included, will not be happy."

"Maybe tomorrow?"

"I doubt it. I think Taylor has a pretty fair idea who took a shot at him. But if he won't put a name forward tonight, he probably won't ever do so. A kind of blind rationalisation will take over."

"If I don't say their names, the bad people will go away?"

"Something like that."

But less than an hour later, Stride and Phelan had the name. Phelan had phoned the Fort before leaving the Taylor house on Leslie Street. Billy Dickson had a message for him.

"It's Mrs. Edward Taylor, Sergeant, and she sounded very agitated. She said she had called Inspector Stride at home but there was no answer. I didn't tell her where you two had gone, but I think she had an idea. I told her to sit tight at home and I would get hold of you and pass the message along. I was just about to call you at Mr. Taylor's house."

"Call her back, Billy, and tell her we're on our way. Probably less than fifteen minutes." Stride was hovering by the front door. "Message from Mrs. Edward Taylor, sir. She's at home."

Joanne Taylor sat in her living room drinking cocoa from a large white mug. George Shaw stood by the window, his hands behind his back. There were deep worry lines in his forehead.

"I asked George to come over," Joanne said. "He's Ned's best friend."

"We've just come from his father's house, Mrs. Taylor," Stride said. The formality bothered him, seemed silly somehow. "Someone attempted to kill Mr. Taylor with a shotgun."

He let the statement dangle in the silence. George Shaw abruptly turned away and looked through the window. A street lamp threw a dull halo of light over two cars parked by the curb in front of the house. Shaw's hands fought with each other, writhing as if in pain.

Joanne did not change expression. She sipped her cocoa, staring straight ahead at the fireplace. She placed the mug on the Queen Anne table and clasped her hands in front of her. She looked at Shaw who now had turned away from the window and taken a seat on the piano bench. Stride tried to remember if he had ever heard Shaw say anything.

"I'll try and make this as short as I can. Tonight at dinner, I told Ned about Jennifer White and the mess that Jack had gotten into with her fifteen years ago. And about Jennifer's mother and brother, Ambrose. And why Ambrose probably had no love for Jack, and probably blamed him for his mother's death. I don't know exactly what reaction I expected from Ned. But he became very angry.

"Then he became very quiet. I cleared away the dishes. Ned poured a large rum and went to his study." She gestured towards the stairs. "We have three bedrooms. Ned made one of them into a study." She seemed about to add something to that, but was silent for a moment, chewing on her lower lip. "After about a half-hour, I went upstairs to see what he was doing. He wasn't there. He wasn't anywhere in the house. When I went outside, his car was gone. I couldn't believe it. I hadn't heard anything. He must have allowed the car to coast down the driveway and then started the motor in the street. I phoned George to ask if Ned was there."

Shaw nodded but still didn't speak.

"I went back to the study and it was then that I noticed that the shotgun was missing. Ned and George hunt partridge in the fall. Ned has two shotguns, one he's had for years that he keeps at the cabin, and a new one that he kept on a wall rack in his study."

"He bought that gun last year." Shaw spoke for the first time, his voice surprisingly high-pitched for a large man. "It's a Remington, double-barrelled. I said he should get one of the newer pump-action guns, but Ned liked the old standard double-barrelled type."

Stride glanced at Phelan, who was thinking the same thing he was. If Ned Taylor had used a pump-action he might have gotten off more than two rounds and Jack Taylor might now be history.

"Where do you think he is now, Mrs. Taylor?"

"I think he may have gone to the cabin at Tors Cove." Joanne looked across the room at Shaw. "George?"

"That would be my guess."

Stride looked at his watch.

"It's been more than an hour since the shooting. If he went to the cabin, he should be just about there by now. Harry, give O'Brien a call and tell him to keep an eye open for Taylor's car. But make certain he understands he's not to try to contact Taylor. Mrs. Taylor will give you the make, model and license number."

Stride turned to Shaw.

"Does he have any other weapons at the cabin? Mrs. Taylor said there was a second shotgun. A shotgun is one thing, but a .303 or a 30/30 is another matter entirely. Taylor could take someone out from a mile or more away if he has a good rifle."

Shaw's discomfort level went up noticeably.

"There are two Lee-Enfield .303s in the cabin. War surplus. One of them has a telescopic sight."

"And now, I suppose, you're going to cheer me with the news that he's a crack shot?"

"Ned knows how to handle a rifle," Shaw replied. He scuffed at the carpet with his foot. "We both had rifle training with the Militia. Ned was one of the better shots." He looked at the carpet, then back at Stride. "Sorry."

Shaw cleared his throat and looked to see if Joanne was in earshot. "The night that Edith was killed, Ned was very quiet on the way home. We sat in the car outside my house for a while, smoking. He still didn't say anything, but I could feel the tension. I said the usual things, you know, to try and make him feel a little better. It didn't help. Then all of a sudden, I realised Ned was crying. After a minute or two he said he was sorry, but that he would be all right. I left him then and went inside."

"Did you tell this to Mrs. Taylor?"

Shaw shook his head.

"That's probably just as well," Stride said.

twenty
five

Stride opened the trunk of the MG and pulled out a pair of heavy leather boots and passed them to Phelan. Then he took out his own. The morning was cool and they donned insulated jackets, military-issue they had purchased from the war-surplus store. With the war over, there was a lot of quality gear on the market. Stride had gotten in early and had persuaded Phelan to do the same. The constabulary had a limited budget, and didn't supply extra clothing and footwear for romps in the forest primeval.

"You're certain that the direct approach is best?" Phelan said.

Stride glanced briefly at Phelan but didn't reply.

"Just asking, sir. It's your call, of course."

They had left St. John's at dawn, stopping at the Bay Bulls station to speak with O'Brien who confirmed that Ned Taylor's car was parked off the road about a hundred yards from the gravel pit. Taylor had driven the vehicle as far into the brush as he could and, O'Brien said, was probably well stuck in the wet spring earth and would need a tow to get back on the road.

Stride leaned against the back of the car and lit a cigarette.

"I think this is the best approach, Harry. If we go in there with a herd of men in blue, Taylor could panic and start a small war. But I'm making this up as I go along. I think the personal approach is best. Just the two of us." Stride stood up and faced Phelan. "In fact, Harry, I think it would be best if I went in alone. As you said, this is my call. I don't want to think about you taking a slug from Ned Taylor's .303. You have a wife to think about. I'd be happier if you stayed here while I negotiated with him. Give me two hours, and if I'm not back, or if you hear gunfire, call in the troops."

"No, sir. We go in together. Two heads are better than one."

"You may be right." Stride laughed. "Two half-wits add up to one moderately intelligent human. We'll have him outnumbered if not out-gunned."

O'Brien had suggested that they avoid the usual walking route from the gravel pit and circle in behind the cabin. The direct route would allow Taylor to see them while they were still more than a half-mile away, easy range for a .303 with a sight. Assuming that Taylor was still in the frame of mind to try and shoot people.

The alternate route ran on a curve far to the left, around a second small pond that fed into the main body of water along a narrow stream. The landscape was scalloped by a series of small hills and hollows in that area. It would give them some cover as they approached the cabin. With luck, they would be able to reach the place without Taylor seeing them. George Shaw had also told them that Ned kept a personal supply of rum and whisky in the cabin, in spite of his father's views on drinking. If Stride and Phelan were really lucky, there was a chance that Taylor might be drunk and out of commission. But they couldn't count on that. He might only be slightly drunk and wildly reckless.

"O'Brien reckons it will take us about forty minutes to reach the place by the long route." Stride grinned at Phelan. "Two brave Boy Scouts about to tangle with a man who has at least three heavy-calibre weapons."

Stride took a Colt Detective Special, snug in its leather holster, from a lock-box behind the front seat. Phelan watched as Stride clipped the holster to his belt and pulled the waistband of the jacket down over it. The constabulary, like its counterparts in Great Britain, did not arm its policemen. Phelan had never carried a weapon, although he had had instruction with both rifles and pistols. Stride sometimes carried the Colt with him on duty. To date, he hadn't had to use it.

"If it comes to a him-or-us decision, Harry, Ned Taylor collects a .38 slug. I will aim for his leg but I might get unlucky and hit a more delicate spot. If anyone asks, you didn't know that I was carrying a weapon."

"We'll hope it doesn't come to that."

"My father liked to say that we humans live in hope. It's what separates us from the beasts of field and forest. I never thought to argue the point."

O'Brien's estimate proved to be accurate. The walking was not easy, but they set a brisk pace. The ground was wet from the recent rains and snow melt, but there was no heavy brush to walk through. Most of the growth was not much more than ankle height.

"Good blueberry picking around here," Stride said. "Just like O'Brien said. I must remember that. Have I ever served you my famous blueberry grunt?" Phelan shook his head. "Didn't think so, but I shall. End of summer, or early fall. Mark the date in your social calendar."

"Done," Phelan said. "Served with Devonshire cream?"

"No other way would do." Stride held up his hand. "Softly now. I think we may have arrived."

Stride dropped to the ground and moved slowly forward on his elbows to the crest of the rise. He could feel the cold water from the ground soaking through his trousers. Better that than warm blood from a bullet hole seeping through in the opposite direction. Phelan crept up alongside him.

The cabin was about eighty yards away. Beyond that, perhaps another twenty yards, was Tors Cove Pond. The small boat they had seen Jack Taylor and Tommy Connars in was pulled up on the shore, the green outboard motor tilted inboard. They watched in silence for a few minutes. Stride looked back over his shoulder. Then right and left. It was very quiet. Too early in the year for flies.

"So far, so good," Stride said. "No sign of our man, though, and I don't like that part. And I also don't fancy dashing across eighty yards of open ground. That's shotgun range and, Mr. Audubon be damned, I harbour no ambition to nourish flocks of his feathered friends with bits of the cherished Stride anatomy."

"We could try the polite and gentlemanly approach," Phelan said.

"Might work. But if he declines our invitation to surrender quietly, we'll be pinned down here until nightfall. I don't fancy a long vigil in wet clothing. At the moment we have the advantage of surprise. I vote we use it."

"Your call, General Patton."

"My guts, your blood?" Stride grinned. "Okay. We take the chance that he doesn't know we're here, and isn't expecting visitors from this direction. I go first. You follow. We aim for the wall to the right of that single window. If Taylor appears, and you see him, shout a warning and then you hit the deck, flat out like a seal on an ice pan. Same goes for me, except I'm the one carrying the artillery. Agreed?"

"Agreed."

"After that, we improvise." Stride took his revolver from its holster, made a final check of the six chambers. "Give me ten yards and then you start. Mind you don't race past me, Mr. Owens."

Stride assumed what he hoped was an acceptable starting position for a world-class sprinter and took off towards the cabin. He kept his profile as low as his six feet two inches permitted, scanning the cabin from right to left and back again, running as hard as he could. He reached the window barely a stride ahead of Phelan.

The door was on the other side of the cabin, facing the pond. Stride started moving to his right. Phelan stayed behind him and kept a vigil over his shoulder on the left side of the cabin. Stride rounded the corner and reached the window on the side wall which they knew looked in on the kitchen. Before he had a chance to look through, Stride heard the sound of metal on metal, a pot being placed noisily on the top of the wood stove. He turned to Phelan and gestured towards the kitchen. Phelan nodded. The two men squatted on their heels beneath the window. Phelan framed a silent question with his hands. Then he pulled at the sleeve of Stride's jacket and pointed to a galvanised pail in the storage area under the cabin.

Stride nodded and picked up the pail. He stood back from the window and hurled it, one-handed, towards the boat on the shore. The metal pail bounced once on the ground before clattering into the boat. It made a huge noise in the stillness.

An instant later Ned Taylor was standing in front of the cabin, staring at the source of the sound, holding a shotgun at the ready. Stride stepped quickly behind him and punched him just below his right ear. Taylor pitched forward and sprawled face down on the ground.

Stride sucked blood from the torn skin on his knuckles and shifted his weight to his right foot, which was planted atop the barrels of the shotgun. He returned the revolver to its holster and pulled the jacket down over it. Taylor groaned and struggled to raise himself on his knees and elbows.

"Take your time, Mr. Taylor," Stride said. "Wait until your head clears."

Taylor rolled over and sat up. He looked at the two policemen and rubbed the back of his head. His eyes did not quite focus.

"I don't feel very well," he said. "I think perhaps I am going to be sick." His face was pale and there were dark circles under his eyes. A stubble of beard covered his face. And then he was sick, his body heaving painfully with the effort, streams of brownish liquid jetting from his mouth and nose.

Stride turned and looked out over the pond while Taylor emptied his system. There was a strong smell of rum and bile in the air. Phelan picked up the twelve-gauge, broke it, and pocketed the two cartridges.

Stride walked a short distance away and looked back at the man kneeling on the ground. He attended to his bloody knuckles again and wondered whether he would have hit Ned Taylor if he had not been married to Joanne.

He walked back to where Taylor was sitting on the ground holding his head in one hand.

"Let me give you a hand there, Mr. Taylor. Walk around a bit. Get the blood circulating. Then you'll feel better."

Taylor sat on the small couch and sipped a mug of steaming soup. There was a trace of colour in his face but he was still not the picture of robust health. Stride thought that he looked thinner than he had on the night of Edith Taylor's murder, but that was probably an after-effect of being ill. And of too much alcohol. Taylor studied the two detectives sitting across the room from him. He went back to sipping his soup, making a small production of the exercise.

"Whenever you're ready, Mr. Taylor." Stride said. "We were at your father's house last night. He's lucky to be alive. You're lucky he's alive. You don't have to answer any questions now, if you don't wish to. You might prefer to wait until you have a lawyer present. But if you do say anything, it can be used in evidence. Do you understand that?"

Taylor nodded. He stared at Stride over the top of his mug of soup. The steam from the liquid cast his eyes into soft focus, giving him a somewhat dreamy expression. He placed the mug on the small wooden crate that served as a coffee table. He leaned forward, elbows on knees, and held his head in his hands.

"I don't know what to say. What do you want me to say?"

"We don't want you to say anything, Mr. Taylor. I want you to be clear on that point. Anything you say to us is voluntary, but it will be noted."

"I understand." He looked closely at Stride. "You knew Joanne before, didn't you? Before all this, before she married me?"

Stride nodded but said nothing. He didn't want to get into a discussion with Ned Taylor about Joanne.

"I thought so, but it doesn't matter. All of this goes back a long time, long before Joanne."

He was silent again. Stride debated simply marching Taylor out of there, back across the barrens to the car, and back to St. John's where he would be charged with the attempted murder of his father. But he sensed that Taylor might want to tell them something. Stride prompted him.

"Your wife told you about the situation with Jennifer White and her family. Is that the reason for last night's events at your father's house?"

"Yes. Partly, anyway. I've known about my father's reputation for a long time. The first time was when I was in school, when I was thirteen. I got into a fight with another boy because of what he said about my father. And I didn't even win the fight. I was given a bloody nose and a black eye for my trouble. What was much worse was the feeling of being embarrassed by my father."

He gently touched his right eye with his fingertips, as though it was still painful.

"But there was worse to come. I had never really accepted that my mother's death was an accident. I remember the day that she died. I was seven years old and I wanted to go with them on the boat. My father told me that it was just for the grown-ups, and he wasn't very patient with me. I never forgot the way my mother said goodbye to me that day. It was as though she was going away for a long time." Ned Taylor picked up the mug of soup, cradled it in his hands, then returned it to the table. "She went away forever. I spent most of that day alone in my room. I cried a lot because somehow I knew she wasn't coming back. Bobby was angry with me because I wouldn't play with him. He kept saying he was going to tell Mom that I was being mean. I didn't pay any attention to him because I knew that wouldn't happen, that he wouldn't ever say anything to her."

"Did you speak to your father about any of this?"

"No. I didn't know how. Years later, when I discovered what he was like, I knew why my mother had died. Why she had killed herself. As far as I'm concerned, he killed my mother." He looked at Stride and Phelan, tears on his face, seeking a sign that they understood what he was saying. Then he looked away. "And now he's killed Edith, too." Taylor fell silent then and concentrated his attention on the soup, taking small sips from the mug.

He had delivered the two verdicts with almost equal passion. It made Stride think of something Taylor's brother had said during their interview.

twenty
six

Bobby Taylor closed the door behind his sister-in-law. Joanne walked to the centre of the room and stood there, one hand by her side, the other holding onto the leather strap of her shoulder bag.

"I'm glad you phoned first," he said. "I don't like surprises. Your call gave me the opportunity to put on my calm and reasoned expression."

Bobby walked up behind her and placed a hand on her shoulder. They stood like that, silent, for a few moments. Then Joanne moved away and dropped the bag on a wooden chair near the table. She still had not spoken.

"I can offer you a very good sherry, Jo. It might lift your spirits."

"Thank you, Bobby. I could use a drink."

Taylor took a bottle from the cabinet and stripped the foil off the top. The cork came out with a crisp popping noise.

"I ran into an old friend from navy days yesterday, on Duckworth Street. I didn't know he was in town, nor he I for that matter. His ship is just in from Cadiz, and he gifted me with two bottles of the best." Bobby held up the bottle. "I've not actually tried it, yet, but I'm certain it will be first-rate."

Joanne nodded and tried a smile. Taylor filled two glasses with the pale golden liquid. Joanne took an exploratory sip and then swallowed a third of the glass.

"It's good," she said. She closed her eyes and let the sudden jolt of the alcohol diffuse through her. Then she gulped the remainder of the sherry in her glass.

"I will interpret that as high approval," Taylor said. "But do take it a little more slowly, my dear. I don't want you pitching face-downward on my rug." He refilled her glass.

"I'll try to pace myself." She slurred the words slightly and giggled. "The thing is, I haven't had a lot of sleep since yesterday. Or a lot to eat."

"I'm not surprised," he said. "I would expect you to be upset. But eating is important. Although I don't hold myself up as an especially good example." He opened a drawer in the ornate walnut sideboard. "I think I have some sweet biscuits. That's not really what you need, but they'll be better than nothing." He took out a square red and black tin and pried open the lid. 'Have you talked to Ned since the arrest?"

"Yes. Just for a little while, though. I'm not sure that he really wanted to see me, but we did talk."

"Have they charged him yet?"

"Not yet." Joanne brushed some crumbs from her skirt and reached for another biscuit. "I asked Eric about that. He told me that Ned's attorney would have an opportunity to confer with the Crown Prosecutor before formal charges are laid." She broke the biscuit into two pieces.

"Is there a chance that he might be charged with something less onerous than attempted murder?"

The word seemed to echo around the room. Joanne took a deep breath, let the air escape slowly in a long sigh.

"I don't know, Bobby," she said. "We'll have to wait and see."

"You know, of course, that this all started a long time ago, Jo? This thing between Ned and Jack?"

"I'm sure," she said. She chewed reflectively on a piece of biscuit. "But it doesn't really help all that much, does it? It's like being run over in an accident. The absence of intent doesn't make it any less awful."

Taylor grunted. He walked to the window and pulled it open a few inches. Fresh air and street sounds infiltrated the room.

"Have you seen Stride since Edith's murder?"

"I saw him yesterday after he brought Ned in. I told you that."

"You know that's not what I meant."

"Yes, I have seen him." She paused. "I went to his flat last week. Ned was at his club, or at your father's—I don't know which—and I went to see Eric. I needed to talk to someone." She drank a little sherry and tapped her finger on the glass. "No, that's a lie. I needed to see Eric, to talk to him."

"How long has it been now? Two years?"

"Almost three."

"That's a long time to be apart from someone and still need to see him, Jo. What do you want from him?"

"I don't know. I went to his flat on an impulse. Well, a sort of a protracted impulse, I suppose. I drove around for almost an hour before I actually went in."

"And how did Stride feel about that? Apparently, he didn't kick you down the stairs, out into the cold and damp. Was he pleased to see you?"

"He wasn't displeased. Cautious, though."

"More cautious than you, certainly."

"Don't be a shit, Bobby." Her cheeks had coloured.

"A rational observation does not make me a shit. Going to Stride's flat was not the wisest thing to do in the circumstances."

"Jesus, Bobby. We didn't fall into bed. All we did was talk."

"A wink is as good as a nod to a blind man."

"That really is brilliant. Are all queers as profound and insightful as you?"

"No," he said. He drank some sherry. "I'm a special case."

She stared at him, then stood up and walked to the window. She pulled the curtain aside and watched the activity on the street. A tired brown horse, his head low, pulled an empty coal cart down the street. Joanne focused on the slow even rhythm of the animal's great shaggy hoofs. The carter sat on his wooden seat, holding the leather reins loosely in his hands. His head was slumped on his chest, and Joanne wondered if he was asleep. The horse probably knew the way in any case. She dropped the curtain back in place and sat down again.

"I shouldn't have said that. I'm sorry."

Taylor shrugged. "I've heard worse. Did Stride come calling on you? Officially, I mean. He came around to see me with his man Phelan the day after Edith was killed. We had a long chat. I think he believes I could be the guilty one."

"Are you?"

"No, of course not. There are indeed a few people on this earth that I consider worth killing. But Edith, for all of her irritating qualities, really did not qualify. But you didn't answer my question."

"Eric came to see me and Ned. With Sergeant Phelan."

"It's a formality. They have to interview everyone in the immediate family."

"It turned out to be not quite a formality."

"Really?" He was surprised, and interested.

"Yes. I had told them I was at a movie at the time Edith was being killed, but that I hadn't seen anyone I knew at the Paramount. The place was almost empty because of the rain. But I remembered seeing two Americans there together, a coloured boy and a white man. Sergeant Phelan corroborated my story with the ticket girl."

"She remembered you?"

"She remembered the salt and pepper."

"And the salt and pepper?"

"They remembered seeing me."

"That was good luck."

"You know what they say. Unlucky in love...."

"I didn't know they said that. And I've always wondered who they are."

They were silent again. Taylor picked up the bottle of sherry and stared at the label.

"Eric will interview anyone he thinks has information about Edith," Joanne said.

Taylor nodded agreement.

"Of course. The police have their set routines." He was watching her closely. She was on her feet again, looking at his collection of books, tapping spines with her index finger.

"I wonder how much Edith told her friends about the odd family she lived with?"

"Aren't all families odd? And does it matter?"

Joanne shot him a glance.

"I think it matters."

"She wouldn't have told her friends anything about you and Ned, surely?"

"Probably not directly, no."

"Ah." Now he was really smiling.

"You are a bastard, Bobby."

"Edith and Ned? It's a joke. That was eons ago, when the world was young. Who would give a damn now?"

"Maybe Ned gave a damn. Has it occurred to you that perhaps that's why he tried to kill his father?"

"Because of Edith? Because the teenager and the housekeeper were having it on fifteen years ago?" The smile had faded and he looked puzzled.

"No. Because Ned and Edith were still having it on."

"Still?" It wasn't so much a question as irritated acceptance. He turned away from her, assimilating the idea of it. "I suppose I'm not really surprised, Jo. Poor Ned. The model of stability and traditional values." Taylor turned back to her, his expression carefully neutral. "Tell me. Did he know that you knew?"

"Yes."

"And you accepted it?" He stood up and closed the window, as if concerned that someone might be listening. "That's not like you."

"Maybe not. But it's complicated."

"I'm sure."

"It started again after I lost the baby." She paused, looked at him, but he didn't say anything, just waited for her to go on. "After that, I didn't want him to touch me, and he didn't. I don't know if that was because he respected my decision, or because he had no more desire than I had." She paused again. "It was mostly downhill, anyway, after I got pregnant." She laughed. "Although we did have a brief spectacular interlude just after I found out I was great with child. It was like a stimulant, knowing that the worst had happened, so why not celebrate. The ideal honeymoon spirit. But it didn't last very long. And then I miscarried."

She sat down and leaned forward, elbows on knees, hands wrestling with each other. Taylor waited for her to go on.

"Ned made one half-hearted overture, a month or so after I got out of the hospital. I said I wasn't ready yet and that I would let him know when I was. Then one night, long after that, when we were getting ready for bed, he said he guessed we weren't going to have a family after all, and I said I guess not. And that was the last time we spoke about it. He moved into another bedroom."

"And that's when he and Edith started again?"

"I suppose so. I don't know for sure. I just know that they did."

"So Ned went back to Edith." Bobby paused, selecting his words. "Back to mother."

Joanne appeared startled, looked away. She was silent for a moment.

"I wonder if that had something to do with it," she said. "Whatever it was, it probably wasn't very healthy for Ned, even if it didn't mean very much to Edith."

"We don't know what it might have meant to Edith. She wasn't as simple, or as simple-minded, as we liked to think."

"Maybe," she said. "And as long as we're talking about life and love, how are you and Raymond getting along?"

"As well as can be expected," Taylor said. "To use the popular phrase. In fact, I haven't seen him for a few days. He's off on one of his mysterious solitudes. He does that from time to time."

"Well, at least one of us is happy, more or less." She stood up suddenly. "I have to go."

"Why?"

"For no good reason. I'm restless, and when I'm like this, I need to do things. Wash a floor, do the laundry." She laughed. "Write a novel, compose a symphony. Whatever." Joanne picked up her shoulder bag and tossed back the rest of her sherry. "I didn't really dislike Edith, you know. Even after I found out that Ned had gone back to her."

"I don't believe a word of it."

"I knew you wouldn't, but it doesn't matter." She looked back at him from the doorway. "Who was it said that in a hundred years none of this will matter because we'll all be dead, and those that come after won't even know about it?"

"I think everyone says something like that at some point."

"You're probably right, Bobby. Thanks for the sherry, and for listening. You're a good friend."

"Come again, Jo." He raised his glass. "When you need a good friend."

She smiled, and closed the door softly behind her.

twenty
seven

Billy Dickson told Stride that Joanne Taylor called while he was talking with Jack McCowan about the latest development in the Edith Taylor case.

The Field Marshal had been intrigued at the turn of events but was at pains to point out that Stride and Phelan were not all that much closer to finding their prime suspect, Ambrose White.

"So, White's sister—Jennifer is her name?—is now on your list of people to talk with?"

Stride said that she was, and they had started looking for her. He told McCowan that Phelan was working on that. McCowan tapped his fingers on the windowsill while looking across the city towards Signal Hill.

"More wrinkles in this case than around an old man's balls," McCowan said finally. "But you say you've at least patched together a history of sorts for White?"

"He was supposed to have died in a motor accident near Friendship Cove in 1939. But the man they pulled from that wreck and buried eight years ago clearly wasn't Ambrose White."

"And you say Corrigan was the constable in Spaniard's Bay at the time? Interesting fellow, Corrigan."

"A diamond in the rough, sir."

"Too bloody true. Mind you, Corrigan is a good copper, for all his faults. Damned good war record, too. Survived almost the whole bloody show from '14 on. Gallipoli, Beaumont Hamel, Gueudecourt. The man has a map of the Western Front carved on his back." McCowan shook his head, remembering his own experiences in France. "He was wounded in 1917, at Arras I think it was, and invalided back to England. Don't sell Corrigan short, Eric. He's been around a long time and he knows a lot of things. And people."

Then McCowan snorted. "But keep him away from me. Much as I respect him, I can't abide the bugger."

Joanne wanted to meet Stride at Middle Cove, a horseshoe-shaped inlet east of St. John's, bracketed by rugged cliffs. It was a place they had liked to visit together. Stride stood in front of the station and looked at the sky. It was a tumbling white overcast punctuated by splashes of bright sunshine. The wind was brisk but it wasn't cold. Not here, anyway. It might be a different matter, though, on the Atlantic shore. He had told Harry that he would be gone for at least an hour.

He drove slowly along Outer Cove Road, then moved the MG slowly down a moderate incline towards the rocky beach. The path was rough, and the small car bottomed out several times. The tide was in, the sea was high, and waves were rolling onto the shore, their crests shattered and white. White caps—white horses, his father called them—decorated the dark blue-green of the cove. Farther out, at the base of the cliffs, the white water leapt into the air and attacked the jagged rock face, fell back, gathered itself, and rolled forward to try again. Gulls circled the cove scanning the water's surface, or sat in crevices on the cliff sides.

Stride walked down towards the water. The beach was deserted, but off to his right, tethered to a fence post, was a brown horse. A small two-wheeled cart stood nearby with the leather harness slung over its front. Stride assumed the horse belonged to a fisherman who was out in his boat somewhere near the cove. Man and horse stared at each other. The horse lost interest first and went back to pulling at the sparse grass around the fence line.

A crunching of gravel told Stride that a car was coming down from the main road. Joanne parked her Hillman beside Stride's MG. She wore dark blue slacks and a light blue sweater. A second heavier sweater was draped over her shoulders, the sleeves loosely knotted across her chest. The large sunglasses she wore gave her an exotic, romantic look.

"I know I'm late, Eric. Sorry about that. I had a flat tire, believe it or not. Fortunately it went down in front of Corbett's Garage and they were able to put on the spare right away. I'll pick up the tire on my way home."

Stride had already noticed that the front left tire was almost new, much less worn than the others.

"We have company of sorts," Stride said, indicating the horse, who raised his head to study the new arrival. Joanne walked over and stroked the animal's soft muzzle.

"Some day, when I am disgustingly wealthy, I am going to have my own riding horses. Two of them." She grinned. "At least two."

"Will you invite me for a ride?"

"Maybe. Maybe not. It depends on how well you behave."

They started walking down the beach, turning left towards the cliffs. There was a rough trail there that meandered up over the rocks and continued on to the cliff edge. It was where they used to climb and walk.

"I haven't been down here since—well, since you and I used to hike out along the shore. That was one of my favourite things. Ned and I never came here." She canted her head. "Do we have time?"

"Yes," he said. "If we have enough to talk about."

"So officious." She seemed about to add something, but paused and smiled instead. "But I suppose you're busy?"

"Yes." He was uncomfortable that she had asked him to come here, and wondered why he had agreed. The place had memories, and the memories had barbs. Joanne had sometimes said that he cut easily and was a slow healer. He knew that had given her a perverse satisfaction at times. And here they were again, the circumstances vastly different, but with some of the foundation bricks still more or less solidly in place. He indicated a large flat-topped rocky outcrop set back close to a grassy embankment. "We can sit there and talk. It's always a pleasure to come here."

Joanne laughed and clambered up the rocks.

"You know the words, Eric, but the music needs a bit of work."

He sat beside her, looked at the sea for a moment, then at Joanne. She smiled, put her hand on his cheek and touched his hair with her fingertips.

"I'm sorry," he said, looking at the ocean. "It's all become very complicated, very quickly."

"I know. We'd both given up on any sort of future together, and here we are all of a sudden, almost falling over each other." She paused, reflecting. "No, it's not quite like that, is it? It's tricky for me, too." She looked out towards the sea. "Well, I don't have to tell you that, do I?"

"No. I'm the one who arrested your husband, after all."

They were silent for a time. Stride took out his cigarettes. Joanne shook her head at the proffered package. She took a chocolate bar from her purse, unwrapped it, set it on the rock surface, and broke it into pieces. Chocolate was one of her things. Stride took a piece and let it dissolve slowly in his mouth. The flavours of milk chocolate and dark tobacco mingled nicely.

"I went to see Bobby yesterday," she said. "I needed to talk to someone about Ned."

"Did it help?"

"Yes. Bobby and I are friends. I can talk to him. Sometimes, anyway, when he's in the mood to listen. He isn't always. He was quite shocked when I told him about Ned. He didn't expect anything like that. Ned has always been the good son. Bobby himself is a different story, of course. He fought with Jack over everything and walked out of his father's house when he was seventeen."

"I've had a man keep an eye on your brother-in-law since Edith's murder," Stride said. He watched for a reaction but she only turned to look at him, eyebrows raised.

"I guess I'm not surprised. You haven't ruled him out as a suspect, then?"

"No."

"Have you learned anything?"

"Some. He has at least one interesting association."

"Really." She was looking away, now, watching the motion of the waves. Or pretending to.

"Do you know the name Franklyn Pincher?"

"I've heard of him." She nibbled at a piece of chocolate. "And, yes, I know who he is and what he does."

Franklyn Pincher had once spent a term in prison for gross indecency. But that had happened a long time ago, when Pincher was young and unwise. He was now in early middle age, had learned a great deal, and was comfortably established. Franklyn Pincher specialised in providing male companionship, sometimes very young companions, it was said, for men who wanted that and who valued secrecy. And who could afford his price. The important lesson that Pincher had learned after his one arrest was how to cultivate friends and clients with influence in the important sectors of society. He was careful never to cross the undefined but clearly recognised line between private vice and public perception. A lot of people seemed to know the name Franklyn Pincher, and what he was about. But his name elicited little more than a knowing look, a shrug of the shoulders, and the subject usually was quickly changed.

"Did you know that Bobby Taylor was acquainted with Pincher?"

"No." She hesitated only a moment. "But I know that Bobby is a homosexual."

He waited for her to say more, but she had propped her chin on her fist, a silent statement perhaps, and was staring resolutely at the ocean again.

"He was observed entering Pincher's place one night, a few days after Edith Taylor was killed. He went there at eight and left just before midnight." He waited to see if Joanne wanted to say anything. "We have no information that he's involved with Pincher in any substantial way," Stride said. Or that he wasn't, but he didn't say that. "Does Bobby have any special companions?" Joanne looked at him. He knew he had phrased the question badly.

"From time to time, yes. He has friends. And from time to time, companions, as you put it. He has a companion of sorts, now. Has had for a while." She looked at him, her hostility almost tangible. "Queers are human, after all."

They were silent for a few minutes. Joanne chewed on a piece of chocolate and then spoke, changing the subject. "Has there been any word, yet, about the charges against Ned?"

Stride shook his head. "Maybe later today. Or perhaps tomorrow. I don't really know."

"I can't believe Ned was really trying to kill Jack. Maybe I'm just whistling past the graveyard, but I just can't see it."

"Well, if he was trying to kill him, he went about it the wrong way. Firing a shotgun through a double window isn't the most efficient method. If he was really serious, he should have gone inside and had done with it." Joanne had watched him while he was speaking. Now she looked away. Stride waited until he caught her eye again before asking the question. "What's the likelihood that Ned would go eyeball to eyeball with his father?"

"Somewhere between not-bloody-likely and no-bloody-way. Ned's never been able to stand up to Jack on anything. As I said: the good and true son."

Stride picked up another piece of chocolate.

"I want to ask you something, Jo. When we interviewed Bobby, I asked him if he was close to Edith and he replied that he was not as close as some. It was an odd thing to say. Do you know what he could have meant by it?"

"Yes." She took a deep breath. "I will have that cigarette, after all. Light one for me, Eric, and I'll tell you the story." She waited until he passed her the lighted cigarette. She exhaled a stream of smoke and watched it disappear into the breeze.

"Ned and Edith had a long history. Maybe you won't be surprised to learn that they became involved when Ned was still just a boy. Well, a teenager, anyway. Are boys still boys when they reach their teens? Ned said he was sixteen when it started. It's supposed to be every teenage boy's dream, if you can believe the popular sexual theology. Teenage boy, older woman, all the sex he could want, beyond anything he could have imagined."

She looked at him. Appraising. He nodded but didn't say anything.

"Except it really wasn't straightforward at all. Ned was essentially an orphan, and Edith was the housekeeper-mother. Play with that notion while you sip your second rum some evening."

He nodded again, but still couldn't think of anything he wanted to say. This was her story, and Ned's, and he would let her tell it.

"It went on for quite a long time. Ned admitted to me that he got very involved in it, even thought he was in love with her for a time. Well, that's not surprising, I suppose. He was very young, and innocent besides. He told me he would get very jealous when she went out with men."

"I'll grant you it was complicated," Stride said. "Maybe it will have some influence on the outcome of the trial, if his attorney decides to pursue it. But I don't know that."

"It's all right, Eric. I'm not asking for anything. I'm just filling in some of the blank spaces for you."

He took a final drag and flicked his cigarette towards the water. Watched it bounce once on the wet stones before disappearing.

"I have to ask the next question also, Jo."

"The one that goes along the lines of, 'Was your husband still having an affair with Edith Taylor?' That one?" She was smiling, but not with her eyes.

"Yes." Her coolness unsettled him. He picked up another piece of chocolate. It had softened under the sun's warmth. He licked the stains off his fingertips.

"Yes, he was. I found out after we had been married for about a year. In a way I wasn't surprised. Not very happy, mind you, even though I knew by then that marrying Ned had been a very bad idea, pregnancy or no."

"And it continued? Even after Jack and Edith were married?" Stride was scrambling to play catch-up with Edith Taylor's collection of lovers. Or whatever they might be called.

"As far as I know. Don't ask me to explain it, Eric. I can make guesses, but that's all they are, really. It was complicated enough that Ned was sleeping with Edith when she was a sort of mother-substitute, but when Jack married Edith, the whole thing changed into something very bizarre. I sometimes think Edith's marriage to Jack made it even more important for Ned to continue his relationship with her."

"It added the element of revenge?"

"I think that may be a part of it." She laughed and twisted a strand of dark hair around her finger. "Inspector Freud."

They shared the last two pieces of chocolate and Stride crumpled the wrapper and put it in his pocket. He mulled over the new information about Ned and Edith and then pushed it into the back of his mind.

"Let's walk for a bit," he said. "Then I really do have to get back." He levered himself off the rocks and held out his hand for Joanne. She held tight and jumped down, landing easily and lightly on a patch of rough grass.

They set off along the beach, then up a small rise to a footpath that ran into a stand of fir trees, and from there to the cliff edge. Ten minutes later they emerged from the trees and stood on a high point of land. Far to their left they could see the rock face that formed the northern wall of Torbay Bight, and to their right the entrance to Outer Cove. A motorised dory was making its way through the white-caps towards Middle Cove. The boatman gripped the tiller in his right hand, holding a steady course against the power of the wind and waves. The horse's owner, probably.

"Do you remember the day we came up here looking for whales?" Joanne pointed across the water. "We saw them spouting and breaching over there, just off Outer Cove."

"Yes," he said.

They had hiked along the cliff almost to Torbay, and swam in a tidal pool where the captive water had been heated by the sun. Then, standing together in a recess under the cliff, they had made love, nervous and hurried, their excitement heightened by the possibility that someone might happen by and see them. It seemed a very long time ago.

"We watched them in the distance and wondered if they would move over here, closer, so we could see them." Her eyes were bright, her expression relaxed. Neither compromise nor contradiction. She turned to him. "Then, whoosh! There was a whale right under our feet, coming from Torbay, steaming towards Middle Cove. He was so close it felt as though I could reach down and touch him. I remember you were quite startled."

Stride laughed. "I was startled. I tripped on a root and almost fell over the cliff."

"And you were fortunate I was there to catch you." Joanne had seized his arm and helped him regain his balance.

"Of course, if you hadn't shouted at me in the first place."

"Sure," she said, tossing her head. "Blame me."

They smiled, sharing the memory, holding it close, then moved away from it, the present realities setting up obstacles again.

"We should go," Joanne said, but she didn't move at once. "I still love this place, Eric. I always will. I hope you do, too."

Stride nodded, and touched her cheek.

"I'm glad," she said. "But the best of the day is behind us. And I know you have to get back to work."

"Yes, I do," he said.

He didn't want to say anything else.

twenty eight

Ned Taylor looked better than Stride had expected he would. He was clean-shaven and wore a crisp white shirt, open at the neck. He looked more rested and relaxed than he had the last few times Stride had seen him. It occurred to Stride that Taylor might have received some good news, perhaps about the nature of the charges that would be laid against him, or about his release on bail.

"As far as I know, my attorney is still talking to the Crown Prosecutor," Taylor said, "but he did say that he would probably have news for me later today, or early tomorrow. And I have the same information as far as bail is concerned."

"I think you can expect to be out of here sooner than later."

"A mixed blessing, really. I've more or less gotten used to being in here. Where all of life's decisions are made for me. It's almost a kind of vacation. The scenery is no hell, and the entertainment is sharply limited, but at least it's quiet, and my family is not greatly in evidence. The one problem I have, and I have had it for a long time, is sleeping. But even that has been taken care of now. Dr. Kavanagh has prescribed a very effective sleeping potion, and it works like a charm. I awake each morning feeling quite refreshed. I shall always keep a supply close at hand, even when I get out of this place. And I've read one book, and I'm well into a second. I used to read a lot, you know. It used to be a passion of mine." He paused. "But that was before I was married."

He stared at Stride when he said that, as if challenging him to offer a response. Stride smiled patiently.

"I need to ask you some questions about your stepmother," Stride said.

"Really? I would have thought that anything I might have to say in that regard would be looked at very much askance. Having just emptied a shotgun through my father's kitchen window. Now, if you had said you wanted more information about that, I would understand."

"We have your statement on that, Mr. Taylor. Any additional information needs will come up at your trial."

Taylor tilted his head back and pretended to laugh. Stride made no comment. He looked quietly at Taylor across the table. Taylor stared at him then.

"Have you been spending any time with my wife, Inspector? It would seem to me that a golden opportunity has been handed to you. Both of you."

"I have spoken with Jo, yes."

"Ah." Taylor's theatrical smile returned. "Jo."

"Yes." They stared at each other in silence for a moment. Taylor was the one to look away. Stride wanted it done with. "I've talked with your wife on several occasions. Mostly as part of the investigation, but we have touched on other things also. I won't play games with you, Ned. I've known Jo for almost four years. There was a time when we thought about getting married. But we went our separate ways instead. You already know all about that, or enough, so we needn't talk around it."

"Right," Taylor said. "It's amazing, the things that happen to people, isn't it? And the things that people do?" He shook his head and smiled again. This time the smile was more genuine, if weary. "Ask your questions, Eric. I'll answer them if I can."

"When Phelan and I interviewed you and Jo, I asked if you could think of anyone who would want Edith dead. You said then you couldn't think of anyone. Do you want to reconsider that answer now?"

"In the bright, cruel light of the new day, you mean? No, not really. I suppose I could say that of all the people I know, Jo had the strongest motive. But you might conclude that I was just being unpleasant."

"What would her motive have been?"

"The fact that I was sleeping with Edith." Taylor looked directly at Stride, assessing his response, his eyes hard. "Ah. I see you already know about that. Can you tell me how you found out?"

"Jo told me. Eventually. But I wasn't surprised. I had already halfway guessed it."

"I see." He frowned and changed position in his chair, uncrossing his legs carefully. Stride remembered Taylor's earlier remark about his back injury. "I take it from what you said that Jo didn't just blurt it out to you? That it was something that she had to think about?"

"She didn't treat it lightly, no."

Taylor nodded his head slowly.

"Well, that's something."

"Yes," Stride said. It was something. "What did Jo think about your affair with Edith? You've suggested it might have given her a motive for murder. Tell me about that."

"I don't think there's much I can tell you that you don't already know." Taylor gave Stride another hard look. "It appears that my wife talks more to you now than to me. Maybe you can tell me things that I don't know."

"Possibly. But you still haven't answered my question. How did Jo feel about Edith, and your affair?"

"That's a hard question for me to answer. Even though we lived together, Jo and I have been estranged for some time." He paused and looked blankly at the window behind Stride, then refocused. "She didn't like Edith much, but I never thought there was a lot of hostility there. More like indifference. I don't know why she would have been very upset that Edith and I were sleeping together. Jo hadn't wanted to sleep with me for a long time. But who knows what people are really thinking? Under the surface."

"Did your father know about your affair with Edith?"

"I don't think so. Not as far as I know. I'm fairly confident that Edith wouldn't have told him."

"And if he had known about it?"

"Would he have been filled with rage? Enough rage to have had her killed?" He shrugged. "I doubt that. But, really, I don't know how he would have reacted. My father and I are not as close as we should be. You'll have to ask him yourself."

"A tricky proposition."

"Yes. I should think so."

"Do you care whether he finds out?"

Taylor took a deep breath.

"Well, I've been thinking about that. A lot." Taylor leaned forward. "Is this off the record? In connection with my own case, I mean?"

Stride nodded. He thought he knew what Taylor was about to say.

"I've discussed this with Geoffrey Hamlyn. My attorney. It will probably be the basis of our defence. I was having an affair with Edith. My father's philandering in the past created the circumstances that led to Edith's death. Just as his infidelities led to my mother's death. It will all be brought out." He sat back and crossed his arms. "It's going to be a very unpleasant business. And if you think that I will find some pleasure in it," he paused again, "you are probably correct. Misery and pleasure in about equal proportion. Miserable pleasure. Pleasurable misery. Sounds odd, doesn't it?"

"A settling of accounts."

"Perhaps."

"That brings me back to my original question, though."

"Who might have killed Edith? I thought Ambrose White, Jennifer White's brother, was your prime suspect?"

"He is. But the evidence says only that he had been in your father's house. We don't know that he was there the night Edith was killed. We have no evidence that he killed her."

"Certainly he had motive."

"Did he? His argument was with your father. Killing your father's fourth wife as an act of revenge stretches credulity a bit."

"Perhaps he was unbalanced," Taylor said. He was smiling again. "In that confused state where black and white blend into grey."

"That possibility has not been discounted." Stride paused. "Do you know the name Emma Jeans?"

Taylor was surprised at the question. He reflected for a moment.

"Edith sometimes mentioned an Emma, yes. I don't remember that her last name was Jeans, but I suppose it could be the same person. She hadn't mentioned her lately, though. Why? Does she have something to do with this?"

"We don't know. She was a friend of Edith's a few years back. A number of people have mentioned her." Stride left out the part about Harvey Button. "Did she ever tell you anything about Emma Jeans?"

"I don't think so. Nothing that has stuck in my mind, anyway."

"Was Edith involved with other men?"

Taylor didn't answer at once. The question obviously bothered him.

"Yes," he said finally. "Our affair, if that's what it was, wasn't an all-consuming passion for her." He paused again. "It never had been."

"There were always other men?"

"Yes. Always and often. Edith lived, as they say, for the moment. Don't you envy people who can do that? People who just dip a hand into the pool and pull out whatever pleases them?"

Stride didn't reply. Taylor's comment had plucked a string and it was still resonating. He wondered if Edith Taylor—Edith Wright—had been that uncomplicated. He asked the question. Taylor sighed.

"Was Edith unburdened by concern or guilt or shame? Those leaden Victorian burdens that so many of us lug around?" Taylor paused and thought about that. "I often thought so. But we never talked about it. Maybe I never wanted to know the answer."

Perhaps, Stride thought, it would have compromised Taylor's sense of being superior to this woman from a small outport community.

"Do you know the names of any of the men Edith was involved with? Was there any one in particular?"

"No." He looked down at the table, frowned, then looked back at Stride. "Yes. There was one man that she mentioned more than once. His name was William. But I don't know his last name. She teased me about him, hinted that he was 'someone.' She gave me the impression that she had hopes for him."

"This was unusual?"

"Yes. You know, Edith had never heard of Gertrude Stein, but they shared an odd point of view."

Stride stared at him, surprised. Taylor laughed.

"A man is a man is a man."

Stride smiled in spite of himself. He was silent for a moment. "Edith's hopes for this William. Were they for marriage?"

"I don't think so. But, as I said, I think her William, whoever he was, had money. Maybe status as well. I think perhaps Edith hoped he would keep her in the manner to which she wished to become accustomed."

"She said that?"

"No. I'm just guessing. Playing with words. It's all the reading I've been doing. And being alone a lot. The mind starts working in unexpected ways when you're not used to it. The being alone, I mean." He smiled again. "I'm getting to like it."

"What happened to William? Was he in the picture recently?"

"I don't know. She hadn't mentioned him in a long time. Perhaps they weren't involved any longer."

"But he was a major item at one time?"

"Yes. I'm sure of that. At least in Edith's view."

Stride sat back and closed his eyes. He thought about William, and about the man who had impressed Emma Jeans sufficiently to cause her to break away from Harvey Button. Harvey had called Emma Jeans an opportunist.

Ned Taylor had said much the same thing about Edith. The danger for Stride was in cutting the cloth for a suit that would only fit an imaginary person. McCowan would say that it was too neat by half. But Stride would see Emma Jeans anyway and ask the questions.

Taylor seemed to have lost his focus, now. He wasn't looking at Stride directly.

"It's interesting, isn't it?" Taylor said.

He seemed about to add something but didn't, and stared through the window behind Stride's shoulder. He took out a cigarette, methodically tapped the end on the surface of the table, then lit it. A cloud of smoke hung in the air between the two men.

t w e n t y
n i n e

Stride recognised Emma Jeans as soon as he and Phelan walked into her shop on New Gower Street. Even without the hat she had worn in the picture with Edith Wright. She was short and trim, and not much changed from the way she looked in the photograph on the dresser. Stride tried to guess her age, and decided that mid-thirties probably wouldn't get him into too much trouble if the subject ever came up between them. Then wondered why that thought had crossed his mind, and knew it had a lot to do with the fact that she was a very attractive woman. He reminded himself that Emma Jeans had managed a brothel for Harvey Button during the war. Among other things.

"You already have hats," she said, "so I am guessing you probably want something else?" She looked at Phelan, smiling. But without much warmth. "Perhaps a hat for your wife, Sergeant? Or is it Inspector? It's important to get the titles right, I know."

"Sergeant Phelan," Harry said. "CID. I never stop hoping it isn't so obvious." He guessed every copper in the world had said something like that at least once. "This is Inspector Stride. And, yes, we would like to ask you a few questions, if it's convenient."

"And if it's not convenient? Will that mean I will be deprived of the pleasure of your company?"

"It will mean that we'll visit another time," Stride said. He tried to place her accent; more correctly, her lack of an accent. He wondered how hard she had worked to discard it. "But only if it's very inconvenient just now."

"Then let's pretend it's not inconvenient at all." She consulted a watch that was pinned upside-down to her lapel. Thomas Butcher's nurse had a watch like that. "Although I do have an appointment in about thirty minutes."

"We need some information about Edith Wright," Stride said. "I believe you knew her during the war."

"Edie." Emma Jeans took a deep breath. "Yes, I knew Edith Wright. And I know that she's dead. I read about it in the paper. I was wondering if someone would remember me. And hoping they wouldn't. Who was it remembered me?"

"Several people, actually."

"Really? I suppose I'm not surprised. Edie was always a bit of a chatter-box."

"I had a talk with Harvey Button a few days ago," Stride said.

There was a pause, and a noticeable stiffening, while she considered that.

"Of course. I knew Harvey, also." She made a decision. "Then you probably know that I used to work for him. And how."

"Yes."

"If you're interested, we can discuss the whys and the wherefores sometime. But not now, I guess."

"Perhaps on another occasion." Stride smiled to show that there was no malice in the comment, but she had looked away from him.

"I met Edie during the war," she said, "probably in 1941. Maybe 1942. I forget, exactly. We went to some of the same places, dances at the Hut—the Knights of Columbus Hostel on Harvey Road. Before it burned down, of course. And the Caribou Hut. And other places."

"You were working for Harvey then?"

"Yes." She seemed about to add something, but didn't.

"Did Edith Wright also work for Harvey?"

"No. Edie never even met Harvey, and she would never have worked for him. Edie was a good girl." A careful emphasis on "good." "Can I ask you a question?"

"Of course."

"Why are you here? I haven't seen Edie in a couple of years. When I first read the story in the papers, I didn't realise right away that it was Edie. I didn't make the connection with Jack Taylor at first. It was only in a later story they said that her maiden name had been Wright."

"It's really just routine, Miss Jeans," Phelan said.

"Janeway," she said. "My name is Emma Janeway, not Jeans. Didn't Harvey tell you that?"

"Sorry," Phelan said. "Janeway, then. We're asking questions of a lot of people who knew Mrs. Taylor."

"I see." She shook her head. "And the fact that I worked for Harvey makes me an interesting candidate, I suppose. So be it. As distant as the past is, it doesn't really go away, does it? But I don't know how I can help you."

"Perhaps you won't be able to," Stride said. "In which case, we will ask our few questions and be on our way."

Emma Janeway treated them to a cool smile and consulted her upside-down watch again.

"Harvey said that you got to know a better class of people during the latter part of the war, and that you worked for him only part-time after that."

"Harvey said that?"

"Yes."

"Really? What else did Harvey say about me, I wonder? I'm curious."

"I'll let you sort that out with Harvey at your leisure, Miss Janeway. We're only interested in your relationship with Edith Wright and whether any of the acquaintances you had in common might have had something to do with her death."

"You want me to tell you the names of people I knew during the war, people that Edie and I knew? So you and your friend here can run around badgering them with questions and accusations? I won't do that."

Her eyes were hard and her face slightly flushed, but Stride wasn't convinced that it was much more than a careful performance. He tried an indulgent smile, looked at her intently without responding right away. She looked away first.

"You met some interesting people. One of them brought three American officers to the house on the South Side one night. I am right in saying he was an interesting person?"

"Yes."

Stride could see that she was resigned now. "What was it all about, Emma?"

She looked up at the small familiarity, smiled thinly.

"I worked for Harvey for three years, running his house on the South Side. Before that I had worked around St. John's, here and there. I'm surprised we never ran into each other, Inspector. I knew some of your colleagues very well, God knows."

She let that hang in the air without embellishment.

"There was a lot going on at the time," she said. "I imagine you and Sergeant Phelan didn't spend the entire war rolling bandages and singing patriotic ballads. It was party time, and a lot of people—interesting people, as Harvey said—wanted to have a good time."

"And you were part of the good time."

"Yes, I was. It was what I did. There was a lot of money being spent in the city, for all kinds of things. Roads, buildings, airports. And different people had different ways of encouraging some of that money to move in their direction. It's an old story, Inspector Stride. Encourage friendly relationships. You know that at least as well as I do."

"Yes," Stride said. "And where did Edith Wright fit into this?"

"Edie liked a good time. I didn't have to kidnap her. But there was a difference. Edie was an amateur and I was a professional. That didn't mean that we couldn't be friends. We were friends, actually. I did it for the money, and Edie did it for fun. Mostly." Her expression had changed slightly, a smile that was rather sad.

"Mostly?"

"Poor Edie. She was nice, and the men liked her. And she was a surprisingly good dancer, given her background." She shook her head, stared into the distance for a moment. "Sometimes Edie persuaded herself that some of the men wanted something more, something permanent. It was crazy, really, because she went with God-knows-how-many men during the time I knew her. Even I was a little surprised. I tried to talk to her about it once, but she didn't understand the question."

"So no one was really interested in anything permanent with Edith Wright? Whatever she might have thought?"

"No. No one was interested." She shook her head more emphatically this time. "But Edie continued to have hopes."

Hopes. Ned Taylor had used the same word.

"Did Edith have hopes for someone named William?"

"William who?" she said. But her reaction had given her away.

"You tell me, Emma. I think you know."

"Shit." Her face was flushed now, and she nervously drummed her fingers on the countertop. "If I tell you, will you please keep my name out of it? Please."

Stride nodded. She wasn't acting now. There was real fear in her expression.

"His name is William Cartwell. But if you decide to ask him questions about Edie, please keep my name out of it. I don't want to be in William

Cartwell's bad books. Life is hard enough."

Stride and Phelan looked at each other.

"William Cartwell? Bertram Cartwell's nephew?"

"Yes." She stared at them. "His nephew. But he's more like Cartwell's son, really."

She looked through the window of her shop, as though she was afraid that William Cartwell might be lurking around the corner.

"Was Cartwell the man who brought the three Americans to Harvey's place that night?"

"No. But he was someone who worked for Bert Cartwell."

"His name?"

"For what it's worth, his name was Gerald Hopkins. But Gerry doesn't live here any more. He moved to the States after the war. I think he lives in Texas somewhere, Houston maybe, or Austin. I'm not sure."

"Edith Wright met William Cartwell through you and Gerald Hopkins?"

"Yes. William came to a lot of the parties. His uncle's business paid the bills. It was natural that he would be there."

"How involved was he with Edith Wright?"

"Edie thought they were involved, but William wasn't involved with anyone. He liked parties and he liked women. Edie was just one of a dozen women he was with sometimes." She looked down at the counter for a moment. Stride didn't ask the obvious question.

"You seem to be afraid of William Cartwell. Why?"

"I'm not really afraid of him, but I don't want him to think that I was the one who sent the police calling on him about Edie. The Cartwells are rich, and they're only going to get richer. I was useful to them in a small way during the war, but I'm nothing to them now. They would want to keep it that way. And so would I." She looked around at her small store, holding one hand out to underline her point. This was a neighbourhood of small stores run by people without grand ambitions, most of whom were just trying to get by. "The Cartwells could buy me out with their pocket change. Think about that, Inspector. I do."

"Right," Stride said. She had made her point. "Did William Cartwell know about Edith Wright's ambitions for him? If that's what they were?"

"Yes. He thought she was joking. He couldn't imagine it. But mostly he didn't give a damn."

"And when he found out she wasn't joking?"

"He was very annoyed. He told me to keep her away from him, to make sure she didn't show up at any more parties."

"And that was that?"

"As far as I know. For him, certainly. He never mentioned her again. I told Edie the way it was, what William had said. She was upset, couldn't understand what was wrong. I explained it to her as best I could, and she got the message after a while. She didn't like it, though, was really angry about it. I didn't see very much of her after that."

"How much do you know about the Cartwells, Harry? Other than the fact that they have pots of money, and own a lot of properties in and around the city?" They were drinking bottles of Coke that they had bought from a corner store. Phelan took out a cigarette but Stride declined the offer.

"Not much more than your average citizen, sir. I haven't been invited to their house for dinner lately. But I read about the family in the paper sometimes, like everyone else. I do know that Bert Cartwell doesn't have a son. Three daughters, but no sons to his name."

"That would explain the nephew's high standing in the scheme of things. A man like Bert Cartwell would probably want a son to carry on after him."

"It sounds like William Cartwell has been doing a deal of carrying-on already. From what Emma Jeans—Janeway—told us."

"What do you make of her, Harry? Do you think she's on the level?"

"You mean, about making hats and dresses for a living? After a career with her legs in the air?"

"Crudely put, but you've captured the sense of it, all right."

"I think she might be, sir. People can change."

"Not a leopard, then."

"Pussy of a different sort, I'd say."

Stride laughed, set the bottle of Coke on top of a postal box and lit a cigarette. He could start to cut back another day.

"Edith Wright," Stride said. He swallowed a mouthful of Coke. It was ice-cold and burned its way down his throat. He liked the sensation, drank some more.

"Sir?"

"I wonder how big an annoyance she was for William Cartwell."

"Edith Wright? Pretty small potatoes, I would think." Phelan flicked ash from his cigarette. "The Cartwells swim in a large pond, sir. An Edith Wright wouldn't make much of a ripple. On the other hand, people swat mosquitoes with great vigour."

"You're probably right about all of that," Stride said, "mixed metaphors notwithstanding."

Phelan laughed.

"I'm Irish, damn it. English isn't my first language."

"Tell that to Bernard Shaw, Harry. And let me know if he's impressed."

thirty

Bern Crotty was cleaning one of his many pipes when Stride tapped at his door. Crotty looked up, smiled, and raised a hand, index finger pointing to indicate that he needed one more minute to finish the job. Stride leaned against the filing cabinet beside Crotty's desk, watched him scrape tar from the inside of the bowl.

"Clean pipe, clean mind." Crotty said. He placed the pipe back on its rack. "What can I help you with, Inspector Stride?"

"Fishing expedition, Bern. Do we have anything on a William Cartwell? Anything at all?"

It was a routine check, and Stride didn't really expect to find anything.

"Bertram Cartwell's nephew? I don't think so. I'm sure it would have stuck in my mind if we had, but I'll take a look."

Stride counted the pipe collection while Crotty went through the files. There were fourteen pipes in various sizes, shapes and woods. Crotty also had two ancient-looking white clay pipes inscribed with names that appeared to be Dutch. Stride was holding one of them when Crotty returned.

"That one, and its mate, I got from a friend during the war, a Canadian infantryman who went into Holland with his regiment. He'd traded some canned beef to a local for them. I met him in England towards war's end." Crotty sat down. "Nothing on William Cartwell, Inspector. But we have a file on his uncle, if you're interested. Although there are no entries after 1928."

"A file on Bert Cartwell? What was he arrested for?"

"He was never arrested as such, sir. But in his early days, he was brought in several times for questioning about fires and miscellaneous damages at the premises of some neighbouring businesses. Nothing was ever proven, and none of the cases ever went as far as a trial. The gist of it is, though, that Bert

Cartwell was a pretty rough-and-tumble fellow when he was starting out. Not above putting a competitor at a temporary disadvantage with a bottle of petrol and a rag stuffed in its neck. So rumour has it, anyway."

Stride sat back and let that sink in. Like uncle, like nephew, maybe.

"What happened in 1928?"

"Not so much what, as who. And the 'who' was Ralph Waldo Hudson."

"Hudson?"

"Yes. Hudson is Cartwell's attorney and advisor, and 1928 is the year he signed on to the Cartwell family dreadnought, if I can put it that way. Up to that point, Cartwell made up the rules as he went along. Since Hudson came on board the sailing has been a good deal smoother."

"I'm not surprised."

"Are you interested in Bertram Cartwell's file, then?"

"Not just now, Bern. But I may be later. It's the nephew I'm interested in."

"I'd like to help, but I don't know much more about the Cartwells than I've already told you. Or that you've read in the papers yourself." Crotty picked up his tobacco pouch and selected one of the Dutch clay pipes. "But if you really want some background on the Cartwell family, Inspector Stride, I'd suggest that you have a talk with Jack Corrigan."

"Corrigan?" Crotty had surprised him a second time. Stride tried to imagine Corrigan in association with one of the island's wealthiest families. He couldn't make it fit easily, bottles of gasoline notwithstanding. "How would Corrigan come to know anything special about the Cartwells?"

"They're old friends is the way I hear it, sir."

"Corrigan and Cartwell? Chalk and cheese I would have thought."

"Yes, that's true enough, now. But Jack Corrigan and Bert Cartwell grew up in the same town. Martin's Harbour. They were pals, so I heard, and they went to the same school, such schooling as they got. Rumour has it that they still get together from time to time to raise a glass."

"Well, you never know, do you, Bern? I'll speak to Corrigan."

"You should do that, sir. He's not in today, though. But I happen to know he's at home working on a personal project." Crotty opened the tobacco pouch and began filling the clay pipe. "Corrigan has a place out towards Logy Bay. Moved there some years back when he got married and stopped living in the police barracks."

Crotty had surprised him again.

"I didn't know Corrigan was married."

"Yes, he was, once." Crotty stopped filling his pipe and looked reflective. "Got married about eight years ago, the year he moved to his house. I was as surprised as anyone when I heard about it."

"But he isn't married now?"

"Technically, he probably still is. Never heard about a divorce. But his missus left him not too long after he bought the house. He doesn't talk about it, though. Best not to raise the matter with him, sir." Crotty shrugged and resumed filling the white clay pipe. "But you should drop by his place and talk with him. He knows a lot about the Cartwells." Then he grinned and struck a match, holding it above the bowl of the pipe. "I think you'll find it was worth the drive."

Stride looked quizzically at Crotty, who continued to grin at him through a cloud of smoke. But Crotty didn't say anything else.

"We have visitors," Phelan said.

"Tell me it's Ambrose and Jennifer White, Harry, and I will love you forever."

"Kit would disapprove, sir. Some nonsense about monogamy. Our visitors are Herbert Rodgers and his missus, come all the way from Portugal Cove. Herbert appears a bit the worse for worry, but Mrs. Rodgers has the look of a wife whose mind's been made up for both of them."

"Let's have at them, then."

Stride's first thought was that Herbert Rodgers looked harried. But then he decided that harried wasn't the word. The man looked oppressed. When Stride and Phelan had met Rodgers at his shop in Portugal Cove, he was dressed for work, wearing the rough clothes of his trade, comfortable in his element. Now he wore a white shirt with a starched collar fastened in place with gold studs, and a dark blue tie that had gone somewhat askew. His black serge suit dated back to an earlier, leaner time in Rodgers' life. He was a portrait of discomfort. The aggressiveness that had marked his first meeting with Stride and Phelan was nowhere in sight.

His wife sat next to him, her right arm looped through his left, as though she was guarding against any potential attempt to bolt for freedom. She appeared to be a number of years younger than her husband, possibly in her late thirties. Although she carried some of the excess poundage that was the established badge of marital solidity, her features were fine and her eyes were bright and lively. And there was no paucity of resolve in them. It didn't surprise Stride that Mrs. Rodgers spoke first.

"Mr. Rodgers hasn't had a comfortable hour since you visited him," she said. She tightened her hold on her husband's arm. "He had hoped all that business with Benjamin Downe was over and done with when the old man passed away four years ago. I told him then that it would swim back to the surface one day, and probably when we least expected it. And now here we are." She squeezed her husband's arm and simultaneously nudged him with her elbow. Carrot and stick.

"After you left," Rodgers said, "I started thinking about Ambrose White again, Mr. Stride. I always felt sorry for the lad, all the time he was working at the shop, but I never did a thing for him, except what I was asked to do as one of Mr. Downe's workers." He rubbed his free hand across his forehead. "I didn't know what I could do, so I did nothing."

Stride looked across the room at Phelan. Harry made a face that was halfway between impatience and tolerance.

"He would come home at night, sometimes, so upset that he couldn't eat." Mrs. Rodgers loosened the grip on her husband's arm. They looked at each other for a moment, exchanged cautious smiles.

"And then one day White was gone, off to St. John's, and to Mr. Thompson's establishment," Rodgers said. "I'm not proud to tell you that I was relieved that he was gone. I thought—hoped—that would be the end of it, but it wasn't. Out of sight but not out of mind. And now it's all come back again."

He was silent for a minute, reflecting.

"I've been sleeping poorly," he said, "and remembering things about that time. I wanted it all to go away, to drop out of recall, but at the same time I found myself looking for anything that might have to do with Ambrose White. It was strange, sir. Part of me was running away and part of me was running towards. And here I am." He put his hand on his wife's arm. "Here we are."

"Mr. Rodgers remembered that we had a photograph from that time. It was there in an album in the cabinet in the living room. It wasn't stuck in the album proper with picture corners, just tucked in between the pages at the back. We'd forgotten all about it."

"Mr. Downe had a friend of his take a picture one day of everyone who worked at his shop. I think he was planning to use it in an advertisement, although he never did. But he had a half-dozen snaps done up and gave one each to the people at the shop. That's how I came to have one."

"Ambrose White is in the picture?"

"Yes, sir, he is. And knowing that you were trying to find him, I thought the picture might be a help. It's old of course, and he must have changed a lot in ten years, but it's a good likeness."

"It's a very good likeness," Mrs. Rodgers said. "He was a nice looking boy. In spite of all that he'd been through."

Stride took the photograph from Rodgers. An older man with a large moustache and a receding hairline sat on a heavy ladder-back chair in the middle of the group. Benjamin Downe clearly. Stride scanned the faces of the other men looking for White. There were two young men who might qualify. He looked up from the picture at Herbert Rodgers.

"White is on the left, Inspector. The lad wearing the bib overalls. The other young fellow's name is Jones. Robert Jones. He went into the air force during the war, but he came home, and he still works in my shop."

You can read all manner of things into a photograph if you've already developed notions about the person you're looking at. Orphan, victim, transient, lost soul, murderer. All of these garlands had been hung around Ambrose White's neck since the afternoon when Kevin Noseworthy first spoke his name. Stride concentrated on the young man's physical appearance. Shorter than average height, slender, fine facial features, and large dark eyes. In spite of himself, Stride pictured White in a wide-brimmed hat. The longer he studied the photograph, the more White looked familiar. He knew this was a trick that the mind could play. Create a space and then conveniently fit a candidate into it. It was easy to do. But there was a familiarity about White's face, a hint of recognition. He tried to capture a memory, but failed.

"This photograph will be returned to you in due course, Mr. Rodgers. We're grateful to you for bringing this in. It could be very useful." He passed the photograph to Phelan. "If you remember anything else about Ambrose White, please get in touch again."

"Like Rodgers said, sir, White could look a lot different than this. It's been more than ten years since this snap was taken."

"Two approaches, Harry. First, we have Noseworthy do an enlargement and make copies of White's picture. Then, I'm going to make a call on Herc Parsons."

Hercules Agamemnon Parsons was in his middle thirties, an artist and portrait painter—the latter activity referred to as his "wattles and wrinkles money line"—who divided his time between Newfoundland and New York City. He was currently living in the family home in St. John's where he had a studio. Parsons' father was a physician and amateur archaeologist, and his mother taught piano and voice in St. John's. A mezzo-soprano with a good voice, Sheilagh Cromwell Parsons had enjoyed a brief career in opera in Chicago after the First World War, until tuberculosis intervened. It took three years for her to shed the disease, and then she returned to Newfoundland and married Ethelbert Parsons. The Parsons family were quietly eccentric, its three members individually gifted in the way that eccentrics sometimes are.

"Good face," Parsons said when Stride gave him a print of the Ambrose White photograph. "Strong features; fine but strong. And I fancy that he still has all his hair judging from the scalp line." He traced the lines of White's face with his long fingers, "feeling" the bone structure that lay under the skin. "Good bones, this fellow has. Tell me his story, Eric."

Parsons nodded and hummed, and prepared a small pot of espresso coffee, while Stride told him all that he knew of Ambrose White.

"It would help if I had photos of his parents, but I expect that's not possible. Anyway, you don't have the time to go haring off to Caitlin's Cove again, and I can work without them. You'll want my sketches as soon as possible, of course."

"His appearance has probably changed a lot, Herc. He might have a moustache or a beard, although our one witness mentioned neither when she described the man we think might be White."

"I would doubt that he has a beard. This fellow is trying to be anonymous, so you say, living under an assumed identity. A beard in this small town would tend to make him stand out. A moustache, though, is common enough. These days, half the Young Turks with functioning gonads cultivate a patch of fur on the upper lip. Fantasies about being RAF Spitfire pilots, I imagine. I'll do two sketches for you, one with a tidy little moustache and one without."

Parsons poured the thick black coffee into two small cups and gave one to Stride.

"Take a seat and I'll have a brace of preliminaries for you in a little bit. You can amuse yourself by looking over some of my most recent." He pointed to a stack of canvasses leaning against the far wall. "I spent a month sketching on Fogo Island last fall."

Parsons started to work, his left hand moving quickly as he captured Ambrose White's face on heavy sketching paper and then began the task of ageing him ten years. Stride watched for a few minutes, sipping his coffee, then walked across the studio and attended to the paintings Parsons had indicated. He took his time, looking at the eleven canvases one after the other, then started back through them a second time. Parsons' technique had changed since his most recent showing, just over a year ago. These paintings were simpler, lacking the busy detail of his earlier creations, but somehow carrying a greater content of expression. Stride lost himself in the pictures, walking over the landscape, along the shore, and around the spare man-made structures of Fogo Island.

Stride looked up to find Parsons smiling at him.

"I am calling it—*sotto voce*—my Hemingway approach. Trying to say more with fewer words. It works for him and, who knows, it may work for me, although my agent is sceptical, as agents often are. Which is one reason why they remain agents. Eventually they catch up, the darlings. It just takes them a small while to lace their metaphorical shoes and get their metaphorical feet moving." Parsons tasted his coffee. "Do you like them?"

"Yes. Very much." Stride sat on the arm of an easy chair. "Will you have a show soon?"

"Yes, but not here. I have in fact promised all of these to my agent in New York, the sweet fellow. But if you're especially taken with one, it shall be yours for the asking. Think about it, and drop back another time when you're less pressed. I don't fly away for weeks yet."

He handed Stride the two sketches.

"These are very good." Stride placed the drawings side by side and compared them. Ambrose White the teenager was still recognisable, but he had truly aged. He studied them for a few minutes. The sense of recognition was there again, very close, but still just beyond his grasp.

"When can I have the finished product?"

"Late this afternoon. Come back around five." Parsons picked up his coffee cup and swallowed the contents in one go.

"I almost forgot to ask. How is Margaret?"

Stride hesitated an instant too long. Parsons raised an eyebrow.

"Oh, dear. Problems?"

"Yes and no," Stride said. "It's complicated."

"It almost always is, dear man, in my long experience. One rejoices on the rare occasion when it is not. Are things damaged beyond repair? And before you answer, I will express the sentiment that I hope they are not. Margaret is very good for you, Eric. And I know you won't resent my saying that."

"I don't resent it, Herc. And I hope it is not beyond repair." And wondered if he really believed that. Parsons looked at him for a moment, then made a dismissing gesture with his right hand, moving on.

"You will be intrigued to learn, Eric, that the Pater has recently become very excited about the possibility that Vikings may have established a colony on the northern tip of Newfoundland, near St. Anthony, sometime back in the mists of pre-history. He's been carrying on an intense correspondence with a Norwegian lady who sits in a chair of some description at Harvard. Nothing will do but that he has to go up to the tip of the Great Northern Peninsula this summer for two weeks to dig many holes in the ground. His Norwegian lady will be there also." Parsons laughed. "I have dark thoughts that the Pater might be entertaining ambitions both naughty and archaeological. Not for the first time, the old rogue. But he has surprised me by asking that I go along and make sketches of the landscape. And I think I might just do that. After the New York thing, that is."

Vikings in Newfoundland? Stride supposed it was possible. The geography favoured it, and the Vikings were great seafarers.

"He's put aside his Greek enthusiasms, then?"

"For the moment, yes. That field is densely populated anyway, and the Pater really is not any more partial to crowds than I am. And you know," Parsons threw his head back and laughed, "it's just occurred to me that if the Pater had developed this Scandinavian obsession a few decades ago, my name might probably be Eric, just like yours. Instead of this sweet Hellenic mouthful that I am saddled with."

thirty
one

The last time the glaciers had moved across Newfoundland they scooped up most of the good soil that had been on the island and dumped it offshore, into the Atlantic Ocean. Which provided good breeding grounds for fish on the Grand Banks a few hundred miles south and east, but left the island without much potential for agriculture. The land west of St. John's, in the area known as the Goulds, had retained most of the few pockets of decent soil and supported a number of prosperous farms. The picture east of St. John's was very different, with little land suited to farming. But there were some small holdings where the basic garden crops such as potatoes, cabbage and turnips could be grown, and these augmented the harvest from the sea. Jack Corrigan lived by himself on one of those plots of land, in a small frame house. Bern Crotty said that it was the remoteness and privacy of the place that attracted Corrigan.

Stride left Harry Phelan at the station making inquiries about Jennifer White and drove east out of the city towards Outer Cove Bay and Jack Corrigan's place. The weather was clement enough for Stride to take the top down on the MG. He liked the feel of the wind in his hair. The road to Corrigan's was unpaved, but the graders had been out recently and the surface was even enough to allow Stride to get his speed up close to seventy for a short stretch before gearing down to a level that was safer for both humans and stray animals.

He pulled into Corrigan's laneway, stopped behind a battered red pickup truck, pumped the accelerator twice and switched off the motor. He had wanted to phone ahead, tell Corrigan he needed to see him. Billy Dickson laughed when Stride asked him for Corrigan's phone number. Corrigan didn't have a telephone, Dickson said. It was one of the attractions of the place he lived.

Jack Corrigan was standing in the doorway of his house when Stride stepped out of the car. He was wearing bib overalls over a red turtleneck sweater and a pair of short rubber boots that looked to be hip waders cut down to ankle-length. Two large, sleek cats, a black and a tabby, sat just inside the door. Corrigan was smoking a hand-rolled cigarette. He picked a piece of loose tobacco off his lower lip as Stride walked towards the doorway.

"Bern Crotty told me I would find you at home today, Jack."

"And so you have, sir." He raised his arm and gestured towards the house. "Be it ever so humble."

"I don't make a habit of bothering people on their day off, Jack, and I apologise for the intrusion. But I need some information on the Cartwell family, and Bern said you might be able to help me."

"Did he, now?" Corrigan shrugged and stepped out into the yard. He held the cigarette between his teeth and stuffed his hands deep into his pockets. "That all he said?"

"He might have said something else."

"No doubt. Silly fucker. Someday I'll pull that wooden foot off his stump and ram it straight up his arsehole. Serve him right, too." Corrigan sucked on his cigarette and exhaled smoke from the side of his mouth. But he didn't look all that upset.

"Was Crotty right about the Cartwells?"

"I know a thing or two. You best come inside and take a load off, sir."

Stride hadn't known what to expect when he drove out to Corrigan's place, but he didn't anticipate the domestic scene that presented itself. The house was small, just large enough for one or two persons in Stride's opinion, although he suspected the place might once have been home to a large family.

The two cats that Stride had seen in the doorway were now sitting on a brightly coloured rug near an upright piano. Three more cats lounged on chairs, variously sleeping or going through elaborate washing rituals. Corrigan casually rolled another cigarette while Stride looked around the place. The piano was very old, made of a dark wood and polished to a high gloss.

"Some day I'm going to learn to play that thing," Corrigan said. "When I was in the army, I had a coupla lessons from one of the boys in the regiment, fella named Cake. Funny little fella, looked about twelve years old, had to lie about his age to get in. Bought it at Beaumont Hamel, poor little bugger. But he could really play the piano." Corrigan drew on his cigarette and walked to the kitchen. "I have some cold ale in the ice box, Inspector. It's home-made, but it's tolerable. Can I offer you a glass?"

"Yes," Stride said. "Thank you." He looked at one of Corrigan's cats. The cat looked back at Stride for a moment and then lost interest. It went back to grooming the region between its hind legs.

"I lived almost a year in England, but I never could get used to drinking warm fuckin' beer." He gave Stride a tall glass of dark ale. "I hope you like it cold."

Stride nodded and raised his glass. Then his eyebrows. Corrigan made very good beer.

"That year I was in England after the First War, I worked in a pub in the Midlands. It was a small place, and all the beer they sold they made right there on the premises. I learned a thing or two. Cheers." Corrigan downed half the glass at one go.

"How well do you know Bert Cartwell, Jack?"

"Well enough not to have to call him Mr. Cartwell." He walked across the room and opened a door to what Stride assumed was a bedroom and turned on the light. "You better have a look at this first, just to make that arsehole Crotty happy. I know he'll ask you about it when you get back."

Stride swallowed another mouthful of beer and walked over to where Corrigan was standing. The room was carefully organised, a small workshop really. There were two quilting frames, one rectangular and the other oval. A table contained a collection of implements of the quilting craft. There was a large pair of fabric scissors, and a small pair of sharp-pointed embroidery ones, spools of quilting thread, glass-headed pins, a measuring tape, rulers and pencils, a protractor and a compass, and a large amount of fabric. Stride looked at Corrigan and grinned.

"You have surprised me, Jack."

"I expect I have, sir," Corrigan said, smiling back. "That was the second thing I learned while I was working at that pub in the Midlands. The lady of the house, with whom I struck up a nice acquaintance, was famous in the area for her quilts. She showed me how." Corrigan stubbed his cigarette in an ashtray made from the end of a 4-inch shell casing. "I can tell you it was fuckin' good therapy after four years in the trenches." He rubbed the back of his neck and briefly grimaced, visiting old memories. "I been doing it ever since."

"That's almost thirty years. You've made a lot of quilts, then."

"Going on a hundred now." Corrigan grinned. "And there's a good market for them. The Yanks love them. I got a friend in Chicago, old army pal, who sells them for me. Fact is, I'm famous for my quilts, Inspector Stride. Or I should say that Alice McGettigan is famous for my quilts. That was my mother's maiden name. It wouldn't help my so-called career as a lawman for it to be generally known that I sit out here in the wilderness with a house full of fuckin' cats, making quilts. My manhood would be in doubt."

Corrigan laughed, turned off the light in the quilting room, and closed the door. He scooped up a grey cat from the floor on his way into the living room and sat in an armchair. The cat settled onto Corrigan's lap and resumed its bathing ritual.

"I've known Bert Cartwell all my life, Inspector Stride, both of us born in Martin's Harbour. We're about the same age, Bert and me, but we've moved along different paths, so to speak. When the fun and games started up in '14, I went straight up to St. John's to enlist. Very patriotic, you understand. Also dumber than a sack of bird shit, but I didn't know that then. While I was off to St. John's, Bert went to see old Doc Fraser. Fraser was so far past it by then he didn't know his arse from a post-hole, but still practising medicine and keeping the coffin-maker busy and rich. Bert got Fraser to write a letter saying he had a collapsed lung and was unfit for military service. He even persuaded the old man that he was the one who had collapsed the lung in the first place. That letter made the rounds. It kept Bert out of the trenches, and no white feather up his nose. I know all this because Bert told me himself over a jar one night after I came back from England."

"You didn't resent the fact that he stayed home while you and the others went overseas?"

"I would have, if I'd heard about it in '14 or '15. After the business on July 1, 1916, though, I'd had my fill of the fuckin' war and the lah-de-dah Limey arseholes who were giving the orders. By the time I got home three years later, I was of the mind that Bert had the right idea all along. I know that's heresy, especially now we've just finished another war with the fuckin' Jerries, but I don't give a shit about that."

"You and Bert Cartwell are friends, though? Just as Bern said?"

"Like I say, I don't have to call him Mr. Cartwell. And Bert knows me well enough."

Corrigan rolled another cigarette, taking his time. The procedure completed, he flicked a match with his thumbnail and inhaled deeply. He turned back to Stride, regarded him through a cloud of smoke.

"You see," Corrigan leaned forward, "when Bert started out thirty-odd year ago in Martin's Harbour, he had as close to nothing as it doesn't matter.

He liked to say, and probably still says it when the occasion demands, that just about everything he owned in this world was wrapped around his arse to keep it warm. The first smart thing Bert did was decide that, come hell or high water, he wasn't going to work for fuckin' wages. And the second smart thing he did was marry Florence Martin."

Corrigan sat back and crossed his legs.

"And if the surname rings a bell, it was Flossie Martin's family that our hometown is named for. Her great-great-grandfather to be precise. Flossie had inherited a florin or two and stood to inherit a lot more, and Bert knew it. Her family was very well-connected businesswise, and not just in Martin's Harbour, and Bert knew that too." Corrigan slapped a large hand against his knee. "It was just fuckin' good luck that he fell in love with the maid, and her with him. But he would have married her anyway, even if she smelled bad and had two heads, each one uglier than the other.

"Don't get the idea, though, that his wife made Bert or owns him. Almost everything that has happened since they got wed has happened because Bert knew where he wanted to go, and knew how to get there. He worked as hard as any three good men to build what he's built. And what he has built now is a tidy fuckin' empire."

"You know we have a file on Bert Cartwell?"

"I know that, and I've read through it. Bert had some of the qualities of a son of a bitch in his youth and he cut more than one corner along his way. I won't offer any excuses for him. If I'd caught him at any of the shit that he got on with, I would've booted his arse into a jail cell, friend or no. And he knows that. His nose has been a lot cleaner in recent times."

"Ralph Waldo Hudson had something to do with that."

"That's certain." Corrigan sat back and scratched his chin, reflecting. He shook his head, then laughed. "Bert Cartwell and Ralph Waldo Hudson. Now there's a fuckin' combination."

"Where does William Cartwell fit into the family enterprise? I'm working on the assumption that he's the designated male heir because Cartwell only has daughters."

"As good a version as any, I suppose."

"There's more to it?"

"There might be. But it doesn't much matter in the final analysis."

"What else is there?"

"Bert has a reputation and a half where women are concerned. Don't get me wrong. Bert loves Flossie well and true."

"But?"

"He has a large appetite. He's slowed a bit as he's got older, but only from a gallop to a canter. And Bert's trotting pace would look like a flat-out gallop to most of us."

"You're suggesting that William might be Cartwell's natural son?"

"He could be. Bert had a brother—long dead now—and the official record says that William is his son. But if you hang around the wharf at Martin's Harbour some evening, pass a bottle around and mention the Cartwell name, someone will likely whisper in your ear that Bert and his brother's wife were as close as close once upon a time. It isn't a state secret."

"What does Cartwell say?"

"Nothing that he doesn't have to say. His sister-in-law lives in a fine house on Rennie's Mill Road and William sits on the right hand of the holy-of-holies. Flossie Martin had no illusions about Bert when she married him, and she's happy enough I dare say. Bert's three daughters, from what I hear, have hats and dresses and shoes enough to open a fuckin' department store, and don't have a care in the world. And some day they'll all get married and make three men as miserable as ever men were."

"What can you tell be about William Cartwell?"

"Not as much as you'd like me to. Only met him a half-dozen times. But I know he's spoiled rotten, never had to work at a job, thinks his shit is ice cream. And if it's female, breathing, and passably human, William will try to stuff his cock into it. If you were being kind, you might say that young William has not yet found his niche, other than the obvious one that young women have under their skirts." Corrigan snorted. "Someday he might have to shape up. For the present, though, William has a very special standing with Bert Cartwell, and whether he's nephew or son don't matter a hill of fuckin' beans."

"Perhaps Bert is reliving his life through William, but with money in his pocket this time around?"

"Could be," Corrigan said. He snorted again. "I was discussing just that with Dr. Sigmund Fuckin' Freud the other night, sir. And that was the very conclusion we come to."

Corrigan rolled another cigarette. The grey cat jumped down onto the rug at Corrigan's feet, and the black cat took its place and began padding around making a comfortable spot for itself. Corrigan put the cigarette in his mouth and absently scratched the cat behind the ear.

"Can I ask a question, sir?"

"Yes, of course."

"What do the Cartwells have to do with the price of tea? If Bert was in trouble I would have heard about it. Maybe William has shit hisself in public, though? Wouldn't surprise me."

"William Cartwell's name has come up in connection with the Edith Taylor murder."

"How so, you don't mind me asking?"

"I don't mind. Before Edith Taylor was married, she had an interesting life, apparently, apart from her modest housekeeping duties with the Taylors. She spent some of her evenings during the war keeping company with William Cartwell, as well as with any number of men that Cartwell wanted to make happy." Stride paused. "Do you know the name Emma Jeans?"

"I've met her," Corrigan said. He tapped ash off the end of his cigarette. "I hear she changed her name recently. And her outlook. Makes dresses for a living."

Stride looked at him, surprised.

"I hear things," Corrigan said, smiling. "Anyway, I knew Emma Jeans had an arrangement with William Cartwell years ago, be his hostess at gatherings of people that Bert did business with. Didn't know about Edith Taylor, though."

"Her name was Edith Wright, then."

Corrigan nodded slowly.

"Now that name I do remember. Might even have met her once or twice. The odd time, Bert would invite me to drop in to William's place to partake of the food and drink at one of his soirees." Corrigan caught Stride's look and laughed. "Just the regular food and drink, sir, I swear. The beaver pie was reserved for the special guests, and I wasn't in that exalted fuckin' category. To coin a phrase."

"Let me ask you something, Jack. If Edith Wright—Edith Taylor—made a noise about her relationship with William Cartwell, would he be likely to do anything about it?"

"Like beat her to death in her bathtub?"

"Or have someone do it for him?"

Corrigan drew on his cigarette and rubbed his thumb on the side of his chin.

"If you have to think about it, Jack, it suggests to me that it's not an impossibility."

Corrigan looked up.

"Well, if I've learned one thing over the years, it's that just about anything is possible, sir," he said. "But I was thinking more about Bert's ambitions for William, and how he's likely to go about realising them. Like I said earlier, Bert didn't mind cutting corners in his early days, and some of it got pretty rough. Boats set adrift of a stormy night, a fire in someone's shed, nets that got cut loose from their floats. And more than once someone would wind up in the hospital with his head stove in. But that was a long time ago. These days Bert beats his competitors to death—if he has a mind to—with a ledger and a sharp pencil. Mostly."

"What about William, though? Are you ruling him out as a possible suspect?"

"I'd be a fool if I did. I do know that William Cartwell has a mean streak. Spoiled brats usually do, my experience. And he fancies himself a man of action." Corrigan dug a finger into his left ear, was silent for a few moments. "Don't think he'd do it himself, though. I don't think he's got the balls for it."

Stride sipped his beer and stared at the ceiling for a minute. Corrigan stroked the cat and waited.

"Tell me about Bertram Cartwell's ambitions," Stride said.

Corrigan paused and scratched his chin again. The cat in his lap glared at him, annoyed by the movement.

"There's big changes coming on this little island. The war's over almost two years now, Britain is broke, in debt to the Yanks like everyone else, and the Brits want to cut us loose. The time is ripe to do that." Corrigan looked at Stride. "I'm telling you anything you don't already know, sir?"

Stride shook his head.

Newfoundland's history was long and complicated. Newfoundlanders liked to call their island "Britain's oldest colony," a descriptive that was recited with a measure of pride. The political history of the island was turbulent, sometimes violent, often pitting Protestant against Catholic, and city dwellers against the majority who lived in rural areas or in tiny villages on the rugged coastline. Responsible government, the essential feature of an independent country, finally came to Newfoundland in 1855 over the opposition of the mostly Protestant merchant class in St. John's, whose interest in democracy ran a poor second to their dedication to the balance sheet. But their self-interest was finally overcome by liberal reformers, most of them Irish by birth or descent, and most of them Roman Catholic.

The Great Depression of 1929 that laid waste the economies of most of the world also helped put paid to Newfoundland's political independence. The country was essentially bankrupt and in danger of defaulting on its international debts, an outcome that Great Britain, the "mother country," could not countenance. In 1934, opting for one of a number of unattractive choices, Newfoundland gave up its independence and accepted a political anomaly called Commission of Government. The elected legislature ceased to exist, democracy departed the scene, and the affairs of the island were run by a British governor and a six-man commission chosen by the Dominions Office in London, three from the United Kingdom, and three from Newfoundland. The Commission was still in place when the war ended in 1945, but it was an arrangement whose day was almost done.

"Like I said, there's changes coming, and we got a couple of choices," Corrigan said. "We can go it alone again, or join up with Canada. A few people think maybe we could join up with the States, but I don't know as there's much chance of that happening. I'm not a betting man, sir, but if I was, I might place a few dollars on Joe Smallwood and his confederation crew when we have the referendum next year. Smallwood don't cut much cheese in St. John's, maybe, but in the outports it's a different story. A lot of the people there think he's as good as gold. He's got the gift of the gab, he's well known through his radio show, almost famous. He's done his homework better than anyone else around, and he has as much energy as any five ordinary men. He might just make Canadians out of us yet. It's what the Brits have wanted for years, God knows."

"What does Cartwell think about it? Like yourself, Jack, he's an outport man, from Martin's Harbour."

"Bert was talking to me about it a while back. We get together now and again over a bottle of the best. Bert don't like Smallwood much, makes no bones about that. He says he don't trust the son of a bitch. Bert's a bayman, like you say, but now he's a St. John's millionaire, too. They say you can take the boy out of the bay but you can't take the bay out of the boy, and that's maybe true. But if the bay-boy has enough money in the bank, it can shift his slant on things."

"You're saying that Cartwell is likely to be in favour of Newfoundland re-establishing itself as an independent country?"

"All I'll say is that he's looking at things very closely. The long and the short of it is that Bert has a keen interest in the future of this island, and he's more of a businessman than a nationalist. If there's handwriting on a wall somewhere, Bert Cartwell will be among the first to read it all the way through, and then read it a second time."

"A pragmatist, then."

"One of the best." Corrigan took a swallow of beer and wiped his lips with the back of his hand. The cat stirred in his lap and glared at him again. "He even has political ambitions himself. Although that's not fuckin' news. Every sizeable businessman on this island has political ambitions, one way or another. Always been that way."

"Cartwell wants to get into politics?"

"Not himself, directly. Bert pulls too much baggage behind him, and he's not a public sort of person, anyway. Told me once he does his best work in dim light."

"His nephew, then."

Corrigan nodded.

"You got it. William will be his front man. I know Bert's thinking about it. But he's got a piece of work to do first, clean the bugger up for the voting public."

"From what you've told me about him, he has a major job on his hands."

"It's been done before, sir, and it will be done again. With the right kind of manager, William's linen can be laundered well enough, and folks will be persuaded to think that he was just one fine broth of a boy, guilty of a few youthful indiscretions. Some clever arsehole will probably come up with a pretty slogan for him, something like, 'when he was young and foolish, he was young and foolish.'"

"But now that he's all grown up, the voting public can trust him." Stride threw his head back and laughed.

"Right on, sir. Some of the voters will secretly admire his stamina, and enough of the rest won't give a shit."

Stride stood up and walked to the window. There was an old iron plough in the front yard and Corrigan had painted it black and fashioned a flower bed around it. Stride imagined it filled with bright, colourful blossoms, but it was still too early in the year.

"Whoever done Edith Taylor in, sir, I'd be a tad surprised to learn it was William Cartwell. But I'd keep an open mind, just the same."

Stride drank the last of his beer. It had gone a bit flat, but it still tasted good, dark and full-bodied. He accepted Corrigan's caution to keep an open mind about the likelihood of Cartwell's involvement in Edith Taylor's death. And what Corrigan had told him about the Cartwells had planted the seed of another thought. He walked to the kitchen and placed his empty glass in the washbasin. Corrigan was standing near the window when Stride came back into the front room.

"Any of that worth anything to you, sir?"

"Yes, Jack, I think it might be worth quite a lot. And you make a damn fine beer, besides." He walked to the door. The two men stood together in the yard for a minute, Corrigan still holding the black cat in the crook of his left arm. Away from the station, he was a different sort of man, the jagged edges smoothed down, decency and intelligence showing through. Stride walked a few paces in the direction of his MG, then looked back and smiled. "Your secret's safe with me, Jack."

"The quilts, you mean?" Corrigan laughed, his eyes bright. "Don't really matter, sir. I don't imagine nobody would fuckin' believe it anyway."

thirty
two

"I think we have a lead on Jennifer White, sir." Phelan was waiting for Stride when he got back to the station. He appeared pleased with himself. "Miss White had severed all her connections with her friends in Caitlin's Cove, but I got onto the lady at the Colonial Stores that Gaffer Fox told us about."

"The one who gave him an earful on the boat the day Jean Taylor drowned?"

"The same. Her name is Mildred Forbes and she's still at the store. Something of an institution there by now. Knows everyone and everything, and has forgotten nothing. She remembered Jennifer White from the time she worked there and she volunteered the information that it was more or less common knowledge that Jack Taylor had been involved with the girl. Apparently he took a lot of quiet heat after Jennifer left the store. She said he was pretty much sent to Coventry for a time, not that it affected his own position there."

"Well, it wouldn't have, would it? By then, Taylor was a part-owner in the company. Did she say where Jennifer White is now?"

"In St. John's, apparently. She got married just after the war started, to a fellow named Ronald Cole. Cole joined the navy not long after that and shipped out. He was at sea for a good part of the war."

"Mildred Forbes stayed in touch with her?"

"On and off, she said. She was a bit reluctant to talk about Jennifer. But I pressed her a little and she said that Jenny slipped into a less than honourable lifestyle for a time while her husband was at sea."

"Meaning?" As though he had to ask.

"Meaning that with upwards of ten thousand foreign troops on the island, a girl with a certain mindset could make a bit of extra money."

"Delicately put, Harry. Is she still married to Ronald Cole?"

"So I was told. I have two addresses for a Ronald Cole. I'm pretty certain we'll find Jenny Cole at one of them, but I wanted to wait for you before going any further."

Stride had been about to light a cigarette. Now he was motionless, his lighter burning brightly in mid-air. The memory he had tried to get hold of when he had spoken with Herbert Rodgers and his wife and looked at their picture of Ambrose White had finally clicked into place.

"Sir?"

"You said Jenny Cole."

"Yes, sir. Jennifer White's married name."

"We've already met her, Harry. We just didn't know who she was at the time."

"Jesus Christ." Phelan thumped his forehead with the heel of his right hand. "Of course. The Petrelli murder. Jenny Cole—Jennifer White—was with Petrelli the night he was killed. There was another girl we interviewed with her. Rita Fleming. They lived on Macklin Place, just up the street and around the corner from the Taylor house."

Stride finally lit his cigarette. He leaned back in his chair and slowly exhaled a stream of smoke towards the ceiling of his office.

"Sit down, Harry, and let's go over this for a bit." He pushed the lighter and package of cigarettes across the desk towards Phelan. "We've been operating on the more or less reasonable assumption that Ambrose White might have killed Edith Taylor."

"We do have the fingerprint evidence, sir."

"Yes. Add to that White's background of hardship and abuse and you have a potentially angry and unstable character. Then, we have the fact that his sister was involved with Jack Taylor, became pregnant, apparently lost her baby, and moved on to something less than a grand lifestyle. At least for a time."

"White has plenty of reason to be angry. And we still don't have any idea what might have happened to him during the war."

"But now we have another piece to add to the puzzle."

"A husband for Jennifer White who also has reason to be pissed off with things. If his wife was earning bread money on her back during the war, he might have become a very unhappy man."

"Depends on the man, Harry. We each know a few who actively encouraged their wives and sweethearts to accommodate our uniformed visitors."

"At least a few. But if Cole didn't like the fact that Jennifer was having it on with Petrelli and company, he might have taken our unfortunate American friend for a one-time excursion to the South Side that night."

"Assuming he was in town," Stride said. "And assuming his wife didn't know about that. I doubt she would have been screwing around with Marco Petrelli if she had known that her husband might have been skulking in the shadows that night."

"Petrelli is one thing, but the Taylor murder is quite another. Can we really stretch this far enough to see Cole murdering Edith Taylor?"

"Cole might have been angry enough to take a swing at Jack Taylor's chin if they happened to meet under the appropriate circumstances. But murdering the man's wife? That is a long stretch."

"How are we going to do this? Bring them in for questioning?"

"We have no reason to bring either of the Coles in at this point. The connections are all circumstantial with the Edith Taylor murder. And even more so with the Petrelli case. In any event, I think we have to keep Petrelli in the background for now. First things first. It's been four years, and Marco Petrelli won't get any deader over the next few days or weeks."

Stride had a familiar expression on his face. Phelan took a chance.

"Two murders in the same neighbourhood, and the same woman associated with both of them. That's right up there on the coincidence scale, sir."

Stride laughed. "Jimmy Peach was right, Harry, you are a bugger and no bloody mistake. You're trying to put thoughts in my head."

The woman who opened the front door of the small house on Pennywell Road was not immediately familiar to either Stride or Phelan. Jenny Cole had changed a lot. They probably wouldn't have recognised her if they had passed her on the street. When they had interviewed her four years earlier, she had been slender to the edge of gaunt, and with an undertow of anger that made her seem leaner still. Now, she had gained weight, and was beginning to show some of the features of a middle-class housewife. She was still fair and still attractive, but in a much different way than four years earlier. There was a wariness in her eyes, still, an echo from the past.

Stride pulled the various images of the Whites into his mind's focus; the photograph of Ambrose, the sketches by Herc Parsons, his memory of Jenny

Cole, and the maturing woman who stood in the doorway. It all seemed to come together.

It took Jenny Cole only a moment to recognise them. Her eyes widened in surprise and then she looked downward, her head hanging. She didn't speak.

"We'd like to talk with you, Mrs. Cole, if it's convenient."

"Is it about Mark Petrelli, again?" She was looking Stride in the eye now. "I told you everything I knew four years ago. Have you found out anything more about it? About that night?"

"Perhaps if we came in for a few minutes, Mrs. Cole," Stride said.

She pulled the door open and stood to one side.

"To answer your question, we haven't learned anything new about the Petrelli murder." Jenny Cole made a small movement at the word "murder." Remembered pain. "Something else has come up. You have read about the murder of Edith Taylor, I suppose."

"Yes."

"You know that she was Jack Taylor's wife?"

"Yes." She closed her eyes and rested her chin on her hands. "Is that what this is about, your coming here today? Mrs. Taylor?"

"Partly," Stride said. "We know what happened fifteen years ago between you and Jack Taylor."

"Do you?" She turned her head away and appeared about to reply, but said nothing more.

"Our information is that you had an affair with Taylor and became pregnant. Am I right so far?"

"Yes, I was pregnant."

"Was there a baby? We're not sure about that part."

"No. I lost the baby. There was an accident."

"An accident?" Isaac Squires had told them about a "terrible row" when Jennifer White last visited her mother at Caitlin's Cove.

"Yes," she said. She focused on a picture on the far wall. "I had a fall." Her voice was firm, the phrase practised.

Stride left it at that.

"When was the last time you saw your brother, Mrs. Cole?"

"Amby?" Her surprise was evident. "What does Amby have to do with any of this?"

"We're attempting to find that out. When did you last see him?"

"Not for a long time," she said. "After our mother died, he didn't want to have anything to do with me. That was after I lost my baby. Amby was living with our Aunt Vera in St. Phillips."

"Mrs. Courtney?"

"Yes." She showed a brief flicker of surprise that they knew who Aunt Vera was. "He didn't want to see me and when I insisted, he wouldn't say very much. He blamed me for everything that had happened. Our mother dying, I mean. He told me to go away and leave him alone, and then he just walked away and went to his room."

"He blamed you? Did he know about Jack Taylor's involvement?"

"Yes. He knew about that. My mother and I had an argument one night, and I blurted out Mr. Taylor's name. I was trying to make her feel better, less angry with me, by telling her that Mr. Taylor was going to pay all the medical bills, and look after us until the baby was adopted. But that only seemed to make her angrier. Amby was in the room."

"And that was the last time you saw him? At Mrs. Courtney's house?"

She started to reply and then stopped.

"I'm not sure."

"What do you mean, you're not sure?"

"I may have seen him."

"Recently?"

"Yes. Last week. A few days after Mrs. Taylor was killed. On the Monday. There was a man standing on the sidewalk, across the street. I don't know how long he had been there before I saw him. He looked familiar, and I went to the window and pulled the curtains back to get a better look. He saw me, and then he walked away, down the street, walking very fast. I went to the door but by the time I opened it, he was gone, out of sight."

"But you're not certain it was your brother?"

"I kept telling myself that it couldn't have been Amby." There was a distant look in her eye, a tiredness. "After all these years, after so much that's happened. But, yes, I think it was him."

Stride took the two sketches of Ambrose White from his pocket and gave them to Jenny Cole. She studied them for a long time, resting her forehead on her hand. Finally, she looked up.

"I think so," she said. "It looks like Amby, years older than the last time I saw him. Where did you get these?"

"I had an artist draw them using a photograph of your brother from eleven years ago."

Stride told her about Ambrose White working at Benjamin Downe's shop, but left out the circumstances of his relationship with his employer. She gave the sketches back to him.

"You don't know anything about him, about his life, since that time in St. Phillips, more than fifteen years ago?"

"No. I went back to Caitlin's Cove only once after the night I had the argument with my mother. I didn't even go to her funeral. I was still in hospital then. I was five months pregnant when I lost the baby, and I was sick for a long time afterward. I almost died." She took a deep breath. "I went back home once, at night, to put some flowers on her grave."

She was silent for a few moments, then looked directly at Stride.

"Why do you want to find Amby? What has he done?"

"We have reason to believe that he was in the Taylor house sometime before the murder. We don't know when, or why. He might not have had anything to do with it. But we need to find him."

"I didn't know it was that hard to find someone." There was an edge to her voice. "You found me, after all."

"Finding you wasn't that difficult, Mrs. Cole. You have roots in the city, people who worked with you, knew that you had married Ronald Cole." Stride waited a moment while her mind retraced the path he and Phelan had followed to reach her house on Pennywell Road. "Your brother is another story. We know he's been in the city but we haven't found any connections for him. So far, we have been able to trace his movements only until 1939. After that he disappears. We have good reason to believe he's living under an assumed name."

"Why? Why would Amby do that?"

"We don't know. We'd like to find him and ask him that question."

"Oh, God." She rested her head on her right hand. Stride suspected the gesture was as much theatre as emotion. But perhaps that was only professional cynicism. Stride looked at Phelan, who shrugged and made a cutting gesture with his right hand. He nodded. He doubted that Jenny Cole could tell them anything more about her brother's whereabouts.

"Just a little longer, Mrs. Cole. Can you tell us where we can find Rita Fleming?"

"Rita?" She sighed and rolled her eyes. "Then it's going to start again, isn't it? Looking for Mark's killer?"

"Yes. There's no statute of limitations on murder. The case is still open."

"And I suppose you'll want to talk to Ron. My husband."

"It's possible." Stride said. "You can give us Miss Fleming's address?"

"Yes, I think so." Jenny Cole stood up and put her hand on the mantelpiece. "That was all over, that business with Rita and me, even before the war ended. It's been more than three years now. I have a new life. We have a new life. Ron and I have worked our way through a lot of things, hard things. All those things that happened years ago, it's all history, almost like it happened to someone else. I don't want to lose what I have. I've lost too much already. Can you understand that?"

"Yes," Stride said. "I can understand that." That wasn't quite true. All he knew were some of the basic facts of the matter. The understanding of it was on a different level. Maybe more than one level. But he was starting to feel like he was getting there.

"We'll have those pictures and sketches of White on the street in a day or two, sir. With luck, we might have him soon."

"Maybe." They were standing by the MG, outside Jenny Cole's house. Stride had that look again, Phelan thought.

"There's some part of this that doesn't add up for you, sir?"

"A couple of bits, Harry. It was in the language."

"Sir?"

"Her language, Harry. She referred to Petrelli as 'Mark'. Someone she knew, and had probably slept with, whatever the circumstances. The intimacy was there. You could hear it and feel it. But Jack Taylor was Mr. Taylor to her. The formality doesn't make a lot of sense if she actually had an affair with the man and carried his child. And when I asked her about having an affair with Taylor, she said only that she had gotten pregnant."

"I noticed that. But if Taylor took advantage of her and left her with a bun in the oven, her feelings towards him might not be all that warm, even if he was willing to foot the bills."

"It's possible."

"You think maybe she didn't have an affair with Taylor after all, then? But she said she was pregnant and that the miscarriage almost killed her."

"I believe that part of it, Harry, but you'll check the hospital records today and confirm it. But, no, I can't shake the feeling that Taylor was only involved after the fact."

They were silent for a minute, lighting cigarettes as a substitute for activity.

"Well, we know for certain that Jack Taylor was involved," Phelan said.

"Even if someone else was the father. He signed an agreement to provide support for Jennifer White. Which leaves the obvious question. If Jack Taylor wasn't the father, who was? And why would Taylor want to be involved?"

Stride leaned against a telephone pole, thinking. Two cats, one black and one tabby, emerged from a laneway and ran across the street, the tabby chasing the black. Stride watched them disappear into a second laneway between two houses. He looked back at Phelan, then skyward at the telephone wires that ran the length of the street. He flicked his half-smoked cigarette towards the middle of the street and watched it bounce across the surface in a shower of sparks.

"I don't know, Harry," he said, finally.

But that wasn't quite true, either.

thirty
three

Ralph Waldo Hudson rested his grey head against the dark brown leather of the back seat of his Bentley and glanced towards the side window. He pulled the curtain part way back and watched the people on the sidewalk, many of whom were staring at his limousine. There were not that many chauffeured limousines in St. John's. It pleased Hudson that he belonged to a small elite group that could afford an expensive toy like a Bentley. The cost of the car was never an issue with him. Hudson, now in his middle sixties, had long since ceased to worry about money. He sometimes worried about other things, but money was not one of them.

The car moved fitfully along Water Street, progressing a short distance, then stopping again. Hudson imagined there was an accident blocking the traffic somewhere up ahead. He tapped the silver cap of his cane on the glass that separated him from his driver. The driver slid the partition open.

"Can you see what the holdup is, Hayward? At this rate, I'll be late for my meeting."

"I'm afraid I can't see that far ahead, Mr. Hudson."

"Well, turn off somewhere, man, as soon as you get the chance. This is intolerable."

"Sir." Hayward slid the partition closed.

Hudson looked out the side window again. A boy on the sidewalk was staring at the Bentley. He was about thirteen or fourteen, Hudson estimated. He was not very well dressed and he wore on his head a soft cap of the sort that labourers wore. Hudson noticed that the boy's trousers were held up with a length of cord instead of a belt, and the sole of one of his boots had come loose at the toe. The boy caught Hudson's eye and they stared at each other for a moment across the gap of age and circumstance. Then the boy grinned broadly, grabbed his crotch, and made an obscene gesture.

Hudson pulled the curtain across the window. He laid his head back on the leather seat again and smiled. On the whole, the boy was rather nice looking, he thought. A savage, of course, like most of his kind, but cleaned up, and taught some rudimentary manners, he would likely be quite acceptable. Hudson closed his eyes and circled the fingers of his right hand around the warm dark wood of his walking stick.

William Cartwell offered Stride and Phelan a drink, shrugged when they declined, and poured a generous portion of gin for himself. He added a small amount of tonic water and stirred the mixture with a long-handled silver spoon. Cartwell was not quite as tall as Stride, and he was a lot lighter. Not thin, exactly, but lanky and loose-jointed. Stride guessed that he was about thirty years old, but that might have been an over-estimate. Cartwell looked like someone who had partied too often and too vigorously and was ageing prematurely. His tailored suit did not quite conceal an expanding waistline.

Cartwell invited them to take a seat, and Phelan chose a straight-backed chair and sat with his legs crossed. Stride shook his head and occupied himself by walking around the room, surveying the large collection of books that filled the tall bookcases lining three of the walls. Many of the books were leather-bound, rich and handsome editions of the classics of English literature. Stride thought that they had probably been purchased in bulk by an agent who knew what an enlightened gentleman would be expected to possess in the way of reading matter. Few of the books appeared to have been opened, their spines in pristine condition, not a crease to be seen. A more canny pretender might have tasked a family retainer with routinely opening the books to give them the appearance of having been read.

"You realise that this meeting will be a waste of your time and mine," Cartwell said. He swallowed some of his drink and sat in an armchair, his feet resting on a leather hassock. Cartwell wasn't really nervous, Stride decided, but neither did he seem very comfortable in the company of two detectives. There was also a level of impatience there that made Stride wonder about Cartwell's political prospects. Long meetings of little consequence were an essential part of the political life.

"Well, I hope not, Mr. Cartwell. We just want to ask you a few questions about a case we're working on. We hope you may be able to assist us."

Cartwell shrugged and picked up his glass.

As soon as Mr. Hudson arrives, we'll ask our questions," Stride said. "And then, hopefully, we'll be on our way."

Stride had chosen his words carefully and was pleased to see that Cartwell reacted with a slight stiffening of his shoulders. He took another long drink from his glass.

Stride pulled out a leather-bound copy of *David Copperfield*. It wasn't a first edition, and it had a long preface by a professor of English literature from Oxford. The leather felt warm in Stride's hand. He flipped the pages until he came to the beginning of the first chapter.

"Well, I hope this isn't some kind of fishing expedition, Inspector. Stride, is it?"

Stride looked up and nodded, then read the famous line. *Whether I shall be the hero of my own life or whether that station shall be held by anybody else, these pages must show.* He closed the book and looked at William Cartwell for a moment. He shook his head and slid the book back into its place on the shelf.

"Hudson is a very busy man. And so am I," Cartwell said. He stared at Stride. "Time is money," he added vaguely.

Stride nodded and smiled again. He wondered what Cartwell would have been doing with his time and energy if Stride had not requested this meeting. He had disliked William Cartwell at first glance. He remembered Jack Corrigan's description of the young man as a spoiled brat with a mean streak.

Stride had phoned William Cartwell and asked to meet with him and Phelan, and with reluctance Cartwell had agreed. Five minutes later Stride received a call from Ralph Waldo Hudson's law clerk saying that Mr. Hudson would also be present at the meeting, and that Mr. Cartwell would not answer any questions until he arrived. The clerk said that it was routine for Mr. Hudson to assist his clients in matters of any significance.

"This is a very impressive room," Stride said, gesturing towards the collection of books. "Do you read a lot, Mr. Cartwell?"

William Cartwell looked blankly at Stride and tapped his fingers against his glass. He seemed to be thinking about his response when there was a soft knocking at the door of the library.

"Come in," Cartwell said. There was no immediate response from the other side. Cartwell leaped to his feet, spilling a small amount of his drink, strode quickly to the door and pulled it open.

"Goddamn it! I said to come in." Cartwell's complexion had coloured noticeably. Phelan tapped his right temple, stood up and smoothed the lapels of his jacket.

"Calm yourself, William," a soft male voice said. "Calm yourself."

Ralph Waldo Hudson walked into the room, every second step accompanied by the practised tap of his silver-headed cane on the hardwood floor. He turned to the young maid who had escorted him to the library.

"Thank you, Phoebe, my dear." He looked at Stride and Phelan. "Gentlemen, I apologise for being late. There was an accident on Water Street that tied up traffic and we were caught in it. Now, William, dear fellow, introduce me to your visitors from the CID."

"I'm sure they can handle that chore themselves, Hudson." Cartwell walked over to the drinks table.

Hudson watched quietly as Cartwell poured more gin into his glass, then smiled at Stride and Phelan.

"I apologise for Mr. Cartwell's brusqueness, gentlemen. He has been travelling a great deal of late and I expect he's rather fatigued. You will understand, I'm sure." Hudson walked over to William Cartwell and placed a hand on his shoulder. He whispered some words into the young man's ear, then came back to Stride and Phelan. "My name is Ralph Waldo Hudson. I have represented Mr. Cartwell—Mr. Bertram Cartwell, that is—for many years. I'm pleased to represent the entire Cartwell family, in fact, in whatever capacity is appropriate to the occasion."

Two business cards appeared in Hudson's left hand. He gave one to each of the detectives. Stride ran his thumb over the embossed print on the card.

"I believe your name is Stride," Hudson said. "We met briefly several years ago in a matter unrelated to the Cartwell family. Perhaps you remember?"

"Yes," Stride said. "The matter had to do with arson. A fire at the warehouse on the South Side. It was a question of insurance fraud."

"Yes, it was. But no fraud was proven," Hudson said. The smile appeared again. "You have a good memory, Inspector Stride. A valuable asset." Hudson looked towards Phelan. "And your colleague's name?"

"Sergeant Harry Phelan," Stride said.

"Ah." Hudson gently tapped the silver handle of his cane against his chin. "You would be Walter Phelan's son. I'm acquainted with your father, Sergeant, in his capacity as a marine engineer. I myself have a modest craft that I like to gad about in sometimes. But only on warm days, and in gentle seas. I confess that I am long removed from sturdy seafaring stock." Another smile. "Please give my regards to your father, Sergeant."

"I'll be happy to do that, Mr. Hudson." Phelan was wearing his official smile.

Hudson walked to a leather armchair and sat down, carefully adjusting his clothing to minimise wrinkling.

"Now, William, if you will be so kind as to pour me a glass of dry sherry, I will be ready to assist you. I spoke with your uncle before coming here, by the way. He will be interested in the substance of our conversation."

Cartwell nodded. He filled a sherry glass with pale liquid. Hudson took a small sip and dabbed his lips with a silk handkerchief. He placed the glass on an end-table.

"Mr. Cartwell told me that you wished to ask him some questions about the murder investigation you are involved in. Perhaps you can explain how this investigation touches on the Cartwell family?"

Stride gave a summary of the Edith Taylor case, including a general reference to William Cartwell's activities during the war. He didn't mention Emma Jeans. Hudson sat with his eyes closed, nodding his head from time to time. He held his cane between his knees.

"Thank you for that, Inspector. I admire concision when it's also appropriately inclusive." Hudson took another sip of sherry and again produced the silk handkerchief. "We are all sorry to hear of the tragedy in the Taylor family, of course, and the need for information from all possible sources. I've discussed the case with William, and I can happily inform you that he was on the other side of the island, in Corner Brook, the night Mrs. Taylor was killed. Not that there was ever any possibility of Mr. Cartwell's involvement in this sad affair, of course."

Hudson looked directly at Stride.

"I understand also that you have arrested Mr. Edward Taylor for an attack on his father, in the wake of his stepmother's demise?"

"That is correct," Stride said.

"And are you not also looking for a man named Ambrose White in connection with the crime? Isn't he in fact the prime suspect?"

"Yes. We are looking for an Ambrose White. But he is not at this point a suspect. We wish to ask him some questions." That wasn't quite true, but Stride and Hudson were playing verbal chess and it had been Stride's move. Hudson smiled at the comment. Stride wasn't surprised that Hudson knew more about the investigation than had been made public.

"I see," Hudson said. He turned to William Cartwell. "Are you acquainted with an Ambrose White, William? I don't recall your mentioning him."

"Never heard of him," Cartwell said.

"No, I thought not."

"Were you acquainted with a woman named Edith Wright?" Stride asked. It was his move again. "We've been informed that you knew her a number of years ago, during the war."

Cartwell and Hudson looked at each other. Stride watched them both. Hudson nodded his head slightly.

"Yes," Cartwell said. He tried on a knowing grin, which suited him only too well. "I knew Edith Wright. I've known a lot of women."

"How well did you know her, Mr. Cartwell?"

"She was a face in the crowd," Cartwell said. He took out a cigarette and lit it with a silver lighter. He reclined in the chair and blew a stream of smoke towards the ceiling. "It was a crowded time. During the war, I mean."

"That doesn't quite answer my question," Stride said. "Were you involved with Edith Wright?"

Hudson held up his hand.

"I can understand that you need to clarify the decedent's relationships, Inspector, but her past involvement with Mr. Cartwell, assuming such involvement actually occurred, might easily be misconstrued. Even distorted." Hudson picked up his glass. "I wanted to express that concern before my client responds."

"Your concern is noted, Mr. Hudson." Stride turned his attention back to Cartwell.

"I wouldn't call it an involvement. But, yes, I slept with her, if that's what you're asking." Cartwell grinned again. "I've slept with a lot of women."

"Who broke off the relationship? You, or Miss Wright?"

"I told you, it wasn't a relationship. We slept together sometimes. It wasn't a big deal. I slept with other women, too. And Edie slept with other men." Cartwell fell silent. The familiar use of her name suggested a level of intimacy with Edith Wright that he had been anxious to avoid. Cartwell angrily stubbed his cigarette in an ashtray and turned to Stride. "This is all a lot of bullshit."

"William, please." Hudson again held up a cautionary hand. Cartwell glared at him, but said nothing more. He propped his chin on his fist and stared at the bookcase on the far wall of the room.

"Did you know that Edith Wright had married Jack Taylor?" Stride wondered if Cartwell would even respond.

Cartwell looked at Stride for a moment.

"Jack Taylor?" Cartwell snorted and shook his head.

"Did you want to add something to that, Mr. Cartwell?" Stride watched him closely. He sensed there was something there.

"About what?"

"About Jack Taylor. Your uncle controls the company that Jack Taylor works for." Stride didn't add that Taylor owned a block of shares in the same company.

"My uncle controls, and owns, a lot of companies." He laughed suddenly, harshly. "He owns a lot of Jack Taylors."

Ralph Waldo Hudson cleared his throat and stood up. He swallowed the last of his sherry, walked over to the drinks table and placed the empty glass on the polished surface. It was a gesture that was casual and imperious at the same time. Hudson smiled at William Cartwell, then turned to Stride.

"We appear to have wandered away from the subject of this meeting, Inspector. I believe that Mr. Cartwell has answered all of your questions, frankly and honestly. Do you have any others that bear directly on Mrs. Taylor's unhappy demise?"

"Not at the moment, Mr. Hudson." Stride stood up. Phelan was already standing.

"Well, then, we can bring this meeting to a close." Hudson stepped towards Stride, right hand extended. "It has been a pleasure to see you, again, Inspector. Sergeant Phelan. Of course, Mr. Cartwell will be pleased to meet with you again, if you feel that he can be of assistance. William?"

William Cartwell was standing by the drinks table, the bottle of gin in his right hand. He grinned at Stride, raised the bottle as though it were a trophy he had just won, then turned away and picked up his glass.

thirty
four

Rita Fleming was still in the business, but on a much different level than four years earlier. She had a record now, three arrests for soliciting, a six-month sentence on the third arrest two years ago, followed by early release for good behaviour. Both Stride and Phelan were surprised to find themselves looking at a young woman who was poised and frankly very attractive. Her flat, comfortably furnished, was on the third floor of a large house in a good neighbourhood.

"I last saw Jenny just over a year ago," she said. "But she must have told you that we've gone our separate ways since that night four years ago. She can't have been thrilled to bits to see you two standing on her doorstep."

She pointed to a love seat with a dark blue patterned fabric. Stride judged that he and Harry would be closer than friendship sanctioned if they both tried to sit on it at the same time. He carried a straight-backed chair into the living room from the small dining area. Rita Fleming grinned at that.

"Not exactly thrilled," Stride said.

"So, is this about Mark Petrelli, again?" She paused for a moment. "Or about the Taylor woman?"

"It's interesting you should mention that," Stride said.

"I read the papers and listen to the radio, Inspector. And I knew that Jenny had a connection with Jack Taylor. She told me about it not long after we met."

"What did she tell you, exactly?"

"Well, I don't remember exactly, but she said that she had known him when she worked at the Stores and that he had been going to help her out when she was pregnant. She was always nervous about running into him and his wife when we lived on Macklin Place. But you didn't answer my question. Are you here about Petrelli or Mrs. Taylor?" She shrugged before he could answer. "Anyway, I answered all your questions about Mark four years ago. And all I really know about Mrs. Taylor is what I read in the paper."

"We're interested in both cases, in fact."

"I guessed as much. Pretty hot coincidence, I suppose," she said, grinning. "Jenny knowing both Mark and Jack Taylor. I'm guessing you two gents don't put a lot of store in coincidence in your line of work. Right?"

"We tend to have suspicious minds, Miss Fleming. But I'm curious. Do you think there's a connection?"

The question surprised her. It was unlikely that her opinions were often sought by the police.

"It's the first thing that occurred to me when I read about Mrs. Taylor. Well, I would, wouldn't I, it being the same neighbourhood and all? But I thought about it and I don't see any connection."

"Did you ever meet Edith Taylor, or her husband?"

"No."

"Was Jenny Cole's husband in St. John's when Petrelli was killed?"

"Ron? I get it. The jealous husband. As far as I know, Ron was somewhere in the Mediterranean on a cruiser when that happened. I know for a fact that he was at sea. But he knew about the murder, and about Jenny and me, because someone had sent one of his shipmates a clipping from the paper. He wrote to Jenny after that and gave her hell. But she had already stopped going around with other men right after Mark was killed. Things were touch and go between her and Ron for a long time, though. But I guess they worked it out OK. I'm happy about that."

"You said that Jack Taylor was going to help Jenny out with the baby. Was he the father?"

"Jack Taylor? No, he wasn't the father." Rita Fleming looked surprised at the suggestion. "Did someone say he was?"

"No. No one has actually said that he was. But if Jack Taylor wasn't the father, who was? And why was Taylor involved at all?"

"I don't know who the father was. I asked Jenny, but she wouldn't tell me. And I don't know how Jack Taylor got involved. It was a good thing he did, though. Jenny needed a lot of help then."

Stride looked at Phelan. Jack Taylor as Good Samaritan was a new concept.

"The night Petrelli was killed," Stride said, "he was waiting for his friend to come and collect him. I've forgotten the friend's name."

"Peter Bergstrom." She laughed. "A big Swede from Minnesota. Most of the Yanks we knew early on were from Minnesota. When Pete got back to Macklin Place, Mark was gone. But you already know all that."

"You said at the time that Petrelli declined your invitation to wait in the house."

"Yes. It was a nice night, and Mark said he wanted to wait outside and look up at the stars." She giggled. "He was a little bit drunk. Not plastered, exactly, but he wasn't feeling any pain. None of us were. Feeling any pain, I mean. Except Jenny. Jenny never drank very much, said it made her feel sick. Which made her a good friend for me to have. I like to drink, and I know I was pretty looped by the time we got home that night. I fell into bed and kinda passed out as soon as Mark left us."

"What was he drinking that night?"

"Who? Mark? Shit, it was four years ago." She thought about it for a moment. "We had a pretty good supply of stuff. I was drinking rum. I remember that well enough." She tapped her forehead with a finger. "Beer. Mark liked the local beer. He always drank beer, now that I think of it. The Yanks liked our beer. It had a better kick than their stuff. Why?"

"Just gathering information. Can you remember anything else about that evening?"

"You know, I spent a year thinking about that night after they found his body. All kinds of stuff went through my mind. The ring he wore on his right hand. It had a blue stone, a sapphire. He said it was his birth stone. And things he said to us because they were the last things he ever said to us. You know, silly stuff. I remembered afterwards that he said 'Don't take any wooden nickels.' It was something he would say when he went off."

Stride looked at Phelan. Rita Fleming's comments about Petrelli had surprised him. Where their investigation four years ago had indicated that the evening she and Jenny Cole had spent with Petrelli and company was strictly a pay-for-play situation, her comments now suggested that there might have been more to it than that.

"How close were you and Jenny to Petrelli, Rita?"

"I don't know if close is the word, exactly, but we got to know him and Pete pretty well. I guess we knew them almost a year." She paused for a moment and looked at the floor. Remembering.

"So it wasn't entirely a casual thing between you. There was more to it?"

"Yes and no. Mark and Pete were both seeing other girls. Especially Mark. And Jenny and I were seeing other guys."

"Seeing?"

"Right." She looked hard at Stride, then grinned. "And sometimes we got paid for it. A girl has to live, after all."

"Who else was Petrelli seeing?"

"I don't know any names, but Mark was a real devil with women. There was a period when he was engaged to one or two local girls at the same time. Of course, he wasn't really engaged to any of them, but I know some of them took it seriously. A lot of the local girls thought that marrying a Yank was their ticket to Shangri-La, to the land of the big PX. Mark was a real charmer, though, and you couldn't stay mad at him for very long. Not that Jenny and me had any reason to, really. He never made us any promises—I mean, who would, right?—so he had no promises to keep, and none to break."

"You didn't tell us this four years ago. Why?"

"We knew that Mark's parents were from a small village in the old country. Italy. They were old-fashioned and really strict about boy-girl things. They wouldn't want to hear that their son was screwing around the way Mark was. Their son was dead."

Stride walked to the mantel and picked up a framed photograph of a younger Rita Fleming sitting on the concrete wall of a gun emplacement near the harbour entrance. He wondered how she had managed to get the picture. There had been strict rules on such photographs during the war. She seemed to read his thoughts.

"That was taken by an army photographer that I went out with a couple of times. He wanted to impress me by giving me an illegal photograph. He was a real romantic, a nice boy. He thought I was a nice small-town girl." She grinned again, the mischievous glint back in her eye. "He was from Kansas. I used to call him Toto, after Dorothy's mutt. You know, in the movie? I don't remember his name."

"Do you remember anything else from the night Petrelli was killed?"

She took a cigarette from a lacquered box on the table and lit it from Phelan's lighter. She slowly exhaled a stream of smoke, thinking. Then she smiled.

"This is cute. When he left us that night, I told Mark to watch out for the Evil Eye."

"The Evil Eye?" Stride wondered if he had heard correctly.

"Yeah, the Evil Eye." She had caught Stride's surprised expression and laughed. "It was a joke. Something Jenny and I used to kid each other about.

One of the old ladies on Leslie Street would often be in her window at night when we came home, just standing there in the dark, watching the street. She thought we couldn't see her, of course, but we could. We nick-named her the Evil Eye. I suppose she thought we were really bad girls, going out with uniforms, the Yanks and the Canadians. She probably thought we were having...," she leaned forward conspiratorially, "...sex." The last word whispered. "Well, guess what? She was right." Then she laughed.

"Was she standing in the window that night, the night Petrelli was killed?"

"I don't remember if she was there that night. I was pretty hammered, like I said. I don't think I even looked."

"The lady in the window. Who was she?"

"I never knew her name, and I never cared enough to find out, actually. But I can tell you which house she lived in. It was the house next to the Taylors, up the street. Sometimes I wondered what her life must be like, if she spent time staring out the window late at night. I almost felt sorry for her, poor old cow, standing there in the dark all alone, just watching. And we were very bad girls, you know."

She laughed again.

thirty
five

Stride turned left off Hamilton Avenue onto Leslie Street and immediately down-shifted to second gear. In a city with many steep hills, Leslie Street is one of several that stands out as especially impressive. Moving south from Hamilton Avenue, the street quickly becomes almost vertical. The small houses on this part of the street are built into the incline and seem to struggle to hold a precarious balance.

Two young boys were riding their bikes up the hill, standing on the pedals for maximum thrust. The younger and smaller of the two was lagging behind, slowing to a halt. When Stride looked back he had given up the struggle and was standing astride his bike watching as his companion continued to make his way slowly to the crest.

The MG's engine whined as if in pain as Stride carefully eased the car down the hill. As he approached McKay Street on his right, a seductive aroma from the Bavarian Brewery on the opposite side filled the interior of the small car. A dump truck had pulled up by the side of the brewery and a stream of steaming mash was cascading from a chute into its box, feed for livestock on one of the farms west of the city.

Stride stood on Jack Taylor's front landing and rang the doorbell. The street was deserted except for a small pack of mongrel dogs trotting up the hill on the sidewalk opposite, heading for Macklin Place. The leader of the pack was a large black dog, part Labrador, part German Shepherd, and part something else, probably. The make-up of the rest of the pack must have encompassed at least a dozen breeds, wildly intermixed. The door opened while he watched the last of the mutts trot round the corner.

"Eric." The voice took him by surprise. Joanne Taylor stood in the open doorway. "Jack's not home, but come in anyway."

They went to the kitchen. "I can make tea," Joanne said. "Or coffee, if you'd rather. I'm afraid Jack doesn't have anything more exciting on hand." She made a face. "Or if he does, he has it well hidden. Not that I've searched the place, you understand."

"It's all right," Stride said. He held up an envelope with the two drawings that Herc Parsons had made. "I have some sketches of Ambrose White."

"Sketches?" Joanne sat on a kitchen chair and crossed her legs. She leaned her elbow on the table.

"They were done by a friend. An artist."

"I remember a friend of yours who's an artist. His name is Parsons. Some complicated Greek name. Hercules, I think. And something else, I forget what. You introduced him to me once when we ran into him downtown."

"Agamemnon," Stride said. "Hercules Agamemnon Parsons. You're right. I did introduce you. I had forgotten about that."

"Can I see them?" Her eyes were bright, interested. "Who knows? Maybe I'll recognise him." Stride hesitated an instant too long. "But if you'd rather wait for Jack, I'll understand, of course. Although I don't know when he'll be back. He was out when I arrived, so I let myself in. It's just a casual visit. I was in the neighbourhood." She caught his expression. "I walked from our place. That's why you didn't see my car. It's not terribly far. Anyway, I like to walk. And today the walk did me good. It took my mind off things."

Stride nodded and pulled the two sheets of sketching paper from the envelope and laid them on the table.

Joanne looked at the sketches, her gaze moving back and forth between the two. She took her time, finally settling on the one with the moustache. She looked at Stride.

"This is Ambrose White?"

"You recognise him?" Stride picked up the second sketch and studied the face again.

"Yes, I think so. It looks a lot like Raymond Butler," she said. She paused and looked at Stride. "Ray is a friend of Bobby's."

"A friend of Bobby's?" Stride went back to their last conversation. He took out his cigarettes, shook one from the package. "Is he the companion you told me about? That day we were at Middle Cove?"

"Yes. He's the one."

"Christ." The word slipped out. "Tell me about Raymond Butler."

"I don't really know him well, Eric. I've met him only a couple of times. I do know that Ray is one of Bobby's few real friends. I think Bobby said that they were in hospital together, during the war."

"They met in the hospital?"

"I think that's correct, yes."

"Jack Taylor said that Bobby was in hospital in Liverpool. Is that where they met?"

"No. It was here in St. John's. Bobby was wounded a second time, in 1944, I think. Ray was also a patient. Bobby said that he had been wounded in Holland. He was in the army, with an artillery regiment, I think. At least in the beginning. Something like that." She was thinking hard now, putting things into context. "Ambrose White—Ray—knew that Bobby was Jack Taylor's son. I wonder if he also knew that his sister was involved with Jack at one time? I suppose he must have." She paused. "Do you have any evidence that Ray actually killed Edith?"

"I shouldn't really talk about this with you." He drew on his cigarette. "But I can tell you that his fingerprints were found at the scene, and we have a witness who claims to have seen someone matching Butler's description walking across Ayre's Field towards the house that evening."

Joanne was silent for a minute.

"Do you suppose it was all a deliberate set-up, Eric? That Ray sought out Bobby just so he could get back at Jack?"

"I can't imagine it was a set-up, Jo. They were wounded in different operations, after all. And realistically, what were the chances that they would end up in the same hospital? But Raymond Butler may have pursued a friend-ship—or whatever—with Bobby after they met because he was Jack Taylor's son."

"So it's possible that Ray killed Edith to take his revenge on Jack?"

"It's possible. But if he did, he made a mistake. This I will tell you in confidence. Jack Taylor wasn't the father of Jennifer White's baby."

Stride watched as this sank in. Joanne stared straight ahead. She didn't say anything for a time.

"But the file in Brendan Madigan's office," she said at last. "It said that he was the father."

"I wonder if that's really what it says. What you told me was that Madigan's file showed that Jack Taylor had signed an agreement to pay Jennifer White's medical expenses and provide her with help, before and after her baby was born. That doesn't mean he was the father. Whatever. It was logical for you to assume that he must have been. Why else would he take on that responsibility, after all? And Taylor had a reputation to make it all seem likely."

"Do you know who the father was?"

"Not for certain, no."

"But you think you know."

"I have an idea, yes. But Jack Taylor isn't going to tell me, and Jennifer White—her name is Jennifer Cole, now—also isn't likely to tell. And then there's the man himself. He might tell me the truth if I asked him directly, but I have no valid reason to do that. With some obvious exceptions, making someone pregnant isn't a crime. And he did arrange to pay Jennifer's expenses."

"Her expenses." Joanne's eyes were hard now. She turned her face away. "The dollar costs, then."

"I spoke with Bobby recently," Joanne said. "I told you about that. He told me he hadn't seen Raymond for a while. But he didn't think that was unusual. He's always said that Ray is unpredictable."

"Unpredictable." Stride rolled the word around in his mind. "Tell me what Raymond Butler does when he's not being unpredictable. Do you know?"

"Bobby told me he makes things, furniture, things like that. He made a bookcase for Bobby. It's in a style from almost a hundred years ago. Early Victorian. He did a really good job."

Stride nodded, remembering the bookcase wood at Taylor's flat on the South Side.

"Did Raymond ever mention the name Thomas McKinley? He owned a local firm that did carpentry and renovations. They did the work here two years ago." He looked around him at the new oak cupboards, the ones that Harry Phelan had admired the night Edith Taylor was killed. He lifted his hand and touched the fine wood, as if seeking some contact with Raymond Butler.

"As I said, I don't know Ray all that well, Eric." Joanne stood up and walked across the kitchen to the window and looked outside, towards the field. The glass had been replaced and the woodwork repaired, but it hadn't been painted yet. Joanne turned back to him. "I only met him on a couple of occasions. But I remember having a drink at Bobby's place one night about a year ago, and Ray mentioned someone he called 'Old Tom'. I know it had something to do with his work."

"Not Tommy Connars, then."

"Uncle Tommy? No. It definitely wasn't Tommy Connars he was refer-ring to."

"What's he like?"

"Ray?" She thought about that for a minute. "He's a lot like Bobby. They even look alike. They're about the same height and age, thin, intense."

"Peas in a pod?"

"No. Similar. Similar, but not alike, really. Bobby can scare people who don't know him very well, and with good reason. But I stopped feeling nervous about Bobby after I got to know him better."

"And Butler?"

She had to think about that.

"Ray made me nervous, even after I had met him a few times. I sensed that he'd had a rough life. And I noticed that he never mentioned anyone in his family. That's unusual. Most of the people you meet, in this part of the world anyway, have family as their reference point. Raymond seemed truly alone. Solitary. I asked him about his family once, just being polite, and he became very evasive. It was obviously something he didn't want to talk about."

"You're right. Ambrose White—Raymond Butler—has had a very rough life. And if, as we suspect, he thinks that Jack Taylor was responsible for wrecking what was left of his family, he's probably very angry."

"Angry enough to kill Jack's wife?"

"Perhaps. He may believe that Jack Taylor killed his mother, in effect, so it might have been along the lines of an eye for an eye. But I'm puzzled that Edith left the back door unlocked for him that night. We've been working on the assumption that they had arranged an assignation while Jack was away at his cabin." Stride paused, choosing his words. "But if Butler is a homosexual, why would Edith have been attracted to him?"

Joanne smiled when he said that.

"Well, almost anything is possible, Eric. Most especially where Edith and men were concerned."

"You think so?" He tried without much success to keep the surprise out of his voice.

"Yes, I do." She smiled at him again. "For one thing, it's possible that Raymond is attracted to both men and women. And attractive to both in turn. It's more common than you might think."

"I guess I'm always prepared to be surprised." He looked away from her. He felt slightly embarrassed. And then wondered why. "What else can you tell me?"

"I don't have much more to tell, really. As I said, I met Ray only a few times." She gave him a steady look. "Are you really asking me if I could be attracted to Raymond Butler?"

Stride nodded. He didn't want her being attracted to Raymond Butler. He wondered if she could see that.

"It's a possibility," she said. "In a different time, a different place, under different circumstances. But that's all hypothetical. As it happens, I'm not attracted to Ray." She laughed, then, her eyes flashing. "Well, maybe just a bit. Ray seemed dangerous, somehow, and a sense of danger can be attractive. Sometimes."

She had made him uncomfortable, now, and not for the first time. And he knew that she knew. He picked up the sketches and slid them back into the envelope.

"Are you leaving?" She was frowning.

"Yes, in a minute. I need to speak to your brother-in-law."

He went into the hall and picked up the telephone, asked the operator to connect him with Fort Townshend, then asked to speak to Harry Phelan. When he was finished he returned to the kitchen. Joanne was standing by the window again.

"I'll speak with your father-in-law some other time, Jo. See what he has to say about Raymond Butler. If anything."

"You seem upset, Eric. Did I say something wrong?"

He shook his head, feeling awkward, and still embarrassed.

"No, Jo. You haven't said anything wrong. You put it well the other night. This is a very complicated situation. Murder investigations are difficult enough." He made a dramatic gesture, arms spread wide. "And with all this history...." He left it at that, let her finish the thought.

"You're right," she said. She smiled briefly. "You should call Bobby from here, though. Make sure he's at home when you get to his place."

"Good thought," he said. He went down the hall and picked up the phone again.

Bobby Taylor had lost none of his cockiness and aggression when he opened the door of his room to admit Stride and Phelan. But the battle pennants drooped noticeably when Stride explained why they had come.

"You think that my friend Raymond might have had something to do with Edith's murder?" He stepped back and held the door open wider. "What do you want from me?"

"Information," Stride said. "To your knowledge, had Raymond Butler ever met Edith?"

"Yes, I suppose he must have. He did some work at the house about two years ago when Jack was renovating. A new kitchen and bathroom."

"He was working for Thomas McKinley then?"

"He had a contract with McKinley for that particular job, yes. But Raymond didn't work for anyone but himself. He rebelled against the notion of wages."

"A free spirit," Stride said. Taylor stared at him, then turned away, staring at the bookcase that Butler had made. "We think it's possible that Raymond Butler may have had some kind of a relationship with your stepmother."

"Really?" Taylor shrugged and took a cigarette from the box on the bookcase.

"That doesn't surprise you?"

"As I think I said before, there is little that can surprise me, Mr. Stride."

Stride and Bobby Taylor looked at each other in silence for a minute. A hint of a smile crossed Taylor's face.

"I will guess that you have been talking to my brother's wife." With an emphasis on the last three words.

Stride nodded and returned the smile.

Harry Phelan listened to the exchange, taking it in, not certain what was going on between Stride and Taylor.

"When was the last time you saw Raymond Butler, Mr. Taylor?"

"A day or two before Edith was killed."

"You said you were out walking by yourself that Saturday night. Do you know where Butler was that night?"

"When Edith was being killed, you mean? No, I don't." Taylor walked to the bookcase that Butler had made for him. He touched the top shelf, running his fingers over the dark wood. His mood had dropped since Stride and Phelan had arrived, worry lines starting to show on his face.

"Have you tried to contact Butler since that Saturday?"

"Several times, but with no success. It appears he's out of town at present."

"Is this usual? Does he often go away without telling you?"

"It's not unusual." He smiled. "Ray comes and goes. Sometimes he tells me, sometimes he doesn't. We aren't married, after all."

Phelan looked from Taylor to Stride, and back. The penny dropped. His expression clouded and he walked to the window and watched the activity on the street. He took out a cigarette, stared at it for a moment, then lit it.

"You didn't find it curious that Butler disappeared immediately after your stepmother was murdered?"

"No," he said. But Taylor's tone had changed. Stride believed that he had thought about it. Or was thinking about it now.

"Did you know that Raymond Butler's real name is Ambrose White?"

This time, Taylor looked almost startled.

"No. I didn't know that. Point to you, Mr. Stride. It is possible to surprise me, after all." He sat in one of his leather armchairs and crossed his legs. He stared at the window for a time before speaking. "Will you favour me with an explanation? Please?"

Stride sat down and summarised what they knew about Ambrose White. Taylor listened intently, resting his forehead on the fingertips of his left hand. When Stride was finished, Bobby Taylor sat silently for a minute. He touched his fingertips to the scar on his cheek. Stride noticed the gesture and he and Taylor exchanged glances. Taylor abruptly stood up and pulled on his jacket.

"Ray lives in the west end, on Craigmillar. I'll take you there."

Taylor unlocked the door to Raymond Butler's flat. The windows were covered with heavy drapes and the interior had the close atmosphere of a place that hadn't been lived in for a while. Taylor flicked a switch that turned on the lights of a four-bulb fixture attached to the ceiling in the centre of the room. He looked around as though expecting Butler to appear from out of the shadows. Stride stood just inside the doorway and took his time looking around. The room was sparsely furnished, with only the bare necessities. Two worn armchairs, a small table with two wooden ladder-back chairs, a hot plate. There was a second room off to the right, the door wide open.

"That's the bedroom," Taylor said, walking towards the door. "Ray shares a bathroom with the tenants of two other flats."

The single adornment in the place was a collection of six framed photographs on one wall, above a small writing desk. They were pictures of Butler and some of his mates from the war. A green beret and a dagger flanked the photos. The whole array was enclosed in a display case with a glass front, no doubt made by Butler himself.

Stride looked closely at the beret and the dagger and then questioningly at Taylor.

"Regimental issue?" Phelan asked. He ran his finger across the wooden frame.

"Not exactly," Stride said. He turned to Taylor again. "I assume you know what these are? Are they just souvenirs, or did Butler earn them the hard way?"

"I know what they are, Mr. Stride. And he did earn them the hard way."

"I guess I'm the odd man out," Phelan said. "These have some special significance?"

"Very special, Harry. This is an F-S dagger. F-S for Fairbairn-Sykes. The dagger and the beret are Commando issue."

"Commandos?" Phelan said. "Jesus Christ."

"Ray volunteered for Commando training in early 1942," Taylor said. "He was involved in a number of operations. He was wounded in November 1944 when his outfit, Number 4 Commando, along with Royal Marine Commandos, attacked Walcheren Island off the Dutch coast."

"He originally enlisted in the artillery, though?"

"Yes. Early in 1940, and sailed to England that spring. He was with the 166th. When the opportunity came to try for the Commandos, he took it. The special training appealed to him."

"And the special danger."

"That, too." Taylor pulled the drapes back from one of the windows and opened it. A freshening breeze infiltrated the room. "It's stuffy in here. I'll leave this open until we leave." He sat on the arm of one of the easy chairs. He didn't look comfortable, all of his cockiness gone now.

"You understand that we have to find Butler as soon as possible."

"Yes." Taylor looked away from Stride and ran his fingers through his hair. "Do you have any evidence that Ray killed Edith?"

"We have his fingerprints from the bathroom. Butler's living under an assumed name also doesn't help his case. We think he also probably had motive. Revenge." Stride sat in the second easy chair. "How much do you know about your father's involvement with Jennifer White?"

"Jennifer White? Is she related to Ambrose White? To Ray?"

"Jennifer is his sister. She married a number of years ago. Her name now is Jennifer Cole."

"I don't know anything about her. Ray never mentioned having a sister. All I ever knew about his family was that his parents are dead. Family was one of the areas we didn't visit together. What does Jennifer Cole have to do with my father?"

Stride took Bobby Taylor on a quick tour through the White family's history. When he had finished, Taylor closed his eyes and shook his head slowly back and forth.

"So you think Ray killed Edith because he thinks Jack put his sister in the family way? I suppose people have killed for less." He lit a cigarette and exhaled a cloud of smoke with dramatic flair. "Poor old Jack. The sins of his youth and early manhood have come back to haunt him in triplicate. It's almost comical. Or it would be if it weren't so fucking awful. But one can see a sort of rough justice in it all, I suppose."

"Poor old Jack?" Stride said. Taylor's sentiment puzzled him, all the more because it appeared to be sincere.

"Appearances and rumours to the contrary, Mr. Stride, I know more about my father, and I'm probably closer to him, than anyone else in our sad little family. Call it our little secret, if you will. But I don't wish to leave you with a false impression of family togetherness. I don't like my father very much, and he doesn't much like me. It won't surprise you to learn that he despises my lifestyle. Once we accepted the realities, though, we began to get along much better with each other. Honesty occasionally has that effect. We became something almost like friends, contradictory as that might seem."

"It is contradictory," Stride said. "But why 'Poor old Jack'? It has a tragic ring to it."

"That might be a bit heavy, Inspector, but never mind. I expect you've learned most of what you know about my father from Joanne. Perhaps also from Ned, poor fellow, cooling his heels now in a cell downtown. They both think that Jack is a womaniser, par excellence, or at least that he was until he had his little stroke last year. As it happens, their information, and yours, is wildly out of date."

Taylor stood up, walked to where Phelan was standing by the window and looked out at the street for a minute. He returned to the chair and sat down heavily.

"My father was an utter bastard when he was young. He cheated on my mother every chance he got. He had one girlfriend after another, sometimes several at the same time. We have reason to think that he knocked up one of our housekeepers, back before Edith came on the scene." He laughed suddenly and shook his head. "Aunt Becky could tell you a story about that." Then he was serious again. "Bastard though Jack might have been, he isn't an idiot, and he knew that Jean committed suicide that day on Conception Bay, whatever the inquest ruled. And the fact is he never got over that. He was responsible for her death, and he knew it." He paused again, seemingly weary. "It's almost biblical, in its way, Old Testament stuff. You see, my father has been impotent since my mother's death in 1924. Poor Jack. He lugs this monster reputation around with him, and he couldn't get it up if his life depended on it."

"Does Raymond Butler know any of this?"

"Not from me. As I told you: Ray and I had an understanding. There were things we didn't talk about. Just like in the military. You know, no talk about religion, politics, or sex. Except, with Ray and me, it was family."

"Then, as far as Butler knows, your father could have been responsible for his sister's pregnancy."

"Yes, I suppose so."

"Has it occurred to you that Butler pursued a friendship with you in order to get closer to your father?"

"I suppose I have to admit that's possible, in light of what you've told me about him. In my experience, people frequently have hidden agendas."

"In any case," Stride said, "we have to find him." He wondered if Taylor was really as coolly pragmatic as he now appeared. "Can you suggest where he might be?"

Taylor shook his head. He smiled unexpectedly, a measure of puckishness returning.

"I wonder if you have any idea just how resourceful Ray can be."

"Probably not. Enlighten us."

"The short answer is, very. I'll give you an example. He told me that the year after the war, after he got out of hospital here in the city and was well again, he walked into the wilderness, and spent four months there, living off the land and the sea. Just for the hell of it. Or maybe to prove to himself that he still had the goods. He went off late in September, and came back in January. He had a knife, a gun and a small axe, some line and some hooks. He improvised everything else. He said it was a fine holiday."

Phelan looked across the room at Taylor and seemed about to say something but he turned away without speaking. He resumed his study of the street below.

"Does he own any firearms now?" Stride asked. "And is he likely to have taken one with him?"

"In fact Ray has a collection of weapons. Souvenirs, after a fashion, but all of them in mint condition. If he felt so inclined, he could stage a small insurrection. He keeps them in the bedroom, behind a false panel." Taylor was energised again, his earlier weariness dissipated. "Let's have a shufti, shall we?"

The false panel was another tribute to Butler's carpentry skills. The casual observer would not have known it was there. Stride wondered if he himself would have noticed it. Taylor removed eight screws with a small knife that he had taken from his pocket. Stride blinked when the panel came down. The collection included eight firearms of various kinds and calibres. Stride recognised all of them. And there was a vacant spot that would have held a ninth, a handgun.

"I can give you the guided tour, if you like," Taylor said, "but I think you're probably more interested in what isn't here." He pointed at the vacant spot. "That was a Beretta, 9mm, an Italian semi-automatic. Ray told me he took it from a German officer on Walcheren. Then he killed him with it. Raymond Butler wasn't taking prisoners that day."

thirty
six

"Armed and dangerous, eh?" Jack McCowan slumped back in his chair and looked at Stride over the top of his desk. He stroked his mutton chops with one hand and tapped a letter opener on the wood surface with the other. He stared at the opener, as if surprised to find it in his hand, then carefully placed it on a pad of writing paper, arranging it so that it was dead centre on the pad, and parallel with the sides. He stood up and walked to the window.

"Potentially very dangerous, sir. As I said, White—as Raymond Butler—was a Commando for more than two years."

"He plays in a different league than our lads, then, doesn't he?" McCowan turned away from the window and took a cigar from the box on his desk. "I don't fancy re-enacting the charge up San Juan Hill with that bugger sitting at the crest. How much help do you think young Taylor will be willing to give us, when we get down to the short strokes and the heavy breathing?"

"He says he'll try to talk Butler into giving himself up, if and when we locate him."

"Can we trust him?"

"I think so. I think Taylor has some personal experience of Butler's violent streak."

"Really? He told you that?"

"No. But he has a scar on his face that he claims resulted from a tavern brawl. I think Butler gave it to him."

"You're guessing, though."

"An educated guess."

"Well, perhaps we can hope that young Taylor will come through for us. But best be prepared for a sudden change-of-heart. It's also hard to guess what Butler, White—whatever—will do if and when, as you say, that moment does arrive. And for Christ's sake, decide what we're calling this fellow. Butler or White? Which?"

"He's been Raymond Butler for a long time, now, sir."

"Then Butler it is. Probably be a relief to his sister, anyway, not to have what's left of the family name bruited around in association with a murder investigation. I take it Taylor doesn't have any idea where Butler is?"

"No, sir. He says that Butler was in the habit of disappearing for various periods of time."

"Interesting friendship. Couple of odd birds, I'd say, and well-matched by the sound of it." McCowan gave Stride an appraising glance.

Stride considered bringing the Field Marshal up to speed on Taylor and Butler, but passed. He didn't want to have a discussion of sexual preferences with McCowan.

"The thing is, Eric, we still don't have any direct evidence that Butler killed Edith Taylor. It's all circumstantial. We don't want to precipitate a bloodletting while trying to bring in some fellow just for questioning. Granted he's being elusive, and that has the smell of guilt, but given his peculiar background, his playing hard-to-get is not really surprising. I want this handled very carefully."

Stride nodded. As if he would play it any other way. But he was relieved that the District Inspector was taking a cautious approach. He had had a moment of concern that McCowan's military background might have lurched forward in the circumstances.

"Then there's the sister, Mrs. Cole," McCowan said. "You say Butler may have made an attempt to contact her a little while back?"

"Yes. She says she's almost certain that she caught sight of him outside her house, but that he left in a hurry when he saw her looking at him. We've alerted the patrols in the area, and Mrs. Cole has been advised to call us if she hears from her brother."

"Will she co-operate with us, I wonder? Blood will out at the damnedest times, and when least expected. Feel better about going into a roll of barbed wire than family conflicts. We can't be certain how she might react if he does make contact with her, can we?"

"Not really, sir, but we've tried to take that into consideration. Mrs. Cole says she doesn't feel that she's in danger, but I don't want to take any chances. We've also gotten word to Henry Thompson that Ambrose White—Butler—may be in the city and that we're looking for him."

"The wood-worker fellow? That's probably wise. Did he ask for protection, I wonder?"

"Yes, he did. But when I asked him why he felt he needed it, he demurred."

"What's your reading of Thompson, Eric? Do you think he's a bloody poofter like his friend Downe from Portugal Cove, has a liking for young boys?"

"Harry asked a few discreet questions around the neighbourhood, and the majority opinion was that his tastes ran that way, yes. But it also appears that he's generally respected as a good man of business."

"A good man of business, you say." McCowan was smiling. "If I remember my Dickens, Scrooge used the very same phrase to describe Jacob Marley. And we know what his ultimate reward was. Well, I expect our friend Butler will tell us a tale or two when we catch him. If we catch him." McCowan stared at Stride for a moment and sighed. "Never know what's going on behind the shutters in the dark of night, even in the most respectable establishments. I could tell you a few stories."

"Yes, sir." But not just now, if you please.

"I just had a thought," McCowan said. He had finished preparing his cigar and had picked up the ornate Ronson from his desk.

"Sir?"

"Fellow named Coveyduck I met at Government House the year the war ended. One of those post-war rah-rah do's where everyone gets pissed on port wine drinking toasts to the Royals and to what's left of the bloody Empire." McCowan pulled on his cigar sending clouds of blue smoke billowing towards the ceiling. "He was British Army in the last show, a major I think. Well-born, family has property and money. He does some kind of roving diplomatic thing, now, political stuff. Bit pompous, of course, typical upper-class Brit, but not a bad chap, really. Quite liked him in fact, once he pulled the ramrod out of his tailpipe and acknowledged me as a human being. I have his card somewhere."

McCowan pulled open the top drawer of his desk and took out a small black portfolio. He muttered to himself as he thumbed through the collection, smiled several times, and then extracted a white card.

"Got him. Major Roger Coveyduck. Make a note of his phone number and give him a call."

"What's his connection, sir? Something to do with the Commandos?"

"What? Sorry. Got a bit ahead of myself. Yes. Coveyduck told me he had been through the Commando training in '42 or '43—forget which year, exactly—but mangled his leg in a parachute jump and never actually went on any ops. Spent the balance of the war training other chaps for the show. Not likely he ever knew our man Butler, of course, but he might be able to help get some information on him. Expedite things, at least."

"I'll give him a call."

"Yes. Be kind, show the proper deference to his imperial self. You know how the Brits dote on protocol. Send flowers, blow him a kiss, whatever it takes."

"Yes, sir," Stride said. Whatever it takes. He turned to leave.

"One more thing before you go, Eric."

"Sir?"

McCowan was leaning forward in his chair, hands clasped on the desktop. He looked unhappy. His cigar lay on an ashtray, sending a thin ribbon of smoke towards the ceiling.

"I had a trumpet call from the sharp end, yesterday. Did you and Phelan interrogate William Cartwell about the Taylor murder?"

"I wouldn't call it an interrogation, sir. His name came up in the course of the investigation and I thought it desirable to ask him a few questions."

"The sharp end might call that an interrogation." McCowan sat back in his chair. He tapped his thumbs together, a familiar sign of agitation. "Enlighten me, Eric. What is the difference between a few questions and an interrogation?"

"From the sharp end's perspective, sir, there probably isn't any difference."

"Or from William Cartwell's perspective, either, I expect. To say nothing of his uncle's, or Ralph Waldo Hudson's. I don't have to remind you, Eric, that Bert Cartwell and his friend Hudson are men of, shall I say, substance and influence?"

"No, sir, you don't. But, on occasion, it's necessary to ask even the highest and the mightiest a pertinent question or two. They aren't above the law and its processes."

"Yes, we like to think that, don't we? Along with our faith in an afterlife." McCowan placed his hands palms down on the desk and took a deep breath. "Enlighten me further. What is, or was, William Cartwell's connection with Edith Taylor?"

Stride gave him a summary of Edith Wright's involvement with Emma Jeans and, through her, William Cartwell. McCowan's expression remained impassive throughout. When Stride finished, he shrugged.

"Odorous stuff, not quite at the level of original sin, although the linkages are clear enough. I know a few things about Bert Cartwell's approach to business, and to life generally. I have great respect for his industry and intelligence, however, whatever doubts I may entertain about him personally. I wouldn't want him around my daughter—if I had a daughter—but he's the sort of man whose enterprise will provide a job for my daughter's husband. If you get my meaning. It's an interesting constant of history that so much of the progress of our civilisation is due to the self-interest of men who are, when you take an unfiltered look at them, a good deal nearer bastards than saints."

"I take it that it was Hudson who made the complaint?"

"Of course. Hudson handles all that sort of thing for Cartwell. But it wasn't really a complaint, nothing as formal as that. A word in an ear over a glass of single malt. That sort of thing. The volume gets amplified, of course, when it moves in-house." McCowan picked up his cigar and savoured a leisurely drag. "Will it be necessary to ask young Cartwell additional questions, Eric? Or are you done with him?"

"In other words, will there be occasion for the sharp end to pick up the trumpet again?" Stride remembered Cartwell's smug attitude when he and Phelan left the house that day. And how much he would have enjoyed bouncing Cartwell off the walls of his well-appointed library. "I have no additional questions for Mr. Cartwell at the present time, no."

"But you may have more questions in the future?"

"I can't say for sure. But it's possible."

"Yes." McCowan tapped his cigar against the edge of the ashtray and stood up. "I'm not leaning on you, Eric, however it might seem. And I don't really mind if the sharp end leans on me from time to time. It's one of the things they pay me for. But if you have to interview Cartwell again, come see me first. Just as a precaution." He walked around the desk and stood close to Stride. "You don't like William Cartwell much, do you?"

"No, sir, I don't."

"Neither do I." McCowan allowed himself a brief smile. "Tell me, Eric. Is William Cartwell a serious suspect in the Edith Taylor case?"

"I haven't ruled him out, no."

"Even though he was on the other side of the island when Edith Taylor was murdered?"

"The Cartwells have deep pockets, sir."

"And a dodgy past to go with their present arrogance. I'm on your side in this, Eric, but my advice to you is to be very careful." McCowan frowned. "Did you know that William Cartwell's uncle is grooming him, if that's the phrase, for some kind of political future?"

"Yes, I had heard that."

"It could happen, you know. I'd be happier to see pigs take wing, to be honest. With the changes that are coming on this island we will see more than one William Cartwell emerging into the light. It needs thinking about."

"How is the Field Marshal feeling about things?" Phelan asked when Stride returned to the office.

"Not unhappy. He's satisfied that we have all the necessary bases covered. As many as we can realistically cover, at any rate. And he gave me a name. A Major Coveyduck, who works out of Government House. He might be able to help us get information on White's war record."

"That won't hurt our cause."

"No, it won't." Stride tapped his fingers on the desk. "We know that Butler was with an artillery regiment until '42 when he volunteered for Commando training, and that he was wounded in November '44 in Holland."

"It would be nice to know where he was in late June of 1943," Phelan said.

"Yes. But it's a stretch, isn't it? What are the chances that he managed to get leave and then somehow catch a flight to St. John's in the middle of the war?"

"I agree that it sounds like a long shot, sir, but it wasn't unheard of. There were a lot of military flights back and forth across the Atlantic. I read somewhere that there was a flight in and out of Gander every minute of every day at the height of the war. It was the world's busiest airport for a couple of years. A resourceful fellow might well have managed to be on one of those."

Resourceful. It was the same word that Taylor had used to describe Raymond Butler.

"I wonder, Harry. At first glance it seems too contrived. But let's think about it. Butler has finished his Commando training and he's slated to take part in a series of operations."

"And his sympathetic C.O. gives him a fortnight's leave and might even have helped him arrange a flight home to see his nearest and dearest since there's a good chance he could buy the farm."

"He arrives in St. John's, intent on re-establishing contact with the sole surviving member of his family and finds her doing frontal manoeuvres with a Yank."

"Which makes him very angry."

"So he picks up a blunt object, caves Petrelli's head in, and dumps the body on the South Side."

They looked at each other in silence, weighing the possibility.

"Creating dead bodies was a Commando speciality, and I've heard less plausible scenarios. We'll have to wait until we get our hands on Butler's service file. Let's just hope that the military's passion for mind-numbing detail holds up in this case. And that the good Major can pull the required strings to speed the information in our direction."

Stride picked up the phone and gave the operator Roger Coveyduck's telephone number.

"While we're waiting to see Coveyduck, Harry, I want to talk to Jack Taylor again."

He turned his attention back to the telephone. "Major Coveyduck, please."

thirty
seven

Jack Taylor didn't smile when he saw Stride and Phelan standing on his landing, but he stepped back and held the door open for them to enter.

"More questions, I suppose?"

Taylor had a grey, unhealthy look, and his breath, when Stride walked past him, was stale and unpleasant. Stride thought he detected a hint of alcohol, gin possibly, but a glance around the living and dining rooms did not find any bottles or glasses in evidence.

"Yes, Mr. Taylor, more questions, I'm afraid."

Taylor regarded Stride through tired, slightly bloodshot eyes but didn't reply. He led them into the kitchen where he sat down heavily on a wooden chair.

"We want to ask you some questions about a murder that took place near here in 1943." Stride sat at the table while Phelan leaned against the sink by the window. The woodwork around the window had been repainted since Stride's last visit.

"A murder in 1943?" Taylor looked surprised and his brow furrowed as he tried to fill in the blank. Then his eyes brightened. "Yes. That American boy with the Italian name. The one whose body they found on the South Side. I remember that. I recall reading that you were the officer in charge, Mr. Stride. You've never discovered what happened to him, have you?"

"No, we haven't," Stride replied. "The fact is, the trail went cold very quickly." He rolled words around in his head before speaking again. "Petrelli was with two young women that night. We've recently spoken to both of them. Rita Fleming and Jenny Cole."

Taylor nodded his head. Stride looked carefully at him when he spoke again.

"Jenny Cole's name before she was married was Jennifer White."

He had Taylor's attention now. His cheeks coloured and he appeared to withdraw into himself. He closed his eyes as though his head had suddenly started aching. After a minute he spoke.

"I will spare us the charade of pretending that I don't know her name. I do, of course, and you obviously are aware of her connection with me. I don't know exactly what you've found out, or been told. Perhaps you will tell me."

Stride nodded and gave Taylor the substance of what they had learned about Jennifer White, and of Taylor's agreement to provide for her and her child.

"We know you weren't the father of Jennifer White's child. Who was the father?"

"I'm not at liberty to say, Inspector. In any event, I can't imagine there is any connection between that incident and Edith's murder."

"What your imagination might encompass, Mr. Taylor, is pretty much beside the point. Jennifer White's pregnancy ended up destroying what was left of her family, and we know that many people believed you were responsible. And it's my opinion that you wanted people to believe that. Why would you do that, Mr. Taylor?"

Stride tilted his head against the back of the chair and pretended to study the ceiling. Taylor's phrase "not at liberty" could mean anything.

"When we talked to you a few days ago, you said you'd never heard of Ambrose White. Do you still say that?"

Taylor grinned.

"What I actually said was that I had never met an Ambrose White. I was surprised that you didn't jump on that then." He made a dismissive gesture with his hand. "But it doesn't matter. I knew that Jennifer had a brother, and that his name was Ambrose. But I had never met him, and never expected to. He didn't mean anything to me. I also knew that he and Jennifer had lost contact with each other."

Taylor's blasé response, his apparent inability to imagine that other people might have agendas, might hold feelings that he didn't share, was hugely irritating. Stride felt a band of heat encircle his forehead. He took a long breath, tried to calm down. He didn't quite make it.

"Has it occurred to you that your wife might have been murdered as revenge for the disasters that struck the White family after Jennifer became pregnant? For which some people held you responsible? That perhaps

Ambrose White decided, using a sort of tortured logic, to even the score?"

Taylor didn't respond and he continued to stare straight ahead, but his expression was clouded, his face turning red. Stride wondered if this was really the first time that the possible connections had occurred to him.

Phelan's expression told Stride that he was starting to lay it on a bit thick. But Taylor had angered him with his smart-ass comment about Ambrose White, so he didn't really care. He managed not to bring up the matter of Jean Taylor's suicide, although the sentences were already forming.

Stride stood up and walked to the window. He looked across the street where he could just see someone standing behind the sheer curtains in the Gatherall living room. A woman, he thought.

Stride allowed his anger to recede before he turned back to Taylor. Tide going out. He took his time.

"I'll leave you with a thought, Mr. Taylor. Your wife's killer is out there somewhere. We can't know for sure who it is, until we catch him. But if it was Ambrose White, you might soon have the opportunity to meet him in person. It's possible that you might have things to talk about. If he gives you the opportunity. I wish you luck."

With that, Stride headed for the door. He stood in Jack Taylor's driveway and lit a cigarette. After a minute, Phelan joined him.

"I know. I went way beyond the protocol."

"Yes, sir."

"He pissed me off, Harry."

"I believe he has a special talent for that."

"Do you think he has grounds for a formal complaint?"

"Maybe. I told him that we're looking for White and that we've circulated his picture. And I made certain he had the number of the station." Phelan drew a circle in the gravel driveway with the toe of his shoe. "I also gave him our home numbers, told him he could call either of us any time, night or day. Just in case White was to show up on his doorstep."

Stride played with the scenario, Jack Taylor phoning him in the middle of the night, worried that Ambrose White was lurking in the shadows. He skipped through a couple of variations, none of them really in line with official protocol. He was smiling now.

"Feeling a little more cheerful are you, sir?"

"Yes," Stride said. "I was just thinking about various scenarios involving Ambrose White and Jack Taylor. They aren't really funny, of course. Unless you have a certain point of view."

Phelan laughed. "I can imagine what the point of view might be."

"I'm sure you can, Harry." He looked across the street at the Gatherall house. He was almost certain that he had seen the figure there again, behind the curtains.

"I noticed her, too," Phelan said, glancing towards the Gatherall house. "I expect the Taylor house is a prime source of local entertainment."

"You're probably right. Anyway, I owe you one, Harry. Whatever happens."

They walked to the car. Stride started the motor of the MG, revved it a couple of times, warming it up before shifting into gear. As the car started to move down the hill, Stride glanced back over his shoulder. Rose Gatherall was standing in her living room window now, the curtains pulled back, watching as they drove away.

thirty
eight

Roger Coveyduck was standing by the office window, hands behind his back, when Stride and Phelan arrived at the station. He was holding a cane of dark wood, and tapping the stainless-steel tip against the heel of his right shoe. He looked as though he was about to review troops on the parade ground, ready to give them hell for being a sliver less than perfect. He turned when Stride and Phelan came into the office. He didn't smile. He consulted his watch and looked at each of them in turn.

"Name's Coveyduck, gentlemen. I'm here in response to your request for information on one Raymond Butler. Our former Commando. Your call yesterday engaged my interest, Mr. Stride. To the tune of a half-dozen trans-Atlantic telephone calls, no less. Not often one can inspire that sort of activity in the government bureaucracy these days. Usually takes a couple of mortar rounds just to get the eyelids fluttering. Of course, things have gone steadily downhill since peace broke out. Bloody Labour Government, what can you expect? Gaggle of union yobboes marching sternly backwards to the jangle of tambourines."

Coveyduck took out a gold cigarette case and placed a cork-tipped cigarette between his lips. As an afterthought, he extended the case towards Stride and Phelan. Both declined. Coveyduck lit his cigarette with a small gold lighter.

"We've had problems with some of the ex-Commandos. You won't be surprised to hear that, of course. Magnificent group of fellows on the whole, highly efficient fighting machines. None better. But for the odd few, it has been hard to meld back into the post-war, work-a-day world. Understandable, of course." Coveyduck permitted himself a fleeting grin. "Mind you, some of them weren't exactly model citizens before they put on the khaki."

"Did you have any luck with Raymond Butler, Major?" Stride pulled out a chair but Coveyduck waved a hand and continued to stand, leaning now on his cane.

"Yes, I have, as a matter of fact. I managed to find exactly the right contact in London on only the third try. Bloody miraculous, really. He located Butler's service record for me and gave me some information over the phone. He's shipping copies of the relevant bits across the pond in a diplomatic pouch, and you should have them in a few days, a week at most. Things can work very well if you know exactly which buttons to push."

Coveyduck picked up a leather briefcase and flipped it open. He took out several pages of handwritten notes.

"Your man Butler volunteered in 1942 and did his initial training in Scotland at the Training Centre at Achnacarry. He also trained in North Wales and Cornwall. I understood that it's the period around the end of June 1943 that you are interested in." Coveyduck turned to a new page. "By then, Butler had been in training for more than a year and there were some major ops coming up. It wasn't unheard of for chaps to get leave before heading out to something from which they might not return."

"So, Butler did get leave around that time?"

"Yes. Quite a long leave, in fact, two weeks all told. I expect the fact that he lived on the other side of the Atlantic might have had something to do with that. He began his leave on 19 June, 1943, and was back with his outfit, 4 Commando, on 3 July."

"Do they say where he went?" Stride asked. "Is it possible that he managed to catch a trans-Atlantic flight, made his way back to St. John's?"

"There's no information on that, I'm afraid." Coveyduck walked across the room, leaning on his cane, and sat on the edge of Phelan's desk. "The military is rigorous on record-keeping, of course, especially in wartime, but there is a limit. Once he was off on leave, Butler was on his own. His outfit would only get interested in his whereabouts if he didn't show up on time after his leave expired. But I will say that I personally know of instances where men on leave managed to jump on trans-Atlantic flights. It wasn't unheard of."

"But we don't know where Butler was for the two weeks."

"No." Coveyduck shrugged. "If he did catch a flight, there's probably a record of that somewhere amongst the crates of documents in England, or elsewhere. I could suggest that you get someone to plough through the local records for the period you're interested in. If Butler did come back to

St. John's, he would have flown into Torbay, I suppose. Perhaps their logs are available. They might tell you something."

Stride looked at Phelan.

"Good project for one of the new men," Phelan said. "Clue him into what a boring job policing really is."

"Got someone good in mind, Harry? It's a long shot, but we don't want it fucked up." He looked across at Coveyduck. "Pardon the language, Major."

"I'll speak to Crotty," Phelan said. "He's been working with a new lad for the past six weeks. His name's Thornhill. Bern says he's a good man, and nothing much gets past him."

Stride looked back at the Major. Coveyduck was leaning against the windowsill, and flexing his right knee. He moved the damaged joint slowly and deliberately.

"Your District Inspector didn't tell me what Butler might have done, just that it was high priority. None of my business, of course, but I like to keep tabs on former comrades. It didn't all end on V-J Day, you know."

"We want Butler for questioning in a murder investigation."

"You must want him for more than questioning, Stride." There was an edge to Coveyduck's voice now. Stride stared at him. He didn't like the change in tone and didn't appreciate being addressed by his last name. "You must have decided already that he might be the guilty party. Surely."

Stride tapped his fingers on his desk. He also didn't appreciate people telling him what he must surely be thinking. Still, Coveyduck had obtained information for them. Stride conjured up an image of Jack McCowan, and put on his official smile. He stepped closer to Coveyduck.

"As a matter of fact, Major, Raymond Butler is our principal suspect in this murder."

"And this took place almost four years ago?" Coveyduck had caught the change in Stride's manner and did a quick reassessment of the situation, marshalling his diplomatic skills, softening his tone. "I'm confused as to why the case has an urgency now. Four years is a very long time. Can you explain things to me, Inspector Stride? I would appreciate it." Punctuated with a cautious smile.

"In fact, we're investigating two murders, Major Coveyduck, one in 1943 and the second very recently. We think they might be related. We know that Butler was in the city when the more recent killing took place, and that he was acquainted with the victim. We would like to know if there's a possibility he may also have been here when the first murder took place four years ago. The dates you gave us suggest that it's possible he was here."

Coveyduck turned away and looked through the window. His hands were behind his back again and he was once more tapping the metal tip of his stick against his heel. Then he turned to face Stride and Phelan.

"Butler's record tells me he was a good man on the whole. He almost bought the packet in Holland, you know." Coveyduck picked up his stick, examined the steel point, then leaned on it again. "There are two items, though. You'll read them for yourself when Butler's file arrives. There's a note on his record to the effect that he used excessive force during the Walcheren operation. Silly bloody phrase for wartime, of course. Probably a term dreamed up by some limp-wristed bureaucratic jackass who wouldn't know which end of a rifle a bullet emerges from. The incident had something to do with the shooting of a German officer. I expect that at the field level, it was less a concern about one more dead Jerry, officer or not, than about the intelligence that might have died with him."

Stride remembered Bobby Taylor's comment about Butler taking no prisoners.

"And the second item?"

"Yes," Coveyduck said, leaning on his stick and frowning. "A publican in a village a few miles from Achnacarry was badly beaten, almost killed in fact, and spent a long time in hospital after that. It seems that the fellow had a predilection for young men, especially young men in uniform. In other words, a bloody queer. Got less than he deserved, in my view." Coveyduck crushed his cigarette in an ashtray.

"Butler was involved in this?"

"It's not certain to what extent he was involved, but he was questioned about it, yes."

"He wasn't charged?"

"No. No charges were ever laid, and the publican didn't press the issue. He was as interested as anyone in letting the matter fade away." Coveyduck gave Stride a searching look. "I was reluctant to pass this bit of information along, had mixed feelings about it. It can't help Butler's case, I realise. But facts, as Mr. Bumble might have said, is facts."

'*And the law, sir, is a ass*,' Stride thought.

"No matter," Coveyduck said. "It saddens me to see chaps like Butler fall onto hard times. But if he's guilty of murder, I hope you bring him in. And if he isn't, I hope you'll be able to exonerate him. Either way, I wish you good luck in your investigation."

Coveyduck gave his notes to Stride, and closed his briefcase. He leaned heavily on his cane while walking to the door. He paused there.

"I am pleased, if not happy, to have been of assistance, Inspector. As I said, you will probably have the actual files in a little while. In the meantime, look after those notes, and please return them to me when—and if—you have no further need of them. I would appreciate it. You have my card."

He raised a hand, half-salute, turned, and left the office. They could hear his cane tapping against the wooden floor as he slowly made his way down the corridor.

Stride picked up Coveyduck's notes and went through them, then passed them to Phelan. He pulled Butler's file from the cabinet and placed the pictures of Ambrose White—the photograph that Herbert Rodgers had given them and the two drawings by Herc Parsons—side by side on his desk. He and Phelan studied them in silence for a minute.

"Are you thinking the same thing I am, sir?" Phelan had picked up a pencil and he tapped the eraser against his chin.

"That we still haven't actually set eyes on Ambrose White?"

"Yes, that too."

Stride looked at Phelan, questioning.

"You're thinking that maybe we won't ever see him?"

"I do think about that. But then I sometimes think he'll turn up when we least expect him to."

"Hold onto both those thoughts, Harry. That way you won't be disappointed."

After Phelan left for the day, Stride pulled the pictures of Ambrose White from the file and lined them up again on the desktop. He went from picture to picture, not looking for anything in particular. He wondered if Harry would be proved right, that they might never actually come face to face with Ambrose White, with Butler. The fact that Butler had been standing in front of Jenny Cole's house only days ago didn't offer a lot of encouragement. If anything, the opposite could be the case. Butler had apparently run away, and for all they knew he might still be running, out of the city to God-knew-where. He thought about Bobby Taylor's story of Butler legging it out into the wilderness for four months, just for the hell of it, fall and winter months, at that. He placed the pictures back in the file and slid the door of the cabinet shut.

When he turned, Margaret Nichol was standing in the doorway.

"All work and no play," she said.

"Makes Eric a dull boy?" Stride said. Margaret wasn't smiling.

"I don't think you'll ever be a dull boy, Eric." She walked into the tiny office and picked up his package of cigarettes. "May I?"

Stride nodded and took out his lighter. Margaret drew on the cigarette and walked to the window. It was starting to get dark, the stage of long shadows, the sun making ready to leave.

"I haven't seen very much of you, Eric, and you haven't called."

"I know. I am sorry." He had not talked to her since their last evening together. "I've been neglectful."

"No, I don't think that's it. You've been neglectful in the past, and I've become more or less used to that. It's part of what you are. You retreat into yourself and stay there for a while, apart from everyone, me included. I don't think there's a great deal wrong with that, it even has an odd charm. Mind you, it's not my preferred choice for a way to live, but, as I said, I've gotten used to it. Caring about you allowed me to do that." She leaned against the window sill and looked at him. "In the past, I've been fairly certain that I knew where you were, that you were coming back. This time, I'm not."

He thought of mounting an argument, tell her that it was a difficult case, tracks leading in a half-dozen directions. But he knew, even before he formulated the sentences, that neither of them could believe it. So there it was again, his patented granite wall of indecision and conflict.

"I understand that," he said, at last. It was beyond feeble, but it was all he could manage.

"Do you?" She straightened up. He could sense her anger, compounded by hurt. For a moment he thought she would flare, loose it against him, and part of him wished that she would do that, hurl it into plain view. But the moment passed. She wouldn't do him the favour. Margaret walked to the desk and crushed her cigarette in the ashtray.

"Well, perhaps you do understand," she said. "In your way." She stood in the doorway, facing him, buttoning her coat, brushing away some ash that had dropped from her cigarette.

"I know that something's going on, Eric. You're more transparent than you think. And this is a small town, after all. I'd prefer you told me about it in person, rather than hearing it from a third party." She looked at him. "But I can see that this isn't going to be the day. I suppose I'll have to wait." She turned, took a single step down the corridor, then turned back. "But I won't wait a long time."

After he left the Fort, Stride needed to talk to a friend. He drove to Thomas Butcher's house on Waterford Bridge Road. Butcher wasn't there. The housekeeper told him that the doctor was attending to four house calls, three of them pregnancies nearing the final stages. She laughed then, said that August had always been a good month for making babies, the warm nights making people restless. She said she would tell Dr. Butcher that he had called.

Still agitated, Stride climbed back into the MG and drove west along Waterford Bridge Road, continued west on Topsail Road, and drove on to Holyrood, at the bottom of Conception Bay. He focused on his driving, accelerating whenever the road ahead was clear. He had left the top down, and with the wind ripping through his hair, he could forget about Margaret and Joanne sometimes, and even about his remarkable capacity for complicating his life. And his inability to resolve personal conflicts.

A small restaurant in Holyrood was still open and he bought a meal of fish and chips. He ate it on the beach, sitting on an upturned dory that was missing most of its planking on the starboard side. Two small boys, both wearing blue dungarees, wool sweaters and rubber boots, sat on rocks watching him while he ate. Stride hadn't entertained high expectations of the restaurant, but the chips were good and the cod was fresh, deep-fried in a light batter. The boys turned away from him each time he tried to make eye contact, looking out to sea, occasionally skipping flat stones across the smooth surface of the water, making a contest out of it.

Stride finished the last of his meal, crumpled the paper into a ball and deposited it under the dory with the collection of rubbish already there. He walked over to the boys and picked up a flat stone and shied it at the water. It struck the surface at a bad angle, skipped three times in a sharp half-circle and quickly sank. Rotten throw. The younger of the boys grinned up at him.

"I got eight just now, and me brudder got ten."

"You've got me beat," Stride said. "I'm out of practice." He picked up a stone, gave it to the boy. "Show me."

The boy took the stone, spread his feet for balance, and shied it towards the water, straight out from the shore, skipping it expertly across the surface, five, six, seven, eight times, before it sank.

"I done nine once," he said. "Me best ever."

Stride picked up another stone, gave it to the older boy, who still had not spoken. He looked at Stride for a moment, still silent, but took the stone and walked closer to the water's edge, crouched low and executed a graceful wrist-throw. The stone skipped eleven times before sinking.

"He's some good," the younger boy said. "He can throw a baseball real good, too." The older brother listened to all this, still said nothing, but picked up a beach stone about half the size of a baseball and casually pitched it two hundred feet out into the bay. He gave Stride a brief appraising glance.

"You like fish and chips?" Stride asked.

"Yah." The younger boy's eyes were shining with anticipation. The older brother glanced in Stride's direction, his expression still neutral.

"My treat," Stride said. He took a dollar bill from his wallet and gave it to the older boy. The boy stared at the bill, then at Stride, and for an instant Stride thought he would give the money back. Finally, he smiled shyly and said a quiet thank you. Then he took his brother's hand and walked him across the road to the restaurant.

thirty
nine

There are times when you sense that something is wrong, that something bad is about to happen, but more often than not the feeling is ignored, or rationalised away. Later, when the bad thing has happened, you want to take a grip on your head and beat it against a hard surface, teach it a lesson. Stride thought briefly about that when he floated upwards into consciousness on the hooked rug in the living room of his flat. He lay on the floor, not moving, trying to order his thoughts. He sensed that the person who had reduced him to his present state was still in the room. The lights were off, the drapes pulled almost shut, the only illumination a feeble dusting of light from the street lamp, diluting the black of night into a neutral grey.

When Stride unlocked his door, he had felt a vague prickle of apprehension at the nape of his neck that whispered, Take care! He hadn't done that. There was a brief sensation of something, then nothing. Now he had a feeling of being unwell, of having received a physical insult that was as unpleasant as it was undefined. He had no sense that he had been struck a blow, no real pain, no blood from a head wound. His hands were firmly secured behind his back, and it took only a moment to realise that his wrists were circled with handcuffs, almost certainly his own. His macintosh and jacket had been removed.

Carefully, slowly, now that his eyes had regained their focus, he looked around him, trying not to move very much, lest he encourage another assault.

"Take your time. You're not badly hurt, but it takes a few minutes. Depends on how good a man you are."

The voice was soft, low volume, male. A melange of accents, Newfoundland, Irish, British. It came from a corner of the room near the doorway to the kitchen. Stride judged the speaker was perhaps only five feet away. Easy striking distance. He closed his eyes and breathed slowly.

More silence.

Stride spoke first.

"Should I call you Ambrose or Raymond?" The question, given voice, had more than a touch of the absurd. Melodrama from the helplessly supine.

"It's a long time since anyone called me Ambrose."

"Raymond Butler, then."

"Sure. Raymond's fine." The sound of quiet laughter.

Stride twisted around, trying to see him, hoping to make eye contact. He could see the shape of a man standing in the shadows by the kitchen door, his arms folded in a relaxed posture. After a few moments, Butler moved out of the darker shadows, nearer to Stride but still not close.

Stride knew from Joanne's description that Butler wasn't a big man, no taller than five-seven, barely a hundred and fifty pounds. But there was something about him, the way he carried himself, that suggested a larger physical presence. Butler pulled a hassock close to Stride and sat, resting his elbows on his knees. He looked at Stride, a hint of humour in his expression.

"I'm curious," Stride said. He adjusted his position on the rug to take the weight off his right arm and shoulder. Butler watched him closely. "What did you do?"

"What did I do?"

"To me. When I came in. The lights went out all of a sudden, but I don't have the impression that you hit me."

Butler smiled, the pleased look of a skilled workman who has been complimented for a job well done.

"Hitting people is, well, hit-and-miss. There are better ways."

"Commando training?"

Butler didn't reply. He clasped his hands between his knees, rocking back and forth slightly, a slow even rhythm. He was looking past Stride now, his head tilted upwards.

Stride's right arm and shoulder were aching. They must have taken the weight of his fall. He adjusted his position, but it didn't help much. "Will you help me to sit up?"

"No."

Silence again.

"Why are you here, Ray?"

"Because I am. Instead of being somewhere else. I like visiting people sometimes." Butler laughed suddenly, as if remembering something amusing. "I had a nice look around your estate while you were resting. Quite the place."

"I like it."

"I dare say you do. It's a nicer house than your average copper can afford. And you have an English sports car on top of that. You must be the envy of all who know you, Mr. Stride. However do you manage, I wonder? I think you must have a secret life."

Butler had surprised him. Stride looked closely, trying to read something in his face, but Butler only looked back at him calmly, his expression telling him nothing.

"You ever been married, Mr. Stride?"

"No, I haven't. Why?"

"Just asking. If you had a wife, she could be happy here, I expect. Women being what they are, of course, a wife would probably want the whole house to herself. I suppose she'd send your tenants packing. Do you think?"

Stride was surprised again, but he didn't reply. Butler prodded him with the toe of his boot. He was smiling again.

"Best to answer when asked, Mr. Stride."

"Yes," Stride said. "I expect a wife would find this a comfortable house."

"I dare say."

Butler took out a package of cigarettes and stood up. He lit his cigarette with a wooden match that he ignited with a flick of his thumbnail. The smoke was heavy and pungent.

"I'd offer you one, Mr. Stride, but you're not really in a position to enjoy a fag, are you? Maybe you wouldn't like them anyway." He held up a blue package. "They're French. Not everyone likes them. They're an acquired taste." He smiled. "Like a lot of things."

He walked to the bookcase and picked up an ashtray. It was made from a brass shell casing, a gift from Bern Crotty. Butler turned it over in his hands, studying it.

"A 25-pounder," Butler said. "I'd be a rich man if I had a dollar for every one of these I've fired. I might buy a sports car of my own." He laughed again and smoked his cigarette, tapping it against the metal ashtray. Then he was silent again. After a minute he sat on the hassock and balanced the ashtray on his knee.

The room was silent again.

"Did you visit Edith Taylor that Saturday night?"

"Edith Taylor?"

"Edith Taylor. You know who I'm talking about, Ray."

"Yes." Butler tilted his head back again and looked at the ceiling. Then he smiled. "Edith was quite the lady. A good sort of wife for Jack Taylor."

"Was she?"

"Oh, yes. Mr. Jack Taylor deserves the best."

"Was Edith the best?" Stride tried to pick his words. "We've found out things about her. Not all of them good. Interesting, though."

"I expect so."

"Did you visit her that night, Ray? The night she was killed."

"You already asked me that."

"You didn't answer, though." Stride paused. "When did you meet her, Ray? When you installed the new kitchen in her house?"

Butler looked at him, for an instant showing surprise. Then he looked away.

"You left fingerprints in the Taylor house." Butler still didn't reply. "You left them with us once before. When we arrested you, in 1936, when you were someone else."

Butler continued to stare at him, but his attitude had shifted subtly, a tension moving through him.

"When you were still Ambrose White." Stride took a chance. "When you worked for Henry Thompson. After you'd moved on from Benjamin Downe."

Butler stood up suddenly and walked to the bookcase. He was gripping the brass ashtray in his left hand. His cigarette sent a thin ribbon of smoke towards the ceiling. Butler looked at the cigarette as if surprised to find it in his hand. He crushed it against the metal and placed the ashtray on the bookcase. He stood for a moment with his fists against his hips, looking through the kitchen door, silhouetted in the dim light from the window.

"We know a lot about you Ray. People leave tracks and when we have to, we can find out a lot about them." Stride paused, waiting for a response. Butler still didn't move. "That's our business, and we're good at it."

Butler turned suddenly, took a long step towards Stride and lashed out with his foot, driving the toe of his boot into Stride's ribcage. The pain tore through him, forcing the air from his lungs, bringing tears to his eyes. Then Butler kicked him a second time. Stride clenched his teeth, stifling the scream that was leaping from his throat, willing himself not to cry out.

"I'll tell you about my business, Sonny Jim. My business is sending people to the other side, and I'm good at it. I'm goddamned good." Butler spun away from him and walked quickly across the room. He stood in the kitchen doorway, his hands clasped behind his head, rocking back and forth. After a minute he turned back.

"You want to be careful what you say, Mr. Stride. A man should be careful."

They stared at each other across the dimly lighted room. Stride worked at controlling his breathing, pulling small breaths through the pain in his chest. They were silent for what seemed a long time. He tried again.

"There are good people as well as bad, Ray. Not everyone is like Benjamin Downe. You don't have to hide away. Come forward and tell your story. You have a good war record. That can work in your favour."

"Oh, yes. I have a grand record. Hand-to-hand combat. The personal touch. And you think that'll work in my favour, do you? But, you know, the war's been over for a while. A long while. Fellows like me, we're yesterday's heroes. If heroes we ever were." He took a deep breath. Stride could sense the tension rising in him again. "And what do you know about it, anyway? You weren't part of it. You stayed home, chased drunks, ran around in your fancy sports car, went to parties. Lots and lots of parties. It must have been a great time. The old town was bursting at the seams, all those Yanks and Canadians and Brits. Christ, the place was crawling with them. I could hardly believe my eyes."

Stride looked at him. "You're right. It was a busy time. There was a lot going on."

Butler laughed and shook his head.

"Yes, I suppose it was. And I suppose someone had to stay here and be a policeman."

"Someone did, yes. Come in and tell your story, Ray. I'll make you a deal. No one has to know what happened here tonight." He shifted his position so that he could look more directly at Butler. "Tell your story."

"Tell my story? Now, that's an interesting thought. But you know, I've told stories to the police before." Butler was very still.

Butler had surprised him again. He ran Butler's—White's—dossier through his mind, skipped past Benjamin Downe's name, then came back to it. It should have been obvious. Stride drew the scene. The orphaned boy consigned to the care of a man who was, in Herbert Rodgers' delicate phrase, "partial to young men." The boy, unhappy, desperate, goes to the police and asks for help, but his tormentor is an established businessman in a small community. If anyone did know about Downe's predilection, they wouldn't want to talk about it. Like Rodgers himself. It wasn't really a surprise that the constable, stationed miles away in Torbay, wouldn't want to pursue the matter. Easier to look the other way, avoid the fuss, send the boy back home. White goes back to Downe. Later on he's traded off to Henry Thompson in St. John's. Variations on an ageless theme.

Butler's eyes were bright as he read Stride's thoughts. He nodded his head slowly.

"I see that a little light just went on," he said.

"Yes," Stride said. "I know it hasn't been easy for you, Ray. I'm not surprised that you don't trust people. I can understand you're being angry. I think anyone would be."

"You say you're not surprised. Now, what does that mean, I wonder? I wonder if you have any idea at all. Maybe I could show you, give you a guided tour."

He walked to the kitchen door again and leaned on it, both hands against the frame, his head bent low. After a moment he stood suddenly erect and turned back to Stride, reached into his trouser pocket and took out a knife. He snapped the blade open with a touch of his thumb. He knelt on the rug close to Stride and held up the knife, turning it slowly, the steel blade reflecting the pale light from the window. He was breathing slowly, evenly. Stride couldn't read his expression. He tried to move away but Butler held him in place with his left hand, his fingers digging deep into the flesh of his shoulder.

Butler slid the blade under the knot of Stride's tie and cut through it. He pulled the tie from under the shirt collar and dropped it on the floor. Then he cut the top button from Stride's shirt and slid the blade down to the next one.

"I expect you never went to the ice, Mr. Stride. A lot of people did, but they weren't the sort who owned big houses and English sports cars. No."

He cut another button from the shirt.

"There was a man in my town, he went to the ice every year for maybe forty years. They said he was that handy with a knife, he could pelt a seal and leave the naked red carcass shivering on the ice-pan, still alive."

The remaining buttons dropped from Stride's shirt as the knife-blade made its way down his torso. Butler paused and looked into Stride's eyes.

"Myself, now, I never really believed that. I think it was just a story."

Butler rolled Stride over suddenly and ran the blade from cuff to collar, both sides, then pulled the shirt away, leaving Stride naked from the waist up.

He placed one knee in the small of his back, slowly shifted his weight forward until Stride was pinned to the floor. Butler leaned forward, speaking softly, his breath warm against the skin of Stride's neck. He had his hand under Stride's chin, turning his head so their eyes were in contact.

"He liked to come at me in the middle of the night. That was his time. He'd sneak up on me in the dark, catch me sometimes after I went to sleep. What do you suppose that feels like, Mr. Stride, having an old man in your bed, an old man with his hands on you, pulling off your clothes, an old man lying on top of you in the dark, old flesh on young, and no one caring, no one giving a damn? All of them knowing, and all of them looking the other way."

Butler ran his hand across Stride's shoulders, along the upper arms, down his sides.

"You must have been a fine-looking boy." He laughed suddenly, a sharp angry sound. "You would have had a grand career in the wood-working trade, Mr. Stride. Oh yes."

He gripped Stride's neck in his hand, the pressure increasing just to the point where pain would start.

"The thing is, you see, the very worst thing about it, the thing that doesn't go away, is that you get used to it, you accept it, and you almost believe that this is the way it's supposed to be, that it's what you're here for. Like looking at the world through a glass with a twist in it, makes everything distorted and strange. And sometimes you can even laugh at it, it's that funny." Butler's face was very close to Stride's now, his sweat dripping onto Stride's cheek. "And then you don't. One day, it changes, and you start to think about getting your own back. Making them pay the piper. All of them."

Suddenly the weight was off his back, and he could hear Butler moving across the room. Stride worked at regulating his breathing, realised that he had drawn no more than two or three breaths while Butler was cutting his clothes off. There were bright lights behind his eyes, flashing. He had tumbled into fear when he saw the knife, moved beyond fear when Butler pinned him to the floor, moved to another place, a place he knew about but hadn't visited for a long time.

Butler was sitting on the couch now, leaning forward, his elbows on his thighs, looking at Stride, sweat glistening on his face. The knife had disappeared. Butler was smoking another cigarette. He blew smoke around its tip, studied the bright red point. The two men stared at each other for a long time. Butler stood up and crushed his cigarette in the brass ashtray, then kneeled on the floor again.

"You won't hang me for Edith Taylor. And I've told the only story I'll tell. You remember it." He put his hand under Stride's chin and tilted his head up, his fingers pressing deep into the flesh. "Imagine the things I could have done to you this night. You think about that."

He placed his right hand on Stride's cheek, stroking him, almost a caress. Stride tried to roll away, the fear rising again. Butler gripped his shoulder again with his left hand and held him in place, the fingers thrusting hard into the muscle. He whispered to Stride, his voice very soft, like a parent comforting a child.

"I have things to do. If you want me, you're going to have to catch me. And I don't think you can do that." Butler's right hand was on Stride's neck. His voice was lower now. "I've heard it said that if a man believes in heaven, there's nothing on this earth he has to worry about. I wonder if you have the faith."

Butler's finger pushed deep into the flesh of Stride's neck, fanning a hot coal of pain that began to spread outwards. And then there was nothing.

The nausea was there again, more intense than before, and his mouth was dry. He tried to swallow, then feared he would be sick if he did that. He rolled onto his side and took small, shallow breaths. His throat hurt. And he was cold, chilling sweat on his temples and his neck. His left arm was aching, the circulation cut off. He flexed his hands, moved his wrists against the steel of the handcuffs.

He wondered how long he had been out this time. It was as dark in the flat as when Butler had been there. Then he realised that he didn't know how long he had been out the first time, had no idea what time it was. And not knowing the time, he became anxious, and with the anxiety the numbing fear returned. He gave up the struggle and laid his head on the rug, breathing slowly, evenly, fighting for control. Tears rolled across his cheek. A taste of salt in his mouth. He lay still for a long time.

The nausea receded gradually and the anxiety dropped. The sense of crisis passed. With that, his frustration and anger began to rise. Stride pulled and pushed against the handcuffs but succeeded only in chafing and bruising his wrists anew. He wrestled himself to a sitting position, tried to roll onto his knees, but fell over onto his side again. His wrists were aflame, and the pain pushed his anger to a higher level. He reared back and kicked the coffee table across the room and rolled across the floor to the couch, braced his back against it and thrust himself upright. He immediately felt dizzy, the room swimming. He fell onto the couch and waited for the sensation to pass.

After a minute, he sat up again, then walked to the kitchen and picked the phone off the wall hook with his teeth and dropped it on the counter. He bent down and listened to the operator ask for the number, then straightened up and asked her to connect him to the police station. The operator asked if this was an emergency. He told her it was.

The desk constable asked for his name, his voice calm and officious. Stride immediately felt like a tragic fool, standing in his kitchen in the middle of the night, beaten, half-naked, manacled with his own handcuffs. Anger and embarrassment in about equal proportions. He leaned his head against the doorjamb and took a deep breath before answering.

forty

"The bloody man might have done you in right there, on your living room floor."

McCowan stood in front of his desk, his arms crossed over his chest. He rocked back and forth on his heels, the only outward indication of his agitation.

"Yes, sir," Stride said. "He could have, but he didn't."

McCowan grunted and stared at Stride. "The question is, I suppose, why not? He's no stranger to killing, God knows. His service record speaks loudly enough on that point, to say nothing of his most recent adventures. What do you make of it all, Eric?"

"I'm not sure what to think, sir."

And that was close enough to the truth. Stride knew that it had given Butler pleasure to have so easily rendered him helpless, to let him know what it was like to be under someone's control. And he had demonstrated how resourceful he was. Stride wondered how much of last night's events had been scripted in advance and how much had been improvised after Butler's arrival. One thing was clear to him. It had been a personal visit.

The question was why. Stride had no answer for that. He couldn't ignore the possibility that Butler might raise the ante now, play a dark game of hide-and-seek with the police. He had said there were things he wanted to do, but he didn't say what. Butler had to know that the attack on Stride would inspire everyone involved to be especially vigilant. Perhaps he would lie low for a time, or simply disappear. He had shown that he could survive in the wilderness through the worst months of winter. Just for the hell of it, Taylor said. The coming months of spring and summer would provide something like holiday conditions for him.

McCowan's voice brought Stride out of his reverie.

"A bright spot in all this is that we at least know that our man is still in the city. Or at least not very far away. Which again raises the question of why we haven't been able to find him. His picture has been circulated. Is it possible that someone is giving him shelter?"

McCowan sat down behind his desk.

"That part bothers me. Do you think it's possible that someone is helping him? There's the younger Taylor boy."

"I believed Taylor when he told me that he hadn't seen Butler since a few days before the murder. And I've had someone keeping a watch on him, on and off. No one matching Butler's description has ever appeared in his company."

"Really? One of our men?"

"No, sir. Someone who owed me a favour." Which wasn't exactly true, and now Stride owed Jimmy Peach another favour. But that wouldn't be a problem. "I don't think Taylor's involved. I think he's almost as far on the outside as we are."

"There's the sister, of course."

"Yes, sir. We can't rule her out entirely."

"Didn't she say she saw him on her street?"

"Yes, but he ran away when he saw that she had seen him. At least that's what she told us. He didn't mention her last night. That might mean something, or not."

"Yes." McCowan looked at Stride and lifted his hands in frustrated resignation. "I'll let you get back to it, then." He smiled thinly. "You look much the worse for wear, Eric. Perhaps you should take the day off, get some rest."

"I'd rather not, sir." Like Butler, he had things he wanted to do.

"Your choice, of course. I suppose one of the advantages of being close to the sharp end is that I get to sit here and wait for results, and leave the real work to others. Like yourself."

McCowan's smile was a little wider than before, but there wasn't much joy in it.

"Butler appears to be at least a step ahead of us, sir, and running faster." Phelan was restless, standing by the window smoking when Stride came back to the office.

Stride sat down and adjusted the bandages on his wrists. He placed a hand carefully on his bruised side. If he didn't move too quickly or breathe too deeply, the pain was tolerable.

"I suppose I'm a popular topic of conversation this morning?"

"Pushed the price of salt cod right off the front page, sir."

Stride settled in his chair and put his feet on the desk.

"It wasn't a total rout last night, Harry. It wasn't any fun, but at least one interesting thing came out of it. Whether he intended to or not, Butler indicated that he was probably here in St. John's during the war. He made a comment about the large number of foreign troops in the city. Taylor told us that Butler sailed to England in 1940. The Americans didn't get here in any numbers until January of '41. I think Butler was back here sometime after that."

"That is interesting," Phelan said. "Is it possible he ran into Marco Petrelli, I wonder?"

"Maybe. It would be very tidy, wouldn't it? It's what we'd like, connect Butler with Petrelli and Edith Taylor both. A tidy package, nicely wrapped, and placed on the Field Marshal's desk."

"Make his day."

"And ours."

"We could bask in the glory, take a holiday."

"Get promoted."

Phelan grinned and pulled a chair close to his desk and sat down. Neither spoke again for a minute.

"Too neat?"

"It's neat, all right. But just because it's neat doesn't mean it can't be true."

"I believe I read that somewhere, sir."

"Speaking of reading, Harry, did you get Thornhill started on the flight logs at Torbay?"

"Yes, I did. After a fashion, anyway."

"After a fashion. Meaning?"

"Meaning that the logs aren't at Torbay. They were removed to the College after the war. About a year ago. A history prof, fella named Anderson, is planning to research a paper on military air traffic in and out of the island during the war. He has the logs on long-term loan from the military. I had a chat with him."

"Planning to research?" Stride explored his sore ribs again and tried not to wince. "What the hell does that mean?"

"I think it means he has an unrealised ambition, sir, that it's still more in his head than his hands. The logs are in boxes at the College, waiting for someone to find the energy to start going through them."

"Give me a time estimate, Harry. Are we likely to see some results here before everyone connected with this case retires, or fades into carefree senility?"

"Too early to tell, sir. Anderson said he hasn't really looked at the material, just that there's a lot of it. On the positive side, he says he can lend Thornhill a senior student to help him find the records we want." Phelan was silent for a moment. "Do you think the Field Marshal might be right, sir, changing the subject again, that someone is helping Butler stay out of harm's way? Giving him refuge?"

"I think it could be that, yes."

"I don't suppose he had any thoughts on who that might be? Maybe the sister? If he went to her and asked for help, do you think she would turn him down?"

"Blood being thicker than pond water, you mean?"

"Something like that."

"I won't say it's impossible, although it would surprise me. And Jenny Cole's husband might not be at all accommodating. But we don't even know that, do we?" Stride took out a cigarette and tapped it against the side of the package. "I wonder. I'm going to drop in on Jenny Cole."

"And if it turns out that Butler really is staying there?"

"Then we'll have the opportunity for another chat. Maybe a bit less one-sided than the one we had last night."

"He might not feel like chatting, sir. And we know he's probably armed." Phelan hesitated. "And I'm not sure that you're in any shape for a return match right now. No disrespect, sir, but you are moving about a bit gingerly."

Stride looked at Phelan and laughed. Even that caused him some pain. "I'll keep all of that in mind, Harry." He picked up his coat and headed for the door.

"Should I wait here until you get back? I could take a walk across to the College and see what progress Thornhill is making with the airport logs."

"Yes, do that." Stride looked at his watch. "Look for me back here in an hour, Harry. If it's much longer than that, you might want to revisit the possibility that Butler is in residence on Pennywell Road. In that case, raise a posse and come looking for me."

The temperature had dropped sharply since early morning, dark clouds rolling in from the north-east ahead of a gathering wind, a post-script from winter. It wasn't a welcome change, but it wasn't unusual. Stride stopped at the bottom of the steps, buttoned his macintosh and turned his collar up. He patted his coat pockets and remembered that his gloves were in the car. He walked quickly across the parking area, holding his collar against the chill.

Stride sat in the MG, smoking, watching the house on Pennywell Road where Jenny Cole lived. With the sudden return of cold weather, the street was almost deserted. In the fifteen minutes he sat there, only two people appeared, housewives walking quickly against the wind, huddled inside layers of clothing, clutching brown paper bags of groceries.

The Cole house was as quiet as the street. The curtains on the front window were part way open and he could see a light from the kitchen at the back of the house. He considered again the possibility that Butler might be there, thought about the weapon he was probably carrying. Stride took his Colt from the lock-box behind the seat, looked at it for a moment, then put it back. There was a time and a place for carrying a weapon, but this wasn't it, not with a third party at the scene. If it came to a confrontation, he would have to rely on his diplomatic skills, such as they were. He stepped out onto the street, the wind whipping his coat around his knees. The temperature appeared to have dropped even further. There was a smell of snow in the air.

Jenny Cole caught sight of him when he walked past her front window and she opened the door as he was about to ring the bell.

"Come in," she said, "it must be freezing out there." She closed the door behind him and stood waiting for him to take off his coat. "Come into the kitchen. I've just made a pot of tea. You look like you could probably do with a cup."

The kitchen was warmer than the hallway. She had a good fire burning in the coal stove and the oven door was open, dispensing heat into the small room. A tan-coloured mixing bowl stood on the counter by the sink, filled with light-brown batter, the long handle of a wooden spoon resting against the rim.

"Ron likes tollhouse cookies," she said, following the direction of his gaze. "It's his mother's recipe." She took off her apron and draped it over a chair, and poured two cups of tea. "We can go in the front room, if you like, but it's warmer here."

"This is fine, Mrs. Cole." He sat at the kitchen table and crossed his legs. There was a complex mixture of odours in the kitchen. Some of it came from the cookies she was baking, some of it from the coal burning in the stove. But he detected something else.

"You can smoke if you like, Mr. Stride." She brought an ashtray to the table. "Ron smokes. I used to, but I quit. It's been almost a year now." She picked up her cup and wrapped both hands around it, warming them. She smiled at him uncertainly, aware of a change in his attitude.

The something else that had caught Stride's attention was an odour of tobacco smoke, heavy and pungent.

"Have you seen your brother this morning, Mrs. Cole?" Stride stood up and moved away from the table, watching, listening, more conscious now of the pain in his side.

Jenny Cole closed her eyes for a moment, then looked at Stride.

"I was going to call you. Really, I was." She returned her cup to its saucer. Her expression was neutral, controlled. She looked tired.

"Is he here now?" He listened for the sound of another person in the house. There was nothing.

"No, not now. But he was here. This morning, just after nine. Ron had already left for work. The doorbell rang, and there he was, standing on the step."

Christ. Bundled up against the weather, Butler could walk past the assembled constabulary and not be recognised. Stride took a deep breath.

"I've just missed him, then?"

"Yes," she said. "He didn't stay very long, just a few minutes." She sighed, picked up her cup and then put it down without drinking. "I've had a feeling for days, ever since your visit, that Amby would turn up here. I suppose I should have been surprised to see him, but I wasn't really. Does that make any sense?"

"I suppose so," Stride said. He wondered again how she felt about her brother. He recalled Isaac Squires's remark. "Chalk and cheese," Squires had said. "Why did he come?"

"He said he was going away soon, and that he wanted to see me before he left."

"Going away?" Stride sat down at the table. "Did he say where or how?"

"No. Just that it was time for him to leave St. John's. He laughed when he said that, said that he had become too popular lately." She looked at Stride questioningly. "He told me that he had seen you. Last night. Did he? Was he telling the truth?"

"Yes. He was at my place last night."

"I wondered if he was making it up. He said he trussed you up like a Christmas turkey. He seemed very pleased with himself."

"It's not a bad description," Stride said. He placed his hand on his side again. "What else did he say?"

"Not very much. We were like strangers, really, two people who didn't know each other. He kept looking at me, as if he was trying to remember who I was. He was very agitated, pacing back and forth. He smoked a lot, all the time he was here, lighting one cigarette off another."

She shook her head, looking closely at Stride, gauging his reaction, slowly turning her cup on its saucer.

"Go on," Stride said.

"There isn't much else to tell you. I asked him if he had anything to do with Mrs. Taylor's death, but he wouldn't answer me. All he did was laugh."

"Did he know that Jack Taylor wasn't the father of your baby?"

She looked at him, surprised, then looked away.

"Rita Fleming told us."

"He knows now. I told him. He seemed surprised to hear it, but he didn't seem much concerned about it. I don't think it mattered to him."

"Do you know where he is now, where he's living? If he's staying with someone?"

"I don't know. I asked him, but all he said was that he had to leave his place, that he was on manoeuvres, like when he was in the army."

"Is there anything else that he said. Something that might help us find him."

She looked at him in silence for a moment, her expression showing the confusion and conflict she must have been feeling.

"We will find him, Mrs. Cole. Sooner or later. It's better for everyone that it's sooner."

She still didn't reply right, just stared at the table. She moved some breadcrumbs around on the tablecloth with her fingertip, arranging them in different patterns. Stride softened his tone and tried again.

"I have to bring your brother in. That's my job. It's the law."

She was silent for another minute, her eyes closed, propping her head up with her hand. Then she looked at Stride and nodded, the last bits of resistance falling away.

"You're right. There really isn't any choice, is there?"

"No, there isn't. Try and think, Mrs. Cole. Did he say anything at all that might help us?"

She was silent, staring at the wall behind Stride's right shoulder, thinking. "Perhaps there was one thing. When he talked about you, about last night, he said he knew that you were looking for him, and that it would be personal now. But he said that you wouldn't find him because he was too close to you. He said he could hide in your shadow. He laughed when he said that."

Stride sat back and stared at her.

"I don't know what he meant by that, Mr. Stride. Does it mean anything to you?"

"I'm not sure," he said. Well, he had to say something.

He got up and carried his cup and saucer to the sink. There was a small amount of tea remaining and he drank it while looking through the window into the small backyard. The scene remained unremittingly grey and wintry, the lights in the houses opposite only accentuating the general gloom. A low picket fence separated the Coles' property at the back from the neighbour's. A white cat was crouched on one of the fence posts, the tip of its tail twitching, its eyes fixed on a sparrow perched on the swaying branches of a leafless tree. Stride put his cup in the sink and ran water into it. He leaned on the counter and closed his eyes for a moment, thinking about Butler's comment. When he looked up again, the cat and the sparrow had disappeared.

Phelan was on the phone when Stride got back to the office. He gestured with his free hand.

"He just walked in, I'll pass you over to him." He cupped his hand over the mouthpiece. "It's Joanne Taylor, sir." He gave Stride the phone, looked at him briefly, then stepped out of the office.

"I haven't heard from you in a few days, Eric. I hope I'm not intruding." It wasn't exactly a question.

"I'm sorry about that," he said. "Things have been hotting up a bit."

"Have you found Raymond? Is that what's going on?"

"No, we haven't, not yet, but we know that he's still in the city. Not far away, at any rate." The problem being that we don't have any idea where he is. Apart from that, we're doing very well. Jenny Cole's words echoed in his mind: Butler hiding in Stride's shadow. He turned the phrase over for the umpteenth time, and still came up with nothing.

"I spoke with Geoff Hamlyn this morning. He says Ned might be released later today." She paused. When she spoke again her voice was rigid with tension. "Eric, Geoff told me that you were assaulted last night. At your flat."

Christ, he thought. How does it happen? By this evening the gossip will have me slumbering at Carnell's funeral parlour, no flowers by prior request of the decedent.

"These things always get embellished in the retelling, Jo. It wasn't all that dramatic."

"It sounded dramatic enough to me, Eric. Geoff said you were knocked unconscious and handcuffed. Is that true?"

He suppressed a sigh. "He's more or less captured the essence of it, yes."

"It was Raymond, wasn't it?"

"Yes, it was Raymond. He was in my flat when I came home last night, waiting for me."

"I don't understand it, Eric. What did he want?" Her voice resonated with a barely controlled urgency. He tried to think of something to say that would calm her.

"I don't really understand it either, Jo. Maybe he just wanted to let me know how clever he is, or take a close look at me. I don't know. I'll have to ask him about that when I catch up with him." The last added in an attempt to lighten the mood.

She was silent then, the faint humming on the line the only sound.

"Jo?"

"I'm sorry." Her voice was low, her tone distant. "I'm finding all this very upsetting, Eric. There's so much going on right now."

"It's good news about Ned," he said. That was lame, but it was the best he could manage. He wasn't sure how he felt about Ned's release from jail. It would make it more difficult for Stride and Joanne to see each other. Maybe that was a good thing. He thought about Margaret's visit to his office.

"Yes, of course," she said. Another silence. "I should let you go, Eric. I know you're busy. But I was worried about you. That was the real reason I called. Not just to tell you about Ned. Can we talk, later? This evening, perhaps, when you have some time?"

"Yes," he said. "Call me at home." He had a sudden urge to drive to her house, or ask her to meet him somewhere. But that would have to wait.

Phelan had been waiting in the corridor, and with the sound of the phone being replaced, he walked back into the office.

"Tell me some good news, Harry. It's looking like being one of those days."

"No joy from Jenny Cole?"

Stride looked at him and drove the cobwebs away with a brisk shake of his head.

"Christ, I feel like I'm in a fog." He lit a cigarette and inhaled deeply, grateful for the jolt the smoke gave him. "In fact, Harry, Mrs. Cole had a visit this morning."

"Butler?"

"Yes. About an hour before I got there."

Phelan sat down. The two men looked at each other.

"Busy lad," Phelan said finally. "I don't suppose he left a forwarding address?"

"No. His sister says she doesn't know where he is."

"Would she tell us if she did?"

"She might. Yes, I think she would. They're brother and sister, and there's an attachment there, but it's been more than ten years since they last saw each other, and I think she wants him found. Not as fervently as we do, but on balance, I think she's on our side."

"Odd that he went to see her, though."

"Yes, it is odd, but not really out of character. Butler told her it was time for him to leave St. John's, time to move on. I wonder if he really meant that."

"A smoke-screen, maybe."

"Maybe. I really don't know what's going on, Harry." He looked at Phelan, frowning, anger starting to grow out of the frustration. Change the subject. "How is Thornhill making out? Any good news there?"

"That project is going to take a little while. I had the quaint notion that the logs would be actual books, with the information set out neatly and chronologically between black covers."

"And now you're going to tell me that's not the way it is."

"I'm afraid so. There are books listing the aircraft that arrived and departed, and when, but the information we want is in supporting documents. There are boxes of papers: flight numbers, flight plans, dates, times, crew and passenger manifests, cargo manifests, all on sheets of paper. Some of it is handwritten, more of it's typed, and a lot of it seems to be the fourth carbon copy of the original. And Thornhill says it wasn't boxed all that carefully."

"Meaning it's not in any particular chronological order?"

"Apparently not. The lads who boxed the stuff didn't care if they never saw it again, or if anyone did. Definitely not systematic scholarly types."

"You're not giving me a lot of cheer, Harry."

"Just telling it the way it is, sir."

"I know. Nothing we can do about it now." Stride tried to imagine the packing process, a couple of bored uniforms yearning for mufti, stuffing wads of papers into boxes, out of sight out of mind. "Maybe Thornhill has a new career. Does he have an estimate yet for when he might sort it all out?"

"No, sir. He can't tell at this point. He's a good man and he put on his best face, but I almost think he'd be happier walking a beat, even in this weather."

forty
one

Dickson phoned Stride's flat from the Fort just after nine that evening. Stride had finished clearing up after a late supper. He was dead tired, but delaying going off to bed as long as possible, in the hope of achieving a decent night's sleep. He'd just poured a glass of rum.

"We've had a call, Inspector Stride, from the Southside Road. A man's been killed, and maybe a woman too. At a house owned by a Mrs. Michael Casey. We've put in a call for Dr. Butcher, given him the particulars. He should be there just about now, sir."

Stride took a breath, added up the pieces as best he could. There was an ache behind his eyes.

"Did you check the address, Billy? Is it the same Mrs. Casey that Bobby Taylor boards with?" Taylor had called her his "gentle hostess," smiling at Stride and Phelan when he said that.

"Yes, sir. Sergeant Phelan was here when the call came in. He checked straight away. It's the same address, all right."

"Phelan's on his way, then? To the Southside Road?"

"Yes, sir. They were going to pick up Noseworthy on the way."

"Right. I'm on my way, too, Billy."

Stride looked longingly at the glass of rum on the kitchen counter, knew if he drank it, he wouldn't be able to function, might not even be able to drive safely. He placed a saucer on top of the glass, picked up his keys, straightened his tie, and headed for the door.

When Stride approached Bobby Taylor's boarding house, the constable standing guard at the front door tapped the tip of his nightstick against the brim of his cap.

"Bloody awful mess in there, sir." He looked over his shoulder, made a movement halfway between a shrug and a shudder. "You'll find Dr. Butcher inside, hard at work. He got here about five minutes ago."

"What's the score so far?"

"Well, sir, the man that boarded here is dead. Back of his head smashed in. The woman who was with him is still alive, but she's seen better days."

Thomas Butcher glanced up when Stride came into Bobby Taylor's room. He was kneeling over the body of a woman who lay on the rug in front of the ornate bookcase that Raymond Butler had made. Only her feet and lower legs were visible. Butcher made a grunting noise, nodded at Stride, and went back to the task at hand. The second body was on the floor about ten feet away. Bobby Taylor lay face down, the back of his head an uneven tangle of blood and hair. His left eye, open but sightless, was just visible where his face rested against the hardwood floor.

Harry Phelan was standing by the window, pretending to be interested in the activity on the street. A small crowd had gathered on the far side, braving the cold, watching the front of the house and the lone constable standing vigil. Phelan's face was pale and he held onto the windowsill, his arms braced. He was breathing heavily. Stride walked over to him and placed a hand on his shoulder.

"Go on outside, Harry," he said. "It won't help matters if we have a third body on the deck."

Phelan shook his head. He took several deep breaths and stood erect, his head tilted back.

"I'll be all right, sir. I got here just before you did. It will take a minute or two more for the room to stop whirling around."

"It's your choice, Harry. But don't try to be a hero."

Stride noticed then that a woman was sitting on a straight-backed chair in a corner of the room, to the right of the door. He hadn't seen her when he first came in. She was middle-aged, early fifties, Stride guessed, and she was wearing a white bib apron over a patterned dress. Stride looked back at the woman on the floor, her identity concealed by Butcher's torso as he tended to her injuries. He walked across the room and spoke to the woman in the chair.

"I've never had anything like this happen in my house, sir. Not ever. It's just terrible. I heard some noises from Mr. Taylor's room and after a while I came up to ask if anything was wrong. And I found them like that. Just as you see them." Her voice trailed away into silence and she dabbed at her eyes with a handkerchief.

"This is your house? You're Mrs. Casey?"

"Yes, sir. It's my house, sure. Mr. Taylor has been living here now for two years. He's my only boarder. It's not like I really need the money, you see, it's for the company as much as anything, and Mr. Taylor was always a gentleman."

Her words tumbled out as she grasped onto the familiar to isolate herself from the horror that filled the room.

"There were some who thought Mr. Taylor was a hard man, but I think it was the war made him seem that way. Like a lot of the men who came home. He was always very kind and polite to me."

She looked up at Stride, her eyes wide, seeking assurance.

Stride nodded and placed his hand on her shoulder, and she covered it with her own. He looked across the room at Harry Phelan. Phelan tried a smile. He appeared to be getting hold of himself. He walked slowly to where Stride was standing.

"Harry, this is Mrs. Casey. This is her house." The woman nodded at Phelan.

Harry Phelan looked at her, then across the room at Butcher.

"Then who's that over there?"

"I don't know," Stride said. But he could guess. "You tend to Mrs. Casey, Harry. I'll speak to Thomas."

Stride carefully pulled his hand away from the woman's grasp. He turned towards the scene being acted out by the bookcase. He walked over.

Joanne Taylor's face was streaked with blood, although Butcher had wiped most of it away. There was a deep cut over her right eye, just on the arch, the kind of cut that bleeds profusely. She seemed to be unconscious, or hovering on the margin, but appeared to be breathing normally. Butcher looked up at Stride. He smiled briefly.

"She's very fortunate, Eric. Bad cut over the eye that will take perhaps a dozen stitches. Facial bruises. There's another cut on the back of her head that also bled a bit, but I don't think the skull is fractured. The cuts look awful, of course, bleeders always do. But considering what befell that poor fellow, there…" Butcher gestured towards Bobby Taylor's body. He shook his head.

Butcher stood up and slowly wiped his hands on a towel.

"What did happen to Taylor?"

"Huge head wound. Caught him from behind, right side. The weapon is almost certainly that thing there." He pointed to the mace, which lay on the floor near Taylor's body. Stride looked towards the wall over the sideboard. The small sword was still hanging there. "It's got blood and hair on it. I'll know the story better after the post, but it looks to me like two or three well-placed blows."

Stride looked down at Joanne Taylor.

"She's breathing normally," Butcher said, "and for the moment it's best just to leave her as she is. No point moving her about until we have the stretcher. The ambulance should be here shortly."

Stride's eyes were aching, and he struggled to maintain control, leaning on the routine for support.

"What do you make of it, Thomas?"

"I can guess at the sequence," Butcher said. He gestured towards the mantelpiece. "There's some blood, some strands of dark hair, on the edge, just there." Stride leaned forward to look at the spot Butcher indicated. The mantel was made of hardwood, and the edge with the stain was quite sharp.

"The wound on the back of her head?"

"That's my guess, yes. I am speculating that the man who killed Mr. Taylor probably delivered a roundhouse punch that split the lady's eyebrow open and also bruised her face. Then she struck her head against the mantel when she fell. That was probably sufficient to render her unconscious. Whether he killed Mr. Taylor before or after he attacked the lady is something only she can tell you."

"Assuming that she can remember," Stride said.

"There is that. The combination of the blows to her head, together with the shock of the attack, might have been sufficient to induce a loss of memory. I've seen it happen."

They were silent, then. Stride badly wanted a cigarette, but pushed the thought away. Then the slamming of a vehicle door was heard from outside.

"I hope that's the ambulance," Butcher said. He walked out of the room towards the entrance of the house. He returned a few moments later with the two ambulance men following close behind.

Stride and Phelan stood beside Mrs. Casey and watched as the stretcher gurney was rolled through the doorway. Stride caught the eye of the lead attendant.

"I expect you'll want to go with them, sir?" Phelan's colour had returned. He managed a genuine smile. Noseworthy was standing next to him.

Stride looked at Phelan and nodded.

"She may have things to tell us, Harry."

"You're guessing that Butler came back to visit his friend Bobby Taylor?"

"That would seem to be the logical conclusion, yes." Stride walked Phelan over to the door. "Get a statement from Mrs. Casey, and anyone else who has something to say. The standard drill. I also want you to go out to Ned Taylor's place. Taylor was supposed to have been released this afternoon. I'll catch up with you at the Fort later." He looked at Noseworthy and nodded. 'I'll call in as soon as I have something to talk to you about."

Stride played with his package of cigarettes and resolved not to smoke another. Not just yet. He picked up a magazine from the table in the hospital waiting room and stared at the cover. The headline informed him that the Allies had made a large amphibious assault against the German positions in Normandy. He sighed and dropped the magazine back on the table. He looked at his watch. It had been forty minutes since he'd arrived at the hospital. He walked to the window and looked down at the activity on LeMarchant Road, the cars driving by, a few people walking quickly through the cold under the pale glow of the streetlights. It seemed wrong that people should still be going about their routines, preoccupied with the details of everyday life.

"Inspector Stride?"

A man's voice, vaguely familiar. Stride turned and looked at the owner. It took him a moment to capture the name.

"My name is Kavanagh, Inspector. We met a little while ago, at Jack Taylor's house. The night of the shooting?"

"Yes, of course."

"I've been the Taylor family doctor for a long time. I was Bobby's doctor also, years ago. Until he moved out on his own." Kavanagh closed his eyes for a moment. "Poor fellow." The words were just audible.

"Mrs. Taylor? How is she?"

"She's conscious now, has been for a while, but I think she's confused, probably still in shock." Kavanagh placed his hand on Stride's elbow and steered him back to the couch. Physician in charge. "I had a talk with Tom Butcher. We concur that Mrs. Taylor's injuries are not grave. Not trivial, don't misunderstand me. But she should recover completely." Kavanagh took off his glasses and rubbed his eyes. He laid the glasses on the table. "The mental part, now, that may take some time. She's had a terrible experience, tremendous shock. Made worse by the fact that she was quite close to her brother-in-law, you see. And there's that business between Ned and his father."

Kavanagh shook his head and picked up his glasses, carefully placed the wire sidebars around his ears and adjusted the position of the lenses.

"Can she answer questions, Dr. Kavanagh?"

"You can try, Inspector. But as I said, she seems confused. And it's important not to upset her unduly. You understand that of course."

Kavanagh looked closely at Stride, seemed about to add something, but only shook his head again, as though the small movement transmitted important information.

"I understand." Stride paused. What the hell, he thought. There won't be any secrets left when this is all over. "I've known Joanne Taylor for several years, Dr. Kavanagh. We're friends, after a fashion." Brilliantly put.

Kavanagh looked at him closely, no expression on his face.

"Well," he said, "perhaps that will help." He patted Stride on the knee, best professional manner, and stood up. "The head nurse is Mrs. Rowsell."

Stride stood up and Kavanagh shook hands with him, an oddly formal gesture, as though they had just negotiated a contract.

"Is Dr. Butcher still here in the hospital?"

"Yes, he is. I'm sorry, it almost slipped my mind. Tom asked me to tell you that he'd be downstairs for a while yet. And that he'd stop by Mrs. Taylor's room on his way out, if he hadn't seen you by then."

Joanne appeared to be asleep so Stride sat by the bedside, watching her. He wondered if Kavanagh, or someone on the hospital staff, had stitched the cut over her right eye. Whoever had done the work had done it well, using a large number of small sutures to minimise the size of the eventual scar. Her face was discoloured, especially around the right eye, and Stride thought the bruising might continue to spread and darken. A white bandage circled her head, holding in place the dressing on the second wound at the back.

Stride badly wanted a cigarette and there was an ashtray on the bedside table. He looked at it longingly, but pushed the thought aside. After about ten minutes, a nurse stepped into the room. She was a woman of middle age, short and stocky, with dark hair greying at the temples. She stared at Stride for a few moments before speaking.

"Are you Inspector Stride?"

"Yes," he said. He stood up and followed her into the corridor.

"Dr. Butcher just called from downstairs and asked me to give you a message."

"He's left the hospital, then?"

"Yes. He had a call from Fort Townshend. He said he had to attend at another crime scene." The nurse looked at him in what seemed almost an accusatory manner, as though the sudden proliferation of violent crime in the city might somehow be his fault.

"Did he say anything else?"

"Just that he would talk with you later." She looked around him into the room and unexpectedly smiled. "Mrs. Taylor appears to be awake now. You'll want to talk to her, I think. I'll be at the desk if you need me." She turned and walked down the corridor, soft-soled shoes squeaking on the linoleum.

Joanne looked at Stride for a long time before saying anything, and when she did speak she told him her throat was dry. He poured some water into a tumbler. She sipped the water through the glass straw.

"Bobby is dead, isn't he?"

"Yes." He paused. Waited for her to go on.

She turned away from him and stared at the wall.

He waited a few minutes before speaking again.

"How much do you remember?"

"I'm not sure." She reached for his hand.

"Just tell me whatever comes into your mind."

"I went to see Bobby early in the evening. We had a drink, and something to eat. I had brought sandwiches. We ate them, and sat in his room talking for a while before I left. That was about seven-thirty, quarter of eight, I think. I know it was just starting to get dark."

"Did you speak to Mrs. Casey while you were there?"

"No. I didn't see her at all. Sometimes she's there when I visit, but I didn't see her today."

"You said you left about seven-thirty. What happened after that?"

"I was driving back from the South Side, crossed over the Mill Bridge, onto Water Street. When I stopped at the intersection, I realised I'd left my purse at Bobby's, so I turned around and went back."

She paused again, asked for more water.

"Was Butler at Bobby's place when you got back there?"

"That part is confused, Eric. I remember going into the house and I think I remember knocking at Bobby's door. After that, I'm not sure. I must have gone into the room, but I don't remember if someone opened the door for me, or if I opened it myself. I have a picture in my mind of Bobby lying on the floor, but I don't know if that was before or after I was attacked. I may have seen him when I was lying on the floor."

"Did you actually see Butler in Bobby's room?"

"I'm not sure. Someone was there. Someone other than Bobby. I'm not sure it was Ray. I suppose it must have been him, though." She looked at Stride, questioning. "It couldn't have been anyone else, could it?"

"You don't remember being attacked?"

"Not really, no. I remember falling, I think, and a very bright light. Dr. Kavanagh said I have a cut on the back of my head. I suppose that's what the bright light was all about."

"Probably," Stride said. "It appears that you struck your head against the mantel when you fell."

"I must look like hell." She attempted a smile.

"Let's just say you are very colourful just now."

"I don't think I want to look." She held his hand tightly. "I can't believe Bobby's dead. I can't believe that all of this is happening."

"Where was Ned?" Stride watched her closely.

"Ned?" She seemed confused by the question.

"You told me this morning he was being released today."

"Yes. Of course. He got home about five. I picked him up at the courthouse. We didn't talk much." She turned her head away for a few moments. "But that's not new."

"He didn't go to Bobby's with you?"

"No. He didn't want to. At first he said he would, then decided he wouldn't."

"Bobby could have come to your place."

"Bobby never comes to our place. He never has."

"You left Ned at home, then?"

"Yes. I made his supper for him, then I went out. Ned said he was tired, that he was going to take a sleeping pill and go to bed early."

Stride remembered his conversation with Taylor at the jail. He had mentioned the sleeping pills.

Joanne spoke again.

"You haven't caught him, have you? Ray?"

"Not yet, no. We will, though." He knew that his assurance sounded hollow. He didn't have a lot of faith in it himself. Raymond Butler was proving a very hard man to find. And finding him was one thing; catching him would be something else. He thought about the Beretta.

Stride wondered why Butler had killed Bobby Taylor. Had Taylor tried to talk him into surrendering? Perhaps he had threatened to call the police himself? A lover's quarrel? Then he remembered the nurse's message from Butcher. Perhaps this latest one was an unrelated incident. Or maybe Butler had been busy again. And, if so, who this time? Perhaps Jack Taylor. That would be the logical progression. Stride felt a tug of anxiety in his chest.

He gave Joanne's hand a departure squeeze and stood up.

"I have to make some phone calls, Jo."

She looked at him and nodded, pulling the blankets under her chin.

He walked down the corridor to the nurse's desk and asked to use the telephone.

Stride's first call was to Fort Townshend. There was a message for him at the desk from Harry Phelan. He listened to the information from Dickson, then hung up and stood by the desk for a moment, thinking.

"You're having a busy night, Inspector." The head nurse's voice brought him back to the here and now. She was reading through a file and her index finger marked the spot where she left off.

"Yes."

"We have our moments here also, as you can imagine. It goes with the territory. If it was quiet lives we wanted, we should have chosen different lines of work." She looked at him and winked, surprising him. "That helps a lot, doesn't it?"

"Puts it into perspective." He grinned at her and walked down the corridor.

Joanne looked as though she was sleeping when he got back to her room, but she opened her eyes when his shadow fell across her face.

"You have to leave, don't you?"

"Yes. I called the station and I have to meet Harry and Dr. Butcher."

"Has something else happened, Eric? Your expression tells me something has."

"Yes," he said again. He looked at her for a moment, considered telling her the substance of the message, gauge the effect, but decided against it. "It seems so. But I don't have very much information at this point."

Joanne went along with the deception. He tried to think of something else to say, but nothing came. She lifted her hand towards him and he held it for a moment, then turned and left.

forty
two

The Black Maria was parked on the west side of Leslie Street, facing down the hill. Tom Butcher's car was parked behind the van. Stride pulled the MG into Taylor's driveway and stood by the car for a minute. The driver caught his eye and raised his right hand in greeting, then made a cutting motion across the front of his neck. The street was deserted, lights glowing in windows, people standing behind curtains, watching. Stride surveyed the scene, then walked to the front steps.

Phelan was talking with Butcher and Noseworthy in the living room. The room was opaque with cigarette smoke. They looked towards the front door when Stride entered the house.

"No one had seen Taylor outside all day," Phelan said. "He's been on extended leave from his job, of course, and it was so bloody cold that it was no great surprise he stayed indoors. It was Connars who called us when he got no answer at Taylor's house."

"Taylor's upstairs," Butcher said. "In his bed. Everything's as it was when we found him. We waited for you."

"Cause of death?"

"Strangulation," Butcher said. He butted his cigarette in the one ashtray they'd been able to find.

"There's no doubt about that?"

"None," Butcher said. "Mr. Taylor was killed by manual strangulation. The personal touch."

Stride looked at Butcher, startled. It was Butler's own phrase. He walked to the staircase and started up the stairs. He stopped on the third step, held there by an unexpected feeling of sadness at the prospect of seeing Jack Taylor lying dead in his own bed. Perhaps it was the sense of intruding on the man's privacy. He took a breath and started walking again.

Jack Taylor lay on his back on the left side of his double bed, the covers thrown aside, one arm dangling, his eyes wide open and protruding obscenely. The four men stood silent in the bedroom.

"It's very cold in here," Stride said after a few moments. He looked around the room. The window was open, a gap of several inches, the curtains moving slightly. Phelan followed his gaze.

"The heat's off, too," Phelan said. "The place has a coal furnace, probably the original one that was in the house when it was built, maybe thirty years ago."

"Check the cellar, Harry. I want to know if the furnace was shut down on purpose." He turned back to the body in the bed. "Thomas?"

"I'm guessing that Taylor was asleep when he was attacked. He put up a bit of a fight, though. There are several broken fingernails, two on the right hand, one on the left. There's no skin under the nails, though."

"What do you make of the open window?"

"I expect you've guessed at that, Eric."

"To drop the room temperature. Make it harder to estimate the time of death?"

"That would be my guess. The question is, why?"

"It would be nice to know that," Stride said. "Can you make a rough estimate of time of death, anyway?"

"Only a very rough one. He's in bed, in his pyjamas, and the gross indications are that he has been dead more than twelve hours, but probably less than twenty-four. I'd say he was killed sometime last night. That's not much help, I know. I may be able to narrow the estimate somewhat when I've done the post." Butcher straightened up and walked away from the bed, massaging his lower back.

"Last night?"

"Yes. He was killed at least twelve hours before his son."

Noseworthy placed his satchel on the foot of the bed and dropped his coat over a chair.

"If you're through, Dr. Butcher, I'll get started in here." Butcher nodded and walked into the hall.

Phelan was in the kitchen when Stride and Butcher reached the ground floor.

"You were right, sir. The furnace is empty, and cold as a witch's tit. And there's a bucket of half-burned coal around the back. I would guess someone shovelled it out sometime last night."

Stride stood idly in the middle of the room, frowning, his hands buried in his coat pockets. He felt weary beyond measure. Presently, Noseworthy came downstairs.

"The room is very clean, sir. Whoever visited Mr. Taylor last night did a thorough wipe-down. I have a few prints, but I'll be surprised if they don't match up with those I collected the first time I was here."

"Anything else?"

"There's this." Noseworthy held out an evidence envelope. Stride looked at the contents, a mixture of dried mud and plant material.

"What is that? Some kind of moss?"

"Peat moss, I think. It was by the side of the bed. Whoever visited Mr. Taylor had been on a nature walk sometime recently. I'll have a definite identification tomorrow morning, but I think my first guess will prove correct."

"I feel like it's already tomorrow," Stride said. "I'm tired. I'm going to call it a night."

"I think that's a wise decision, Eric. No offence, but you don't look a lot better than our late friend upstairs. I'll be here to greet the ambulance when it arrives."

"They should have been here before now."

"Yes, sorry," Butcher said. "Slipped my mind. A three-car pile-up on the Topsail Highway. The injured take precedence over the deceased."

Stride nodded and walked back into the hall.

"Harry, I'll leave it to you to make the necessary calls. Get a couple of extra patrols out. I want a man posted at the Grace. And Henry Thompson might need babysitting."

"Jenny Cole?"

"Yes. I don't think she's in any danger, but it's just as well to be cautious. Call her and send a patrolman to watch the house." He started for the door, then turned back. "You did talk to Ned Taylor earlier?"

"Yes. It took a while to get an answer at his place. He was in his pyjamas. Seemed a bit groggy, said he'd been asleep for a couple of hours. I gave him the news about his wife and his brother. He appeared to be shocked. He phoned his father while I was there, but there wasn't any answer." Phelan shrugged. "Now we know why. I called the Fort from his place, then came here."

"Right. The one thing we do know for certain is that Taylor was in jail when his father was murdered. Everything else is still more or less up for grabs."

"You're not convinced that Butler is responsible for all this, sir?"

"I'll be convinced when he tells me he is." He started for the door again.

"Look after yourself, too, Eric." Butcher placed a hand on Stride's shoulder. "Butler's generous attitude towards you may have changed in the past twenty-four hours. You'll be careful?"

"We all need to be careful, Thomas," Stride replied, half-smiling. "But I appreciate the sentiment."

Stride had fallen asleep on the couch, fully dressed, a large glass of rum spinning his head in circles. Now he jolted awake with a suddenness that was almost physically painful. He was immediately certain there was someone in the flat with him, in another room, behind a door, in the shadows. He reached for the Colt in its leather holster, but it wasn't where he had left it. He lay still, holding his breath, listening, heard no sound other than the pounding of his own heart. He slowly moved his hand behind the cushions and found the Colt wedged far down against the back of the couch. The cool metal against his hand gave comfort and relief.

Stride lay there a minute longer. He knew his sense that someone was in the flat was nonsense, born out of the fear and tension of recent days. He sat up and looked at his watch, dimly illuminated by the light from the kitchen. He rubbed his eyes until they could focus well enough to read the time. Two-thirty. He had been asleep for almost three hours, enough to blunt the edge of his fatigue. He stood in the middle of the living room, rubbing the back of his neck, trying to stop the grinding behind his eyes that was the footprint of anxiety.

He went to the kitchen, ran water into the kettle and turned on the hot plate. He opened the cupboard and looked for the yellow tin of cocoa and the sugar. While the kettle chugged to a boil, he walked through the flat, checking each room, still certain that he was alone, but with the Colt in his hand, just in case. He stood in the bedroom for a minute, looking at the bed, covered with a green eiderdown. Looking at it, he was reminded of Corrigan and his quilts, the small house near Outer Cove, and the assortment of cats that lived there with him. Steam whistling from the kettle broke through his reverie.

Stride sat on the couch, drinking hot cocoa, his feet on the coffee table. He picked up the Colt, opened it, and spun the cylinder round and round, pleased with the smooth action. He took each bullet out of its chamber, then slid it back in, and snapped the cylinder into place with a flick of his wrist. He targeted various items in the room while he drank, pretending to fire at each one before moving on to the next. He swallowed the last of the cocoa, deposited the mug in the kitchen sink and filled it with water. He leaned on the counter for a minute and thought it all through, from that first Saturday night until now, laying the events out like coins on a long table. He looked towards the telephone, half-expecting it to ring again, considered taking it off the hook, stuffing it in a drawer, out of hearing. But he couldn't do that.

He took off his tie and began undoing the buttons of his shirt as he walked to the bedroom. On his way, he picked up the Colt from the coffee table.

forty
three

Constable Walter Williams trudged along the Southside Road, flapping his arms against his body like some large black bird stripped of the gift of flight. The sky had cleared over the past hour and the moon and stars shone high above, but it was still bloody cold, and no mistake. Williams consulted his watch for the umpteenth time, felt the cold air on the skin of his wrist, quickly pulled his sleeve back down. Just past three, almost five hours before his shift ended. Still, he didn't really mind the cold all that much, and it was almost always peaceful this time of night. Not like the war years, when it never seemed to be quiet, always something going on. A mixed blessing. Almost never bored, but almost always expecting trouble.

He heard the motor before he saw the van. A scant minute before he heard it, he had stepped around the back of a shed on the Cartwell property, not far from the Navy docks, to relieve his bladder. He had finished painting a large wet heart on the wood surface, and was about to add love's precious arrow when the sound of the motor interrupted his concentration, and his creation was spoiled beyond redemption. He peered around the corner of the shed, heard the sound of tires crunching on gravel, and then finally caught sight of the van moving slowly down the access road onto the dock.

It was common enough for vehicles to be moving around this hour of the night, if there was a ship in port, but there was no ship at the Cartwell dock just now. By the time Williams had finished shaking his member and buttoned his fly, the van was on the wharf, lights out, but with the motor still rumbling softly. Three men stood on the wharf by the van, two of them short, heavyset men wearing the caps and rough clothes of labourers. The third was taller than his mates, slender, much better dressed, wearing a three-quarter length coat and a quiff hat.

Probably nothing to it, Williams hoped, but with that optimistic speculation moderated by the cautious hand of his eighteen years on the constabulary. Williams had seen all manner of things, especially on this beat. He'd just take his time and move a little closer, and see what was what. If someone was up to something on Cartwell's property, Walter Williams wasn't going to be the copper who didn't pay attention, and then have his arse shoved through the ringer of Bertram Cartwell's righteous wrath.

Williams stepped gingerly around the corner of the shed, tip-toed across a strip of broken asphalt and crouched down behind a collection of 50-gallon drums. He canted his head to the best angle for sound and sight, and cupped a leather-gloved hand behind his ear. The voices carried the distance, just clear enough for him to hear.

"I found him, Mr. Cartwell, sir, just there, where he lies now, when I did me rounds. Face down he was, and I thought probably he was only drunk, sleeping it off, and I coopied down, like, to have a look, stir him awake, and send him on his way afore he perished. That's when I saw the blood on him, and knew he wasn't drunk. No sir. Dead, says I to meself, dead as gurry is what he is."

"And Sid, here, he rang me, Mr. Cartwell, sir," the second workman said.

"Yes, sir," the first man spoke again. "I rang up Mr. Maunder, here, on the phone in the watchhouse, and told him what it was I found, and asked what should I do. I wanted himself to know about it, you see, afore I called the constabulary. Thought that was the proper thing to do, sir." He paused for a moment, looked at Maunder, then at Cartwell. "Should I call them, now, Mr. Cartwell, sir? The constabulary?"

Williams looked at the man they were calling Cartwell. Too tall and thin for Bert Cartwell, and much too young. Had to be Cartwell's nephew, Williams decided, what was his name? He squeezed his eyes tight shut. William.

"How the hell did he get in here," Cartwell said, "if you were on the job? Were you here all evening?"

"No, sir, Mr. Cartwell, not all the evening." The watchman's tone was edgy, but firm. "I has the three properties to look out for, you see. This one and the two others, down the road, one of them past the Navy docks. I starts at six when the regular crew goes off for the day, and I moves about between the three, sir, one after the other. Used to be there was three of us, one for each of the properties, but the other two lads, they was let go last year. Just afore Christmas, that was."

"Shit," Cartwell said, then again, "Shit!"

"There was plenty of opportunity, you see, sir, for him to come in here, when I was off to one of the other places." The watchman's tone had perked up, evincing a hint of pleasure at laying the blame on the company. "Should I go ring the constabulary, now, sir?"

Cartwell didn't reply at once. He lit a cigarette and walked a few paces away. After a moment, he turned back to the workmen.

"Fucking constabulary," Cartwell said, throwing his cigarette away. The two workmen exchanged glances, shifted uncomfortably, wary of Cartwell's tone. "Where is he? Where's the body?"

The watchman pointed down the dock. Williams straightened up a bit, looked in the direction the watchman had indicated, then crouched down again and looked back at the men. William Cartwell made a gesture with his arm, and the three men set off together.

They had moved some distance down the dock now, out of earshot, but not quite out of sight. It was a bright, clear night, the moon adding illumination to that produced by three lamps high on poles along the perimeter of the property. Williams hesitated, pondering. He knew he should have moved onto the scene at the first mention of a body, but if he presented himself now, he could create a situation, one that might make Bert Cartwell unhappy. Better, maybe, he should hold his place, see if William Cartwell would decide to call the Fort, report having found a dead body on the property. Give him the opportunity to do the right and proper thing, and everyone would be smiling in the morning.

He thought about it some more, and winced. Blood, the watchman had said, blood on the dead man. If that was the case, then this might be a crime scene, and those three would muck it up, moving things, destroying evidence. God damn it. Williams knew he had to make a decision, and that made him unhappy. Decision-making wasn't his strong suit. Give the great and grand Cartwells a bit of elbow room, and he maybe risked the wrath of his own superiors, perhaps all the way up the Chief himself. Williams sighed, and made his decision. Time to shift his arse. Might have waited too long already, but no one would know when he had actually come onto the scene. Williams himself wouldn't spread the word.

He straightened up and walked smartly in the direction of the three men who were now at the end of the dock. He could see that the two workmen were bent over, arranging themselves to pick up the body. Williams accelerated to a trot, holding his nightstick high above his head.

"Here, now," he shouted. "Here!"

Williams increased his pace to a gallop, coattails fanned out behind him, heavy leather boots with metal-capped heels thumping on the wooden beams of the dock. Maunder and the watchman had lifted the body, struggling to stand upright, and both turned to stare at the policeman running towards them. Cartwell saw Williams at the same moment, took a reflex step backwards, and caught his foot on a coil of rope. He uttered a frantic "Jesus Christ!" his arms flailing wildly. He stumbled further backwards, and disappeared over the end of the dock. An instant later he hit the frigid water with a loud splash.

For a moment, the scene was frozen into comic immobility under the cold light of the moon and the pole-suspended lamps. Williams had come to a full halt, nightstick pointing towards the sky. Maunder and the watchman still held the body, the lifeless head and limbs dangling obscenely. The two men stared at Williams, then looked at each other, and gently lowered the body onto the dock and stood upright. A cacophony of frantic thrashings and shrieks informed them that Cartwell had survived his plunge into the harbour.

"Lord liftin Jesus," Maunder shouted. "Sid, boy, take a hold of that rope and make a bowline." Maunder knelt at the end of the dock. "Hang on, there, Mr. Cartwell, sir. We'll have you out in no time." A torrent of strangled obscenities floated upward from the surface of the water.

Maunder took the loop of rope from his mate and lowered it to the surface of the water. Cartwell was silent now, treading water frantically, looking upward as the line came closer to his head.

"Grab on to it, Mr. Cartwell," Maunder said, his voice calm and persuasive, almost a fatherly tone. "Grab on, sir, and get it under your arms."

He turned towards Williams and the watchman who had taken hold of the free end of the line, each looping it a turn around their waists. They braced themselves, their heels wedged against the edges of the dock beams.

"Right, now, lads. Heave away." Maunder gestured with his hand and the two men walked backward across the dock. In a few moments, Maunder grasped Cartwell's hand and pulled him onto the dock where he lay shuddering with cold and shock. Maunder and Williams pulled off their coats and tucked them around Cartwell's body. Cartwell closed his eyes, the muscles of his jaw twitching, his teeth chattering audibly.

"I'll get the van," Maunder said. "Best take him straight to the hospital, I'd say. Have him looked at." Maunder looked at Williams, who nodded his agreement. The watchman, his eyes wide and frightened, knelt beside Cartwell's prostrate form. Williams hesitated for just a moment before running after Maunder.

"Damn close to having two dead bodies on the dock," Williams said.

"Too bloody true," Maunder replied. Then he laughed, slapping himself on the thigh. "Don't know anything about the stiff, but wouldn't have been no great loss if Cartwell went south."

"That so?" Williams looked at Maunder.

"William Cartwell?" Maunder snorted, not smiling now. "Stunned as me arse, and twice as ugly. I knew we shouldn't have touched that body. Didn't want to, neither of us, but Cartwell said he'd have us both fired if we didn't do what he told us. He would have, too. Proper bastard when he don't get what he wants." Maunder halted suddenly and looked hard at Williams. "I s'pose Cartwell will try and lay all this on me and Sid? We'll be in shit up to our eyes, I s'pose, and he'll smell all roses. Is that the way it's going to be?"

Maunder continued to stare at Williams, the challenge laid out, sharp and clear. Williams remained silent, groping for words. He stepped back a half-pace.

"How'd you happen to come on us, anyway?" Maunder said, his eyes narrowing. "And how long was you there watching? That's what I'd like to know."

Maunder really had a look in his eye now, and Williams's awkward silence told him everything he needed to know.

"I 'llows you was watching the whole goddamned thing, likely saw us when we come onto the dock." Maunder planted his fists on his hips and stepped close to Williams, looking up at him. Williams was a head taller, but Maunder was a good ten years younger, solid as new timber and hard as nails. "You son of a bitch," Maunder went on. "You just stood there and let that arsehole Cartwell have his way. Well, Sonny Jim, if me and Sid catches shit over this, you'll catch it too, make no bloody mistake about that. And maybe some dark night you'll find yourself in the harbour, and without no friendly hand to pull you back out. You hear me?"

After a moment, Maunder stepped back and grinned at Williams, slowly nodding his head.

"Oh, I can see you hears me. And you knows how to add two and two. You're not as stunned as you look."

Williams looked back to where Cartwell lay on the dock, the watchman still kneeling beside him. He felt the cold air cutting into him now, and he turned up the collar of his jacket. He wanted his coat back. Bloody Cartwell. Williams thought about his eighteen years on the constabulary. He could retire after twenty-five. Lately, he had started looking forward to that. He looked at Maunder and drew himself up to full height. This would make two decisions in one evening.

The sky was greying in the east, the passing of night, the promise of morning. There were three vehicles on the dock now, semi-circled around the body, their headlamps casting a broad sheet of light over the scene.

Stride was the last to arrive. He had been lying on his bed, wide awake, sleep gone for the night, when the call came in at four o'clock. He parked his MG between the Black Maria and Thomas Butcher's Rover, walked over to the small group standing in the wash of the headlamps.

Raymond Butler lay on the dock, on his back, his face cruelly pale in the unnatural light. Stride looked down on the man, matching the grim reality of his appearance in death with the memory of the night in his flat. He looked up when Butcher spoke.

"It appears to be a suicide, Eric. A single gunshot to the temple. The pistol was near his right hand."

"It's a Beretta, 9mm," Noseworthy said. "Probably the one that Taylor said was missing from the collection. Just one bullet fired. We found the spent shell." Noseworthy held out the brass casing for Stride to look at. Stride held it in his hand for a moment, turning it over and over, then gave it back.

Stride knelt beside the body and turned the dead man's head to look at his face. He seemed even smaller than Stride remembered him, but their situations were reversed, now, Butler lying on the deck, Stride hovering over him, his memory skewed by the perspective. The entrance wound was small, not much blood, and the indication of powder burns that told of having been shot from very close range. The exit wound showed a lot more damage, a ragged gouge on the opposite side of Butler's head, towards the back. Stride looked at the timbers that made up the end of the dock. The area was littered with gurry: fish entrails and blood. The stench was impressive, even in the cold air.

Noseworthy caught the direction of Stride's gaze.

"They were gutting fish here most of the afternoon, sir. No chance of identifying Butler's blood in that mess."

Stride lifted Butler's left hand, turned it over and examined it, then the right, touched with his fingertips the unblemished skin. Butler's hands looked like those of a writer or a musician, fine and unmarked. For some reason, he had not noticed his hands the night that Butler had invaded his home. But he had other things on his mind then, survival sitting at the top of the list.

Stride nodded and stood up. He rubbed his hands together in a washing motion, then wiped them with his handkerchief.

"Time of death?" He looked at Butcher.

"Sometime last night, Eric, but I probably won't be able to estimate closer than several hours, even after the post. It's been near-freezing since yesterday morning."

Stride thought of the open window in Jack Taylor's bedroom.

"No witnesses, I suppose?" He looked at Phelan, then at the others. Phelan shook his head, then gestured towards the watchman who was standing off to the side. Stride walked over to him. "Your name?"

"Sid Barter, sir." He made a half-step forward and touched his cap. "I come on duty at six, sir. I didn't see the fella here, then, and I had a good look around at the time. I always does that when I gets here. And I does the same at the other properties. He must have come in after that. When I was at one of the other places, it must have been, or on the road."

"What time was it when you can say for certain that he wasn't here?"

Barter took off his cap and scratched his head.

"Well, I'm not sure I can answer that, sir. You see, it's this way. I come on at six, took a good look round, then I come back to the watchhouse there, and made some tea and had my supper. And then I did the same for the other places I looks after, the other Cartwell properties. It were dark by the time I got back here, going on for eight. And bitter cold outside. I was half-froze." The watchman looked towards Butcher, as if seeking corroboration on the severity of the weather.

"All right," Stride said. He could feel the man's discomfort. He draped an arm over Barter's shoulders and walked him a dozen paces down the dock. "Just between you and me and the famous gatepost, Mr. Barter, let me run through this with you. You came here at six, took perhaps five, ten minutes to set up your things in the watchhouse over there, put the kettle on the hot plate for your tea, and while it was boiling you made your round of the property." Barter nodded. "What I want to know for certain is whether there's any possibility that the body was there at that time. Say six, six-thirty."

Barter shook his head vigorously. "No, sir. I can say for certain sure that he wasn't there then." Barter pointed to the body. "I knows that for sure, you see, because the crew that went off at six, they left the rope at the end of the dock in a proper tangle. I took the time then to clear that up, coil the line neat, like it should be. The dead man, now, you can see he's lying right handy to where the coil of line sits."

"Good. Now tell me when you did your next inspection of the area."

"That would be when I found him, sir."

"And what time was that?"

"Going on three, sir."

"You're certain of that."

"Yes, sir, indeed I am." Barter was looking worried now. "Mr. Cartwell might not be too happy to know that, though. If you get my meaning."

"I suppose not," Stride said. "But he won't hear it from me, Mr. Barter."

"I appreciates that, sir. Thank you."

Stride looked at the watchman. He shook his head.

"You work long hours, Mr. Barter. Here at six, and still here at three. What time does your shift end?"

"Six in the morning, sir, when the regular crew comes back to work for the day."

"Twelve hour shift. That's the standard here, is it?"

"Yes, sir," Barter said. "Twelve hours. That's the way of it."

"Right. Thank you, Mr. Barter. I don't have any more questions just now. But if you think of anything else, you know where to reach me."

"That I'll do. And thank you, again, sir." Barter's relief that the interview was over was almost tangible. He turned and walked towards the watchhouse at the opposite end of the dock.

Noseworthy came up to Stride when he rejoined the group near Butler's body.

"You'll want to see this, sir." Noseworthy gave Stride an evidence envelope. "I took this off Butler's shoes. It was caked against the heels. Mud and some bits of peat moss. Similar to the stuff I found on the carpet in Taylor's bedroom."

Stride looked at the material, pursed his lips as though whistling, although he made no sound. He gave the envelope back to Noseworthy.

Butcher had been examining the body, and the area around it, and now he stood up, rubbing the small of his back. He took out a cigarette and offered one to Stride.

"You were doing that at Taylor's house yesterday, Thomas. Not serious, I hope."

"Lumbar disk. I'd like to say it's a war injury, but it first happened when I was lifting a case of claret out of the boot of my car."

"Well, a noble wound, Thomas, if not a heroic one."

"Sounds almost acceptable when you put it that way. Well, I've finished here. I'll do the post tomorrow morning, but you already have the gist of it. Gunshot wound, apparently self-inflicted." Butcher buttoned his coat and took out his gloves. "This would appear to wrap things up for you, Eric."

"Yes, it does appear that way."

The wind was picking up a bit, now. Stride turned his collar up and dug into his pockets for his gloves.

"Are you done here, Kevin?"

Noseworthy nodded, picked up his satchel and walked to the Black Maria.

"Lately, we seem to have spent a lot of time waiting for ambulances, Eric." Butcher took a final drag on his cigarette and tossed the butt over the end of the dock. He looked towards the road. A pair of headlamps was visible in the distance.

"Well it's over now," Stride said. He took a final look at Butler's prostrate form.

"And none too soon to suit me." Butcher looked at the body again. "That lad walked a long, hard road from Caitlin's Cove to here. But he didn't do the whole journey by himself. From what you've told me, he had a lot of assistance, most of it bad." He looked at Stride. "That doesn't excuse him, though. Murder is murder."

Butcher flicked his lighter and lit another cigarette, exhaling a long stream of smoke into the chill morning air. Stride patted Butcher on the shoulder, then walked to his car.

forty
four

Stride attended the funeral for Jack and Bobby Taylor at the General Protestant Cemetery. He parked the MG on Topsail Road and walked down the slope to the Taylors' grave site in the south-west corner. Jack and Bobby Taylor would lie in an area that already had received the bodies of Jack Taylor's four wives. Stride had gone to the cemetery the day before, and asked the caretaker to show him where the interment would take place. The two men had stood by the single open grave, Stride smoking a cigarette and the caretaker pulling on his pipe. Jack Taylor and his son would lie in the same place, closer in death, Stride thought, than they had been in life. Then he remembered that Bobby had told him and Phelan that he was probably closer to his father than anyone in the family.

Now he stood off to the side, three or four graves away, removed from the group of mourners. There weren't a lot of people there, many of the family's friends and colleagues intimidated perhaps by the grim circumstances that had produced the occasion. Two naval veterans attended, a lieutenant-commander and a petty officer in full dress uniform, a row of medals across each of their chests. The petty officer carried a wreath.

Joanne and Ned Taylor stood together by the graveside as the minister read through the service. Joanne held onto her husband's arm with her right hand. Her face was still badly discoloured from the evening that Bobby Taylor had been killed, but the veil she wore muted the effect. Only once, when the service had ended and the small assemblage was dispersing, did she catch sight of Stride. She glanced at him, nodded quickly and turned away, then walked with Ned towards the cars parked on Topsail Road. She didn't look back. Stride felt something like a sense of finality as he watched her walk away, a feeling that their time together might now truly be over. And with the feeling came the familiar biting sensation of loneliness and regret.

After the service, Stride drove back to the Fort. Phelan greeted him with news that he had had a call while he was out.

"Rita Fleming would like to talk to you, sir," he said.

"Rita Fleming?" Stride looked at Phelan, sitting there smiling at him, his eyes twinkling. Stride wasn't in the mood for humour, however light-hearted it was intended to be, and he felt his irritation start to grow. That wouldn't do. He clenched his fist and punched himself on the thigh. "Give me a cigarette, Harry. And don't give me a hard time. I'm tired."

"I've never been a great fan of funerals, myself, sir, any more than hospitals. A good Irish wake, now, that's a different matter. A few pints of cold beer chasing whisky down the little red road usually dispels the oppressive gloom." He held his lighter out to Stride, then lit his own cigarette. "Any surprises at the funeral?"

"Not really. There weren't a lot of people there, which didn't surprise me." Stride leaned back in his chair and lifted his feet onto the desktop. The aches and pains inflicted on him by Raymond Butler had faded.

"Kit and I are taking in a movie this evening, sir. At the Paramount. Why don't you join us? Take your mind off things. First show, seven o'clock."

Stride looked at Phelan. A movie wouldn't be a bad idea. He wondered if calling Margaret might also be a good idea, a better idea perhaps than going to a movie with Harry and Kit. But he didn't know what kind of response he might receive from her. He also didn't want to think about Joanne, but her image rested just behind his eyes, not quite out of sight.

"What's playing?" Stride asked, pushing his thoughts aside.

Phelan started to reply, then laughed suddenly.

"*The Killers*," he said. "Which I guess makes it a busman's holiday."

Stride stared at him, and then he laughed too.

"Kit picks most of the movies we see," Phelan said. "She says this one's gotten good notices. And it stars a new guy, a dreamboat, Kit says. Fella named Lancaster."

"Hemingway," Stride said after a moment. "Ernest Hemingway wrote a short story called *The Killers*. One of the Nick Adams stories. Wouldn't have thought they could make a movie out of it, though. I might take you up on that, Harry." He dropped his feet to the floor and sat up, picked up the piece of paper with Rita Fleming's number. "The lady didn't say what she wanted?"

"Just that she wanted to tell you something. In person."

"In person? As in, in the flesh? A phone call won't do?"

"Apparently not."

"You asked her?"

"Yes. She didn't want to talk on the phone. And she didn't want to talk to me at all."

Stride frowned and pulled on his cigarette.

"Well, I can't really say that I blame her, I suppose, in her line of work. About the phone, I mean. Some switchboard operators have large ears."

"You'd better call before you go to her place, sir, just to make certain she's alone. You never know who you might find leaping around in her boudoir. Might be embarrassing."

"Tell me something I don't know, Harry," Stride said. He picked up the phone.

There wasn't anyone leaping about in Rita Fleming's bedroom when Stride arrived at the flat. Although it was likely that someone had been not too long before. She was wearing a satin dressing gown. She closed the door behind him and leaned against it. She had a glass in her hand.

"Can I get you something, Inspector? I'm having a rum and Coke. A very tame one, though. It's mostly Coke." She grinned, eyes sparkling. "I'm between appointments."

Stride shook his head. And then almost wished he hadn't declined. The fatigue that had accumulated over the days leading up to the death of Raymond Butler lay heavy behind his eyes. And he still was unable to sleep well. A glass of rum might just do the trick, cut a swath through the gloom. Or knock him flat on his ass. She led him into her living room and perched herself on the love seat. Stride sat in an armchair.

"You've had a busy time of it, Mr. Stride. Two murders and a suicide since Edith Taylor was killed. It's all over the papers. And on the radio. You and your pal have become quite famous."

"It's the kind of fame we can do without, really. Four people are dead. We're not celebrating." Five people if you counted Petrelli. He thought again about the rum that she had offered.

"I'm sorry," she said. "I hope I didn't offend. I didn't mean to. I was trying to lighten your mood, actually. You do look very strained, you know." She wrinkled her brow and managed to look vaguely maternal. "I would guess that you haven't been sleeping well."

"As a matter of fact, I haven't." His response surprised him. Why was he telling Rita Fleming this? He looked at her sitting across the room on the love seat in her satin gown, shapely legs tucked underneath her. To his further surprise, and no little dismay, he felt a sudden surge of desire. And probably something more, all of it honed to a fine edge by the turmoil of recent days. He tried to think about Margaret, but Joanne Taylor's shadow fell across the image. He stifled a groan and turned his head to stare at a picture on the wall, counting slowly from one to ten, then back to one again. In a minute he would ask for a double rum, and then he would be the one leap-frogging around Rita Fleming's boudoir. Harry would be amused. He carefully crossed his legs.

"You said you had something for me, Miss Fleming." That sounded so bloody officious, but he needed to derail his train of thought. Rita Fleming continued to smile at him, but now there was a pensive look in her eyes. "Was it something about the Petrelli murder?" he asked.

"Yes and no," she replied. "Like I said, I've been reading about the murders in the paper." Her smile was brighter now, her eyes shining, a certain pleasure evident again.

"Yes?"

"The reporters have done a fair job of it, haven't they?"

Stride nodded. He had read all of the articles, and he had been impressed.

"I was surprised at how much stuff they came up with," she said. "Right back to when Jack Taylor's first wife drowned in Conception Bay, in 1924. They even found out that Jenny's father was lost years ago, off Cape St. Francis. Poor Jenny. She came to see me yesterday, the first time in years. She told me that her phone has been ringing off the hook. Reporters hanging around her house." She paused, starting to look serious again. "I guess the Taylors have been busy, too. The two of them that's left, I mean."

Stride uncrossed his legs and sat forward. There was something more in Rita Fleming's expression now, just behind her eyes, a look that told Stride that she knew something. He knew about that look, that feeling. It came when the pieces fell into place, and a coherent picture emerged out of confusion. He was conscious of a burning knot in his stomach, as a feeling, part excitement, part dread, stirred inside him.

Rita Fleming jumped off the love seat, skipped across the living room and into the kitchen. When she returned, she was holding a newspaper, folded over to an inside page.

forty
five

Lynch's Pond was maybe a mile and a half east and north of the city centre, not quite in the country, but close enough. Not far out of the city proper, the pavement came to an end, and the road from then on was potholed and rough. Stride geared down and reduced his speed, navigating the MG around the holes and ruts in the surface. The car bottomed out twice, hard enough to worry him, but he didn't think he had done any damage. After the second thump, though, he stopped and looked for any sign of an oil leak. He drove even more carefully after that.

There were only a few houses in the vicinity of the pond, small structures that were widely spaced. Stride shifted down to third gear and drove slowly along the road by the pond, the motor keening, noising impatience with the slow pace. The house he was looking for was set back about fifty yards from the road. A gravel path, narrowed now by encroaching vegetation, led to the front steps. The house was separated from the water by another fifty yards, a landscape covered with low growing bushes, and punctuated by the occasional small tree.

It had been several years since Stride had driven out this way, and the area seemed to have changed somehow. About seventy yards from the house, he pulled over to the side of the road opposite the property, and surveyed the scene. It took him a few minutes to decide that the changes in the landscape were probably the result of a disruption of the water table, a consequence of the road having been widened, the tons of fill corrupting the natural flow. The land around the house now had more the appearance of a bog than he remembered, more peat moss, fewer low-growing bushes, and fewer trees. Many of the trees that had survived were stunted, their growth slowed by the changed environment.

He stepped out of the car and looked up at the sky, a pastiche of white and blue. The weather had improved over the past several days, warmer now, edging tentatively towards real spring.

Stride walked up the gravel path that led to the house. There was no indication that a car had been here recently, no tire marks at all. He went back to the road, then, and walked slowly up and down, both sides. He found what he was looking for about twenty yards from the path on the side opposite the house. The shoulder of the road was softer than the driving surface, and the multiple tire marks there were deeply etched. A car had stopped there more than once. One of the tires appeared to have left a sharper tread pattern than the others. Alder bushes lined the road at that spot. The ends of a few branches were broken, nipped off by the closing of a car door.

Stride walked back up the path and stood by the front steps of the house and looked back towards the road. Two other houses were visible, but they were far enough away to give a degree of privacy. The front door was padlocked, the metal on the lock heavily rusted. He grasped it in his right hand and shook it, tiny flakes of red rust falling from the metal.

He went around to the back of the house, scanning the ground as he walked. The back door, like the front, was padlocked, and that lock was rusty also. But it had been opened recently, and he could see that oil had been applied to cut through the rust and to lubricate the moving parts.

Stride knew that the correct thing to do now was to drive back to the city and obtain a warrant, return with Harry and Noseworthy, cut the lock off the door and conduct a formal search of the premises. Except that he had no reasonable grounds on which to base a request for a warrant to search this property, none that was likely to cut any cheese with a judge. That was the problem with hunches and gut feelings. He had tried it a couple of times, with mixed success. One judge, not known for his support of iffy property searches, had suggested to Stride that if his motivation was a strong gut feeling, he should take a dose of salts and wait for the problem to resolve itself.

A tire iron was a useful alternative to the likely absence of judicial sympathy. Stride had brought his along. It took only one determined effort to snap the lock open. Vandalism was rife in the post-war society. There had been articles in the papers about that. He pushed the door open and walked inside.

The place had been cleaned up, the kitchen table and chairs were free of dust, and the stove had been washed down. Stride went through the entire house, found evidence of habitation in only two rooms, the kitchen and the adjoining parlour, which had probably served as a bedroom. The floor opposite the parlour window was cleaner than the rest of the room and Stride guessed there had been a mattress or a sleeping bag there. But there was nothing else in the room to suggest that someone had lived there. The kitchen was also almost bare. There was no food, no tins or packages; no cutlery, cups, saucers or plates; no kettle, no pans. Beside the black iron stove stood a coal scuttle, holding a small shovel and an iron poker, and a few small pieces of coal.

The house had been uninhabited for years, and someone might have broken in and set up residence for a few days, even weeks. Stride didn't really believe that—squatters weren't famous for cleaning up after themselves. That someone had recently been living in the house was clear enough. But a faceless, nameless someone wouldn't do. Stride needed a connection with a specific person. He needed to know that Raymond Butler had been in this house.

He wondered if Noseworthy would be able to find fingerprints, and thought it possible that he might, although he would have to look very hard. The cleanup job had been very thorough. He went back to the parlour and knelt on the floor where he thought the mattress or sleeping bag might have been. If Butler had been here, perhaps he had left a mark, initials carved into the wood, something, anything. He inspected the baseboard, taking care not to touch the wood. There was nothing.

After a few minutes his knees were aching. He shifted his weight backwards and sat on the floor cross-legged. He lit a cigarette, fighting frustration, and then decided to go through the house again, more carefully this time. A half-hour later he had very dirty hands from the accumulation of dust in the unused rooms, but nothing else to show for his efforts.

He sat on the floor in the corner of the parlour again, smoking. It was a small room, in a small house, even smaller than he remembered it. The feeling he had now reminded him of a visit to his parents' home, years after he had moved out on his own. How tiny their house seemed then, the rooms shrunken, the ceilings lowered, the property itself somehow diminished.

He stubbed his cigarette on the floor, brushed the ashes into a corner, and held the butt between thumb and forefinger. He sat back against the wall, facing the door that led to the kitchen, playing catch with the cigarette butt. Thinking. He noticed then that the moulding at the top of the door was similar to that in his parents' home, a concave adornment that had a shallow well, maybe three inches deep and about as wide. When he was a boy, he would toss pennies up into the moulding, using the well as a kind of secret, surrogate piggy bank.

Smiling at the memory, Stride took careful aim and tossed the cigarette butt towards the top of the door, but it fell short. He sighed, stood up and looked again at the moulding, thinking to take a second shot, from closer range this time. And saw something blue, just visible over the top edge. He took out his handkerchief, reached up and retrieved it. It was a paper package, crumpled loosely into a ball. Stride imagined someone sitting or standing in the room, tossing the paper ball at the moulding, amusing himself, killing time. He walked to the parlour window where the light was better, and unfolded the ball, careful to keep the cloth between his fingers and the paper. It was a cigarette package. The brand name was Gitanes. They were manufactured in France.

Stride got back to Fort Townshend just after six that evening. Phelan had left for the day, but Kevin Noseworthy was still there, tagging and filing a collection of evidence envelopes. On his way to see Noseworthy, Stride asked the desk constable to phone Phelan at home, have him come back to the Fort as soon as he could. He asked the constable to tell Phelan that he was sorry about the movie, tell him that real killers took precedence over those on the silver screen. The constable looked puzzled when Stride said that, but he didn't question the instruction.

"Bern Crotty takes me to task on a regular basis about my file-keeping," Noseworthy said, leaning back in his chair. "And, before I forget, sir, Crotty was looking for you earlier today." Noseworthy pushed the pile of envelopes to the back of his desk and stood up and stretched his arms over his head. "I've been at this half the afternoon, and it's still not done." He shrugged. "Is there something I can do for you, sir?"

"I hope so." Stride took the cigarette package from his jacket pocket. It was still wrapped in the linen handkerchief. He placed it on Noseworthy's desk and unfolded it.

"Gitanes," Noseworthy said, making a face. "Awful bloody things. I smoked a couple one night when I'd had a wee bit too much to drink. Made me sick as a dog." He looked questioningly at Stride.

"I found this in a house near Lynch's Pond," Stride said. "I think it was the house where Raymond Butler was holed up after Edith Taylor's murder." Stride gave Noseworthy a quick summary of his visit with Rita Fleming and his tour of the house at the pond.

"Just far enough from the city to be out of the way," Noseworthy said. "But easy walking distance for someone as fit as Butler was."

"Yes," Stride said. "It fits. Do you think you can raise fingerprints from this material?"

"Shouldn't be a problem." Noseworthy picked up the package with metal tweezers and held it towards the light. "Typical post-war paper, poor quality, porous and crude. This stuff makes a good surface for capturing prints, and for holding them." Noseworthy walked over to a bench on the opposite side of the room. "Did you know that they've lifted the latent prints of ancient Egyptians off papyrus scrolls?"

"Yes," Stride said. "I read about that."

"So, unless our man was wearing gloves while smoking, an unlikely possibility even in this frigging climate, we should find his mark." Noseworthy took several three-by-five-inch lift cards from a box and passed them to Stride. "Just fill in the appropriate information, sir—the where, the when, and the how—and I'll get at this." Noseworthy sat at the bench and took an applicator with fingerprint powder from a shelf. He dusted the surface of the cigarette package, humming a tune while he worked. Stride filled in the cards and initialled them, occasionally glancing in Noseworthy's direction. After a few minutes, Noseworthy sat back, smiling.

"Success?" Stride stood up and walked across the room.

"Yes, indeed. A nice thumb print, and three fingers. Along with some partials that won't be very useful." He took the lift cards from Stride and transferred the prints from the cigarette package. He initialled the cards, then went to the cabinet and pulled out Raymond Butler's file. He compared the new prints to those he had taken from Butler the morning after they had found his body on the dock. He was humming the same tune again. "Left thumbprint is a match. Left index finger. Middle finger, left hand. All good matches." He looked up at Stride. "More or less what you'd expect if Butler was right-handed. Which he was."

"The fourth print?"

"Not Butler's." Noseworthy looked at Stride, questioning.

"Get the file," Stride said. "See if we have a match."

Noseworthy went to the cabinet and took out a second file, went back to the bench and opened it. He began the process of comparing the fourth fingerprint from the cigarette package to the ten prints on the cards in the file. Stride leaned one hand on the bench and watched over his shoulder. After a minute Noseworthy turned and looked at him.

"Middle finger, right hand," he said.

Stride straightened up and took a deep breath.

"You're certain. No chance of a mistake?"

"No, sir. It's a good match." He closed the file and stood up. "It's Joanne Taylor's."

"Joanne Taylor?" Harry Phelan was sitting across from Stride in their office. Harry was wearing the same dark suit he'd worn earlier in the day, but he had changed his shirt and tie for his night out at the movies. Stride had given him the results of the fingerprint analysis. "You're telling me that Joanne Taylor is the one?"

"I'll start with Rita Fleming," Stride said. "You remember when we interviewed her, after we found Jennifer White? She told us that Petrelli was quite a ladies' man, had been engaged to more than one of the local girls."

Phelan nodded.

"Joanne Taylor's picture was in the papers this week, along with the stories about the murders, and they included her maiden name. Rita Fleming recognised Joanne Bartlett as one of Petrelli's girlfriends. After I left her place, I spent an hour at a house near Lynch's Pond. Joanne's house, her family's home. Joanne inherited it when her mother died. She never actually lived there after that, but she held onto the property. We went there once."

Stride paused, remembering an afternoon by the pond. They had brought a picnic lunch, and had eaten it sitting on a patch of grass near the water's edge. Joanne had seemed ill at ease all the time they were there, but she hadn't wanted to talk about that.

"After I left Rita, I went to the house, because I guessed that Raymond Butler must have been there, had used the place to hide. It would have been a good spot."

"You think that Butler and Joanne Taylor were in this together, then?"

Stride looked at Phelan. He didn't say anything for a few moments, was wondering how Harry would respond to what he was thinking. He took out a cigarette, played with it, rolling it back and forth on the desktop.

"No, Harry, I don't think they were in it together. I don't think Butler had anything to do with it. I think Joanne gulled him. Used him."

"You think she did it all on her own?" Phelan was staring at him. Stride could see the doubt in his eyes.

"Yes," he said, finally. "Yes, Harry, I think she did it on her own. I can't know that for certain, but that's what I think."

"Starting with Petrelli?" Harry was sitting forward now, resting his elbows on his knees.

"Yes," he said again. "I think she killed Petrelli. We've been trying to construct a scenario that had Butler coming back to St. John's during the war, killing Petrelli because his sister was involved with him."

"But you don't believe that any longer."

"No, I don't. I still think Butler might have come back here, just as we thought. But he said enough that night in my flat to persuade me that he hadn't seen his sister since the time at their aunt's house in St. Phillips, long ago, when he wasn't much more than a boy. Butler probably didn't even know about Petrelli."

"And the rest of it? Joanne's alibi for the night that Edith Taylor was murdered?"

"Yes, that," Stride said. "I think Joanne was at Jack Taylor's house that Saturday night. After she killed Edith Taylor she drove to the Paramount, waited until the film ended, and was standing under the marquee when the two Yanks came out."

"And then made certain that they saw her."

"It wouldn't have been difficult. Joanne's an attractive woman, and like most attractive women, she can catch a man's attention if she wants to. It was her good luck that there were two very conspicuous Yanks at the Paramount that night. It was almost made to order for her. But she could have made it work with someone else. It doesn't take an Olivier to pull it off."

"And she faked the attack on herself after killing Bobby Taylor," Phelan said. He stared at the ceiling, thinking. "It is possible. I remember one time, a few years ago, when we visited Kit's uncle in Ferryland. Her uncle has a liberal hand with the rum bottle. I had a couple too many and walked into a doorpost looking for the can in the middle of the night. Split my eyebrow wide open, blood all over the place. It's easy enough to do." Phelan sat back and was silent for a moment. "Once she got started, she moved awfully quickly, though. Jack Taylor, then Bobby, and then Butler. If you're right about her having done it all alone. It's almost as though she panicked or something."

"I think Butler's coming to my flat that night must have done just that, threw her into a panic, and she decided that he was becoming dangerous for her. I think he forced her hand. Butler knew that he hadn't killed Edith Taylor. I think he must have started to suspect that Joanne had."

"So Butler was just a convenient scapegoat?"

"Yes, I think he was a scapegoat. Joanne met Butler through Bobby Taylor. Butler was a lonely man, and seriously disturbed. If she had found out that he was having an affair with Edith, it was something she could take advantage of. I think she saw an opportunity, turned on her charm, and took it from there."

He waited for Harry to make a comment.

"Now, that part really bothers me." Phelan was uncomfortable, agitated. He stood up and walked to the window, touched the glass with his fingers, then turned back to Stride. "For Christ's sake, sir, we know that Taylor and Butler were a couple of bloody queers."

"To coin a phrase," Stride said.

"Yes, to coin a phrase." Phelan's face was flushed, his cheeks bright red, glowing with anger. "Are you telling me that you actually think there was something going on between Butler and Edith Taylor? And between Butler and Joanne?"

Stride waited for a moment before replying. The issue had come up before, in other contexts, and it was something they avoided talking about. When they could.

"It's possible, Harry," Stride said, finally. "It is possible. Joanne gave me a lecture one afternoon about sexual preferences. There's irony for you."

Phelan stared at Stride, shaking his head, then turned back to the window again.

Stride's mind went back to the morning in Jenny Cole's kitchen. Butler had said that Stride wouldn't find him because he was so close that he could hide in Stride's shadow. It made sense now.

Phelan spoke again. He had calmed down, his colour almost normal again.

"All right. I'll buy into your theory that Butler and Joanne Taylor might have been involved." He made a dramatic gesture. "Anything's possible, I suppose. But, queer or not, Butler was a very tough guy."

"Yes, he was," Stride said. "I was lucky that he took me by surprise that night, and decked me. If we'd gotten into a fight, I might have come out the other side in even worse shape."

"You're probably right about that." Phelan sighed and sat down. "She took him by surprise, then. Shot him with his own gun, then put his body in the trunk of her car."

"Yes. I think that's what happened."

"And waited for an opportunity to dump him on the Cartwell dock."

"It wouldn't have been all that difficult. The watchman had a set routine. Joanne had plenty of time to dump Butler while he was doing his rounds on the other two properties."

"Christ." Phelan got up and walked to the window again, and stood there looking out. Or at his reflection in the glass. Stride thought he looked tired. Reason enough for that. "Petrelli makes some kind of sense to me, sir. He betrayed her. She had reason to hate him, maybe. But why the Taylors? Was it just the money?"

The same question, with multiple variations, had been spinning around in Stride's head since he had left Rita Fleming's flat. He knew that Joanne liked nice things, had not been shy about spending Stride's money. Her family had not been well off, a small cut above the poverty line. Her mother had raised her on her own from the time she was in her early teens. But he still didn't have an answer to Harry's question that he was comfortable with.

He raised his hands in a gesture of helplessness.

"I don't know, Harry. Money is a great motivator. Jack Taylor had a lot of money, and Joanne probably knew more about his finances than anyone in the family, working in Brendan Madigan's firm, having access to his files."

"But you're not satisfied that's really it, are you?"

"No, I'm not. The money might have been part of it. But I don't think it was just the money. I don't know what the answer is." He imagined asking Joanne the question after they made the arrest. That was the next step, but he couldn't get his mind around that just yet.

"How are you feeling, sir?" Phelan sat down again and stretched his legs out, relaxed now. He and Stride had long ago learned to disagree about some things, and still be able to get on with it. "This can't be all that pleasurable for you."

"A mixture of feelings, Harry. I'm as certain as I can be that we've got it right now. Most of it. That part feels good. But there's the other side of it. When you turn on a light, you make shadows."

Phelan pulled open the bottom drawer of his desk and reached into the rearmost compartment. He and Stride kept a bottle of dark rum there, hidden under a sheaf of papers, for important occasions. Phelan held up the bottle, eyebrows raised. Stride nodded and took two glasses from the side drawer of his own desk. Phelan uncorked the bottle and poured several fingers of rum into each glass. He placed the bottle on Stride's desk.

"I'd like to be able to say that I wasn't really satisfied that Butler was the one," Stride said. He sniffed at his glass before drinking a small amount of rum. "But the truth is, I persuaded myself I was satisfied. I wanted Butler to be the one."

"Fella breaks into your home and kicks your ribs in, pulls a knife on you, you're going to want to hang him from the highest tree. I'd say it's a natural response, sir."

"That's part of it, yes." Stride picked up the cigarette he had been resisting and lit it. "I was angry enough. Even if I also felt sorry for Butler." Phelan nodded and drank some rum. "The other part, the bigger part, is that I let Joanne get too close to me. I should have been able to stand back, keep my perspective."

He tapped the cigarette against the ashtray, carefully sculpting the glowing tip. He knew there had always been something about Joanne, even during their best times, a small sharp stone of discomfort that surfaced painfully from time to time, but he had become practised in pushing it away.

"Don't know that you behaved much different than any other man would have, sir. She knew where all your buttons were, knew which ones to push."

"I suppose so," Stride said. Acknowledging that didn't make him feel much better. He drank more rum, allowed the liquid to burn its way slowly down the back of his throat. "But I'd like to think I could stand back from all that. When it comes to the job."

He swallowed a large portion of the rum, then placed the glass on his desk, turned it round and round and watched the dark liquid swirl against the sides.

"What I have to decide is where we go from here, Harry. We know that Butler was in Joanne's house, and the cigarette package puts the two of them together. But we need more than a single fingerprint to make a case for murder."

Stride looked at his watch. It was eight-twenty-five. "You and Kitty can still make the second show at the Paramount if you want to, Harry. We don't have to do anything more tonight." Even if he knew what to do.

Phelan tossed back the last of his rum and stood up.

"Why don't you join us, sir? Take your mind off it for a few hours."

"No," Stride said. "I think what I need to do is put my mind on it for a while longer. You go ahead." He gave Phelan what he hoped was an encouraging smile.

After Phelan left, he uncorked the bottle and poured out another two fingers of rum. He picked up the glass and raised it to his lips, then put it down without drinking. It occurred to him that he hadn't eaten since lunch. A second drink of rum might just knock him on his back. And while that prospect had a definite attraction, it didn't really suit his mood.

He placed the glass on the desk and sat back in his chair, thinking about food, and about the fact that he really wasn't very hungry. It was then that he saw the brown manila file folder in his in-basket. He remembered that Noseworthy had said that Bern Crotty had been looking for him that afternoon.

Stride picked up the folder and read the name on the tab. Bartlett, Alice. He pulled his chair close to the desk, opened the folder and began to read.

It was almost eleven when Stride drove from the parking area at Fort Townshend. He had read through the file that Crotty left for him, then brewed a pot of strong tea and read through all of the material on the Taylor and Petrelli murders again. A constable looked in on him once, about nine-thirty, and asked him if there was anything he wanted. Stride shook his head, said thank you, and the constable went back to his desk. Stride finally put the files away, switched off the light in the office, and left the building.

When he reached Harvey Road, he looked towards the Paramount, scanned the street, both sides, for Phelan's car. He spotted it on the south side of the street. He lingered at the intersection for a minute, debating whether he would wait for Harry and Kitty to come out of the theatre, invite them to his place for a nightcap so that he could talk to Harry about the new information that Crotty had brought forward. But this was something he wanted to deal with on his own. He turned right onto Harvey Road, heading west towards LeMarchant Road and Cornwall Avenue.

Ned and Joanne Taylor lived in the west end, off Cornwall, in a two-story home in one of the new subdivisions that had been constructed after the war. The area had been carefully planned, avoiding the jumbled, if oddly charming, aspect that characterised much of the old city. The houses were new, the layout efficient and rational. But there were few trees, and the area had the cold, sterile appearance of something that was not yet quite alive. The charitable view was that everything would look much better ten years hence.

Stride parked on the street about seventy-five yards from the Taylor house, switched off the lights and the engine, and rolled the window down. He had driven here on an impulse, acting on a strong sense that he had to talk to Joanne, lay it all out for her, gauge her reaction, perhaps even make an arrest. But the closer he got to her house, the less certain he was of his purpose, caution damping the surge of energy that had grown after he read the file on Alice Bartlett.

He lit a cigarette and watched the house, thinking. The neighbourhood was quiet, few people out at this time of night. Several cars drove past. One couple walked by, led by the family dog on a leather leash. After they had passed him, Stride watched their progress in the rear-view mirror, saw the woman turn around to look at the car, then say something to her husband. The couple stopped for a moment, both of them looking back at the MG, talking. Then they walked on.

A half-hour passed, Stride watching the Taylor house, the two cars parked in the driveway. Ned's was a black four-door sedan, a Dodge, and it was parked nearer to the house. Behind it was Joanne's light blue Hillman. A "little English car," Corporal Tom Addams had called it. Stride looked at his watch. It was almost eleven-thirty. He lit another cigarette, made up his mind that he would go home after he finished it, bring the vigil to an end, postpone decisions and action until he had talked with Harry in the morning. Then the front door of the house opened and Joanne came out. She was wearing dark-coloured slacks and a short jacket. She walked quickly to her car, opened the trunk and looked inside, appearing to check on something. Then she closed the trunk and walked around to the driver's side.

Stride had a moment of anxiety. He knew that if Joanne turned right she would drive past him, and she would recognise his car. He tried to think what he would say to her, account for his presence. He heard the Hillman's engine grind into life, saw the headlights flash on, watched as Joanne backed her car slowly down the driveway onto the street. She turned to the left.

He waited until she moved far down the street before he started his engine. He eased away from the curb, drove down the quiet street, his headlights off. He followed her to the intersection with Cornwall Avenue, watched as she turned left, heading east towards LeMarchant. He didn't turn his headlights on until he had merged with the traffic, light at this late hour, and he stayed well back, keeping at least one vehicle between himself and the Hillman. Joanne's car was a two-door model, almost new, and the taillights were distinctive. He would have no trouble staying in contact with her. They continued to drive east on LeMarchant Road, onto Harvey, then left onto

Rennie's Mill, heading north.

Stride had a feeling now that he knew where she was going. When they had left the city proper, and had reached Torbay Road, Stride switched off his headlights, drove with extra care, and stayed well back. But he kept the taillights of the Hillman clearly in view. It was obvious now that she was heading for the house at Lynch's Pond.

Stride pulled off the road about a hundred and fifty yards short of the house and nestled the MG into a grove of alder bushes. Joanne had driven past the house and stopped some distance beyond. Stride didn't wait until she had parked. He was on his way on foot while the red taillights were still visible. He had left his coat and hat in the car, started walking quickly towards the house, jogging when the terrain and the vegetation permitted, staying as far off the road as possible.

He reached the house before Joanne, approaching it from the rear. There was a small stand of fir trees at the back of the property, close enough to the house to allow him a clear view, at the same time giving him cover. It was a dark night, the moon and the stars hidden behind clouds. He crouched low behind the trees and waited.

He heard Joanne's footsteps on the gravel of the laneway before he caught sight of her. Then she came into view, a tall, slender figure against the dark horizon. A knapsack was slung over her right shoulder and she was walking quickly. Halfway along the laneway, she stopped abruptly and looked to her right, down the road in the direction of the MG. She walked back to the road, and looked again. Then she turned and started walking again.

She stopped at the back door, dropped the knapsack on the ground, and took a key ring from her jacket pocket. The keys made a jangling sound as she searched for the one she wanted. Then she saw that the lock had been pried open. She stood still, holding the ring of keys in one hand, the useless lock in the other, looking around as if half-expecting to see someone standing beside her. It was a reflex movement. She waited, silent and still, listening. Stride wondered if she would change her mind now and leave, postpone whatever it was she had come here to do. But after a minute she dropped the keys into her pocket, and the lock into the knapsack where it clanked against something metallic. She pushed the door open, picked up the knapsack, and stepped inside the house.

Stride watched a small beam of light moving about inside the kitchen, then moving farther away, into the parlour. He stood up, worked the stiffness from his legs, and walked to the door. He waited for a moment, watching and listening, then went inside. The beam from Joanne's flashlight was motionless now. She was in the parlour, the flashlight lying on the floor in the far corner of the room, pointing towards the kitchen door. It filled the room with an opaque light. Stride edged closer to the parlour doorway, stepping carefully, making no sound. He stopped when he saw Joanne kneeling on the floor in the centre of the room.

She had taken two candles from the knapsack, each one about two inches long. She struck a wooden match and held the flame to the bottom of one candle until enough wax had melted for it to stick to the floor. She repeated the process with the second. She took a long piece of cord, coiled like a lariat, looped one end several times around the bases of the two candles, and ran the cord across the room, around the corner into the hallway that led to a ground-floor bedroom. She took the knapsack with her.

Stride went into the parlour. He touched the cord with his fingers, then brought them close to his nose. The smell of gasoline was unmistakable. He moved quickly to the corner of the room where the flashlight lay and stood behind the beam of light.

It was obvious what she was doing. The set-up impressed him. It would take ten, maybe fifteen minutes for the candles to burn down and ignite the cord running into the bedroom, where it would reach a pile of newspapers or rags soaked in gasoline. Stride suspected the old house would burn like a torch. Guy Fawkes Night, five months early. By the time anyone noticed the flames, Joanne would be long gone. The constabulary and the fire department would investigate the destruction of the old Bartlett property, and the official verdict of the investigation would probably be vandalism.

Joanne walked back into the parlour, screwing the cap on a metal container with her right hand. She knelt on the floor and slid the container into the knapsack. The beam from the flashlight cast her giant shadow against the far wall. There was a smell of gasoline in the room. She took another match from the box.

"That's far enough, Jo," Stride said.

"Jesus!" Joanne stared at him, stood up and glanced quickly over her shoulder towards the kitchen.

"Yes, that was me, Jo," he said, following the direction of her look. "I was here this afternoon. Sorry about the lock," he added. He moved out of the shadows towards her.

She timed it perfectly. Stride glanced downwards as he stepped around the flashlight and Joanne swung the knapsack with her right arm, catching him on the left side of the head. The padlock gave the sack enough weight to knock Stride off balance and stun him, and he stumbled backwards and to his right. She hurled herself against him, knocking him further off balance, his arms flailing to regain control. The flashlight skittered across the floor, throwing a kaleidoscope of shadows against the walls and ceiling. Joanne struck him again and he was conscious of an intense, searing pain near his left eye. It took an instant to realise that she had gripped the ring of keys in her right hand, and the sharp metal points had torn into his face. Stride fell heavily to the floor, the back of his head slamming against the wall at the corner of the room. Joanne was sitting astride his chest now, clutching his hair in her left hand, her right hand rising and falling.

He struggled to push her away, astonished at her physical strength, at the fury of her attack. He held up his right hand to fend off another blow to his face and the metal points slammed into his palm. He fought the reflex to pull his hand away from the pain, increased the pressure of his grip on her fist. She reached under his wrist with her left hand, her nails sinking into his cheek. Stride caught her left hand in his own, and with all of the strength and energy he could manage, he threw her away from him.

She tumbled across the floor of the parlour and instantly was on her feet, running through the doorway into the kitchen. The parlour was almost completely dark now, the flashlight casting its beam into a far corner of the room, a small intense circle of light on the faded wallpaper. Stride struggled to his feet, fighting the nausea and dizziness that spilled from the shock and pain of Joanne's attack. His hand came back wet when he touched it to his face. He heard the door to the outside slam shut.

He ran from the parlour into the kitchen, and tripped over something in the middle of the room. The sound of metal clattering across the canvas told him it was the coal scuttle. He was fighting for his balance again, stumbling like a bird with a broken wing. The image of the coal scuttle with its iron shovel and poker flashed across his mind. When he had been in the house earlier that day, the scuttle stood beside the stove.

His reflex reaction to the image in his mind's eye, a defensive hunching of his shoulders, saved him. The poker glanced off the side of his head, and his left shoulder took most of the force of the blow. But it was still enough to send him reeling across the room where he collided with the far wall. Joanne came at him out of the near-darkness, the poker raised, ready to strike him again. He rolled along the wall, his hands scrabbling for something he could use as a weapon. He had a desperate, almost wistful thought of the Colt hidden in the MG. The second blow took him across his left arm just below the shoulder as he slid along the wall, intense pain and fear tearing through him. Joanne stalked him, her face a strange pale mask in the near-darkness, her expression calm, the poker ready for a third strike.

He reached the corner of the room and his right shoulder jammed against the adjoining wall. He made his decision. He wedged his heel into the corner and launched himself towards her, seized her upraised right hand with his left and grabbed a handful of her jacket, pulling her close to him. For an instant they seemed to hang suspended, their faces almost touching, staring into each other's eyes, breathing the same air. Then Stride lifted her off her feet, swung her around in a half-circle and hurled her across the room. From the noise of the impact, he knew that she had landed against the cast-iron stove.

He stumbled backwards until the far wall stopped his progress. He leaned against it, then slid downwards until he was sitting on his heels. He took a deep breath and held it for a long time. The pain resurfaced in every part of his body. Blood and sweat dripped from his chin onto his shirtfront.

Stride raised his head and looked across the room. Joanne was sprawled motionless against the iron stove, her head turned away from him, her chin resting on her shoulder. He was glad that he could no longer see her face.

forty
six

Stride was at his desk, working on his report on the Taylor case when Phelan arrived at the Fort at eight-thirty. He had been there since he had left the hospital, sleeping fitfully in his desk chair for several hours before dawn. Phelan sat down slowly and stared at him. Stride hadn't been home and he still wore the same bloody shirt from the night before.

"Go ahead and say it, Harry."

Phelan shook his head, and continued to stare.

"For once, sir, I'm at a loss for words."

Stride's right hand was bandaged, and blood had seeped through the gauze in the region around the palm. There was a bandage on the left side of his head, where Joanne had struck him with the poker, and his face was bruised and cut. His left eye was badly swollen. He had taken off his tie at the hospital and had forgotten to retrieve it.

"What the hell happened last night? The last time I saw you, you were here, sitting at your desk, drinking a glass of rum."

Stride pushed his chair back from the desk and clasped his hands across his belt buckle, the bandaged right hand on top of the left. He told Phelan the story.

"I could have rousted you out of your bed at midnight, Harry," he said. "But I took pity on you. And on Kit."

"I appreciate that, sir. And I'm sure that Kit will appreciate it even more. What's the news on Joanne Taylor? How serious are her injuries."

"A lot worse than mine," Stride said. "She has a fractured skull and a concussion. An hour ago she was still unconscious. Thomas wouldn't give me a prognosis."

He picked up the file on Alice Bartlett and gave it to Phelan.

"Read that through, Harry. It's not long, just two pages."

Phelan shook a cigarette loose from his pack and lit it. He opened the file and began to read, smoke curling around his head.

The file dated back to 1932, when Joanne Bartlett was twelve. Her mother, Alice, had been brought in for questioning about an attack on Wendell Bartlett, Joanne's father. She had used a kitchen knife, the closest weapon to hand at the time. Bartlett's life wasn't in danger, but the injuries were serious enough to require treatment, and the attending physician called the police. Gaffer Fox was the investigating officer. Alice Bartlett was held overnight, but she wasn't charged.

While Phelan was reading the file, Stride walked to the window where he could watch the activity in the parking area. He saw Fox's Morris coupe pull into the lot. Stride turned and looked at Phelan, who had placed the file back on Stride's desk.

"You think this might have had something to do with the Taylor case? It was a long time ago, sir, fifteen years."

"Yes, I think this might have something to do with it. I don't know what, and I don't want to start making guesses. Gaffer's just arrived. Perhaps he'll have something more to tell us about it."

"Perhaps I will, Eric," Gaffer Fox said. He stood in the office doorway. He stared at Stride, shook his head in dismay, then sat on the chair that Stride held out for him. "It was myself who told Bernard about the Bartlett file, of course. That was yesterday, after I read the stories in the paper on the Taylor case. I remembered I had questioned Mrs. Alice Bartlett fifteen years ago, about the attack on her husband."

"This file doesn't say a whole lot, Gaffer." Phelan picked up the folder and opened it again. He ran his index finger down the first page, then did the same with the second. "Says here that Mrs. Bartlett attacked her husband, he was treated at the hospital, he was released, and then he disappeared. And then Mrs. Bartlett herself was released from jail."

"The bare essentials," Fox said.

"The first date in the file is July 12, 1932, and the last notation is almost two months later, first week of September." Stride looked at him. "What went on in between?"

"At first, I thought it was pretty much an open and shut case of assault. Domestic violence," he said. "Not the first such affair I had to deal with, certainly, although most of the cases of that kind, it was the other way around, the husband beating up on his wife." Fox was silent for a moment. "You see, Wendell Bartlett didn't have very much to say for himself when I questioned him. That's not necessarily unusual in a case like that. Fella gets chopped up by his missus, he might not feel all that talkative. All he would say was that they had an argument, and then she went at him with the knife she was using to slice the potatoes." Fox smiled briefly. "Potatoes. Mr. Bartlett was very specific about that."

"And Alice Bartlett didn't have much to say, either?"

"No, the lady didn't have a lot to say. I explained to her that she might be charged, might even go to jail for a spell. That part upset her, of course. I encouraged her to tell me what had happened, the why of it, but still she didn't want to say very much. Which didn't give me a lot of choice in the matter. So I put her in a cell for the night, give her a chance to think about things. In the meantime, her husband was released from the hospital, and he went back home. To the house at Lynch's Pond."

"Where was Joanne while all this was going on?"

"There was an aunt lived near by, Alice Bartlett's sister, a widow, and the girl went to stay with her. Her mother asked me to look after that, asked me to make sure Joanne went there. It was about a half-mile away. The lady had no children of her own, lived alone. I saw to it that the girl was looked after, just as her mother had requested. Next day I went out to the house to have another talk with Wendell Bartlett, but he wasn't there. I thought he was probably at the aunt's house with the daughter, but he wasn't there either, and the lady hadn't seen him since a few days before the attack."

"Was Joanne there?" Phelan asked.

"Yes, she was. And she was the one who told me that her father had gone away. She said he had packed a suitcase the same afternoon he came home from the hospital, and he told her that he was going away."

"Joanne told you this? Not her aunt?"

"Yes, Eric. It was Joanne Bartlett told me that he'd gone away." Fox scratched his head, wincing as if in pain. "I can still see her as she was then. A pretty girl with long black hair. Tall for her age. Very quiet. More than a bit shy, I thought."

"You said Joanne moved to her aunt's house after the incident," Stride said. "How did she know her father had packed a suitcase and left?"

"She told me she had gone back to the house that afternoon to get something." Fox closed his eyes, remembering. "A book it was. Her father was at the house when she got there. He was packing a suitcase, she said, and then he left. That's what she told me."

"He didn't tell her where he was going?"

"No. Just that he was leaving. We looked for him, of course, made all the usual inquiries. We talked to his family—they lived near Torbay—the people he worked with. We looked for him, off and on, for the next two months."

Gaffer Fox sat back in his chair and rolled a cigarette, all of his attention focused on the task. Stride and Phelan watched him closely. Fox wiped sweat from his forehead with his right hand, then dried his fingers on his trouser leg.

"Tell us the rest of it, Gaffer."

Fox nodded slowly, took a match from his jacket pocket and lit it with his thumbnail.

"I talked to a lot of people, you see," Fox said. "After not very long, I got a bad feeling about it. It wasn't what anyone said, really, it was more what they didn't say, and the way a few of them looked when they didn't say it. It was the aunt who finally told me the truth."

"Wendell Bartlett abused his daughter," Stride said. He stood up and walked to the window again, looking out, staring at nothing in particular, trying not to think, wincing at the images that floated unbidden across his mind's eye. He concentrated on breathing slowly, fighting against the anger that grew inside him.

"Raped her, Eric. He raped her. The aunt told me that it had been going on for at least a year." Fox shook his head. "It's more common than people think. Than they would want to think. Gave me a sick feeling, then, and it does still." He fell silent for a minute. "So, when I found out about that part of it, I was just as happy that he'd lit out for parts unknown. Good riddance, I thought. Good bloody riddance. But, you know, I've sometimes wondered what might have become of the son of a bitch. Nothing good, I hope."

Phelan was tapping his cigarette against the side of the ashtray. He stared at Fox, then looked at Stride. Stride turned from the window and looked back at Harry, nodded, then turned away again. His right hand was aching now, and fresh blood had seeped through the bandage. He walked back to the desk.

"I'll speak to the Field Marshal," he said. "We'll need at least a half-dozen men." He looked back towards the window. The sun was shining, and there were only a few small clouds in the sky. "We have a good day for it, at least."

Gaffer Fox looked back and forth between Stride and Phelan. He sat upright suddenly, then slumped back in his chair, his face pale.

"Oh, Christ," he said. "Jesus Christ Almighty."

forty
seven

Stride left Harry Phelan in charge of the search party at the Bartlett house. It looked like being a long day, with almost an acre of land to probe and search, most of it covered with brush, some of it very wet as a result of the road construction.

"A lot will have changed around here in fifteen years," Stride said. "On the other hand," he said, digging at the stony ground behind the house with the toe of his shoe, "there probably aren't a lot of places where she could have buried him. It's going to be a case of probe and dig."

"Could take a couple of days, though," Phelan said. He looked at Stride. "And we might never find him."

"I'd rather not think about that just now," Stride said.

"Maybe when Joanne regains consciousness."

Stride stared at Phelan for a moment, then shrugged.

"If she does."

Stride walked a short distance away and looked out over the pond, his hands buried in his jacket pockets. Gulls circled overhead, bleating their annoyance with the presence of so much humanity near the pond. Stride watched them for a minute, trying not to remember the struggle with Joanne, the sound of her body colliding with the iron stove. He looked at the activity around the pond. The six policemen had formed a line and were moving slowly through the brush in an area demarcated with rope, probing the ground with metal rods.

"I'll leave you here to look after things, Harry. I need to have a bath and change my clothes. I'll stop in at the Fort after that. I'll come back here later." He gestured towards the road. "There's a telephone in that store we passed on the way in here. If you have anything to report."

Rex Thornhill peered around the door of Stride's office a few minutes after he got back to the Fort. Thornhill didn't look the part of someone who received his best thrills poring through dusty files, ferreting out bits of information. He was almost as tall as Stride, and heavily built. He gave the impression of both physical strength and a high energy level. His dark brown hair was closely trimmed and he had a neat military moustache. Stride recalled Herc Parsons' comment about Young Turks and Spitfire pilots.

"I have the information you were looking for, sir," Thornhill said. He gave Stride two sheets of paper. "The top one is for the flight that Raymond Butler arrived on, and the second one is for the flight out of St. John's."

Thornhill's voice did not match up with the rest of the man. It was high and reedy, with an odd sing-song quality.

Stride looked at the constable for a moment and quickly scanned the four pages. Then he went back to the beginning and read them carefully, one at a time.

"This says that Butler arrived in St. John's on the 28th of June, 1943, and left on June 30th."

"Yes, sir," Thornhill said. "There's more documentation at the College, but this gives you the meat of it."

"More documentation? What's in that?"

"Additional information on flights in and out of Torbay for that period. It appears to have been a bad few days around the end of June that year. For three days nothing got into Torbay because of fog, and not much got out. It must have been a real traffic jam there for a while. Butler's DC-3 was turned back to Gander twice before it finally touched down early in the morning of June 28th."

Six days after Marco Petrelli was killed. Not that it mattered, really, not to the case against Joanne. Still, it confirmed the fact that Raymond Butler had indeed come back to Newfoundland in the summer of 1943. The question was why? Butler hadn't made any attempt to contact his sister directly. Jenny Cole had been definite about that. And their aunt had been dead for two years.

Stride looked again at each of the four pieces of paper, then placed them on his desk. He closed his eyes and tilted his head back. The bath and the clean clothes had helped lift his mood, but there was an ache behind his eyes that intermittently rose and fell in intensity.

"Sir?"

Stride opened his eyes.

"Was that the information you wanted, sir? Does it help?"

"Yes. It's what I wanted, Thornhill. And it does help. Thank you."

"Is there anything else I can do for you, sir?"

"Not just now," Stride replied. Thornhill nodded and turned to leave. "Unless you can tell me why Raymond Butler came back to St. John's in 1943. He went to a lot of trouble to get here. All the way from England." He motioned to Thornhill to sit down. "How much do you know about this case?"

"I've read the file, sir, and all the newspaper articles, of course. And I've talked about it with Bernard Crotty." He smiled patiently. "Although I guess it would be more accurate to say that I've listened while Bernard talked to me about it."

"So you know the background?"

"Pretty well, sir, yes. And Sergeant Phelan explained that you wanted to find out if Butler was here around the time the American was murdered in 1943."

"Yes. That was the hypothesis we were working on originally. That Butler might have killed Petrelli. But we know now that Butler didn't have anything to do with it."

"My brother was in the war," Thornhill said. "My older brother, Cyril." Thornhill pronounced it "surl," his reedy voice giving the name a strange twist, making it sound almost girlish. "He was in the air force, the RAF. Bombers." Thornhill was silent for a few moments, staring at his feet. "He didn't make it back. His Lancaster was shot to pieces over France and they had to ditch in the Channel. None of the crew survived."

Stride waited, not sure where Thornhill was going with this. But he wasn't about to interrupt.

"We had a letter from him, written not long before he was killed. He'd already been on a lot of operations, over France and Germany, and the casualty rates were very high. Much higher than anyone was willing to admit at the time. Or even now, for that matter." He looked at Stride and smiled shyly. "You're probably wondering what I'm on about, sir."

Stride nodded, returned the smile.

"In his letter, it was his next to last, he talked about how he often didn't expect to survive the war, how so many planes were being lost on bombing operations. They were sitting ducks a lot of the time, the bombers, and the German night fighters had a field day with them, especially early on in the war. Later on it got better for our side, when the bombers had fighter escort. But Cyril was dead by then."

Stride raised his eyebrows. "The censors allowed a letter like that to get through?"

"They didn't see that one. It was hand-delivered to my Mom and Dad by one of Cyril's friends who was invalided home. One of the things he said in his letter was that sometimes he would lie on his bed thinking about the operations, the likelihood that the next one would be his last, and how sometimes he wished he could make a trip home and settle a couple of scores before his number came up."

"Settle scores?"

"Yes, that's what he wrote. It surprised me, Cyril thinking about that in the middle of a war. But maybe it wasn't so unusual, I don't know. Cyril didn't say what they were, the scores. But I would guess almost everyone has one or two he would like to settle before he passes on. Maybe when you're older, all grown up, you don't think so much about things like that. But Cyril was still young, only twenty."

Stride thought about what Thornhill had said. Raymond Butler had had a pretty rotten life, his family all dead save for a sister he didn't want to have anything to do with. The people closest to him in and around St. John's were not his friends. Quite the opposite, in fact. It made a kind of sense that Butler might want to settle some outstanding scores before he went into the long dark night. Which, given his situation in the Commandos, was more than a possibility.

"Benjamin Downe," Stride said.

Thornhill nodded.

"I don't know all that much about it, sir, not from Butler's point of view, certainly. But from what I do know, it wouldn't surprise me to learn that Butler might have wanted to come back here and have a word with Benjamin Downe."

Stride took his notebook from his inside jacket pocket and flipped through the pages until he came to the first interview with Herbert Rodgers, the day he and Harry had driven to Portugal Cove, the day that had almost ended in a donnybrook with Rodgers and two of his workmen. Rodgers had told them he bought Downe's business in 1943, that Downe had died early that summer. He closed the notebook.

"There is something else you can do for me, Thornhill."

"Sir?"

"Find out when Benjamin Downe died, and how. All the relevant information. And let me know as soon as you have it."

Kevin Noseworthy called in to Fort Townshend just past three in the afternoon. He told Stride that they had found a shallow grave in the bush about fifty yards from the Bartlett house. The body was that of a mature male, and there appeared to be sufficient damage to the back of the skull to suggest that he had died a violent death. There was a wallet in a pocket of the man's jacket. The wallet contained several papers with the name Wendell Bartlett. The papers were difficult to read, Noseworthy said, but one of them clearly bore the letterhead of the General Hospital and was dated July 12, 1932. Noseworthy said that Thomas Butcher had been called and was on his way to the pondside.

The next morning, Rex Thornhill told Stride that Benjamin Downe had died on the night of June 29th, 1943, the day after Raymond Butler had arrived in St. John's. He was seventy-one years old. Downe's body was found by his housekeeper when she came by at seven-thirty the next morning to make his breakfast, an established routine. The cause of death was recorded as cardiac arrest. Thornhill, enhancing his reputation as a diligent pursuer of information, also told Stride that Downe had been in good health up to the time of his death, had consulted his doctor regularly, and had never presented with symptoms of heart disease. He added that Downe's father had lived to be eighty-eight, and that his mother was still alive when her son died, and was ninety-two years old at the time. An autopsy had not been performed.

forty
eight

Joanne Taylor died without regaining consciousness an hour before midnight on the day after her father's body was found near their family home. Stride was home alone when Butcher called from the hospital to give him the news. It wasn't unexpected. Butcher had tried to sound optimistic in the several conversations he had with Stride that day, but Stride had sensed the caution in his voice, heard the unspoken words. Butcher also told Stride that Ned Taylor had been with his wife when she died.

And so it was over. At least that part of it.

A short while after he spoke with Butcher, acting on an impulse, Stride left his flat and drove through the dark and silent city to Leslie Street. Ned Taylor's car was parked in the driveway of his father's house. Stride wasn't surprised. It was what he would have done, taken himself back to the family home, to think about everything that had happened. There was a single light on inside the house, in the kitchen at the back. Stride parked across the street and sat for a minute in his car, looking at the house, uncertain now about what he should do. Taylor might want to have someone to talk to, or he might prefer to be left alone with his thoughts and his sorrows. Stride would let Taylor make that decision. He stepped out of the car, walked across the street and up the front steps. He rang the bell.

If Ned Taylor was surprised to see Stride standing there, his expression didn't show it. He looked at Stride for a few moments, his face pale, his eyes heavy with fatigue. Then he stepped aside for Stride to enter, closed the door after him, and led the way to the kitchen. A cigarette was burning on a glass ashtray on the kitchen table, a thin ribbon of smoke trailing upwards to the ceiling. Taylor picked up the cigarette and walked over to the counter that fronted the window that looked out onto the back yard. He leaned against the counter, facing Stride.

"It's the first time I've been here since that night," he said, finally. "I mean, the night Edith was killed." He paused, looking at the floor now. "The night that Joanne killed Edith."

Stride nodded but didn't reply.

"I was at the hospital tonight," Taylor said. "I've been there most of the day. Dr. Kavanagh told me this morning it was only a matter of time. So I spent the day at the hospital with her. I didn't want her to be alone." He looked at Stride. "Does that make any sense?"

"I think so. Yes. It was right that you should be there. In spite of everything." He wondered if he should have added that.

Taylor looked at him for a few moments.

"Everything. Yes." He tapped cigarette ash into the sink and turned on the water to wash it away. "That other night, the night I tried to kill my father. I thought at the time that he was responsible for Edith's death, that the things he had done, years ago, had been the cause of it. But I was wrong."

"We were both wrong. I thought the same thing."

"Did you ever suspect her? Joanne?"

"I did at first, but then she came up with an alibi for the night Edith was killed."

"The two Americans."

"Yes."

"Dr. Butcher was at the hospital tonight. We talked for a little while, after Joanne…" He didn't finish the sentence. "He's a friend of yours, isn't he? Butcher?"

"Yes. Thomas and I are friends."

"He told me that all of this, all these murders, it goes back a long time, to before Joanne and I were married."

"Yes, it does. It goes back at least fifteen years, to when Joanne was a girl."

Ned Taylor looked at Stride. It was apparent that Butcher hadn't told him the story. But Taylor, more than anyone, had a right to know. So Stride told him all that he knew of it, piecing it out carefully, avoiding embellishment. When Stride had finished, Taylor sat down at the kitchen table. For a few minutes he only sat there silently, leaning on his elbows, looking at nothing.

"Joanne almost never talked about her family," he said, at last. "Except about her mother, sometimes. I don't think she ever mentioned her father. Now, I can see why." He looked at Stride. "Did she ever say anything to you? About all that? When you were together, I mean?"

Stride shook his head. "No. She didn't tell me anything."

Taylor took out another cigarette and lit it. As an afterthought, he offered the package to Stride. Stride took a cigarette and lit it with Taylor's lighter.

"The night I tried to kill my father," Taylor said, "I was angry, about the things he had done, or that I thought he had done, the people he had hurt. My mother, me, Bobby, even Edith. It was a kind of rage. I'd never felt like that before."

Butcher had used the same word—rage—when he had described Edith Taylor's injuries. Stride pulled out a chair and sat down at the table.

"It all goes back to Joanne's father," he said. "All of it. I'm certain of that. Her father was supposed to be her protector, someone she could trust. Instead he raped her, brutalised her. I don't think she ever recovered from that. On the outside, perhaps, but not entirely." He could feel the anger rising inside him, now, just as it had when Gaffer Fox had told him and Harry about Wendell Bartlett.

Ned Taylor looked at Stride, sensing the change in his mood.

"You think Joanne's father is responsible for all this?"

"It's as good a word as any I can think of," Stride said.

They were both silent for a minute.

"There were so many people," Taylor said. "Even Bobby. She liked Bobby, they were friends. Why him? I don't understand it."

Taylor looked at Stride through a haze of cigarette smoke, waiting for a response.

"I don't have the answer, Ned. Joanne tried to kill me too. And she almost succeeded."

"But, instead, you killed her." Taylor started at his own words. "I'm sorry, Eric. I didn't mean it to sound like an accusation. I know you didn't have a choice."

"For what it's worth, Ned, I wasn't trying to kill her. I was only trying not to be killed." Stride stared at the wisp of smoke rising from his cigarette. A memory of that night flashed behind his eyes, the fury of Joanne's attack, her cold rage, the fear that had engulfed him. It was hard to speak now. "I couldn't recognise her. I was fighting with a stranger, someone I didn't know."

"Christ!" Taylor stood up and walked back to the window. He leaned on the counter, looking at his reflection in the glass. After a minute, he turned back to Stride. "She'll always be a stranger, won't she? Even to us. That isn't much to hold on to."

"No, it isn't," Stride said. "But it's what we have."

e p i l o g u e

When it was over, Stride took a ten-day leave. He was tired and dispirited and wanted nothing more than to be left alone. His first thought was that he would barricade himself in his flat with books, music, food and drink, and pretend that the rest of the world no longer existed. But even as he formed the thought, he knew that it wouldn't work, that he would be climbing the walls within a day, the voices in his mind howling at him relentlessly. So he packed a small suitcase and had Thomas Butcher drive him to the harbour, where he booked passage on a small freighter that made a regular run along the south coast of the island, stopping at ports along the way.

Stride disembarked at Fortune on the Burin Peninsula and boarded a ferry for the short trip to St. Pierre. Jean-Louis Marchand met him at the dock and they drove in the Citroën to his house in the town. They drank more wine than usual over dinner that night. Marchand left the next day for Montreal and New York City on a business trip.

St. Pierre was a good place for Stride to be. He had the solitude he needed, and he was far away from the source of his most recent miseries, in a foreign country, in another world almost, an outpost of France in North America. He knew the place well from his years in the smuggling trade, and it had good memories for him.

He spent much of his time walking on the shore and over the hills of the island. He borrowed Jean-Louis' bicycle and cycled, furiously at first, later at a more leisurely pace, over every road and path that existed in the place. He went to bed early every night and greeted every dawn. He devoured elaborately cooked meals that he mostly prepared himself. He let his beard grow.

When Stride came back to St. John's, he felt rested, and if the fierce and bitter memories of Joanne Bartlett, and the tragedy of her life, had not gone away entirely, the tumult and the pain had at least diminished to levels that he could tolerate most of the time. He phoned Harry Phelan the night he arrived and told him that he was taking one more day of leave because there was one piece of unfinished business that he had to attend to.

Bertram Cartwell's office was in a modest three-story building in the east end of the city, on the north side of Water Street. Cartwell owned that building and several more in the area, including the Colonial Stores, almost directly across the street. Stride had phoned and asked Cartwell for a few minutes of his time, and his secretary suggested he should come on ahead. He parked the MG in front of the building and stood beside it for a few minutes, thinking of what he would say. It was possible that Cartwell would simply tell him to leave. He might even pick up the phone and tell Hudson to make life as unpleasant as possible for the bothersome Inspector Stride.

Cartwell's secretary smiled at Stride and asked him to take a seat and wait for a few minutes. Mr. Cartwell was on the phone, she said, talking long distance with a client in Boston. A rectangular black plate with white letters on the front of her desk told Stride that the secretary's name was Mrs. Chambers. She was a pleasant looking woman, her dark hair flecked with grey, carefully permed. Stride guessed she was in her late thirties. He settled in the chair and took out his notebook, ran through the several points he had made in preparation for the meeting with Cartwell.

"Your picture really doesn't do you justice, Mr. Stride," Mrs. Chambers said.

He looked up at her, surprised.

"In the newspaper," the secretary said. She was smiling at him while she folded single sheets of paper and inserted them into envelopes. "Your picture was in the paper a few weeks ago. Two or three times."

"An occupational hazard sometimes," he said. "Having one's picture in the paper."

"We were very shocked to hear about Mr. Taylor and his family. What an awful business that was. Mr. Cartwell had known Mr. Taylor for a long time, of course." She looked thoughtful for a moment. "I met Mr. Taylor myself, you know, when I worked at the Colonial Stores. But that was years ago." She smiled again and patted a strand of hair into place. "Well, not too many years. This is a much better job, more interesting." She sealed the last envelope and dropped it onto the small pile in a wire basket on the corner of the desk.

The door to Bertram Cartwell's office opened then. Cartwell walked a few paces into the reception area and stood, fists on hips, staring at Stride. He was a stocky man, not as short as he appeared at first glance, with a large head, thick grey hair, impressive black eyebrows, and a weather-beaten complexion. Bright red suspenders and a heavy leather belt secured the waistline of Cartwell's black serge trousers against the topography of a prominent pot belly.

Until now, Stride had seen Cartwell only at a distance, and in the occasional newspaper photograph. Up close for the first time, he tried to square Cartwell's appearance with his reputation as an ardent and successful womaniser, and got nowhere. There must have been more to Bertram Cartwell than met the masculine eye. Stride thought the man looked enough like Jack Corrigan to be a close relation. Perhaps the rumours of enthusiastic inbreeding in some small outport communities were not too far off the mark. Cartwell's secretary was looking at her employer with unalloyed affection. Stride found himself wondering about the history of her promotion from the Colonial Stores.

"Your name has lately come up a couple of times, Mr. Stride. You'll be an old friend soon." Cartwell's tone was light but not quite friendly. "I believe you know my nephew, William?"

"I've met your nephew, Mr. Cartwell. How is he feeling? No lingering ill effects, I hope."

"I expect he'll live," Cartwell said. "If a dip in the harbour is the worst he has to deal with, he'll lead a charmed life. Not that St. John's harbour is famous as a source of healing waters."

Cartwell stood to one side and made way for Stride to enter his office. Two wooden armchairs with black leather seat pads stood in front of the desk. Cartwell gestured towards the chair on the right, then sat in the other and crossed his legs. He wore heavy black boots and grey hand-knit socks, holdovers, Stride decided, from his early days in Martin's Harbour. Or calculated posturing.

"You had a talk with William a few weeks back, Mr. Stride," Cartwell said. "I wasn't too pleased about that at the time, as maybe you've heard." A hint of a smile crossed Cartwell's face but lost momentum before it reached his eyes. "Is it this miserable Taylor business you want to talk to me about today? If it is, then you're wasting both our time, sir. William had nothing to do with it, and neither did I. And that's all I will say about the matter."

"No, Mr. Cartwell. I don't want to talk about the Taylor murders. In fact, I'm not here on official police business. It's more along the lines of a personal inquiry."

The heavy black eyebrows rose slightly. Stride had taken him by surprise, but Cartwell wasn't the sort of man who could be kept off balance for long. He nodded, staring at Stride, the dark brown eyes sharply focused. Stride wondered if Cartwell had already guessed the purpose of his visit. There can't have been much about the Taylor case, and everyone involved in it, that Cartwell and Ralph Waldo Hudson didn't know.

"Do you remember a young woman named Jennifer White, Mr. Cartwell?"

Cartwell's expression didn't change, but there was a tiny flicker in his eyes.

"Jennifer White worked for a time as a maid for the Harristons," Stride said. "For John Henry Harriston and his family. Then she got a better job, at the Colonial Stores. That was some years ago, before the war."

"Jennifer White." Cartwell was grinning now. Then he laughed, suddenly, a sharp, raucous outburst. "Well, don't you have balls of brass, sir, walking in here and asking me about Jenny White? By Christ, you have. Yes, I knew Jenny. And what tales has she been telling you, I wonder?"

Stride waited a few moments before responding.

"She hasn't told me anything, Mr. Cartwell. Not a word. But I know she became pregnant not long after she moved to St. John's from Caitlin's Cove. And I know it was generally believed that Jack Taylor was the father."

"Ah," Cartwell said, smiling. "The bold Jack Taylor, may he rest in peace. A grand fellow with the ladies, so I was told."

"That was his reputation, and very convenient for you. And you know as well as I do that Jack Taylor didn't father Jennifer White's baby."

"Do I, now?"

"Yes, you do. I think you were the father. And I think you persuaded Jack Taylor to take on the responsibility, letting you off the hook. Taylor's reward was the opportunity to buy into the Colonial Stores at a bargain price."

Cartwell looked at Stride for a moment, shaking his head.

"Balls of brass," he said again. "Not a bad quality in a man. Indeed it's not. But we both know you can't prove any of this, and it wouldn't matter a fiddler's fart if you could. It's ancient history." Cartwell stretched his legs out and crossed one ankle over the other. "And suppose it is all true, Mr. Stride. Jenny White wasn't the first young maid to find herself in the family way, and she won't be the last. Flowers are grown to be plucked, and that particular blossom was short a petal or two afore I got handy the garden gate. And I can tell you she was looked after a damn sight better than if she'd made a kitten with some young tomcat back in Caitlin's Cove."

Cartwell stood up and walked around the back of his desk. He picked up a letter opener in the shape of a small dagger, tested the point with his index finger.

"You said it was a personal inquiry. What's Jenny White to you, if I might ask? It would surprise me to learn you have a personal interest in the maid, you being a righteous man of the law, and her a married woman now. Or is your interest in me? If it is, I won't say I'm flattered." He grinned again, the dark brown eyes suddenly mischievous. "But I won't say I'm not interested."

"No, I don't have a personal interest in Mrs. Cole. She and her brother were associated with these murders from the start, albeit as more or less innocent bystanders as things have turned out." Stride stood up and walked to the window and looked across at the red-brick facade of the Colonial Stores. The display windows were filled with the new spring fashions. A streetcar rumbled past, eastbound, sparks shooting from the cable connection. He turned back to Cartwell. "We originally thought that Jennifer White's pregnancy was a key element in the case, that Edith Taylor's murder might have been a revenge killing. We were wrong."

"But you still wanted to know who made her pregnant."

"Yes. It was a loose end that I wanted tied up."

"A loose end?" Cartwell snorted. "When loose ends was a problem, my old dad would dose us with extract of wild strawberry. I hand you that bit of wisdom for free."

"I'll keep it in mind, Mr. Cartwell." Stride said. He hesitated for a moment, and then thought, what the hell? In for a penny. "I have been told that your nephew, William, is considering a career in politics."

Stride had surprised Cartwell again.

"I would guess you've been talking to my good friend Jack Corrigan, then." Cartwell tapped the letter opener on his desk blotter, then put it down. "We're giving the matter due consideration. Politics is not against the law, last time I looked. Borderline, some would say, but not quite a crime." Cartwell was regarding Stride very closely, trying to guess where he was going with this.

"I imagine there's a bit of housekeeping to be done before your nephew jumps into the public arena. Or so I've been told."

"William's led a full life. No law against that, either."

"A chip off the old block, as the saying goes."

Cartwell started. He picked up the letter opener again, holding it in both hands, testing the flex of the blade. Stride tried to gauge his mood, decided he didn't really care what Cartwell was thinking. He recalled William Cartwell's smug comment that his uncle owned a lot of Jack Taylors. In for two pennies.

"It was convenient, then, Jack Taylor marrying Edith Wright. It had been a few years since she and your nephew were involved, but safe is always better than sorry, isn't it? Especially if you have a loyal friend who's open to persuasion."

Cartwell stared at Stride for a moment, then threw his head back and laughed.

"Well, I will be goddamned, Mr. Stride. Indeed I will. Not just balls of brass, but twice the regulation number." Cartwell shook his great head slowly. "You know that I could pick up that phone and make your life a lot more interesting than you would like it to be?"

"Yes. But you're not going to do that, Mr. Cartwell. In the first place, it isn't worth your trouble. And in the second place, I would give an interview to any journalist who asked me. I might not even wait to be asked. I'm guessing you don't want that, and we both know your nephew doesn't."

"A truce, then," Cartwell said.

Stride nodded.

"We shall be living in interesting times soon, Mr. Stride. Especially if that little bugger, Smallwood, has his way. A brave new world it will be." He placed the letter opener on the desk between his hands. "I believe there's a chance our paths might cross again. Perhaps you'd consider coming to work for me. I expect I could find uses for a man like you."

Stride shook his head, but acknowledged the compliment. He knew that Bertram Cartwell was a ruthless son of a bitch, but there was a quality about the man. He remembered McCowan's and Marchand's comments.

"No?" Cartwell smiled. "I suppose I'm not surprised. You seem well suited to your line of work, Mr. Stride, and that counts for a lot. And you don't need the money, so I hear." It was Stride's turn to be surprised, and Cartwell's to look satisfied.

Stride smiled and picked up his hat. He opened the door and left Cartwell's office, said goodbye to Mrs. Chambers and walked out onto Water Street.

Now that he had tied up the last loose ends, he felt empty. Bearding the lion brought only a transitory satisfaction. He stood on the sidewalk, watching the people on the street, feeling the warmth of the spring sunshine. A couple walked by, holding hands, smiling at each other. He watched them for a few moments, felt the familiar tug of loneliness, and considered going back to work after all. No, he decided, he wouldn't do that. It was still his day.

He jogged across the street to the Colonial Stores, pausing to let a taxi drive past. He studied the window display for a few minutes, and thought this might be a good time to do some shopping. As he turned away from the window, he felt a hand on his elbow. Margaret Nichol was standing beside him. She wasn't smiling exactly, but she also wasn't as grim as he thought she might have been. He looked down the street, then back at Margaret.

"I thought I might do some shopping," Stride said. He couldn't think of anything else to say. He looked back at the street. A west-bound streetcar rumbled past. Two schoolboys in blue blazers and grey trousers stood on the platform at the back, sharing a clandestine cigarette.

"Shirts," Margaret said.

"I suppose so," Stride replied. He hadn't actually thought of what he might buy, hadn't really decided to go into the store, for that matter.

"Yes, you need shirts, Eric. The collars and cuffs on half the ones you own are badly frayed."

"You're right," he said. "I do need shirts."

"And ties. You could use a couple of new ties."

"Ties, too. Do you have anything else in mind?"

"Yes. Maybe." She touched the right side of his face, just under the eye. The cuts had healed, but the marks were still there, the swelling not completely gone. "But the shirts and ties will do for a start."

"I suppose so," he said again, smiling now.

He pulled the door open, stood to one side, then followed her into the store.

acknowledgements

I want to acknowledge the considerable number of people who offered advice and encouragement during the writing, and extensive re-writing, of *Undertow*. I am especially grateful for the expert advice given me by Jim Lynch, who served with the Newfoundland Constabulary during the period covered in the narrative, and by Sergeant Bob Morgan, currently with the Royal Newfoundland Constabulary. To the extent that *Undertow* accurately reflects the Constabulary of the period is in large part due to their input. Deviations from historical fact, unintentional and otherwise, are my responsibility alone. Special thanks to Terrence Thomas, Kathryn Guthrie, and Anna M. Curren for their insightful and critical comments on the text, to Constance Auclair for her assistance with manuscript preparation, and to Penelope Edwards for final proofreading. Thanks also to Betty and Michael Corlett, John DeGrace, Kristen Douglas, Ruth Fawcett, Fredy Kerr, Stephen Knowles, Janet Martin, Barbara Pilek, Margi Young, and my two daughters, Kristina and Meredith. I am grateful to Clyde Rose and his staff at Breakwater Books, and especially to my editor, Carola Kern, for her enthusiasm and expertise during the final stages of manuscript revision.

During the writing of *Undertow*, I consulted a number of books in an effort to get historical and other facts correct. The following were especially useful: Arthur Fox's *The Newfoundland Constabulary* (Robinson Blackmore Printing & Publishing Ltd., Newfoundland, 1971); Harold L. Lake's *Perhaps they left us up there* (Harry Cuff Publications Limited, St. John's, 1995); Peter Neary's *Newfoundland in the North Atlantic World, 1929-1949* (McGill-Queen's University Press, Montreal & Kingston, London, Buffalo, 1988); Paul O'Neill's *The Oldest City and A Seaport Legacy, The Story of St. John's, Newfoundland* (Press Porcépic, Erin, Ontario, 1975, 1976); A.B. Perlin's *The Story of Newfoundland* (The Guardian Press, St. John's, 1959); Helen Porter's *Below The Bridge—Memories of the South Side of St. John's* (Breakwater, St. John's, 1979); Frederick W. Rowe's *A History of Newfoundland and Labrador* (McGraw-Hill Ryerson Limited, Toronto, Montreal, New York, 1980); and E.R. Seary's *Family Names of the Island of Newfoundland*, Corrected Edition, edited by William Kirwin (McGill-Queen's University Press, Montreal & Kingston, London, Ithaca, 1998).

A number of fictional Newfoundland places are included in the book, including Caitlin's Cove, Martin's Harbour, Friendship Cove, Harrows Bay, and Lynch's Pond.